June Francis was bro   north-
west England. Altho   career
by writing medieva   o also
write family sets   inating
historical background, especially as she has several mariners
in her family tree and her mother was in service. She has
written twenty sagas set in Merseyside, as well as in the
beautiful city of Chester and the Lancashire countryside.

Visit June Francis's website at: www.junefrancis.co.uk

JUNE FRANCIS

A Mother's Duty

EBURY
PRESS

1 3 5 7 9 10 8 6 4 2

First published as *Kitty and Her Boys* in 1996 by
Judy Piatkus (Publishers) Ltd

This edition published in 2015 by Ebury Press, an imprint of Ebury Publishing
A Random House Group Company

The Random House Group Limited Reg. No. 954009

Addresses for companies within the Random House Group can be found at:
www.randomhouse.co.uk

A CIP catalogue record for this book is
available from the British Library

The Random House Group Limited supports the Forest Stewardship Council®
(FSC®), the leading international forest-certification organisation.
Our books carrying the FSC label are printed on FSC®-certified paper.
FSC is the only forest-certification scheme supported by the leading
environmental organisations, including Greenpeace.
Our paper procurement policy can be found at:
www.randomhouse.co.uk/environment

MIX
Paper from
responsible sources
FSC® C016897

Printed and bound by CPI Group (UK) Ltd, Croydon, CR0 4YY

ISBN   9780091956370

To buy books by your favourite authors and register for offers visit:
www.randomhouse.co.uk

Chapter One

Kitty Ryan glanced around the room and was satisfied with its appearance. She had polished the tallboy and oval-mirrored dressing table with a power of elbow grease of which her mother would have been proud, and her cousin Annie had done the same to the linoleum. Kitty straightened a towel on the washstand before moving over to the window and gazing out on Mount Pleasant. It had once been called Martindale Hill and surrounded by countryside but now it was at the heart of Liverpool, only five minutes from Lime Street railway station and half an hour from the docks.

On the opposite side of the road a yellowish sun was reflected in the windows of the YMCA and below in the street a nun was panting up the Mount in the direction of the Convent of Notre Dame. The faint sound of her voice and that of Mr Fyans, theatrical wigmaker, exchanging greetings, came to Kitty but she did not heed them because out of the corner of her eye she had caught sight of her eldest son Mick racing up the cobbled road. Her heart seemed to leap into her throat because she had been expecting something else to go wrong and this looked like being it. Her mother had always said bad things came in threes. First there had been her death six weeks ago, then early this morning Kitty's brother-in-law Jimmy had told her he was leaving. Now here was Mick in the devil of a hurry and that usually meant trouble.

Kitty fled downstairs and was in the lobby when the vestibule door was flung open, crashing against the wall.

Mick stood in the hotel doorway, red-faced and panting, his dark hair damp with sweat. 'Ma, you'd best come quick! Our Teddy's at it again.'

'What's he done this time?' She did not pause to untie her apron strings but hurried outside, trying to make sense of Mick's babbled explanation as they ran past the numerous temperance hotels, dental establishments and shops strung out down the Mount.

'I told him not to do it,' gasped Mick. 'I said we're both too old for that sort of game! But he called me a coward and told me to shut me mouth! I should have hit him but he's smaller than me, Ma, and I don't—'

'It's all right, son. You don't have to explain.' She marvelled at how this eldest boy of hers was ever ready to take on responsibility for his younger brothers, who seemed unable to recognise fear even when it stared them in the face. Mick was a gentler soul, more like his father who had died three years ago.

Roscoe Gardens came into view, named after one of Liverpool's most famous sons who had instituted the Liverpool Botanical Gardens and found fame in America. Several grinning children, one with an elbow out of his frayed jacket sleeve and a couple with boots on but no socks, gathered where Teddy clung with both hands to a railing. He was trapped by a spike which had torn right through the fabric of his trousers and was sticking out near his groin.

'Do you always have to be putting me to shame?' said Kitty in a seething voice whilst her heart hammered in her breast. She could not see if the spike had caused any damage but she feared the worst and her fear made her speak more scathingly than she would have normally. 'You think you'd have more sense at your age! You're a blinking nuisance! How am I going to get you down from up there?'

Beads of sweat had formed on Teddy's forehead despite the cold. 'I'm sorry, Ma. You'll have to cut me trousers and lift me off. I'm scared to move. The spike's scraped the skin off right along the inside of me thigh an – and further in.' He looked anguished.

'I knew it,' she cried and for a moment everything swam around her. Then she took a deep steadying breath and weighed up the situation, wishing not for the first time she was six inches taller.

A man in a pinstriped suit and a bowler hat paused in front of Teddy and wagged a finger. 'Children have no respect for public property.' His bulbous nose twitched and he sniffed. 'Get your husband to give him a whipping, madam.'

'My man's dead,' said Kitty in clipped tones. 'And if you've got nothing better to say get out from under me feet and let me be thinking how to get him down.'

The man spluttered indignantly and said something about finding a constable.

Kitty turned her back on him and climbed onto the sandstone kerb into which the railings were cemented. Mick jumped up beside her and they both put a hand beneath Teddy's bottom and attempted to push him up off the spike but they could not quite do it, despite his being small and wiry for his thirteen years. Then seemingly out of thin air came a long arm which barely brushed the flaxen hair Kitty had inherited from her Norwegian father and heaved Teddy from his perch, tearing his trouser leg apart in the process.

Kitty glanced up at least a foot into an austere, weather-beaten face and eyes which were more green than brown, before switching her glance to her middle son. There was blood on his underpants, which were also torn, and her stomach turned over.

The man planted Teddy on the pavement and there were tears of mortification in the boy's eyes as his rescuer knelt and inspected his injuries. 'Let me go,' said Teddy through gritted teeth.

The man released him. 'Next time, laddie, don't be worrying your mother. You nearly lost your manhood there. Think first and don't be such a daftie.' He nodded in Kitty's direction. 'He should see a doctor and have that wound cleansed and stitched.'

She cleared her throat. 'Thank you. He will.'

A faint smile lightened the man's eyes and he doffed his tartan bonnet before picking up a violin case from the ground and walking away with his kilt swinging, past the Shaftsbury Hotel and out of sight round the corner.

Kitty and Mick stared after him. 'Wow!' exclaimed

Mick. 'Fe-fi-fo-fum! Was he a giant or wasn't he?'

'I hate him!' said Teddy, pulling the flapping trouser leg so that it covered his bloodied underpants and slashed inner thigh. 'He shouldn't have looked at me like that and, besides, men shouldn't wear skirts. They're for cissies!'

For a moment Kitty forgot Teddy had been hurt and clipped him across the ear. 'You ungrateful little monkey!' she scolded. 'Next time you mightn't be so lucky. Now get off up home and wash that blood off and change those trousers. I'll have to take you to see Doctor Galloway.'

Teddy's mouth set stubbornly. 'No doctor's going to mess with me there. Gran wouldn't have allowed it. I'll see to it myself.'

'You'll do as you're told,' she said firmly.

He shook his head and, elbowing a couple of kids aside, he ran limping up the road. Mick followed him swiftly but a still-shaken Kitty trailed slowly after them, wishing her mother was still there to turn to at such times. Tears caught her unexpectedly by the throat. Her mother had been so strong and it still seemed incredible to Kitty that she could have died so suddenly. Her husband Michael's death had been so much easier to accept. He had been weak and suffered long. She eased her throat. What was the point of dwelling on sad times? There was work to do and Teddy to deal with.

She quickened her pace and hurried inside the Arcadia Hotel, which her mother had taken over seven years ago, three years before the Wall Street Crash. Times had been hard since then but somehow Kitty had managed to keep her head above water, although she had had to postpone the improvements she would have liked to have made. Still, having the hotel to run was what kept her going. The hotel was her boys' future. It would provide them with jobs and an inheritance.

She went in search of Teddy but the kitchen and basement were empty. She ran upstairs and found the boys' bedroom door closed against her. 'Are you in there, Teddy?' she cried.

'Go away, Ma. I'm dealing with this myself.'

'Don't be silly. You could end up with septicaemia.'

'No, I won't.'

Mick spoke up. 'I got him some whiskey, Ma, from the shelf. You know how Gran only ever used it for medicinal purposes.'

'Don't you dare be drinking any of that,' commanded Kitty, rattling the doorknob.

'We won't,' said Teddy. 'Just go and get on with the dinner, Ma.'

Kitty gave in and went downstairs, considering how controlling her elder two sons had been much easier when they were younger. She went into the room she had been preparing for the Potters, whose liner from New York had been due to dock that morning, and checked once again that everything was spick and span. A rumbling of wheels on the cobbles and her brother-in-law Jimmy's deep voice in the street below caused her to hasten out of the room.

Annie, with her rusty-coloured curls unruly beneath a mop cap, appeared in a bedroom doorway at the end of the landing. 'He's back, Kit. Is there anything else you want me to do up here or can I go down?' she said eagerly.

'You go.' Kitty had guessed months ago that Annie was head over heels in love with Kitty's good-looking Irish brother-in-law. If Jimmy did leave as he had strongly hinted then Annie was going to be upset.

In the lobby Jimmy was hauling a large trunk along the floor with Kitty's seven-year-old son Ben doing his best to help. Since his father's death he had followed Jimmy around everywhere. They had just been to the docks with the handcart for the Potters' luggage.

'Enough, Ben,' panted Jimmy, coming to a halt near the foot of the stairs and collapsing on the trunk.

Immediately Ben scrambled up beside him. 'Now give us a ride upstairs,' he commanded.

Jimmy raised dark eyebrows, took a cigarette from behind his ear and lit up. He shoved the boy along with his backside until he fell off the other end of the trunk. Ben laughed before perching once more beside him.

'Where are you putting them, Kit?' asked Jimmy.

'First floor. I take it you're not going to manage that trunk on your own?'

'Not on your Nelly! It weighs a ton.'

'I'll get Mick. Teddy's hurt—'

'Don't bother.' Jimmy got to his feet. 'I've a job to do for Annie's ma in Vine Street.' He glanced at the girl who was looking at him with sheep's eyes and away again to Kitty. 'I'll see to the trunk later.'

'But it's going to be in the way there,' she protested. 'Can't you hang on for half an hour. Besides we've got to talk.'

'Not now.' His tone was short. 'I'll see you later.'

'OK! I suppose now isn't the right time – but what about the Potters? Where are they?'

'They're finding their own way – said they wanted to have a look at Liverpool and the Shakie. He says he's a magician. And this —' he tapped the trunk with his boot, 'contains his props. I'll see you later.' With a wave of a hand he strolled down the lobby and outside.

Ben slid off the trunk and ran after him. Kitty called him back but he took no notice and by the time she reached the front door he was running up the Mount at a fair lick. She let him go, wondering if she was losing complete control of her boys and how she would cope if Jimmy did leave. She went back inside, to be confronted by a serious-faced Annie. 'What's up with Jimmy?'

'He might be leaving.' Kitty's tone was as calm as she could make it as she headed for the kitchen.

'Leaving! B-but he can't be,' cried Annie, dogging her footsteps.

Kitty did not reply but went over to the sink and washed her hands before taking the lid off the pan of steak and kidney she had cooked earlier. She began to spoon it into two shallow dishes. 'Put the kettle on, love.'

'But what'll we do without him?' said Annie.

'We'll manage somehow.' Quite how, Kitty was unsure. Since Michael had returned from the war with gas-damaged lungs he had been unable to work. So it had been Jimmy who had done all the odd jobs and heavy lifting around the place, but he had been with them longer than that. He had been too young for the Great War so he had lived with Kitty and her mother in the lodging house in Crown Street which had been their home at that time, whilst his brother had gone off to Flanders.

Annie looked as if her whole world was disintegrating. 'But where will he go?'

'I don't know. He hasn't said.' Kitty took lard from the gas refrigerator and flour from a cupboard shelf. 'That's what I wanted to talk to him about – as well as to try and persuade him not to go.' She measured out ingredients and her fingers began to work lard into flour.

Annie's soft mouth set. 'It'll be difficult for him anywhere else. You must tell him that.'

'He doesn't need me to tell him.' Kitty did not lift her head. 'You know how touchy he is about not being able to read or write but never would he allow me or Ma to help him. His pride got in the way. You know the way it is with the whole male race. Have you made that tea yet?'

'No, I don't know,' said Annie, her tone agitated. 'You're forgetting we're all girls in our house. People could cheat him, Kit. We can't let him go.'

Kitty was silent, considering how Michael could have taught his brother to read and write, but Jimmy's vitality in the sick room had only served to make her husband more aware of his own physical weakness.

'We have to do something,' said Annie, placing a cup and a buttered scone on a plate near to Kitty's hand.

'I'll speak to him,' said Kitty.

'You make him listen!' Her cousin stared at her unhappily over the rim of her cup and was about to say something else when the bell rang in reception.

Kitty wiped her hands on a cloth and went into the

lobby. A man was sitting on the trunk and a woman was gazing at a Victorian watercolour of wild flowers on the wall nearest to her. Both heads turned as Kitty entered.

'Mr and Mrs Potter?' enquired Kitty.

'Sure are,' he said, not bothering to rise. 'You the help?'

'I'm Mrs Ryan,' she said with dignity and whipped off her apron, concealing her annoyance. She rolled down long black sleeves, fastening the buttons on the creamy lace cuffs and resisting the urge to smooth her hair. She moved towards the chiffonier which acted as a reception desk and opened the register on top of it. 'Did you have a pleasant voyage?'

'It was rough,' drawled Mr Potter in an American accent. He was floridly handsome with a pencil moustache and glistening dark hair.

'That's the sea for you! Who'd be a sailor?' She smiled politely, thinking how her father had been a seafarer on a whaling ship. He had been washed overboard when she was seven years old and it was after that her mother had taken in lodgers in the house in Crown Street. 'Now if you'd like to sign the register, I'll show you to your room. If you'd like some tea – in a quarter of an hour, say? – I'll have it served in the Smoking Room where there's a good fire.' She indicated the room's position with a wave of a hand.

'That sounds just the ticket,' said Mr Potter, rubbing his hands and grinning, showing a mouthful of large teeth. 'But I want this trunk taken to our room as quick as spit. Don't want no one interfering with it.'

Kitty felt indignant as she watched him sign the register

with a flourish. What kind of establishment did he think this was? Her regulars were dependable and honest folk unlike some that were around these days. As for her other guests she had to take them on trust, just as she did him – despite the fact that since the depression there were reports of a crime somewhere or other every day in the newspapers. She reached for the key to room four and led the way upstairs. She did not linger once the Potters said everything was to their satisfaction but hurried back to the kitchen.

There was no sign of Annie and she wondered if her cousin had gone off home in search of Jimmy, hoping perhaps that she could persuade him to change his mind about leaving. Kitty put on the kettle before going through the door under the stairs which led to the family living quarters in the basement. She found Mick and Teddy sitting in front of the fire.

'Find Jimmy,' she ordered Mick. 'He said he was going to your aunt's house. Ask him can he move himself fast? That trunk has to be shifted. Mr Potter's complaining. Besides someone might hurt themselves falling over it and I can't afford to be sued for damages. If Annie's there, tell her to get back right away. I need her.'

Mick departed and she turned to Teddy. 'What about you? Can you walk?'

'If I have to,' he said, gazing at her with his father's dark eyes and struggling to his feet.

'Perhaps not,' she said, and pushed him back down into the chair with a sigh. 'I hope you cleansed that wound properly.'

'It stung, Ma. Dad would have said it was a waste of good whiskey but Gran used to say they cleaned wounds in the Bible with alcohol.'

She smiled faintly. 'Your gran was right but just in case – if that wound does start going bad you must tell me right away. Embarrassment or not, son. I don't want you dying on me.' Even though he was forever getting into mischief she loved the bones of him. He had what her mother had called spunk and she admired that in him.

He nodded and she left him and went upstairs to see to the Potters' tea herself before finishing the steak and kidney pies and popping them in the oven of the grey-enamelled range.

Mick and Annie arrived a few minutes later but her cousin promptly disappeared into the dining room to set the tables. 'Jimmy wasn't there,' said Mick. 'Aunt Jane said he came and went in half an hour.'

Kitty's brows knitted. What did Jimmy think she was paying him for? It certainly wasn't for him to come and go when he pleased or to sit staring into space the way he had done since her mother had died. He was not the only one having to work harder whilst grieving. She remembered the days when he had been dependable and they could have a good laugh about the difficult guests. 'Did he say where he was going?'

'No. Only that he wanted to leave our Ben with her but he wouldn't stay and went after him. Will I see to the fires now, Ma?' She nodded and left him to it, determinedly putting thoughts of Jimmy aside whilst she went on with her preparations for the evening meal.

*

The guests had been fed and the dishes washed and stacked away. There was nothing to do until hot water bottles needed filling, and tea and biscuits were served at ten. Kitty was toasting her toes on the fender, trying to relax but giving only part of her mind to reading the *Liverpool Echo*. Jimmy and Ben were still not home and Annie had left half an hour ago. Even as Kitty's eyes scanned an article about an Austrian called Hitler being made Chancellor of Germany, she was worrying about the two missing males in her life. She glanced at Mick who was reading a couple of pages of her newspaper and wondered whether to send him in search of them.

As if aware of her scrutiny, her son looked up. 'You're not worrying about those two, are you, Ma? I'm sure there's no need.'

'You're probably right.' She forced a smile, considering what a comfort he was, which reminded her in a peculiar way of Teddy's torn and bloodied underpants and trousers. She should have put them in to soak, she thought wearily, but hopefully the blood would still come out. She might as well mend them first, though. She reached for her work basket.

'Edward G Robinson's on the pictures next week,' said Mick.

Teddy glanced up. 'In that new gangster film?'

Mick nodded.

'Could we go, Ma?' said Teddy, looking at her eagerly. 'It seems ages since we've been to the pictures.'

'I don't think you deserve a treat after getting stuck on

those railings,' she said, squinting as she threaded a needle with grey cotton and wondering whether she should get glasses. Her eyesight was definitely not as good as it used to be but giving in and buying a pair would be tantamount to admitting she was no longer young.

'That damn Scottie made me feel a fool.'

'That Scottie saved your bacon,' said Mick, stroking the cat as it landed on the sheet of newspaper spread across his knees. 'And you shouldn't swear in front of Ma. Dad would have said it's not gentlemanly.'

He would have too, thought Kitty as she set jagged large stitches. He had believed women needed protecting from the harsher side of life despite the reversal of their marital roles.

'I don't count damn as a swear word,' said Teddy.

'It is, you know. You're cursing the Scottie and condemning him to hell,' said Mick earnestly.

Kitty pictured the Scotsman and thought there was a man who could certainly protect a woman if she needed protecting. He had been so big and strong and for a moment she had been physically stirred by his presence in a way she had not been by a man for a long time.

'Oh shut up, know-all!' Teddy kicked out at Mick and the next moment his arm was about his elder brother's neck, attempting to drag him off his chair and onto the floor. The cat yowled and struggled free.

Kitty was thoroughly incensed and not pleased at being roused from her daydream. 'Teddy, don't be stupid! You'll hurt yourself.' She jumped up from her chair and flicked him across the head with his trousers, but part of her mind was still thinking about the Scottie and wondering what he had made of her when his greeny-brown eyes had passed over her. Thoughtful eyes, seeing eyes! Had they only seen her outer appearance, though? The wispy-haired, anxious mother nudging middle age.

At that moment the door to the outside railed area opened and Jimmy's face appeared in the gap. Teddy freed his brother and Mick straightened his collar.

'What's going on?' Jimmy slid round the door carrying Ben.

'Nothing!' chorused the brothers, sitting down feet away from each other.

Kitty crossed the room and took her sleeping son from Jimmy. 'Where've you been? I've been worried sick. It's almost half past nine.'

Her brother-in-law squared his jaw. 'Ask no questions and you'll get told no lies!'

Never had he spoken to Kitty in such a way and her temper rose. 'And what's that supposed to mean?'

'What I said. You're not my keeper and I've a right to me privacy.'

'You've got a cheek,' she said, sitting down with Ben on her knee. His eyelashes flicked open and then closed as he snuggled against her. 'Privacy is a luxury none of us have in this household. As for being your keeper that's the last thing I want to be. Besides I was worried about Ben, not you. It's well past his bedtime.'

'You should know I wouldn't be letting any harm come to him.' He scowled. 'And anyway he shouldn't have followed me.'

'He's fond of you! You must know how fond. I can just imagine how he'll feel if you leave. You won't will you, Jimmy?' she said quietly. 'You know how much I depend on your help.'

'My help,' he grunted, his cheeks flushing. 'That's all I am, though, isn't it, Kit, a help?'

'What's wrong with being a help?' she demanded. 'I pay you, don't I?'

'Yeah, but—' He stopped abruptly. 'I *will* be leaving, Kit, unless things change. But I'll tell you when in my own good time.'

'As long as you do.' Her voice softened as she wondered what things he wanted changing. Hopefully he just wanted more money, but he'd have to pull his socks up to get it. 'You'll be wanting your dinner,' she said. 'It's your favourite, steak and kidney pie.'

He looked uncomfortable. 'Me and Ben've ate.'

'Ate!' She could not believe his thoughtlessness. Food cost money and she could not afford to waste it. 'Where did you eat? Not at Annie's?'

His chin came up again. 'Last thing I'd do. Her family's another one that would interfere in a man's life. Families have no right to interfere. Now is there anything you want me to do?'

Kitty was starting to feel puzzled as well as annoyed. Who could have said that about family not interfering? But perhaps now was not the right time to ask. 'The Potters' trunk. Mick'll give you a hand.'

She watched them go out, wondering if there was a girl involved. Someone as good-looking as Jimmy was bound to have had women interested in him. Suddenly Ben opened his eyes and looked up at her. 'Where's Jimmy gone?'

'He's gone to do a job. Where did you go with him?'

'Out,' he said, and wriggled down from her knee.

Kitty placed herself swiftly in his path and carried his struggling, chubby, little body back to her chair. 'Where's out?'

He gave her a measured look. 'Jimmy said it was a secret and not to tell.'

Did he indeed? thought Kitty and brought her head closer to Ben's. 'You could tell me. I'll keep it a secret,' she whispered.

He shook his head and a blond curl fell on his forehead. 'Secret means don't tell *anyone*.' He smiled angelically. 'I want my cocoa. Miss Drury's cook doesn't have cocoa.'

'Doesn't she now?' Kitty's heart gave a peculiar jump and she added grimly. 'You mean Miss Drury who lives in Princes Road?'

Ben clapped a hand over his mouth and his expression was anguished. 'Don't tell Jimmy I split,' he said in a muffled voice.

'Split!' exclaimed Kitty wrathfully. 'I'll have him split! What's he thinking of taking you to Myrtle Drury's house?'

Myrtle and Kitty had been in the same class at school but Myrtle's father had owned several properties in far from salubrious areas of Liverpool and Myrtle had looked down on Kitty who had in turn disliked her intensely. An arrogant little bitch and no better than she should be was what Kitty's mother's employer had called Myrtle. Her father had been a widower and there had been a time when he had shown an interest in Kitty's mother, after her employer had died and left her the house in Crown Street and a little nest egg. For a short while in her adolescent years it had looked like Kitty and Myrtle might have become stepsisters but it had not happened. He had died a few years back and Myrtle had inherited his pile. Immediately she had put up her rents, despite the houses being broken down and often rat-infested. A year ago she had employed a bully boy to frighten those who complained or would not pay up.

'What did Jimmy go and see Miss Drury about?' asked Kitty.

Ben shook his head.

'You tell Ma,' intervened Teddy who had been listening. 'Or do you want Jimmy to leave? I bet that Miss Drury's behind this idea of his to go, Ma.'

Kitty thought he was probably right and was about to attempt to prise more information out of Ben when the door opened and Jimmy and Mick entered.

'The Potters would like tea,' they both chorused and pulled faces.

'He's a queer one,' said Jimmy and shook his head.

Questions hovered on Kitty's lips but she decided they would have to wait and hurried upstairs.

In the kitchen a bell was buzzing. It belonged to one of her regulars, a travelling salesman in patent medicines who, like Ben, enjoyed his bedtime cocoa. She put on a couple of kettles and lifted stone water bottles from a shelf near the floor, wondering if Ben could be mistaken about Myrtle Drury.

There was a sound at the door and she turned to see Jimmy standing there looking defiant. 'Ben said you know.'

'Miss Myrtle Drury,' she said with distaste. 'How could you? You must know the kind of a bloodsucking vampire she is!'

'Gossip!'

'Gossip or not, it's true!'

His mouth tightened. 'True or not, I don't care! She's taking over a hotel in Rhyl and wants me to help her. Plenty of good clean air and the holiday trade bucking up again. I could make a packet.'

Kitty said grimly, 'She wants to get you away from me. I bet that's it. We've never liked each other. I can offer you another five shillings but that's it.'

'It's not just money,' said Jimmy, toying with a stopper from one of the bottles. 'And you're insulting me thinking it's only because of you she wants me. She's prepared to share things with me. Everything in fact.'

'She's what?' Kitty did not believe it.

'You heard me! I'm not a noggin, you know, just because I can't read or write. She wants to marry me.'

Kitty was flabbergasted. 'Marry you! But – but she's not a nice person, love. I could accept your leaving for anyone else but not her. Any nice girl would do but – but not her!' She repeated the last few words, getting more annoyed with him. 'She'd eat you for breakfast. Now what about Annie? She loves the bones of you.'

He scowled and his dark brows hooded his eyes. 'She's another reason for me to get out of here, looking at me all the time with spaniel eyes when all the time it's—' He hesitated before continuing in a rush. 'It's you, Kit, I want you looking at me like that.'

'Like a spaniel,' she could not help saying and then wished she could have recalled the words because from the expression on his face he was deadly serious. Her heart sank.

'No!' he yelled. 'It's you I'd like to be partners with! Me and you married and running this place together.'

Kitty stared at him, barely able to believe she had heard the words. 'You and me married?'

'Yes!'

'But – but you're Jimmy. You're Michael's brother. We couldn't,' she babbled. 'It just wouldn't be right. Besides haven't you been running this place with me since Ma and Michael went?'

'No, I haven't. You're the boss.'

There was a deathly silence. So that's what this is all about, she thought. Suddenly she was angry. 'You want to be the boss? You think I'm not making a good job of it now Ma's gone?'

He flushed. 'I didn't say that. I'd settle for running the place alongside you.'

'You mean you want to be part owner?' She was thinking how, after only a few years of marriage, her widowed mother and herself had had to support themselves and their offspring. 'Even Michael was not that,' she added forcefully.

'Michael was sick. His lungs—'

'It wouldn't have made any difference,' she cried

scathingly. 'Ma bought this place so nobody could throw us out of it. Michael accepted that it would be mine if anything happened to her. *Mine,* Jimmy, mine for the boys! It's all I have for them!'

'But they could still have it,' he said in a pleading voice. 'Think about it, Kit. You and me together.'

She shook her head.

He looked stricken. 'I might have stayed for a maybe. But not now.' He left her.

Kitty hesitated before hurrying after him. 'Jimmy, think twice. I know Myrtle from old. She's a prize bitch. Sooner or later she'll decide you're not good enough for her. She's mean and ruthless and'll make you unhappy.'

He halted at the foot of the stairs. 'I'm unhappy now. Married to her I'll at least have a husband's rights.'

Kitty hissed, 'I don't believe she'll marry you. More likely she'll string you along and get as much work out of you as she can – and if you step out of line she'll have her bully boy onto you.' She could tell from his face he was not convinced and decided to try a different tack. 'Anyway, think what Michael would have thought about all this?'

As aware as Kitty was that guests might be listening at doors, he said in a low voice, 'I wondered when you'd say that. I don't give a fig what Michael might have thought.' He reached out and touched her shoulder and his voice dropped even further. 'Have you ever wondered how it might have been between us if I'd been the elder brother? I've always found you attractive, Kit.' His hand moved and touched her cheek. 'I know I'm a few years younger than you but you've kept yerself well.'

'Thanks very much!' Those words had surprised her! 'But stop right there! I wouldn't feel right about it.'

'Why? Michael's dead and I'm very much alive! You don't have to be madly in love with me. But I've been like a father to your lads without any of the advantages. You don't know what it's been like lying in bed knowing that you were sleeping only a wall away in the next room. There were times when I just couldn't get you out of my mind.' He sounded desperate and suddenly he pulled her against him and kissed her, taking her completely by surprise.

For a moment Kitty was passive in his embrace. She had been lonely for a man's touch for a while now and if she had felt something she might have reconsidered her decision, but it just did not feel right being held by Jimmy. He had fulfilled the role of the brother she had never had for too long. It was a pity but there it was. It would have to be a clean break, she realised, because things could never be the same between them again. She dragged herself out of his arms. 'Perhaps it's best you do leave and maybe you shouldn't come back,' she said quietly.

A flush rose in Jimmy's neck and spread to his face. 'God! I never thought I'd hear you say that,' he said hoarsely. 'Right, I'll go to Rhyl and make pots of money and have a helluva good time without your kids hanging round my neck!' He turned and ran upstairs.

For a moment Kitty stared after him, hating herself for having to hurt him. But what other choice had she? She stood indecisively for a moment before remembering the kettles were on and marched into the kitchen. Number two's bell was buzzing again and the kettles were boiling.

She made a jug of cocoa and a pot of tea and tried to put aside what had happened in the lobby but the memory was too close and Jimmy had shaken the facade of iron-like control she tried to have over her emotions.

She went out of the kitchen and under the stairs, calling down to the basement for Mick. When he appeared she told him to see to the hot water bottles whilst she took in a tray to the guests in the Smoking Room. Her mind was buzzing with all Jimmy had said as she exchanged small talk with some of the guests and gave information concerning the best places for bargains to a mother and daughter from Wales. Part of Kitty wanted to cry because she felt emotionally drained. Then she heard the front door slam and suddenly found herself making her excuses and she fled out onto the step. She looked up the lamplit road and saw Jimmy, a rucksack bobbing on his broad back, and called to him.

He turned. 'Have you changed your mind?' he yelled.

She hesitated, reluctant to let him go. He was Michael's brother and they had shared a past which contained two people she had cared for dearly. So many memories! She was going to miss him but he could not stay on his terms. 'No!' she cried. 'I just want to say if you're ever stuck you know where to come.'

He made no answer but turned and walked away.

With her cheek pressed against the doorjamb and an obstruction in her throat, Kitty watched until he was out of sight before going back indoors. She found Ben sitting on the bottom stair. 'Jimmy didn't come back with my cocoa,' he said sleepily.

'He forgot, sweetheart.' How could she explain to him, to any of the boys, about Jimmy leaving them for Myrtle Drury and Rhyl? She pulled Ben to his feet and took him into the kitchen where she made fresh cocoa for the pair of them and for number two. She was tired out but her mind was busy allotting Jimmy's workload for the next day. Teddy would have to be up early to clean the guests' shoes, despite his injury. Mick would have to fill the coal scuttles and light the fires in the downstairs rooms. Her eldest son would also have to write a notice to put in the front window advertising for an odd-job man. At least there shouldn't be any difficulty in finding someone with the way unemployment was. Somehow she would manage.

But what about Annie! Her spirits sank. How on earth was she going to explain Jimmy and Myrtle to her? She couldn't! She wouldn't! It would break her cousin's heart. Lord, how was she going to cope with it all? For a moment she longed for a strong shoulder to lean on and wondered if she had been a complete fool letting Jimmy go. Then in her mind she heard an echo of her mother's voice saying, 'You can do it, girl! We're strong, you and I.'

Yet, as Kitty sipped her cocoa, she did not feel strong at all, she just felt tired and weepy. There were tough times behind her but she guessed there were going to be even tougher ones ahead.

Chapter Two

'I can't believe it! I don't believe it,' cried Annie, her small pointy face crumpling and her fingers screwing up a corner of her apron. 'Why did he have to go?'

Kitty avoided her eyes as she slid a fried egg onto a plate. 'I told you, more money. There's not much here at the moment.' She had sworn Mick and Teddy to secrecy concerning Myrtle Drury's part in Jimmy's leaving and was praying that Ben would not think about mentioning his visit with Jimmy to Annie. Kitty would not be able to cope if her cousin went to pieces, knowing Jimmy had another woman.

'Well, I never thought Jimmy the type to put money before us,' said her cousin.

'Me neither,' said Kitty blandly. 'But you know how he loves the seaside. And perhaps he wants to spread his wings before it's too late. He is over thirty. We'll just have to try and forgive him.'

'Yeah, we'll have to. But I do think he's mean leaving us in the lurch. I'd never leave you like that, Kit.' Annie sniffed back her tears, smoothing her apron before taking the plate to place on a tray beside another.

Kitty was touched as well as pleased to hear it. With

part of her mind she had worried about letting it slip that he had gone to Rhyl fearing Annie might go chasing after Jimmy there.

Her cousin paused in the doorway. 'I'm not going to be the only one missing Jimmy, though, Kit. We're going to have trouble with Ben. I can just see it coming.'

Kitty had already had trouble with Ben. Upset about Jimmy's departure, her youngest son had soon got up to mischief. She had not known about it until his yells had penetrated the kitchen and she had dashed to the coal hole which ran under the pavement to discover him tear-stained and covered in coal dust. He had flung himself at her, dirtying her apron and yelling that Teddy had locked him in! Five minutes later Teddy had informed her in an equally furious voice that Ben had taken all the shoelaces out of the guests' shoes and knotted them together *and* he'd left fingermarks on the glossy surfaces *he* had spent ages achieving. She was exasperated with them both and, despite what she had said to Annie, she felt far from forgiving towards Jimmy for his leaving her to cope with them alone.

She broke another egg into a frying pan and glanced up as Annie bustled back into the kitchen. 'You're going to have to get someone to fix that wobbly chair, Kit. I put it to one side but someone's moved it back again.'

'Mick's doing a notice for the window. Someone's bound to answer it. You OK now?'

Annie nodded. 'What's all this about a notice? Mam was saying me uncle Horace's still out of work. He'd probably appreciate anything you can throw his way. I mean most men can repair things, can't they? Might as well keep it in the family.'

Kitty did not think that it was an absolute truth that all men were handy but she only murmured, 'I don't really know your uncle Horace.' She slid another egg onto a plate.

'I don't know him much meself.' Annie picked up the plate. 'He's hardly ever in when I go there but I know Mam's worried in case Dad starts slipping money me aunt's way. It's hard enough for Mam to cope as it is with the six of us girls and her having to take in sewing.'

'I can imagine,' said Kitty, but Annie's words clinched the matter because her mother and Kitty's had been sisters who had come to Liverpool from St Helens in Lancashire, which was renowned for its glass and coal. They had both ended up in service but Kitty's mother had come off the better financially so she had always tried to help her sister. 'Tell your uncle to call round,' said Kitty with a smile.

'Right!' said Annie returning her smile, which pleased Kitty because it meant her cousin was perking up again.

With the breakfasts finished Kitty was about to go down to the basement to check on the boys when Mr Potter came out of the dining room.

'Wunnerful breakfast, Mrs Ryan. You sure are a good cook.'

'Thank you, Mr Potter.' She smiled and made polite conversation. There were guests and guests and she had taken an instant dislike to this one, so it was an effort. 'I suppose you and your wife'll be going to the theatre this afternoon to rehearse your act?'

He placed his hands behind the wide lapels of a striped cream and navy blue jacket. 'Things can go missing in theatres, Mrs Ryan, and the tricks in that trunk are too precious to let any Tom, Dick or Harry set their blinkers on. Good day.' He hurried upstairs.

Kitty was surprised and pulled a face at his back. She had never known a theatrical not to take props to a theatre and rehearse. Most were also friendly and keen to talk about their work. The boys would have enjoyed learning some magic tricks, so it was a pity Mr Potter had to be different.

She went down to the basement, wondering whether to offer the boys a reward for good behaviour. There was that film Mick had mentioned? Although it would be too frightening for Ben. She decided to leave it a little longer. After all it was only yesterday since Teddy had got into trouble.

Mick was disappointed his notice was not to be displayed because he prided himself on his lettering but he and Teddy responded to the promise of an outing to the pictures in a week or two. Ben, though, was quiet, putting on his coat and balaclava, and going outside and up the area steps. There was such a forlorn air about his plump little figure that, despite having the Sunday lunch to prepare, Kitty hurriedly donned her own hat and coat and went after him.

Church bells pealed across the city calling the faithful to prayer, but despite having a faith Kitty had little time to worship in church. Her life had been so taken up with looking after other people's needs in one way or another, most of her praying was done at the kitchen sink because if she left it until bedtime she fell asleep before she had finished,

She caught up with Ben halfway down the Mount and took his hand, determined he would not wander off. They walked round the centre of town looking in shop windows and dreaming. In Great Charlotte Street, Ben gazed longingly in the window of Bee's cycle shop. 'When I'm bigger,' he said, pointing to a blue and black Raleigh tricycle. *When I'm richer*, she thought wistfully. But right now a tricycle for Ben was definitely out of the question, however much she might want to please him; improvements to the hotel had to come first.

Almost a week passed before Annie's uncle Horace made an appearance. It was Saturday and Kitty and Ben were in the kitchen having just finished making gingerbread, which was something they both enjoyed. Annie entered and announced grandly, 'Mr Horace Roe!' before withdrawing.

Horace was older than Kitty had imagined and was short and squat with fat rosy cheeks clustered with fine purplish veins. He wore a frayed-at-the-sleeves brown jacket and grey baggy trousers. When he removed a greasy-looking cap it was to reveal straggling grey hair. 'How-de-do, missus?' He blinked his eyelids rapidly and appeared none too steady on his feet. 'T'niece said yer had a job for me.'

Kitty's lips twitched but she quickly straightened her face. 'Have you brought your tools?'

He took a small screwdriver from his pocket, held it up and took a step forward. Kitty caught a whiff of something intoxicating and her doubts as to his suitability doubled. Still she had to give him a chance with him being Annie's uncle. 'Do you want to start with the doorknob? And do you like boys, Mr Roe?'

'I can take them or leave them, missus.' He looked startled by the question.

'Then take Ben,' she said, pushing her son forward and hoping for the best. 'He'll show you which door.' Horace went with the small boy, who had behaved beautifully so far that day.

No sooner had they quit the kitchen than Teddy entered. He sniffed ecstatically. 'Lov-e-ly gingerbread.' He placed an arm round Kitty's waist and hugged her before snaffling a square of gingerbread from behind her back. 'Is that Annie's uncle Horace I caught sight of in the lobby?'

'Who else could it be?' she murmured dryly, wondering where he had been. 'How's the leg?'

'Getting better,' he said shortly, then he grinned. 'I've seen Horace coming out of Yates Wine Lodge hardly able to stand up. Gran would have thrown him out on his ear.'

Kitty's heart felt sore at the unexpected mention of her mother. 'I guessed he drank a little.'

'A little!' Teddy weaved a drunken path across the floor and fell down, only saving himself from hitting the ground at the last minute by spreading his hands. He levered himself up slowly.

Her eyes twinkled. 'There's no need to be smart. We've got to be Christian about this. Sometimes men – not that I agree with it – have this need to drown their sorrows. They don't seem able to cope with problems like us women do.'

She was remembering how Michael had enjoyed a drop of the hard stuff – the real Irish whiskey which an uncle used to bring over from the Emerald Isle and pass to him under cover of the bedclothes, away from the sharp eyes of Kitty's mother.

'Oh come on, Ma! Not all men drink, but I agree Horace should be giving the money to his wife and kids not spending it at the ale house.' He reached for another piece of gingerbread.

She rapped his knuckles with a wooden spoon. 'Stop that! Anyhow, let's not judge him too much and see how he copes with that doorknob.'

Horace managed the doorknob and afterwards downed two cups of tea and a piece of gingerbread. Drink did not appear to have spoilt his appetite, thought Kitty.

'I'll be needing glue for that broken chair, missus, so you'll have to be giving me the money,' he said.

'I'll have my eldest son buy the glue,' said Kitty with half a mind on Yates Wine Lodge. 'You come back here in the morning.'

He shrugged, pocketed the coin she gave him and left.

Kitty looked at Ben and smiled, thinking perhaps Horace could be a surrogate uncle to him. 'Did you have a nice time with Uncle Horace fixing the doorknob?'

He shook his blond curls and said with childish candour, 'He knows nothin' and he's too fat. He'll never shift the Potters' trunk. You'll have to get Jimmy back.'

She was disappointed but for once Teddy was in sympathy with his brother, ruffling his hair and saying equally, 'No dice, kid. I know how you feel. I miss Jimmy but he chose to leave so you'll just have to put up with us and fat Horace.'

Ben's bottom lip quivered and he flung himself at Teddy and pummelled him. Kitty dragged Ben off and hugged him tightly. 'I want Jimmy back.' There was a sob in his voice.

Kitty remained silent, smoothing back his hair and wondering if she had made a mistake in letting Jimmy go. She could have offered him a partnership without the marriage bed, but almost instantly she knew that it would not have worked. She was just going to have to learn to cope with Ben better.

When Sunday arrived, being nice to Horace proved beyond Ben and he squeezed wood glue inside one of the man's jacket pockets. Horace demanded compensation so Kitty gave him a jacket which had belonged to her husband and which she had intended asking Aunt Jane to alter to fit Mick. The man grumbled and asked for money. When she refused he turned nasty but she stood her ground despite her trembling knees. It did not come naturally to her to be tough but, with her mother and Jimmy gone, she was just going to have to be. She felt in a stronger position when Teddy mentioned the chair leg had been glued on back to front. So Horace left, grumbling about mean, bossy women, which really annoyed her because it had been a good jacket she had given him.

'Won't I be able to go to the pictures now?' asked Ben, sighing gustily.

'I'll have to think about that,' she said severely, despite being convinced he had done her a favour in getting rid of

Horace. 'Let's see how you behave this week.'

Ben obviously tried to be on his best behaviour during the next few days so she decided his efforts needed rewarding. The gangster film was no longer showing but Gracie Fields was on in a film called *Looking On The Bright Side.* It was advertised as bubbling with laughter and music. *Just what we all need,* thought Kitty, considering how much her mother would have enjoyed such an outing. She had been strict with her grandsons but she had always found pleasure in their company, although she had grieved with Kitty for the baby girl which had been stillborn. It still felt odd not having her there to share things with and Kitty felt vulnerable and lost for a moment.

As expected, with such a popular star in the film there was a lengthy queue outside the Futurist cinema in Lime Street but Kitty had come prepared. From her handbag she took four bags made up by the girl in William's Sweet Shop. They contained tiger nuts, creamy whirls, Spanish laces and sticky lice. If that was not enough to keep them all quiet there was entertainment at hand. A fiddler was playing a tune vigorous enough to set toes tapping on what was a chilly evening.

Chewing on a tiger nut, Kitty craned her neck in an attempt to catch a glimpse of him but her lack of height made it impossible and she felt frustrated. The toe-tapping rhythm changed to a tune that was meltingly sad and evoked a longing for what she did not know. Dreams not realised perhaps? But she had given up expecting dreams to come true a long time ago and all she hoped for now was that one day her ambitions for her hotel would be realised and that her sons would find happiness. She realised how much her life was wrapped up in those two things, but of course they were all she had. It was too late to expect romance at her time of life. In four years' time she would be forty and some would say past it. She sighed for the unattainable even as she told herself romance did not really exist outside a Ginger Rogers and Fred Astaire musical in these tough times.

The music changed and she began to hum a Scottish air. The busker came into view and she gasped in surprise for he was, as Mick had said on another occasion, a giant of a man.

Ben pulled on her coat and said excitedly, 'Ma, he's got a monkey! Can I put money in its hat?'

Kitty dug into her pocket and handed him a penny without hesitation. She had been truly grateful to the Scottie for rescuing Teddy. Ben stepped forward with an important air. The monkey was a tiny, dainty creature clad in a plaid jacket and matching cap, carrying in its scrawny paw a larger tartan bonnet with a feather in it.

'Ma, it's that damn Scottie,' said Teddy, in a sibilant whisper loud enough to cause the man to glance their way. His gaze caught Kitty's and held it, before he lowered an eyelid in a wink. *Cheek!* she thought and looked away despite the sudden lift to her spirits. He thanked Ben for his contribution in a grave voice, before moving on down the queue.

When they emerged from the cinema Kitty felt a vague disappointment that the Scottie was nowhere to be seen. He had intruded into her thoughts while watching the film and she had questioned why a man who was obviously fit

and strong should need to busk, despite times being hard.
She wondered if he had a home to go to on such a night?
There was a freezing fog and it was slippery underfoot. She
shivered and tried to hurry the boys along the pavement but
they would not be hurried, making the most of the night
out, and suddenly she realised that they needed time to act
daft. The two elder boys especially had little time for play
since Jimmy had gone. So she let them enjoy themselves
re-enacting parts of the film, mocking Gracie's singing and
fighting imaginary crooks, and in their pleasure she found
enjoyment. Even so it was a relief to get home and find that
Annie, who was staying the night in Jimmy's old room,
had kept the fire in the front basement room burning.

'Everything OK?' asked Kitty, her hands curling round
her cocoa cup after the boys had gone to bed in their attic
bedroom.

'That Mr Potter complained about the biscuits, and
there was nothing wrong with them, Kit, honestly!'

'Perhaps he's hoping I'll knock something off the bill?
He probably thinks because I'm a woman on my own
that I'm fair game. Well, it's not going to work,' she said
determinedly.

'I don't like the man, and that's the truth. He complains,
then smiles, showing all them teeth of his. Seems to me he
has twice as many as anyone else.' Annie pursed her lips
in disapproval. 'And I've yet to get a complimentary ticket
off him despite his boasts about the tricks in that trunk.'

Kitty yawned. 'I'll have to find someone to bring that
precious trunk of his down soon. They can't be staying
much longer, thank God.'

A deep sigh escaped Annie. 'It's now we need Jimmy. Imagine him in Rhyl in this weather. Perhaps it's not as cold there as it is here.'

'We don't need him,' said Kitty firmly. 'I'll find someone. As for the weather in Rhyl, I hope it's freezing. Just don't mention him to Ben.'

She drained her cocoa cup and went to bed, hoping that her youngest son would continue to behave himself.

But a week was long enough for Ben to be good and the next morning he threw a tantrum. 'I'm not going!' He drummed his heels on the floor in the basement.

'Yes, you are! Get up and do as Ma sez!' Teddy seized the back of Ben's collar and hoisted him to his feet.

Ben made a choking noise and kicked out at his brother.

'Stop that!' roared Kitty, darting across the room. 'If I've told you once I've told you a thousand times, I won't have you fighting.'

Teddy loosened his grip. 'He's refusing to go to school and if I'm to get him there and meself back to Pleassie Street before the bell, we've got to go now.'

'I want Jimmy,' said Ben, stamping his foot. 'He gave me a ride on his shoulders and my legs didn't get so tired.'

Kitty gazed at him feeling a sudden helplessness. 'It's not so far, love, and you're not a baby anymore. Walking will make your legs stronger and on Monday I'll go with you myself. Today I have to go the fish market and I should have been there by now.'

He looked at her mournfully but she determined to be stern with him. 'I'm telling you straight if you're not on your way in three minutes, there'll be no ha'penny for sweeties later!' She reached for the black velour cloche hat she had bought for Michael's funeral and dragged it over her fair hair. 'Now get going.' She took the basket from the table and, seizing Ben by the shoulders, propelled him in the direction of the area steps. But he proved stubborn and dug his heels against the bottom step, resting his full weight against Kitty, almost forcing her off balance. She slapped his leg but he did not flinch.

'I want Mick to take me instead of Teddy,' he yelled, gazing up at his eldest brother who stood at the top of the steps.

'I can't,' said Mick. 'I'll have to leave now or I'll be late. You're making life tough for Ma, Ben, when you could make it easier. Don't be such a selfish little so-and-so.' He vanished from their sight.

Ben lowered his boots one by one and said beseechingly, 'Can't we go the seaside and see Jimmy?'

'No, we can't!' said Kitty who was angry and determined not to make promises she could not keep.

He made a noise which seemed to come from deep in his boots and slipped his hand into hers. 'Can I see that monkey again instead?'

Her anger subsided. 'What monkey?'

'The one with the little jacket on.'

Teddy groaned. 'You're not still going on about that, are you?' Kitty glanced at him and he muttered, 'That damn Scottie's monkey, Ma.'

She had not really needed reminding who it belonged to because the Scottie had popped into her thoughts unbidden several times in the last few days. It was that wink he had given her. It had made her feel attractive, sexy even! Daft as that might seem to anyone with a sensible head on their shoulders.

Ben beamed at her. 'That's right. It was a clever monkey collecting money the way it did. Perhaps if you take us to the pictures again we'll see him?'

'Ben,' she said as patiently as she could, ready to explain that there was no guarantee that the monkey would be there even if she could afford a trip to the pictures again so soon.

'Please?' he pleaded.

She got down to his level and gazed into eyes which were a purer blue than her own and her heart melted. 'Perhaps,' she murmured. 'If you're good. We'll see.'

'It's a promise,' he said jubilantly.

'No, it's not,' said Teddy.

Kitty kissed Ben and ran up the steps. She felt guilty for not going with him and it was an effort not to turn back, but she had a busy day ahead of her.

Ben gazed moodily at Teddy, who grinned. 'It seems you're stuck with me, Shrimp. Now let's git!' He knuckled Ben in the back, which had the effect of sending him scrambling up the steps and up the Mount in the direction of the workhouse and convent school in double-quick time. Teddy kept at his heels and Ben didn't dare stop, but he felt more cheerful. The thought of seeing the monkey was like a diamond shining in a dirty gutter and that made him feel less unhappy about Jimmy.

Kitty was thinking about the pictures and money and the Scottie when she reached Ranelagh Place. She eased the basket of fish on her arm and knew she could not really afford the time or the money for another outing to the cinema. Ben might create a fuss but she would have to deal with him firmly. She tried to be a little more optimistic about the control she had over her youngest son but knew herself unable to keep his exuberant nature completely in check. She sighed and looked up at the sky. At least the weather was brightening up, she thought, gazing at a patch of blue revealed by scurrying grey clouds.

She turned the corner into Mount Pleasant and paused outside the pawnbroker's to gaze at the jewellery on display there. She fingered the locket which had belonged to her mother and hoped things would never get so bad that she would have to pawn it. Its presence was a constant reminder not only of her mother but also of the father who had died so young. She felt sad thinking that she had never really known him and sorry, too, for those poor people who had to pawn even the shirts on their husband's back to buy food for their children. She wondered how different her life would have been if her father had lived. She might have had brothers and sisters, but in that case there would never have been that special relationship she had shared with her mother, and the Arcadia would never have been hers.

Kitty was about to turn away when she saw reflected in the window two figures on the opposite side of the road. There was something familiar about them but before she could pinpoint who they were they vanished off the edge of the window. She spun round and immediately recognised the Potters. He was carrying a portmanteau and they appeared to be in a hurry.

Her curiosity and suspicions aroused, Kitty crossed the road and followed them along Lime Street. They went inside the railway station and she went in after them, hoping they had not already purchased tickets. Once inside she was relieved to see Mr Potter standing in a queue in front of a ticket window. His wife was several yards away and was holding a small mirror up to her face, applying lipstick. The portmanteau was on the ground in front of her.

Kitty eased the basket on her arm and walked towards her, determined they would not get away with diddling her. She steeled herself and picked up the portmanteau, saying, 'Going somewhere, Mrs Potter?' The mirror slipped from the other woman's fingers and broke into glittering shards on the ground. 'What bad luck!' said Kitty sweetly. 'Seven years of it with a bit of luck.'

Mrs Potter's arm shot out. 'Give me that bag,' she snapped, surprising Kitty by her lack of American accent.

Several heads turned and Kitty tightened her hold on the portmanteau as her eyes searched for a policeman. The other woman reached for the bag with both hands, got a grip and tugged. Kitty felt desperate as the bag began to slip from her grasp and had to let the basket of fish slide down her arm so she could get a better hold.

Then Mr Potter arrived on the scene and Kitty despaired as without a word he began to prise her fingers from the handles. 'Let me go,' she gasped. 'You no good thief!'

With a sharp wrench that hurt Kitty's shoulders he

tugged the bag from her. 'Come on, Dolly, let's be going
and leave Mrs Ryan to something that smells extremely
fishy.' He grinned, showing all his teeth.

Kitty was furious and pulling the cloth from the basket
she took out a fish and threw it at him, knocking his hat
askew, but he only paused to straighten it before hurrying
on without a backward glance. She reached for another
fish but, before she could hurl it, her wrist was seized. 'Do
you mind!' she said angrily, struggling to free herself.

'It's a waste of good fish, lass. If you're wanting to
speak to the man I'll fetch him for ye.'

If she had not known his face she would have known his
voice. Her eyes sparkled up into his. 'Thanks! I'd appreciate that. He's a no good thief.'

His expression stilled and for a moment they just stared
at each other, then he said, 'R-rright!' and released her and
went after the Potters.

Feeling as if the battle was already won, Kitty picked
up the fish from the ground and placed it on top of the
cloth in her basket. The Scottie had caught up with
the fleeing couple and she watched with joy as he rammed
Mr Potter's hat down over his ears before spinning him
round and relieving him of the portmanteau. He pushed
him in Kitty's direction, accompanied by Mrs Potter who
was screeching at the top of her voice.

'Planning on doing a vanishing trick, Mr Potter?' said
Kitty in a lilting voice. 'My money, please.' She thrust her
hand beneath his nose.

'Don't give her any, Alf,' screamed Mrs Potter. 'And
you—' She aimed a punch at the Scottie – 'You just give

me me husband back. Or – or I'll have the poleece on yer.'

'Don't get common, Dolly,' panted Mr Potter, having managed to free himself from his hat. He eased his collar, scarlet-faced, but obviously trying to maintain some dignity. 'We've been caught so let's act like civilised beings.' He took a wallet from an inside pocket. 'Will you accept two pounds, Mrs Ryan?'

'You have to be kidding,' said Kitty. 'Five pounds minimum.'

'But you were recommended to us as a charitable woman,' he protested. 'And you can sell the trunk. That'll fetch a bob or two.' His voice no longer contained an American twang and she realised what a good act he had put on.

'I still want five pounds,' she said firmly. 'You haven't been the easiest of guests to look after.'

Mr Potter sighed heavily. 'We had to hock everything to buy our tickets home from the States.'

Kitty strengthened her resolve. 'Don't give me any sob stories. I've kids to feed. If you wanted charity you should have gone to the Sally Army. Now if you don't mind – five pounds.' She twiddled her fingers under his nose.

Mr Potter glanced at the man looming above him and then at the station clock before delving into an inside pocket and bringing out a bag of coins. He counted five pounds onto Kitty's palm. She thanked him with a radiant smile and indicated to her rescuer that the portmanteau be handed back to its owner. Mrs Potter gave her a dirty look before hurrying away with her hand tucked inside her husband's arm.

Kitty did a little tap dance before looking up at her rescuer. 'So that's that,' said the Scotsman.

'Not quite,' she said boldly. 'You're just the man I've been looking for and I'd like you to come with me.'

'How's that?'

She could see that she had taken him completely by surprise. 'You have a monkey – and I'm in need of a strong right arm.' She thought how despite his lack of kilt and doublet he still cut a wonderfully impressive figure in a well-worn Harris tweed jacket and brown corduroy trousers. He was at least six foot two inches. His face was attractive more than it was handsome, but he had a distinctive nose and a rather nice mouth that made her wonder what it would be like to be kissed by him. He was probably in his late thirties.

'Not mine.' His smile was puzzled, slightly amused. 'I'm John McLeod by the way.'

She stretched out a hand which was immediately swallowed up by his in a grasp that was reassuringly firm. 'Kitty Ryan. I'm in your debt.' She decided that she had to continue to be bold. 'Can I offer you a cup of tea and a bite to eat? I have a hotel up Mount Pleasant and was on my way back there when I saw these two doing the equivalent of a moonlight flit.'

He did not hesitate, which pleased her. 'I'd like that fine,' he said. 'Here, let me carry that basket of yours. It looks heavy.'

Even more pleased with him, she handed her shopping over without demur and they began to walk towards the exit. She searched for something to say, wanting discover more about him. 'You weren't aiming on catching a train, Mr McLeod?'

'Trains are for people with money, Mrs Ryan. I was just taking a short cut.'

So he was hard up. 'You live in Liverpool?'

'For the moment.'

What did that mean? she wondered. 'Are you looking for work?'

'Not really.'

He had surprised her and she stared at him, wide-eyed. 'But you were busking! You must be short of cash?'

'Off and on.' His eyes crinkled at the corners. 'You mustn't concern yourself about me, Mrs Ryan. I have enough for my needs and possessions can be a burden.'

His words flummoxed her because most of her life her mother had instilled in her the need to build a nest and feather it as best she could for her family. But perhaps he had no family? No wife, no children. 'What did you mean you don't have a monkey? I saw you with one. Unless, do you have a double, Mr McLeod?' she said with a touch of humour.

'Ach! What would God be thinking of making two of me?' he said with a lazy smile. 'The monkey belongs to my god-daughter. Her mother has a pet shop near Scottie Road. Tell me, Mrs Ryan, is your hotel anywhere near the size of this one?' He glanced in the direction of the towering edifice of the Adelphi Hotel.

Kitty's eyes twinkled. 'I think you're trying to change the subject. Do I look that rich? My place could fit into a corner of *that*! Even so I have great plans.' Her tone was enthusiastic. 'Although, with one thing and another it isn't easy.' She heaved a heartfelt sigh.

There was a silence before he murmured, 'You don't have a husband, Mrs Ryan?'

She shook her head and said softly, 'He died a few years back. Influenza. It was what took my mother a short while ago too.'

'I'm sorry.'

'Me too.' She smiled up at him and reminded herself that she was going to be bold. 'Do you have family, Mr McLeod?'

He hesitated. 'Sort of.'

She laughed. 'How do you sort of have a family?'

'They exist but you don't see much of them.' A smile lurked in the depths of his hazel eyes. 'I have a sister in the south who doesn't approve of me. A brother in Canada whom I haven't seen since I was four years old. He has a daughter whom I've never seen. Then there's my uncle Donald in Scotland. We correspond. And there's my grandfather, although he—' There was an indefinable something in his voice and his smile had vanished.

'He what?' she said curiously.

His expression was suddenly less than friendly. 'Do you always ask a stranger so many questions, Mrs Ryan?'

For a moment she felt as if she had received an unexpected slap in the face and her cheeks reddened. 'I'm sorry. I was interested that's all. You aren't quite—'

'Respectable?'

'No! Not my idea of a busker.'

'You've something against buskers?'

'Did I say that?' she responded swiftly.

'Words aren't always necessary.'

'If you wish to play in the streets,' she said in a hoity-toity voice, 'that is your business but I could think of more comfortable ways of making a living in winter.'

'I'm sure you could but I like my life the way it is.' He sounded amused again. 'Are you sure you want me to come to this hotel of yours?'

Her eyes glinted. 'I'm no snob! Perhaps we should change the subject and talk monkeys again.'

'That suits me fine. Just tell me why you're so interested in Joey?'

She stared at him, thinking that she did not want to talk about monkeys – she was far more interested in him – but there was nothing for it but to answer his question. 'Because of Ben, my youngest. He's missing his uncle who lived with us, and has taken a shine to the creature.'

'You weren't thinking of buying him, I hope,' said the Scottie swiftly. 'I wouldn't recommend him as a pet. He might look the daintiest thing but he can give a nasty bite and would climb your curtains and tear them to shreds.'

'Not buy,' she said hastily. 'I couldn't have a monkey on my premises. Would it be possible for Ben to see Joey?'

'I don't see why not.'

'You can arrange it for me?'

'I can arrange it.'

They had reached the Arcadia by now and both looked up at its frontage which was badly in need of a coat of paint.

Kitty said, almost apologetically, 'It was run-down when

we took over but I've promised myself it'll be painted after the Grand National this year. I'd also like window boxes filled with flowers.'

'Sounds a good idea.'

'I'm glad you think so.' She smiled warmly at him before turning the handle of the vestibule door. He moved forward quickly and held it open for her while she stepped inside. *Another tick for nice manners,* she thought.

Annie was brushing the stairs. There was a cup of damp tea leaves at her elbow to sprinkle on the carpet to help bring up the dust. 'There's a family come, Kit. I gave them room three. They've gone down the Pier Head, something about emigration.'

'That's fine. Mr McLeod, my cousin Annie. Mr McLeod helped me with the Potters, Annie. They were doing a flit.'

'Fancy that!' Annie gaped at John. 'You're a big fella if you don't mind me saying so.'

'I'm used to it. It's nice meeting you, Annie,' he said in a friendly way before turning to Kitty. 'You'll be wanting this fish in the kitchen?'

'Yes, please.' With a wink at her cousin, Kitty went ahead of him to put on the kettle.

She was extremely aware of his presence as he paused in the middle of the quarry-tiled floor and knew him to be watching her as she spooned tea into the pot. She felt all fingers and thumbs and dropped a spoon. 'Do sit down, Mr McLeod,' she said, pausing to pick it up. 'You're making me nervous.'

'Am I?' He looked amused but made no move to obey her. Instead he went over to the sink and placed the basket on the draining board before turning on the cold water tap.

'What are you doing?' she asked, startled.

'Washing the fish.' He lifted the cloth from the basket. 'How will you be cooking them? They're fine big ones. I remember my grandmother's cook used to stuff herring with a mixture of oatmeal and herbs.'

His grandmother's cook! Her mind seized on that bit of information. She cleared her throat. 'I'll be cooking them in the Scandinavian way which my father showed my mother.'

'And how'd that be?' He began to wash the fish.

'I bake them with a little melted fat and mustard.' It was a pleasure to her to talk about cooking. Michael and Jimmy had never shown any interest in how the food on their plates got there.

'And to go with them?' He glanced over his shoulder at her.

'Boiled potatoes with a vinegar sauce and parsley.' There was a quiver in her voice as she took her apron from its hook. 'Do you want to know what's for pudding?'

One of his eyebrows lifted interrogatively.

'Baked jam roly-poly. Does that meet with your approval, Mr McLeod?' Her eyes smiled up at him.

'If it's the food you're offering me, aye.'

'It was not. I was offering you lunch which is ham bone soup with lentils,' she said with mock severity. 'The herring are for my guests' main course this evening. If there's any left over you can share it with us in payment for work. That's if you wouldn't mind doing the odd job?'

She could not conceal her eagerness. 'Since my brother-in-law left there's some things that the boys just can't do. I'd really appreciate it if you could help me.'

'I might be interested as long as you don't think I'm stopping.' There was a warning note in his voice. 'I'll be hitting the road as soon as the weather improves.'

'I wasn't thinking of you stopping,' she lied, adding in a persuasive voice. 'There's only a few little odd jobs. You remember Mr Potter mentioning a trunk?'

'No, but go on.'

'I need it moving.' She busied herself peeling onions for the lentil soup. 'My brother-in-law said it weighed a ton.'

'Why did he leave?' John slapped a fish down on the draining board.

Kitty turned her head. 'A woman. I wouldn't mind if she was any ordinary woman but—'

'Are you sure about that?'

She remembered how Jimmy had kissed her and inexplicably blushed as if she had a guilty secret to hide. 'Of course I'm sure,' she snapped. 'The woman involved is called Myrtle Drury, but you won't have heard of her although she's quite well known by some in Liverpool.'

'But I have heard of her,' he said softly.

She could not believe it and as she stared at him their eyes met, but his expression was hard to read. 'She was dunning my god-daughter's mother, who's hopeless with money and fell behind with her rent. Charley, that's Miss Drury's bully boy if you didn't know, got nasty. I had to scare him a little. I don't think she was pleased with him.

In fact I know she wasn't because she offered me his job. I turned it down, of course, with me not wanting regular work.'

'That wasn't your only reason, surely,' said Kitty. 'You must have realised she was no lady.' The kettle began to hiss and Kitty dropped the knife on the table to make the tea.

'Naturally. Ladies don't threaten to have you thrown in the Mersey.'

'Is that what she did?'

'Haven't I just said so.' His eyes teased her.

She found herself blushing. *At my age*, she thought, and said hurriedly, 'I wish Jimmy'd had as much sense as you.'

'Ach, you make her sound like the whole German army. I'd left home and seen death when I was twenty-one. I'm sure he can cope with one woman if he's any kind of man.'

'He's over thirty but that doesn't mean anything with some men,' said Kitty, cutting the remains of a sponge cake into three before calling Annie.

Her cousin entered the kitchen. 'That there doorknob's worked loose again, Kit.'

Kitty pulled a face and resting an elbow on the table she looked at John with a question in her eyes. 'Please?'

'I'm no expert at doorknobs,' he said woodenly. 'But if it's only a loose screw I'm sure I can manage.'

She smiled as she filled his cup almost to the brim and murmured, 'A whole herring for you, Mr McLeod. But first that trunk. After you've drunk your tea of course.'

The trunk stood in a corner of the bedroom, large and imposing. John took a grip on a handle and lifted one side before lowering it carefully. 'I'll need help if it's downstairs you want it.'

'Along the passage will do,' said Kitty, thinking he really was strong. She had tried to lift one end of it before and had been unable to shift it. 'There's a small room I never use unless we're absolutely full, and we haven't been that for ages, since the last Grand National.' She *rat-a-tatted* on the trunk with her fist. 'I wonder what's really inside? Mr Potter had to be lying about props.'

'Have a look.' John leaned against the wall, his tongue in his cheek. 'Perhaps there's a body in it?'

'You think so?' She was half inclined to take him seriously as she slowly turned the key in the lock before lifting the lid. Her heart seemed to miss a beat as she gazed inside. 'Ohhh!' she exclaimed.

'What is it?' He moved hurriedly and lowered his head as she lifted hers. Their heads bumped and she winced. He took her arm and led her over to the bed. 'You sit there. I'll deal with this.'

She rubbed her head and watched him go back to the trunk, glad to leave it to him. As he looked inside she said, 'My eyes didn't deceive me, did they?'

'What do you think you saw?' he said carefully.

'A body as you said.' The words came out in a whisper.

He reached inside the trunk. 'Don't!' she cried, jumping to her feet.

He surprised her by grinning and producing a ventriloquist's dummy.

She laughed. 'I've never liked those things.'

'It was lying on what looks like a hundredweight

of bricks,' he murmured. 'It's crazy the lengths some people'll go to con others.' He dropped the dummy on the floor. 'Where d'you want the bricks?'

'The back yard. Perhaps we can build something with them?' She was so relieved, so pleased with him that she added, 'For the extra work you can have a bed for the night. A comfortable bed, better than you'd get at the Sally Army.'

There was a silence and their eyes met. 'You're taking a risk, aren't you, Mrs Ryan?' he drawled. 'You don't know me from Adam.'

'I don't know the majority of my guests from Adam,' she countered.

'Of course you don't! Stupid me!' He sounded vexed. 'Thanks but no thanks. I could get too comfortable here and besides I'm not staying at the Sally Army but with friends.'

'Those at the pet shop?' she murmured and then could have bitten off her tongue.

He said seriously, 'That would be the last thing I'd do. What do you want doing with this dummy?'

'Sling it in the yard.' She decided it was time for her to go. Time perhaps to stop being so friendly. She did not want him to feel hunted. She nodded regally and allowed her skirts to brush his leg as she left the bedroom.

By the time John had cleared the bricks, moved the trunk and fixed the doorknob, the soup was ready. Watching him eat, Kitty wondered why he had taken to the road. There was little of the vagrant about him. He was strong, quick-witted, well-mannered, clear-eyed and with no smell of drink on his breath. He fascinated her. She wanted to question him further about himself and the way he lived but she held back.

After their meal she showed him the chair with its back-to-front leg and when he had sorted that out and still appeared willing to be of help she handed him some newspapers and a bottle of vinegar and asked him to clean the front windows. He was still at work when she realised Ben would be coming out of school in five minutes and went to meet him.

She hurried up the Mount, thinking of the man she had left behind. He really could be useful to her but she was not sure how to handle him. He was different to anyone she had met before. She knew she would have to take things slowly, although if he planned on leaving Liverpool she did not see how she could do that.

By the time she reached the school gates there was only a trickle of children coming out. She waited a while but when there was still no sign of Ben she turned her footsteps homeward, thinking how once again she had fallen down on her responsibilities towards her youngest son and all because she had got too interested in a man who seemed to have no sense of responsibility at all.

Chapter Three

Ben had returned home by a different route to Kitty and arrived at the hotel to find John cleaning the basement window. 'Who are you?' demanded the boy, pausing at the top of the area steps.

'Don't you remember me, laddie?' John tossed the used newspapers into a bucket and came up the steps. 'I'll have to be going. You tell your mother that Mr McLeod will be back for that meal she promised him.'

Ben nodded and trotted beside him as he went indoors. 'Have you come in place of Jimmy and Horace?'

'Who's Horace?' asked John, making for the kitchen.

'Annie's uncle and he was useless and had a fat tummy. Teddy said he liked his drink too much and he didn't do the jobs properly so Ma got rid of him. Are you here for a trial p-pe-riod?' Ben stumbled over the word.

'Your mother might think so,' said John dryly, washing his hands at the sink.

The boy stared at him and then crowed with laughter. 'I know you! You're the man with the monkey!'

John smiled faintly, 'You're spot on, laddie. Now I've got to be off to get changed and fetch my fiddle and Joey, or I won't be catching the first-house queues.' As he dried his hands Annie entered the kitchen. They nodded at each other as she took potatoes from a box.

Ben said earnestly, 'Can I come with you? I won't be any trouble. Just let me see the monkey.'

'You'll be Ben. How old are you?' said John, hanging up the towel. 'And tell me, what time do you have your evening meal?'

'I'm seven. And after the guests. We have what's left over.' Ben sighed. 'Generally Ma's here now and I have a buttie.' He followed him out of the kitchen and onto the pavement.

John halted and looked down at Ben. 'This is as far as you go. Tell your mother to keep my food in the oven. I'll be back about half nine.'

'But I want to come with you and see the monkey,' pleaded Ben. 'Did you say his name's Joey? I like that name. It sounds right for a monkey.'

'I'm thinking it would be more than my life's worth to take you with me. Maybe I'll take you to see him in the morning.'

'But I want to see him now.'

'I said no, laddie.' The tone of John's voice brooked no argument.

Ben sighed and sat on the step, oblivious to its chill, and watched him go down the hill. After several minutes he rose and followed him. Teddy, whose school was only round the corner from the hotel, was playing marbles in the gutter with a couple of his mates but Ben did not speak to him and his brother did not look up as he passed.

The boy trotted in John's wake across the centre of

Liverpool, past St John's Gardens, the free library and the technical school, and on up Byrom Street. Despite the cold Ben was beginning to get hot and his legs ached but he had no trouble keeping the man in sight because he was head and shoulders above anyone else. They were now in an area Ben had visited with Jimmy but knew only vaguely. He felt hurt when he thought of his uncle. The Scottie passed a couple of churches and Ben began to feel uneasy. Wasn't the man ever going to stop? The lamplighters were out now and street lamps shed pools of light on pavements.

Ben was just starting to think of finding his way back home when John turned a corner. The boy hurried after him and to his relief the Scottie stopped outside a shop halfway up the street and went inside.

The boy paused outside to get his breath back and gaze in the window. Delight brightened his sweaty little face as he stared at a litter of puppies curled up in straw. Immediately one came over to the window and, rearing up on its hind legs, barked shrilly at him. There were not only puppies but rabbits, a cockatoo chained to a perch and a cage of canaries. There was no sign of the monkey so Ben decided to go inside.

A bell tinkled as he entered. There was a big girl behind the counter and a woman talking ten to the dozen to the Scottie in a shrill voice. Ben was delighted to see the man was in the act of clipping a lead to the monkey's collar.

The girl looked in his direction before coming over to him. 'What do you want, little boy?' She smiled and he did not know what to say. It had suddenly struck him that the man might be angry with him for following him. 'Cat got your tongue? I bet it's a white mouse? All the boys want a white mouse.'

Ben nodded and followed her over to a large cage which stood against a wall in a far corner. Instantly he was captivated and gazed enraptured at the mice, wishing he had some money.

'Well, do you want to buy one?'

'Can I think about it?' He had heard his mother say that when she wanted something but couldn't afford to buy it.

The girl nodded and moved away. Ben stared at the mice, desperate to hold one. He glanced around and saw he wasn't being watched and opened the cage. The mice's reactions were swifter than his and several of them escaped. 'The mice! The mice are out!' he shrilled, and dropping on his hands and knees he scrabbled about the floor.

The others spun round and the woman shrieked, 'Shut the cage, Celia, and be quick!'

The girl shot across the floor and closed the cage. John slammed the shop door. The woman approached Ben with her hand raised. 'You pest! You nuisance!'

Having managed to catch one of the mice, Ben rose to his feet and held it out beaming up at her. 'Here's one. Isn't he lovely? Or is it a she?'

The woman stared at him seemingly lost for words as he stroked the teeny creature's back. 'What about the rest?' she said.

'I'm sorry. I didn't think they'd be so fast.'

'I bet he didn't think at all, Ma,' said Celia.

John's expression was exasperated as he gazed down at

Ben. 'What were you thinking of following me all the way here? Your mother's going to be worried sick.'

'I wanted to see the monkey.' He held the mouse out to the girl and smiled up at John who did not return his smile.

'Mrs McDonald is right. You're a pest and a nuisance. What am I going to do with you?'

'Take me with you,' said Ben eagerly, wiping his hands on the sides of his trousers. 'I'll be good. I'll look after your monkey for you.'

'Ach, I can't do that. Your mother wouldn't like it and it would take you past your bedtime.'

'You know this boy?' said Mrs McDonald, pursing her lips.

'Barely at all,' said John, taking up his fiddle. 'And I've no urge to become better acquainted. Ben, you're trouble!'

'I'd take him with you,' said Celia with a grin on her freckled face. 'With that smile, Little John, he'll win hearts for you.'

John stared at Ben who was holding out a tentative hand to the monkey. 'I'll take him so far then he can go the rest of the way on his own.' His tone was decisive. 'Come on, Ben. If we don't get going I'll be late catching the crowds.' He nodded in the woman's direction. 'I'll be back with the monkey. You'll know it's me by my knock.' He pulled the girl's plait gently and then pushed the boy before him and out of the shop.

John's eyes searched doorways as he strode along the darkened street with the monkey scampering behind him and Ben trotting at his side. Even this early in the evening one could never be too careful and he had made a dangerous enemy. He was also pretty sure that spunky little widow Mrs Ryan would have his life if anything happened to her son. He thought back over what had happened since he had met her and it was only gradually he became aware that Ben was panting in such a way that it was impossible for him to ignore. John halted and gazed down at him. 'Are your legs tired?'

Ben nodded wordlessly.

'Up with you then.' John almost doubled himself. Without any more encouragement Ben scrambled on his back and clung tightly as any monkey. The man hurried on faster than before, across St John's Gardens and on up Lime Street until they came to the Futurist where a queue was shuffling slowly along in the direction of the cinema entrance. For a moment he hesitated, wondering whether to skip playing that evening and take the lad home to his mother, but then he thought how he needed new boots. He lowered the boy to the ground and told him his mother would be worrying about him and to skedaddle.

Ben walked slowly away but only went a few yards before stopping in a doorway. He watched John take his fiddle from its case and begin to play. The monkey reared up on its hind legs and performed a kind of dance so that Ben was entranced by the creature all over again. He forgot about food and his mother worrying, and a few moments later came out of hiding and joined the monkey, jigging along and following John along the queue as he played tune after tune.

Kitty was in a panic. She had seen no sign of Ben on the return journey and when she arrived home he was not there. Annie was not around for her to ask about him and Teddy and Mick were not in yet. She searched high and low, looking in the most unlikely places, such as the pantry, because Ben liked hiding. She even checked the Smoking Room, although it was forbidden to her youngest son when guests were around. In the end she went back down to the basement where she found that her two elder sons had arrived home and were listening to the Brown's wireless which Mick had put together with his father's help in 1929 before the Crash.

'Ben's missing,' she said loudly. 'You're going to have to look for him. I've got fish to cook.'

Teddy opened his eyes. 'He's nothing but a worry is our Ben but he probably hasn't gone far.' He stared into space and got to his feet slowly. 'I've got a feeling he went past me when I was playing ollies in the gutter. I remember thinking those fat little legs looked familiar as they went down the road.'

'Why didn't you stop him?' cried Kitty, even more worried as she tied her apron on. She seized Teddy by the shoulders and hustled him out of the door to the area. 'Go and look for him. You too, Mick.'

'Hang on, Ma! Let me get me coat,' cried Teddy.

'Where are we supposed to look?' asked Mick, shrugging on an overcoat.

Kitty stared at him, thinking with half a mind that his overcoat would not last another winter and perhaps she had been wrong in agreeing to him staying on at school another year. What was the use of a grammar school education when she needed him here? 'Anywhere! Everywhere!'

She waved her arms about. 'Use your common sense! You were his age once, weren't you?'

'Yeah! But I never did half the things he does,' protested Mick.

'I know that! Ju-just try and think like him,' said Kitty and headed upstairs where she found Annie in the kitchen.

'I see that big fella's fixed the chair,' said her cousin.

'Yes, of course he has,' said Kitty and realised that for a whole twenty minutes she had forgotten about the Scottie. 'Where've you been? You haven't seen Ben have you? Only he's gone missing.'

'I just slipped out on a message. Your Ben was here not half an hour ago mithering the life out of the big fella. Something about a monkey. He wasn't going to take him with him, though. Didn't want him from what I could make out.'

Kitty stopped in her tracks. 'Mr McLeod's left?'

'I'm sure he has.'

Of course he has, thought Kitty. She had not seen sight nor sound of him as she searched for Ben. 'I bet he's followed him,' she groaned and sank onto a chair. 'I hope he doesn't get lost in the dark.'

'Perhaps the big fella's noticed him,' said Annie.

'I hope so.' She felt a bit brighter thinking that he had and rose to her feet again. 'I wonder where he's gone?'

'I don't doubt you'll find out sooner or later,' said Annie cryptically.

Kitty was not so sure but hoped she would and that it would be sooner rather than later.

Mick and Teddy returned half an hour or so later,

empty-handed and famished. Kitty told them that Ben might be with the big Scottie.

'You let that Scottie come here!' exploded Teddy. 'You must be mad! For all you know he might have been out to rob us and has kidnapped our Ben.'

'Don't be daft!' said Mick, sprawling in a chair and yawning. 'Our Ben would be more trouble than he's worth.'

'You just never know,' said Teddy darkly, thrusting his hands in his pockets. 'Everybody keeps saying these are hard times and some people would do anything for money.'

Kitty disputed that. 'Mr McLeod isn't like that. He helped me get my money from Mr Potter.'

The boys looked at her. 'Why did he have to help you?'

She told them. 'It was a good job Mr McLeod was there. Otherwise I don't know what I'd have done.' She smiled at them. 'You should have seen him ram Mr Potter's hat down over his eyes. I could have cheered.'

Teddy looked disgruntled but Mick said, 'I suppose we should be grateful to him.'

'Yes, you should,' she retorted. 'I don't know where I'd have been without him.'

There was a silence which Mick broke by saying, 'So Potter wasn't a magician after all. That figures. Most magicians would have shown off with at least one trick. He had nothing up his sleeve.'

Teddy threw a cushion at his brother's head. 'What happened to the dummy?' he asked.

'In the yard. And don't throw cushions. Let's hope Ben'll be back in time for supper. He must be starving.'

But Ben was not back and Kitty was really worried by

then. Perhaps he wasn't with Mr McLeod after all. She put on her coat and told the boys to do the same.

'But what about our supper?' protested Teddy. 'Couldn't we eat first?'

'I couldn't eat at a time like this! You'll just have to wait.' She rammed on her hat and despite their groans the boys did as they were told.

It was outside Mount Pleasant Post Office they met up with John. Ben was perched up on his shoulders with his arms clamped round his neck and his head drooping against his plaid bonnet.

A rush of relief and anger surged through Kitty. 'I've been worried sick,' she cried. 'Where on earth have you been?'

Before John could speak Ben lifted his head and said, 'I've had a luv'ly time. Me and the monkey collected piles of money for Little John.'

'You've what!' Kitty could scarcely believe her ears. There was her worrying all this time and this – this busker had been using Ben. She was disappointed in him. 'How could you?' she cried, gazing up at the man. 'He's only seven years old and you've had him begging in the streets. What will the neighbours think?'

'Why should the neighbours think anything? They probably haven't seen him,' said John. 'Calm down, woman! He did it off his own bat. I didn't know he was there until it was too late. He'd been singing and dancing a fair treat for ages, so some woman said, but he kept out of sight behind me. You should keep a better watch on him if he's prone to wander.'

His words went home and guilt was now a lethal ingredient in the cocktail of her worry and anger. Her eyes blazed. 'How dare you suggest I don't look after my children properly! I went to meet him but I was late because of you.'

'It was you that wanted me to go back to your place,' said John.

Ben interrupted them, 'The girl in the pet shop said I'd melt their hearts and I did, didn't I, Little John?'

'The pet shop! Melt their hearts,' gasped Kitty. 'So it was suggested to you, you use my son and you've just said—'

'I know what I said,' said John, 'and it's true.'

'So you say! How do I know you're telling the truth? You could have deliberately exploited him! You might as well have sent him up a chimney!'

'Don't be daft, woman. There's no comparison between singing and dancing and sweeping chimneys.'

'It's child labour and there's a law against it! I'll pay you for the jobs you've done and after that I don't want to see you again.' She turned on her heel and marched up the Mount. Over her shoulder she called, 'And don't you dare bring that monkey onto my premises!'

'Phew!' said Mick. 'She's in a real paddy.'

'She was worried,' snapped Teddy. 'You know she's always worrying about our Ben since Jimmy went.'

John swore under his breath and hoisted Ben from his shoulders. He held Joey's lead out to Mick. 'You look after them both.'

He loped in Kitty's wake and caught up with her outside

Mrs McKeon's corset-making premises. He seized her arm and brought her to a halt. 'You are one unreasonable woman,' he yelled, exasperated. 'Chimney sweeps! I've never heard the like. Didn't you hear a word Ben said or see his face? The lad enjoyed himself! Doesn't that mean anything to you after what you said about him missing your brother-in-law?'

She realised guiltily that she had not given thought to how Ben had felt, but that still did not make her feel any better about her youngest son begging in the streets. 'I'm not against him enjoying himself,' she said stiffly, tilting back her head and staring up at John, 'but doing what he did wasn't what I had in mind. I've my reputation to think about.'

'Your reputation comes before your son I suppose.'

'That's unfair! My reputation is my livelihood and if it got about what Ben had been doing, people might think I'm short of money.'

'And would that matter?'

'Of course it would matter,' she said, suddenly remembering where she was and lowering her voice. 'I have to appear to be making a success of things with my mother and Jimmy gone – and Mr McLeod, I'd appreciate it if you could keep your voice down. I don't want to be heard arguing in the street.'

'It's you that started this, Mrs Ryan,' he hissed. 'Shrieking at me like a seagull! You should be *proud* Ben's got some initiative. He won't sit and starve if he's ever in a fix.'

'I am proud of him,' she whispered. 'Anyway, why did

you have to busk tonight when there was no need? I said
I'd feed you and give you a roof over your head.'

'I don't want reforming, Mrs Ryan,' he whispered back.
'I like my life the way it is and I don't want no woman
chaining me to her apron strings.'

Kitty gasped. 'You've got a cheek suggesting such a
thing! Winking at me and looking at me in such a way
that – that . . .'

'So it's a sin now to look? You're an attractive woman. I
could kiss you right now instead of just looking at you but
that would be a fool thing to do.'

He had succeeded in taking her breath away and she
found herself blushing like a young girl paid her first
compliment. Her hand went to her hair where it curled in
the nape of her neck. He had disarmed her and she knew
that she would have liked him to kiss her. 'You really think
I'm attractive?' she stammered.

He smiled. 'Even when you're biting my head off – but
don't go thinking I enjoy you acting like a shrew.'

'I'll have you know normally I'm an even-tempered
woman.'

'Like when you throw fish.'

'Some people would try the patience of a saint.' Her
tone was mild but she was feeling gloriously alive. 'Now
will you let go of my arm because you're hurting me?'

He released her. 'So where do we go from here?'

'I thought we were going to my hotel? You want paying,
don't you?'

'A labourer is worthy of his hire,' said John. 'That's from
the Good Book so my granny taught me. But don't make

the mistake of thinking playing the fiddle isn't labour, too. I practised damn hard to get that good.'

'You are good,' she said generously. 'I'm sure you could play in a dance band.'

He frowned. 'There you go again trying to turn me respectable.' He fell into step beside her. 'I don't want to play in a dance band.'

'What do you want?' she asked impulsively. Because surely there must be something more he wanted from life than busking in the streets.

For a moment she thought he was going to tell her, then the warmth that had lingered in his eyes died. Without another word he walked on and his stride was so long she had no chance of keeping up with him.

The boys came up to her. Ben was dragging his feet, scuffing the toes of his shoes as Mick and Teddy tried to keep him upright and control the monkey, whose lead had wrapped itself round Mick's left leg. 'I want Little John to stay,' said Ben, his bottom lip quivering. 'If he goes he'll take Joey with him and I don't think I'll be able to find the shop with the white mice again.'

She almost said, 'I don't think he wants to stay,' but she did not trust her voice because for some reason she felt near to tears. She took Ben's hand and they walked slowly up the Mount together.

They found John sitting on the stairs with his hands looped between his knees, and Kitty came over all maternal as she looked at him. 'You're tired, Mr McLeod,' she said softly.

'It's all that work you threw my way,' he murmured with only the faintest of smiles.

'You'll sleep all the better for it.' She hesitated. 'Are you going to stay for supper?'

He hesitated too before answering. 'Herrings cooked the Scandinavian way?'

'That's what I said.'

He rose to his feet and she felt an overwhelming gladness.

She turned to the boys. 'Ben, leave that lead alone. Mick, take that monkey downstairs. Teddy, get that scowl off your face and show Mr McLeod the way. I'll be with you in ten minutes.'

She did not stay to see her orders carried out but hurried into the kitchen. She sang softly as she placed the covered dish of fish and a tureen of potatoes taken from the oven onto a tray. After the barest of hesitations she got out a tumbler before going to a cupboard and standing on tiptoe. She could just about manage to reach the next to highest shelf standing on an upturned bucket and considered how someone tall in the kitchen would be an asset. She poured an inch of liquid into the tumbler and replaced the bottle. Then she diced some fruit into a dish before making a jug of cocoa.

As she entered the front basement room she was aware of the two elder boys' eyes upon her, but neither of them spoke and she was thankful for that. She glanced at John who was slumped in the rocking chair with his eyes closed and decided to leave him for the moment. First the monkey. She had noticed that despite the cat's arched back and hissing protests, Ben was trying to persuade the monkey to sit in the cardboard box which was the cat's bed. She placed the fruit on the hearth and immediately the monkey scampered towards the dish.

She served the boys their meal before going over to the man in the rocking chair. His long legs were stretched towards the fire and she noticed there was a dirk thrust down a stocking. Did he walk where danger lay or was it purely for show? Her eyes reached up to his face and she noticed that his eyelashes gave the impression of having had their ends dipped in gold paint. Part of her wanted to leave him sleeping, to enjoy his rest, whilst another part wanted him awake and noticing her. She realised then what a mess her emotions were in. She glanced at the dinner table where she had dished out their supper and saw that the cat, having given the monkey's plate a disdainful sniff was preparing to spring. 'Scat, cat,' she hissed. It hesitated but the temptation was too much and it sprang. 'Mick, get that cat!' she yelled.

The Scotsman shot up in the chair. 'I'll be with you in a minute, dammit! I've only got one pair of hands!' His eyes were wide open and immediately Kitty fell on her knees beside his chair. She had seen such fearful apprehension before. 'It's all right, Mr McLeod. The war's over. You can relax. But if you want that dinner I promised, you best have it now or the cat'll yowl the place down.' She reached out with both her hands and covered his shaking ones. 'It's all right,' she repeated. 'I promise you. You're safe with me.'

It seemed a long moment before he appeared to recognise her and he freed a shaky breath. Even so there was still a haunted look about his face.

'I've a drop of whiskey here if you'd like it?' said Kitty calmly. 'It's Irish, though, not Scotch. I thought it might help keep out the cold.'

He nodded and took the glass from her, downing it in one go. Then he rose and went over to the table and sat next to Ben who was eating with his fingers and drowsily watching the monkey.

Kitty poured cocoa and made conversation as she began to eat. 'Michael used to have a wee dram sometimes to help him sleep. His uncles who live in County Cork brought a bottle over every time they stayed for the Grand National.'

John forked up a mouthful of fish, chewed, swallowed, and said huskily, 'I've been to Ireland.'

'When was that?'

He hesitated and she thought he was not going to answer, but after a moment he said, 'After the war. I went to see the mother of a soldier who'd died on me.' He chewed with slow deliberation.

'The Black and Tans would be in Ireland then,' said Kitty, wanting to find out more.

'Aye. It was a dirty fight they were involved in and the civil war which followed wasn't much different.'

'You stayed on in Ireland for that?' She was surprised.

'I was needed,' he muttered. 'Let that suffice.'

Kitty fell silent because she knew a little more about him now and guessed it would be a mistake to force his confidence, even if she could. Who was he? What was he? She had a name but that told her only that he was of Scots descent. He had fought in the war, had been to Ireland, had a sprinkling of relatives whom he didn't have much to do with. Perhaps they were all ashamed of the life he led? But what had caused him to lead such a solitary life? Had it solely been the war? That moment back there when he had wakened, she had been reminded of Michael after the worst of his nightmares. Then she had had to hold his shaking body and soothe away his fears.

Ben's sleepy voice startled her into remembrance of her sons' presence. 'Can I go to bed now and take Joey with me, Ma?'

She smiled at him tenderly, forgiving him for having worried her. He was still her baby after all. 'Yes to bed. No to Joey. Mick, you take him up. Teddy, you can give me a hand in the kitchen. We'll leave Mr McLeod to finish his dinner in peace.'

She ushered them out, hoping when she returned the Scotsman could be persuaded to talk a little more about himself. But when she returned he had gone.

Feeling disappointed and now too restless to go to bed despite her weariness, Kitty decided to do some paperwork. She hated paperwork. It was something her mother had always dealt with, although she had taught Kitty the rudiments of bookkeeping. She sat down at the table in the basement determined to do her accounts, but no sooner had she started than she felt an urge to weep. She swallowed the sudden lump in her throat. What on earth was the matter with her? She could not now start weeping all over again for her mother. She had to cope! She gazed down at the accounts book and a tear splodged some figures. Quickly she blotted the spot and concentrated her mind not on that still figure in the coffin but on John

McLeod. He had said she was attractive and had wanted to kiss her but perhaps it was all baloney. Why else had he just upped and left without saying goodnight?

With an unsteady hand she picked up a pen. She was being stupid and all over a man who had told her he didn't want to be tied down. Was that the kind of man she needed right now?

She rose and went over to the sideboard set against a wall and took up the photograph. Michael looked handsome, smart and upright in the wedding photograph and she looked good too. She wore a cream crêpe de Chine suit and a large hat with overblown artificial roses round the brim. They both looked familiar but not like anyone she really knew well anymore. They were so young, untested, but soon to be put through the mill.

She replaced the photograph and gazed unseeingly across the room. It had been terrible saying farewell to the keen-eyed youth she had loved when he went off to war but it was even worse when he returned. That farewell had really been goodbye because the man he became had been so ill, so weak, had found it such a struggle to breathe sometimes that there had been days when she could not bear going into the room where he lay because it hurt so much. Of course she had gone but it had torn her apart watching him suffer, slowly dying in front of her eyes. It had been a relief when the influenza took him from her.

The tears rolled down her cheeks and she picked up her pen again and dug it into the blotting paper. She remembered what Jimmy had said about Michael being weak and told herself fiercely that was not true. Yet as she sat at the table she felt miserably unconvinced. He could have been more of an emotional support to her and the boys, but everything involved in their rearing had been left to her and her mother. What would her life have been like now if Michael had not died? He had been surprisingly demanding in bed and how would she have coped if there had been another child, with him being no help at all? She longed for someone strong to lean on, to replace her mother and Jimmy. A man who would be able to do all the jobs necessary but control her boys. He would need to have a sense of humour and plenty of patience, to have seen a bit of life. It would also be useful if he knew something about the internal combustion engine because Teddy had a growing interest in engines. Mick, on the other hand, enjoyed reading, writing and listening to the radio, acquiring knowledge on any subject under the sun. Whilst Ben – he was into everything! But John McLeod knew that and still he had said she was attractive. He must feel something for her whilst she . . .

Kitty pulled herself up short. What on earth was she thinking of? He had left and she did not know where he had gone. It would be best if she stopped thinking about him altogether.

Chapter Four

Ben was up early the next morning and after breakfast sat himself on the area steps, despite having been told by Kitty he must never sit on stone. By ten o'clock there was still no sign of the big Scottie and he was getting restless and thinking of going to look for him.

Annie appeared with a bucket of steaming water. 'You get up off them steps,' she ordered, 'or you'll end up with piles.'

Ben did not know what piles were and could not have cared less but he went down the steps and indoors anyway. There was no one in the basement so he went up to the kitchen where he found Mick and Kitty.

'He hasn't come,' he said, standing next to Mick's chair and resting his chin on the newly scrubbed table.

'Who hasn't come?' murmured Mick, not looking up from his book.

'Little John. I want to see Joey and the white mice again.'

'Hard luck,' said his brother.

'I want to see them.'

There was no response from Mick but Kitty, who had known exactly who he was talking about, said, 'He probably has something else to do, son.'

'He said he'd take me.'

'Are you sure?' She knew Ben could convince himself something was true when it was not. Although she had not forgotten that Mr McLeod had said he would fix it for Ben over the monkey but, of course, that had been before yesterday evening.

'He said maybe,' said Ben.

'That's not definite.'

'It almost is.'

'It isn't! And that's enough,' said Kitty, getting to her feet. 'You've already blotted your copybook, my lad, so you just be careful. No wandering off on your own. Why don't you go down the Pier Head with Mick to watch the boats? Then when you come back we'll have something on toast by the fire downstairs and play Snakes and Ladders.'

Ben considered the suggestion and tugged his brother's sleeve causing him to spill some milk. 'Eejit,' said Mick without rancour.

'Let's go now,' insisted Ben.

'Go where?'

'The Pier Head like Ma suggested. Please, Mick,' he said coaxingly.

Mick sighed and closed his book. 'What's the rush?'

'I want to get there.'

Kitty smiled as she watched the pair of them. 'Go on, love. I could do without him under me feet.'

Mick drained his cup and led the way out of the kitchen, not averse to an outing but wishing it was not always him that was chosen to look after Ben. He wondered what had gone on between her and the big Scottie after they had gone

to bed. Perhaps nothing, he thought hopefully. Otherwise
Ma would have said something about him calling round
later for Ben.

Mick put the two adults out of his mind and began to
work out which way to go down to the river. He liked a
bit of variety so considered taking a different route than
normal. He would go along Ranelagh Street and Hanover
Street to the Custom House in Canning Place, then Strand
Street, past the Goree Piazzas where it was said negro
slaves had once been put up for auction and then on to the
Pier Head.

But they were only halfway along Ranelagh Street
when Ben tugged his sleeve. 'Not that way.'

'Why not?' said Mick. 'What's on your mind now?'

'I want to go the pet shop.'

Mick groaned. 'No dice! Forget mice and monkeys and
think on ships. It'll be more exciting down by the river.'

'You'll like the mice, Mick,' said Ben earnestly and
smiled beguilingly. 'And I think I can find the way.'

'You only think?'

'More than think,' said Ben, knitting his brows. 'We
go across St John's Gardens and up the road that way. It's
straight along.'

'Is it far?'

Ben hesitated. 'Not too far. I walked it and your legs are
longer than mine.'

Mick stared at him, not trusting Ben's estimation and
wanting no complaints from him that his legs were getting
tired, which meant he would end up having to give him a
piggyback. 'Couldn't you be happy with the puppies at

the back of the market?' Ben gave him a reproachful look. 'OK, OK!' said Mick. 'Puppies are too ordinary for you but I'm telling you if we get lost you're in it, kid.' Mick had a horror of getting lost ever since he had been swallowed up in a crowd in New Brighton as a toddler. He had only vague memories of it now but there had been a big, bluff policeman who had towered over him and frightened the life out of him. He had wanted his mother and his gran, who had always been there when he needed them.

Ben beamed up at him. 'I knew you'd say yes. You're the best brother in the world.'

'You don't have to give me any soft soap. Just don't get us lost or we'll be late for lunch and Ma'll get cross.'

Ben swore that he knew where he was going, but when they came to St Anthony's Church on Scottie Road he could not remember in which street the pet shop was situated. Everything looked different in daylight with the pavements busy and women doing their weekend shopping. He stopped on a street corner and gazed about him.

'You're lost, aren't you?' said the exasperated Mick.

'We went up one of these streets.'

'That's a great help.' Mick glanced up at a pub sign. 'What about this place? Do you recognise it?'

'There *was* a pub.' Ben's expression brightened.

He began to walk up the street but Mick grabbed his shoulder. 'Hang on! Are you sure this is the right one? There's a pub on every corner along Scottie Road.'

'We'll have to try every street then.'

'You're a noggin,' muttered Mick, thinking he must have been daft to agree to come.

'I've got us this far,' said Ben, thrusting out his chin. 'Let's go right up one and then down the next and I bet we find it.'

Mick decided to throw his natural caution to the wind, because deep down he admired his younger brother's determination to get what he wanted. 'OK! But if we do find it we won't be able to stay long because Ma'll start worrying if we're late for lunch. Have you got that, our kid?'

Ben nodded.

There was no sign of a pet shop on the first street but at the other side of Great Homer Street there was a street market. Mick's face lit up and he felt in his pocket for the shilling his mother had given him for the work he'd done that week. He hurried across the cobbled thoroughfare.

'Hey! Wait!' cried Ben, doing his best to slow his brother down by hanging on to the tail of his overcoat. 'Where are you going? We're suppos-edd-ly looking for the pet shop.'

'We will in a minute,' murmured Mick, pushing his way through the crowds with a bony shoulder and dragging his brother with him. He was heedless of the feet he trod on. Up one aisle and down another he went in search of secondhand books. At last he found what he was looking for and began to browse.

Ben looked up at him in disgust, knowing that once his brother got his head in a book then they could be there for ages. He rested his elbow on a row of books which slowly fell on their sides like a row of dominoes. A girl stopped the end ones from sliding to the ground and the stallholder rapped the back of Ben's hand with his knuckles and told him to beat it. Ben tugged on Mick's pocket but his brother only flicked a page.

The girl smiled at Ben. She was a lot bigger than him with long dark plaits, freckles and a wide smiling mouth. 'I've seen you before,' she said. 'I'm Celia from the pet shop. You freed some of our mice and we had the devil's own job trying to catch them. Ma reckons a couple are still missing and perhaps have gone behind the skirting board.'

Ben's face lit up and he pulled hard on Mick's pocket, until eventually his brother said in a vague voice, 'Stop it, Ben, or I'll belt you.'

'No, listen, Micky! This girl's name's Celia and she's from the pet shop.' Mick ignored him so Ben pinched his arm.

'Ouch!' The book slid from Mick's grasp and his hand caught Ben on the side of his face. 'What the heck did you do that for?' He rubbed his arm.

Celia frowned at him. 'There was no need to go and hit him like that. He's littler than you.'

'He pinched me!' cried Mick. 'Besides it was a reflex action me hitting him. Anyway I don't see what it's got to do with you. You should mind your own business.'

The girl flushed. 'He's already been in trouble with Mr Elias but you were too wrapped up in a book to notice.'

Mick glanced down at his brother. 'Trust you! I suppose we'd better shift.'

'Let's go the pet shop,' said Ben, turning towards Celia and slipping his hand into hers. 'You'll show us the way, won't you? I'm Ben. He's Mick. Will we find Little John there? You were funny last night calling him that 'cos he's big.'

Celia smiled. 'There was a big fella like him in the story of Robin Hood and he was called Little John.'

'If he's going to be there, I'd rather not go,' said Mick.

'Why not?' asked Celia pushing her way through the crowds.

Mick made no answer. He could not have put his feelings into words but he had felt uncomfortable seeing his mother kneel in front of the Scottie last night. The way she had taken his hand and spoken so gently to him had been in such contrast to her former anger in the road that it had confused him. He could not understand why he should feel like this. His mother was more nice to people than not. It was part of the job she had once said, and he knew she liked meeting people and looking after them or she wouldn't be doing what she did.

'He's OK, you know,' said Celia earnestly. 'I know he's big and that can be a bit threatening-like but he's really a gentle giant. Although—'

'Although what?' said Mick, pouncing on the word. 'What's he done wrong?'

She shrugged slender shoulders. 'I've seem him punch Charley – but that fella deserved it. He was destroying things and threatened to cut all the puppies' throats. He slashed right through a sack of pigeon feed with a knife!' She shuddered. 'We was terrified until Little John came in with his fiddle like an avenging angel sent from God.'

'You should have sent for the police and they'd have clapped him in jail,' said Ben with relish. 'They do that to bad men.'

Celia shook her head. 'He's too canny for that, little

fella. Anyway, Charley hasn't been back and hopefully he never will be. We heard on the grapevine that his boss has left Liverpool, but I doubt whether *she's* gone for good. She has her finger in too many pies round here.'

'Little John's still around, isn't he?' said Ben anxiously.

She smiled. 'At the moment he is but sooner or later he'll be moving on. He was a friend of me dad's. Not that I remember me dad because he was killed just after I was born.'

Silence fell. It was broken by Mick. 'What do you know about this Little John? I mean besides him being a tough guy, a friend of your dad's and a busker.'

'I know he's got other friends in Liverpool. Rich friends but money don't mean nothing to him. He's me godfather and that's why he comes and sees us every time he's in Liverpool. Him and me dad met at some field hospital during the war. They were both in the medical corps with Scottish regiments.'

'Was your dad a doctor?' asked Ben.

'No!' said Celia, smiling. 'Would I be living round here if he had been? Me gran said he could have done better for himself if he'd had the education but Ma doesn't believe that. She says Gran fantasises, but she never says that in front of her because she wants her to leave her savings to us when she dies.' Her mouth tightened. 'I told Ma I'd rather have me gran than her money and she said I was like me father – daft!'

They came to the pet shop and the two boys gazed at the puppies in the window. Celia went inside saying that her mother would have a face on her if she was any later.

Mick barely noticed her going because he was gazing at a white puppy with a black patch round one eye. He had always wanted a dog but knew Ma would not countenance one in the hotel. She had told him several times that dogs brought fleas and needed looking after almost as much as a child did.

Ben tugged on Mick's sleeve and they went inside. Celia was tying on a large white apron. There was no sign of the big fella and her mother barely glanced their way before flinging a knife on the counter. 'You can carry on with this horsemeat, Cissy. It fair turns me stomach cutting it. I'm going for a lie-down.' She disappeared through an opening at the back of the shop.

The girl picked up the knife and spoke to the shabbily dressed man in front of her. 'How much do you want, Mr Lang?'

The man murmured something and Ben nudged his brother. 'Let's go and look at the mice,' Mick followed him over to the cage and he had to admit the mice were cute. 'Wouldn't you like one?' whispered Ben. 'You've got money. We could go shares. I've a ha'penny.'

'Ma wouldn't allow it.'

'She doesn't have to know. One could live in your pocket or mine and it wouldn't eat much, not something as teeny as a mouse.'

Mick looked at him askance. 'And how do you think you're going to keep it from Ma?'

'I'll hide it.'

'Mice make dirt and if I was going to spend my money on an animal it'd be a dog. Forget it, Ben.' He moved away from the cage and over to the window to look at the puppies once more.

Celia came over and asked did he want to buy one. He looked with longing at the one which had captured his heart but he shook his head and left the shop. Ben joined him a couple of minutes later and Mick told him to hurry or else Ma would start to worry.

Kitty was not worrying about them at all. She had just been shopping in St John's market and was now loaded up. She was thinking about National week in a few weeks' time when her hotel was bound to be bursting at the seams despite the Depression. The punters would come from here, there and everywhere and she would need more help, especially where shopping was concerned. In the past Jimmy had used the sledge stored in the outhouse to carry all that was needed, and she supposed Mick and Teddy could do the same, but she would not be able to trust them on their own to get the right price and to recognise the good cuts. Really she needed a man she could train who could take the chore of shopping off her shoulders. Her thoughts turned to John McLeod. Then as she passed the fur shop on the corner into Ranelagh Street she heard the strains of a violin.

He was standing outside Central Station, a little way up from where several Mary Ellens were selling flowers. For a moment Kitty was undecided what to do, then she made up her mind and walked towards him. She dropped a penny in the plaid bonnet held by the monkey and John acknowledged her offering by elevating an eyebrow.

'I know I owe you more than that,' she said with a smile. 'But if you want your money you'll have to call for it. I don't have more than threppence on me.' John made no answer but fiddled away as if his life depended on it. He was wearing his kilt and his tweed jacket, and gloves with the fingers cut out of them. An involuntary sigh escaped her. 'You don't want to call?'

He lowered his violin. 'Don't sound like that.'

'Like what?'

'Like I've disappointed you,' he said roughly. 'I've disappointed enough people in my life.'

She was silent, uncertain what to say. She could fib and say she was not disappointed but she had been brought up to believe that fibbing often got you into more trouble than telling the truth; although there were ways of skirting round the truth. 'I don't like being in anyone's debt, Mr McLeod, and that's the truth. I still owe you for helping me out.'

'I don't want your money.' He flicked back a hank of nut-brown hair which he wore unfashionably well past his ears, and began to play again. A woman avoided looking at him but her child dropped a penny in his hat. He thanked her.

Kitty stared at him indignantly. 'You're busking!' she said loudly. 'You could be moved on by a bobby! You must need money, so what's wrong with mine?'

His eyes ran over her slowly before he lifted them to the sky, fiddling away at something that sounded like an Hungarian Rhapsody. Kitty reminded herself that he had said he found her attractive. 'You're scared,' she said.

The music stuttered to a halt and he frowned at her. 'And you, Mrs Ryan, are too used to ruling the roost.'

His words silenced her for a moment. Was he saying she was a bossy woman? She did not like to think she was, but since her mother died she *was* the boss. It wasn't an easy position to be in and she needed help. 'I only want to give back,' she said quietly. 'Last night you said a labourer is worthy of his hire! It was out of the Good Book; so shouldn't you take notice of what it says, Mr McLeod?'

He lowered his violin again. 'If you remember my saying that, then perhaps you'll remember I also said that I liked my life the way it is?'

'On your honour, you really enjoy standing here in the freezing cold?' There was a note of disbelief in her voice.

Their eyes met, held. 'You're one stubborn woman,' he said and a heavy sigh escaped him. 'That was a fine way of cooking fish you had, Mrs Ryan.'

'Pardon?' He had startled her.

'You're a good cook and I'm hungry.'

A slow smile curved her mouth. 'Are you saying you want feeding?'

'What do you think?'

'I think that maybe you could drop in at my place about one o'clock?'

He nodded and she went on her way with a spring in her step, reassessing what she would cook for lunch.

When Kitty entered the kitchen it was to find Teddy spreading jam on bread. 'You'll spoil your lunch,' she said, whipping the bread from under the knife and placing it in the enamel bread crock.

His face fell. 'Ma, I'm starving with all that sea air down at the Pier Head.'

'You'll enjoy your lunch all the more then. And if you're still hungry afterwards you can eat that buttie.' She began to unpack the shopping as he went over to the sink. 'Did you see Mick and Ben on your travels?'

'Nope!' Teddy glanced over his shoulder. 'But I saw someone else we know.'

'Who?'

'Jimmy with Miss Drury. They were on the luggage boat and he was looking real pleased with himself. He looked good all dressed up to the nines in a camel overcoat and a trilby. He was leaning against this real wizard open roadster, all cream and chrome.'

Kitty hesitated. 'Did you happen to notice if Myrtle was wearing a wedding ring?'

Teddy's brows creased in thought. 'She wore gloves. I remember because she had her hand on Jimmy's arm and the sleeve of her coat was trimmed with black fur.'

'Did Jimmy notice you?'

'I don't think so.' He added wistfully, 'I bet it'd be fun whizzing along the coast in that car.'

Kitty forced a smile. 'Not at this time of year it wouldn't. They'll freeze to death.'

Teddy agreed with obvious reluctance. 'In spring it would be good.'

'Definitely.' She smiled. 'Perhaps one day, son.'

He came over to her. 'Just think, Ma, once the tunnel's finished there'll be no need for the luggage boat and all those jams round the docks.'

'No. It'll be good – speed things up.' She began to peel potatoes.

Teddy watched her. 'Is Annie staying for lunch?'

'You know she always goes home on a Saturday.' Kitty added almost casually, 'Mr McLeod is joining us.'

She heard the sharp intake of his breath. 'What d'you want *him* here for?' he demanded. 'He's not a bit like Dad or Jimmy.'

Those words surprised her. 'Why should he be? Are you like our Mick?'

His ears reddened. 'Our Mick belongs here! He fits in. The Scottie doesn't. Besides we don't need him. Me and our Mick can do any jobs that want doing.'

'You're both a great help to me and I wouldn't be without you but you can't do everything, son. Besides Mr McLeod isn't coming to work. I'm paying him in food for work he's already done. Now shift yourself and see to our fire – and while you're down in the basement, set the table.'

Teddy went but with obvious ill-grace and Kitty prayed he would not get into a mood. She wanted the boys to get on with John McLeod and for him to like them. She knew that he already had a head start with Ben. She needed a man about the place and couldn't see why the other two, given time and the will to do so, could not get on with John.

Mick and Ben arrived only minutes in advance of the one o'clock gun, which told the workers in Liverpool when that hour struck. John turned up as it went off with an enormous bang. There had been talk of getting rid of the gun but the powers in charge had changed their mind. She gazed at John with a quickening pulse and for several seconds neither of them spoke. Then he said shortly, 'I'll put Joey in the outhouse, shall I? He won't be distracting Ben then. I've bought him fruit and nuts and he'll busy himself eating.'

'It sounds a good idea.' Her breathing eased because what could be more sensible and down to earth than what he had just said. There was nothing lovey-dovey about it and yet there had been a definite something there between them. 'Perhaps you'd like to wash your hands in the kitchen and follow us downstairs?'

'Yes, ma'am,' he drawled, saluted mockingly and went out.

She held her hands to hot cheeks a moment before hurrying downstairs with a tray.

'It's nothing exciting,' she said once they were all seated round the table and she had begun dishing out crispy fried potatoes and buttered eggs.

'It smells luv'ly,' said Ben, sniffing his plate.

'And looks good,' said John.

'It's only boring ol' egg and potatoes,' muttered Teddy, resting an elbow on the table and taking up a fork in his right hand as Kitty approached him.

'Then you won't want any,' said John. 'I'd miss Teddy's plate out, Mrs Ryan. I'm sure Joey would appreciate his share.'

Teddy looked alarmed. 'I didn't say I didn't want any!'

'Then show a bit of appreciation,' said John laconically. 'Your mother's slaved over a hot stove to produce this meal.'

'And there's children in Liverpool hungry,' put in Ben,

nodding his head sagely. 'We're blessed, that's what Annie says.'

'We are that,' said Kitty, nudging Teddy's elbow off the table with her own and spooning out the minutest portion of potatoes for him. There were times when she felt positively guilt-ridden because they had full tummies but told herself her family going hungry wouldn't help the poor and she gave where she could, supporting the *Echo*'s Goodfellow's Appeal at Christmas.

Teddy sat up straight and stared at his plate in disgust and then at John with dislike before glancing up at his mother. 'You keep telling me I'm a growing boy!'

'You'll have to say "pretty please" if you want any more.' said Mick, grinning at him.

'Don't provoke him,' murmured Kitty. 'Just an ordinary please will do, Teddy.'

He glowered at her and she wondered why he had to be like this. She frowned at him.

'Sorry, Ma. Please may I have some more?' he muttered.

She dropped a kiss on his head and topped up his potatoes and egg before dishing out bacon and beans.

All were silent as they took the edge off their appetites but Kitty's mind was working busily despite all that John had said about not wanting his life changed. She imagined what it might be like to have him sitting where he was every day, a very visible, authoritive figure to help mete out discipline when she wearied of making the effort to do so. She hoped her thoughts did not show in her face.

Plates were soon empty. 'Cup of tea?' She stood, resting her hand on the back of a chair.

'You look tired,' said John.

She straightened with a smile. 'Only a bit.' How could she tell him that she had not slept very well because he had filled her dreams.

'Milk, please,' said Ben.

'Is there any afters seeing as how we've got a *guest*?' asked Teddy, managing to infuse a scowl into the question.

'Marshmallows,' said Kitty. 'You can toast them and play Snakes and Ladders with Ben.'

'What about you?' said Teddy. 'Aren't you going to play? Or are you going to be doing something with *him*?' He glanced in John's direction.

Kitty frowned at her son. 'I'll be doing the washing up,' she said with a toss of her head. 'As for *Mr McLeod*, he may do as he wishes.'

'I'll dry for you, Mrs Ryan,' murmured John, his expression uncompromising as he eyed Teddy. 'Then I'll be off.'

'There's no need for you to lift a finger,' said Kitty briskly. 'As Teddy said you're here as a guest but if you'd like to come up to the kitchen and tell me something about your travels, I'd enjoy that.'

'We went to the street market,' said Ben before John could agree or disagree to Kitty's suggestion. 'We met Celia from the pet shop and she said her dad was in the war like ours and he was a doctor.'

'She didn't say that,' said Mick, toying with a fork and wishing everything could be as it used to be when his gran was alive. 'She said he was in the medical corps like Mr McLeod but not that her father was a doctor.'

Kitty glanced at John but his expression showed nothing about how he felt at having that bit of information from his past let slip. She turned to Ben. 'So you found the pet shop without Mr McLeod's help. Clever Ben.'

He dropped his eyes to his mug. 'Mick wouldn't let me buy a mouse. He said you wouldn't like it but I think you would 'cos they've the twitchiest little noses and are cute.'

She ruffled his hair. 'I'm sure they are but Mick's right. Now drink your milk.'

Ben buried his face in the depths of his mug and drained it to the last drop before gasping, 'Can I go and see Joey now?' Before she could reply he had shot across the room and was out.

'I'll go with him,' said Teddy and hurried in his wake.

'Mick, go and watch them,' said Kitty. 'The monkey could bite. Don't let them tease it.'

Mick hesitated but Kitty said, 'Go on, son.'

He went with obvious reluctance. There was a silence after he had gone which Kitty hastened to fill. She wanted to know more about this doctor business. 'More tea?'

'Thanks.' John glanced across at her then hooded his eyes. 'Before you ask, I'm not a doctor either.'

'Who said I was going to ask?'

He smiled faintly and toyed with his fork. 'My grandfather wanted me to be a doctor. I used to go on his rounds with him and got as far as starting my training in Edinburgh but the war came and I volunteered.'

'Couldn't you have finished your training afterwards?'

'I had no money and Grandfather wouldn't give me any.'

'Had he before?'

'Yes. But he was dead against my volunteering. He was a pacifist, you see.'

'But you weren't in a fighting unit,' she said rapidly, 'so surely—'

'It made no difference!' He threw down the fork and looked angry. 'I went and married a Sassenach just like my father and that finished me completely in his eyes.'

She suffered a severe shock. 'You're married?'

He hesitated. 'Was married. My wife died. But even that didn't make Grandfather change his tune.'

'That's sad. Couldn't your grandmother have done something?'

'If she'd been alive – but she died when I was fourteen.' He glanced across at her. 'My grandparents brought me up from when I was seven. That was why it was so terrible when Grandfather wouldn't support me.'

'Your parents were both dead?'

He nodded. 'My mother died when I was seven and my sister certainly didn't want the responsibility of me. My father was still alive then but he was in the navy. He wrote to his mother who lived in Scotland asking could she look after me. It was a big shock I can tell you, going from the south of England to live on the west coast of Scotland.'

'Poor little boy,' she said softly.

His cheeks darkened. 'No need to pity me. I was *happy* living there once I got used to it. Gran, although strict, took me to her bosom as they say. Her brother, my uncle Donald, was also good to me. He taught me woodwork and how to fish and play the fiddle. He told me company would always find me if I had music.'

'You said he was still alive.'

'Aye! It's he who keeps me informed about Grandfather. They're both in their nineties, don't speak and are determined to outlive the other.'

'Your grandfather must be a lonely, miserable old man.'

John's mouth set. 'Proud and stubborn more like.'

'Probably that too,' she murmured, eyeing him sympathetically. 'You never thought of going to see him? The sight of you might have made him change his mind.'

There was the barest hesitation before he said, 'Never!' He drained his cup and rose to his feet.

He's lying, thought Kitty. 'Regret is a terrible thing to live with, Mr McLeod,' she said before she could stop herself. 'Time goes so quickly and your grandfather mightn't live much longer.'

'Forget it!' His tone was harsh.

He's been terribly hurt, thought Kitty, *and he's stubborn*. She began to collect the crockery together. 'You had no friends who would have lent you the money so you could have finished your training?'

He raised both eyebrows. 'I would never ask friends for money. Especially when times are hard. Maybe if I'd have done as you said earlier, and gone to see Grandfather, then maybe . . .' He shrugged. 'It's too late now. I've wasted my years.'

'It's never too late,' she said.

There was a silence. 'What about you?' he said. 'We've talked about me. What about you? I guess your life hasn't been easy.'

She could have told him just how difficult it had been at times but all she said was, 'I've coped.'

A slight smile lighted his face. 'I can see that.'

She wanted to say, 'But you can't see everything.' Instead she asked would he like another cup of tea. He shook his head, took the tray from her and went ahead of her upstairs. When she got up there he had gone and she wondered whether he felt that he had told her too much about himself and regretted it.

But he came again that evening. She fed him and they talked some more and she discovered he was staying with friends who were from Ireland and connected with shipping. He spoke of the places he had been and the poverty he had seen, of marching with the men from Jarrow, but not once did he say anything about staying or how he felt about her.

Then she did not see him for several days and thought that maybe he had left Liverpool because he did not consider or want their growing friendship to be of enough importance to him to inform her of his departure.

It was on a Friday he arrived on her doorstep with a potted white hyacinth in his hand, astonishing her utterly. 'I thought you might like this.' He handed it to her with a slight bow and a touch of embarrassment.

She did not know what to say. He had a rucksack slung over his shoulder and his violin case was strapped to it. The significance of which was not lost on her. 'You're leaving?' She tried to make the words sound casual.

'I'm going to Scotland.'

'To see your grandfather?'

He shrugged, looking at a point somewhere six inches above her head.

She struggled against asking him outright would he be back. 'How long will you be away?'

He gazed down at her. 'It's a long hike.'

'You're walking!'

'I bought a new pair of boots. I've been breaking them in the last few days.'

Her eyes dropped to his brown boots and she turned the plant round between her hands, wondering how long it would take him to walk to Scotland. She wanted to offer him the money for the train fare but guessed his pride would result in a refusal. 'Have you time for a cup of tea?'

He followed her in and she placed the hyacinth on the kitchen table where its strong scent mingled with the smell of fried bacon and eggs. As she fiddled with cups and things there was a silence which she did not know how to break. She wanted to ask him not to go, but of course he was doing the right thing if he intended seeing his grandfather.

They sat at the table across from each other, drinking tea and eating buttered bread. She cleared her throat. 'If he wants you to stay in Scotland, will you?'

'I haven't thought about it. I'll have the whole journey to consider what to say and what he might demand.'

'You think he'll make demands?'

He raised his eyes and looked into her face. 'If he gives me money he will. That's his way, but he's not going to last for ever. And then . . .' His voice trailed off.

And then what? she thought. Would he come back to

Liverpool? The city was a good place to study medicine. She remembered Dr Galloway from Rodney Street telling her that it had been the first place in the country to have a Medical Officer of Health – a Dr Duncan who had been a Scot. He had shocked the unsuspecting of Liverpool and the nation in the 1840s with his revelations of sickness and death in the working-class slums of the city. 'Is it very important to you to be a doctor?' she asked.

'It was, but I'd almost stopped wanting it. Perhaps I've seen enough of suffering in my time?' His greenish-brown eyes were opaque. 'But there's always research if I could make the grade. Although I don't know if I could cope with studying at my age.'

'How old are you?'

'Thirty-nine.'

Too old to begin all over again? thought Kitty with relief but she said, 'Doesn't it depend on how much you want it?'

He smiled. 'You're right. And I won't know that until I know whether it's possible or not.' He leaned across the table and brushed his lips against hers. 'You're good, Kitty. Thanks.' He got to his feet and hoisted his rucksack onto his shoulder, gazing down at her with an unreadable expression in his eyes. 'Don't come to the door. I'll see you when I see you.'

She nodded, refilled her cup with a hand that quivered slightly and did not watch as he walked out of the kitchen.

Chapter Five

'You'll keep the room for me a couple more days then, Mrs Ryan?' said the tall thin man with a bloodhound expression. He was a commercial traveller selling such things as Ritz cigarette papers to the small tobacconists and newsagents that abounded in Liverpool.

'You're one of my regulars, Mr Smith,' said Kitty, smiling and wishing he would go about his business. She had a headache and Ben had been especially naughty that morning, pestering the guests at breakfast with the ventriloquist dummy. There was the washing still to peg out on the line before she could go shopping, but she could not hurry Mr Smith because she needed the business and it was a while before she was able to escape.

It was a fine drying day with a stiff breeze and a sun which was playing peek-a-boo with the scurrying clouds. Kitty hoped it was shining on the big fella wherever he was, although she could have done with him here. The back door was sticking with the damp and was starting to get on her nerves. She would have to advertise for an odd-job man.

It was late afternoon before Kitty thought again about Mick's notice, which she had placed in the front window.

The bell in reception rang and she left the apple pies she was making to answer it. A man with fair hair which stuck up like the bristles of a yard brush, and whose good looks were spoilt by a broken nose, was standing in the lobby. He didn't have any baggage so she decided he must be an odd-job man. 'You've come about my notice. I hope you're good at unsticking doors?' she said with a smile.

'Don't know nothin' about any notice, missus.' He glanced about him and squared broad shoulders. 'As for doors they ain't in my line of business.'

'Then what do you want?' He really didn't look like a salesman, she thought.

He fixed pale blue eyes on her face. 'You's a friend of the big Scottie?'

The question took her by surprise. 'Why do you ask?'

He moved the tobacco he was chewing to the other side of his mouth. 'Haven't seen him around for a couple of days.'

'Mr McLeod's left Liverpool that's why,' she informed him helpfully, thinking that maybe the man was the son of a soldier friend of John's.

His reaction to her words were not what she expected. He spat out some tobacco juice, which annoyed her, and said, 'Wharrit is – is I've come to offer yer me protection.'

'I beg your pardon! And don't spit in here,' she said crossly, reaching for a duster she kept handy in a drawer of the chiffonier.

'I've bin watchin' this place,' he said, swaying backwards and forwards on his heels with his hands in his pockets. 'Yer a woman on yer own so yer needs looking after. Get me drift?'

'No,' she said bluntly, as she wiped the spittle away. 'And I'd like it if you left now.'

He sighed heavily. 'Let me put this another way. I told Jimmy boy I'd look after yer.'

'Jimmy boy?'

'Jimmy Ryan. He's yer brother-in-law, ain't he?'

'Yes, but . . .' She could not make this out. What had Jimmy to do with this man? 'How d'you know Jimmy?'

'I've worked with him.'

'You mean you really are an odd-job man after all and Jimmy sent you?'

'I'm no 'andy man I told yer! But Jimmy has been worried about yer.'

'You do surprise me,' she said, squeezing the duster into a ball and placing it in her pinny pocket for washing. 'I didn't think he'd be giving us a second thought now he's gone off with that woman.'

'Well, yer wrong. He has been thinking of yer and I'm here to look after yus.'

'I don't need anyone to look after me thanks all the same,' she said firmly, not thinking much of Jimmy's choice. 'You can tell him we're managing perfectly well without him. Ta-ra!' She moved past him to open the vestibule door but he was after her in a rush and shoved his backside against it.

'Let's forget about Jimmy,' he snapped. 'And listen to me. I'm here as I said to offer yer protection and that costs money.'

'Dammit!' said Kitty, getting angrier by the minute. 'Are you deaf or something? I need an odd-job man *not* a bodyguard. We seldom have trouble here except for the odd drunk on St Paddy's night and New Year. Now get out!'

'Yer don't get me, do yer?' He thrust his face close to hers. 'I could cause yous a lot of trouble. Yer've got a nice place here. Yer don't want it spoilt, do yer?'

Kitty's head jerked back, recoiling from his odious breath. She could not believe this was happening. 'Are you threatening me?'

'Yer've got it in one.' He grabbed a handful of her pinny, pinching her breast as he did so and bringing tears to her eyes as he dragged her against him. 'That big Scottie lost me me job and Jimmy boy's wormed his way into the boss's good books. Now I'm short of dough and I need some fast. Five quid that's all I'm asking.'

'Five quid! You're joking,' she said through gritted teeth. 'Now let me go or I'll have the law on you.'

'Don't make me laugh!' His eyes were hard as pebbles. 'They'll have to catch me first and you won't be looking so good then.'

'You're so tough when it comes to threatening women,' she sneered, scared but unable to take his words lying down. 'If the big fella was here he'd have your guts for garters and so would Jimmy.'

The man shook her. 'Jimmy said you were a bloody stubborn bitch,' he yelled. 'Well, I've tried being nice so now we'll try the other way.' He produced a knife seemingly from thin air and flicked it open, scratching her cheek with it before pressing it against her throat and saying, 'Where's yer handbag, luv?'

Kitty knew then she had no choice but to give him money. She wanted him out of the way before the boys or any guests arrived on the scene. She did not want her children hurt and, besides, having his sort around was not good for business. 'In the kitchen! And don't call me luv,' she said defiantly.

He grinned. 'I thought yer'd be sensible if I tickled yer with this.' He brandished the knife, loosened his hold about her neck and pushed her so she went flying up the lobby.

Kitty landed on the floor but managed to save her face from scraping the carpet, although one of her knees received a terrible jolt. He made to drag her to her feet but she avoided his hand and limped into the kitchen, thrusting her hands into the large pocket of her pinny, thinking to protect her face with its folds if he threatened her with the knife again. The fingers of one hand curled on the duster in its depths.

'Well, where is it?' he demanded, seizing her shoulder.

'In the dresser cupboard.' Now she was in the kitchen she remembered the rolling pin on the table but he was in the way of her reaching it.

'Get it.' He pushed her in that direction.

Kitty took out her handbag but as she went to hand it over to him, she pulled out the duster and flicked it in his face. He started back with a curse, blinking his eyes. She made for the table but never reached it because he seized her from behind and flung her on the floor. Kitty tried to get up but all the breath had been knocked out of her and she slumped down again.

Ben approached the area steps with a hop, skip and a jump as he tried to avoid the cracks in the pavement. Then he saw Teddy down in the area. 'Ma, didn't come to meet me,' he said.

'She was probably busy or maybe she had to go out. Come in this way.' Teddy pushed open the door to the basement and was greeted by the lovely smell of newly ironed cotton. Annie was singing, 'It was on a Friday morning when I beheld me dar—' She stopped ironing. 'Hello you two. How was school?'

Teddy wondered why it was that grown-ups always had to ask you about school. Sometimes it was as if nothing else existed outside school when you were young. 'OK! Has Ma been baking?'

'She's up there now slaving away,' said Annie, placing the iron on the hearth.

'I think I'll go up,' said Teddy.

'Me too,' said Ben. 'I'm starving.'

'I'll be up in a minute,' said Annie.

'Race you, Teddy,' challenged Ben.

'You've no chance,' said his brother, taking the indoor steps two at a time and racing along the passage leading to the kitchen, aware that Ben was coming up behind him fast.

Teddy opened the door and froze in surprise. Then he recovered himself and yelled at the man rummaging through his mother's handbag whilst she struggled to get up from the floor. The man shoved a banknote in his pocket and dropped the handbag, lunging towards Teddy, who felt something hit him in the back which sent him colliding into the man. They both fell to the floor and Ben, who had butted Teddy, only just managed to stop himself from falling on top of them. He ran towards his mother and saw her remove a clasp knife from the table and place it in her pocket.

Teddy struggled to his feet as Annie entered. 'What's going on?' Her eyes went from one face to another in bewilderment.

'*He* was going through Ma's handbag!' said Teddy, moving towards Kitty, his finger pointing at the man struggling to his feet.

'He's a thief and a coward,' said Kitty in a trembling voice. 'He attacked me and cut me with a knife.' Her hand strayed to the blood on her cheek.

'You big fat bully!' shouted Ben, resting his sandy head against Kitty's stomach and glaring at his mother's assailant.

A look of intense dislike kindled in the man's eyes. 'You little whippersnapper! I could break you in half!'

Kitty's arms went protectively about her sons. 'Don't you dare threaten my children. Get out of here and don't ever come back.'

'I'll be back, girl,' he said, clenching his fist and shaking it at her, causing the boys to press closer to her. 'And it'll be yer windows if you don't give me the rest of the loot.'

Annie reached for the rolling pin on the table and wacked it against the wooden surface. 'You just get out, me fine boyo, or it'll be the worst for you!'

The man's eyes shifted from Kitty to Annie and he said menacingly, 'I'll remember you.' And he turned and left the kitchen.

'Phew!' said Annie, her shoulders sagging as she plonked herself on a chair.

Kitty sat down too but only for a moment. She hurried out of the kitchen and was just in time to see the man going out of the front door. She took the snib off and closed it. 'The guests'll have to ring,' she said to Annie and the boys who had followed her out.

Annie nodded. 'Who was he? How did he come to be here?'

She hesitated, not wanting to mention Jimmy in front of her cousin. 'He was once Myrtle Drury's bully boy and seems to have been following Mr McLeod around. He said the big fella lost him his job.'

'But what's that got to do with us?' said Annie.

Kitty shrugged. What indeed! She realised she should never have told him that John had left Liverpool but it was too late now to recall her words.

'What are we going to do?' said Teddy, his fists clenching and unclenching. 'He might keep his word and come back. Are you going to get the police?'

'I'll have to think.' Kitty ran a hand over her hair, feeling all to pieces now the man had gone. 'We don't know where he lives to report him to the police and the last thing I want is them hanging round here waiting for him to come back. The guests won't like it and it could damage our reputation.'

'I wonder what the big fella did to lose him his job,'

said Annie, who was looking a bit pale now.

'Let's get Little John,' said Ben, squeezing Kitty's hand tightly. 'He'll give that man two black eyes.'

Teddy frowned. 'We'd be better getting the police.'

'I don't know what to suggest,' said Annie, biting her lip. 'Although I agree with yer mam we don't want the police hanging round here.'

'But you heard what that bloke said,' yelled Teddy. 'He'll be back!'

'Keep your voice down,' hissed Kitty. 'Let's go into the kitchen.'

Ben tugged on her hand. 'Little John'll sort him out.'

She looked down at him. 'He's not here, love. He's gone to Scotland.'

'He might be back by now.'

Kitty shook her head, not in the mood to explain just how far Scotland was if you were walking. 'Let's have a cup of tea. Then we'll really have to get cracking or the guests won't get fed tonight.'

Ben followed her, not wanting to let her out of his sight. It would be terrible if that man came back and he broke their windows and hurt Ma. As he drank his tea he kept looking at Kitty and the scratch on her face, thinking of the big Scottie and whether there was a way of getting in touch with him. He drained his mug and went upstairs to the attic bedroom he shared with his brothers. It was cold in the room but he was hardly aware of it as he wriggled under the large double bed and brought out a shoebox with holes punched in its lid. Inside, nestling in the straw, was a white mouse which he had managed to smuggle out of the pet shop. He placed some breadcrumbs on the linoleum and lifted out the mouse which he had called Twitchy. The tiny creature began snuffling crumbs and as Ben watched he was thinking of Celia. He stroked Twitchy a moment before placing him back in the box and under the bed. Then he hurried downstairs.

Mick was walking up the Mount as Ben was coming down it. 'Where are you going?' asked Mick, pouncing on him.

'To the pet shop!' He seized his brother's coat. 'Come with us, Mick. We've got to help Ma and we've gorra do it now in case he comes back!'

Mick was already fed up because footie practise had been cancelled at the last minute, so he was in no mood for any of his brother's shenanigans. 'What are you talking about? Who's "he"?' he said irritably.

'A baddie man!' Ben hung on to his sleeve. 'He hurt Ma and took her money.'

Mick stared at him. 'You're kidding!'

'No, I'm not,' said his brother indignantly. 'Cross me heart and hope to die! He pinched money from Ma and said he'll be back for more.'

Mick could barely credit it. 'If that's the truth then why hasn't she sent for the police?'

'She's worried about the guests and our reputation.' Ben's quick tongue stumbled over the words. 'So I'm going for Little John.'

Mick's shoulders sagged and his satchel and footie bag slid down his arm onto the ground. 'I don't believe this!

You know he's gone to Scotland. Besides what d'you think he can do?'

'Frighken him off.'

'Frighten,' corrected Mick.

'He's frighkened him before. Remember Celia telling us about the man who was going to slash the puppies' throats?'

Mick screwed up his face. 'Somebody called Charley wasn't it? Myrtle Whatsit's bully boy.'

Ben nodded. 'He's got it in for Little John and's been following him around. He mustn't know he's gone to Scotland. I thought Celia might know where he is. We've got to try and find him, Mick!' Ben's bottom lip wobbled. 'I'm really frighkened. Frighkened Charley'll hurt Ma and break our windows!'

'OK! OK!' said Mick crossly. He was fed up and hungry but Ben's apprehension had got to him and he could see his brother was pinning all his hopes on him at least trying to get in touch with the Scottie. 'I'll go to the pet shop but you're not coming. You go back home and sneak my stuff upstairs. You don't have to tell Ma you've seen me. She's not expecting me home yet but if you go missing she'll worry herself sick.'

'OK.' Ben was happy to do as his brother said.

Mick draped his satchel over one of Ben's shoulders and his bag over the other, ruffled his brother's hair, and then with cold hands in his pockets hurried in the direction of St John's Gardens.

When he reached the pet shop he was reluctant at first to bring up the reason for his being there, so he looked at the puppies. He would have much rather dealt with the matter himself than get in touch with the big Scottie and wished himself older and stronger.

'Are you going to buy one?' called over Celia after Mick had been there for five minutes.

'No.' He sighed and went over to her. 'I need to get in touch with the big Scottie.'

'What d'you want him for?' Celia rested her arms on the counter and smiled at him from lively grey eyes.

Mick felt like telling her not to be so nosy. 'He left something at our hotel in Mount Pleasant,' he said in weary tones. 'It's Ma who insists I get in touch with him.'

'What did he leave?'

'What's it to you?'

'Just curious. I won't tell you how to get in touch if you don't tell me.'

'Then I won't bother,' he said, exasperated. 'I'll just tell Ma he's vanished! Vamoosed!'

'That would be a fib!' Celia straightened. 'What's so deadly secret about this thing? I bet you want him for something else. Is your family in trouble?'

'You really are nosy,' burst out Mick. 'I'll leave it! We'll cope without him.' He turned and walked out of the shop.

Celia hurried after him. 'Hold your horses. You don't have to tell me if it's that much of a secret. I could give you the telephone number of those Irish friends of his.'

'It doesn't matter,' said Mick. 'Go back and look after your animals.'

'You really are irritating,' she said.

'Same to you with knobs on!' He waved his hand in the air without looking back.

Celia could have hit him. Instead she wrote out the telephone number on a scrap of paper and hurried after him. 'Here!' she said, thrusting the paper at him. 'I hope yer get things sorted out.' She ran back to the shop.

Kitty lifted her eyes from the scrap of paper and gazed across the table at Mick. 'Do you think I should telephone?'

'It's up to you, Ma.' He moved aside his maths homework book. 'Our Ben's worrying, and according to him this Charley has it in for the big fella. I think *he* should know that it's down to him that we've had trouble here.'

Kitty was not so sure if it was all down to John but she was not going to bring Jimmy into the conversation with Annie still there. 'I don't see what good it'll do,' she murmured. 'The big fella'll be miles away now but I doubt if he's got to where he's going. If that's true these Irish friends mightn't be able to get in touch with him.'

'Perhaps he'll telephone them? Anyway, it's worth ringing them if it makes our Ben happy.'

She nodded. 'You're right. Although I'll feel a right prune ringing up this number without knowing the name of the person who's going to answer at the other end.'

'I suppose Celia thought we knew their name with knowing about them,' said Mick.

Kitty glanced at him. 'What's this Celia like?'

'OK. A bit nosy but OK,' he said, lowering his head to his homework.

Kitty hesitated, wanting to know a little more. After all

the girl was the big fella's god-daughter, but Mick seemed to have lost himself in his work now and she decided not to disturb him.

The next morning she went down to the Post Office and put a call through from there. It was answered by a woman with a hint of an Irish accent who repeated the number Kitty had dialled and asked could she help.

Kitty hesitated before plunging into speech. 'You don't know me but I'm trying to get in touch with Mr McLeod, a Mr John McLeod, and I've been given your number.'

'Your name?' said the voice.

'Ryan. Mrs Kitty Ryan.'

'Never heard of you,' said the voice cheerfully. 'But I suppose that's not so surprising. What is, is that you have our number.'

Kitty was taken aback. 'Celia gave me it. You do know her?'

'I know her.'

For a moment Kitty did not know what to say next. Then realised it might be helpful if she knew the woman on the other end of the line's name. 'Who am I speaking to, by the way?'

'Mrs Rebekah O'Neill.'

'Are you a widow?' She did not know why she asked.

The voice sounded amused. 'Are you?'

'Yes. But—' Kitty was wishing she had not asked now and said stiffly, 'I don't really know what that's got to do with anything.'

'Oh, I think it does if you're asking me the same question and wanting to get in touch with John. You wouldn't be the first widow to ring this number wanting him to help her.'

What was that supposed to mean? thought Kitty. Her heart was starting to thump in an uncomfortable way and she felt terribly embarrassed. What was this Mrs O'Neill thinking and what was she to the big fella?

'Are you in trouble?' asked the voice at the end. 'If you are perhaps—'

Kitty replaced the receiver and left the booth. She had been daft to telephone. If John McLeod had wanted her to be able to get in touch with him then he would have given her the number or an address where she could reach him. She would have to deal with Charley herself.

Kitty told Mick and Ben she had not been able to get hold of John. 'It's as I said and they don't know where he is.' She did not look up from buttering bread for a bread and butter pudding.

'Couldn't they send a letter to where he's going?' said Ben anxiously.

'They might do that,' she said brightly. 'Don't you be worrying. Everything'll be all right. You'll see.'

Despite her words Kitty felt as if a dark cloud hovered over her during the next few days, due not only to her concern over whether Charley would return but also to her wondering if she might have found out more about John if she hadn't been so hasty in cutting short her telephone call.

The weather changed for the worse and there were blizzards, which were so bad that all football fixtures throughout the country were cancelled. Kitty found her imagination running riot, picturing the big fella frozen in a snowdrift. She sent up a prayer for him, comforting herself with the thought that he was used to being out in the open and would surely have found shelter.

A slow thaw followed and Monday morning found Kitty, Annie and the girl who came in to help with the laundry, hanging washing on the back basement room drying racks where there was a copper boiler and a deep white sink and small fireplace. Outside it was damp and miserable. When they were finished Kitty went up to one of the bedrooms belonging to a guest who had checked out that morning. It was whilst she was in there she heard the sound of breaking glass. She ran in the direction of the noise and cautiously opened the door, relieved that the room was empty. She bent to pick up the brick which lay among the shattered glass before gazing out of the window. Cold air came through a jagged hole, chilling her hot face. She had no doubts about who had thrown the brick. What a mess! Was that Charley? Her eyes rested on a brown-coated back on the other side of the road. Without thinking twice she ran out of the room still clutching the brick.

'What's up?' called Annie and the girl coming out of the door under the stairs.

'That swine Charley's broken one of our windows.'

Annie's mouth tightened. 'What are you going to do?'

'Go after him, of course,' said Kitty, opening the front door. She gazed about her and saw the man she thought was the culprit making his way down the Mount. She sped across the road, narrowly avoiding a coal waggon. The man went round a corner and she was just in time to see him disappearing inside Lewis's departmental store. She made to cross the road only to be stopped by the policeman on point duty.

'And where d'you think you're going with that?' he said. 'It's an offensive weapon.' He tapped the brick with his truncheon.

'It's only a brick,' said Kitty. 'And the man—'

'Don't be smart with me,' he interrupted. 'I can see it's a brick. What I want to know is were you thinking of smashing a shop window with it?'

'Don't be daft! I'm chasing someone. He—'

'Going to hit him with it, are you?'

Kitty's patience began to slip. 'A fat chance I have of that with you stopping me,' she said scornfully.

The policeman hunched heavy brows. 'I don't like your tone.' He prodded her with his truncheon. 'And I've a good mind to take you down to the station.'

Kitty lost her temper. 'Don't poke me!' she yelled. 'Why don't you try catching a real thief if you're so worried about crime! As for this brick! Here, take it!' She shoved it against his chest and ran, but by the time she was inside Lewis's it was too late. The man had vanished.

Annie was on the front step leaning on the yard brush when a shivering Kitty arrived back at the hotel. 'Well?' demanded her cousin. 'Yer didn't catch him, did yer?'

'No, thanks to some stupid policeman,' said Kitty crossly. 'My feet are soaking and I'll have to change my stockings. I'm splashed up to me thighs!'

'Yer were wasting yer time. It wasn't him. He's been back here demanding money and threatening me. I stuck me brush in his face and told him to get lost.' She gave a satisfied smile. 'He didn't like that one little bit.'

Kitty stared at her with a sinking heart but she did not say what she was thinking. Instead she said, 'You gutsy thing! Let's go and have a cup of tea and then I'll have to get out the glazier and have that window fixed.'

Kitty was feeling intimidated but was nevertheless determined to carry on as if nothing had happened once she had seen the glazier. At ten minutes to four she put on her wellies and went to meet Ben from school.

She was standing at the junction of Bedford Street and Oxford Street when she heard her youngest son shouting her and caught sight of him on the other side of the road where there was a crowd of children. She waved, keeping her eye on him, only for him to be obliterated from her vision by a large shiny black car splashing its way between them. When the car passed there was no sign of him.

She hurried across the road, surrounded by children coming in the opposite direction and searched their faces but Ben's was not among them. Where had he gone? Was he hiding like he did sometimes? She reached the opposite pavement and hurried first one way and then the other, searching steps and doorways. She began to feel scared remembering the way Ben had spoken to Charley and what his response had been. She told herself to calm down. She was letting her imagination run away with her. How could Charley possibly know Ben would come this way from school? Unless – unless he'd been keeping a watch on the house and had seen Teddy taking him to school? Her fear intensified and she ran homewards, slithering down the slippery pavements until a stitch in her side caused her to slow down.

Then suddenly Ben was there jumping out on her and saying, 'Stick 'em up!'

Kitty caught him by the shoulder and shook him violently. 'What have I told you about wandering off?' she yelled. 'You've had me worried sick!'

'It was only a game!' He stared up at her with wide reproachful eyes.

'A game! How did you get past without me seeing you?'

'I crouched down and pulled me coat over me head and hid among the others. I was being a bandit that's all,' he said, clutching at her. 'Don't be angry with me, Ma.'

'There's enough bandits around! I want you to be good, good!' She seized his hand and hurried him along, trying to behave normally but inside she was trembling. Then she received another shock. Outside her hotel a car was parked and Teddy was talking to a woman and a girl.

'It's Celia from the pet shop,' said Ben, and hid behind his mother.

'Ma, this is Mrs O'Neill,' said Teddy as Kitty approached. 'She wants to speak to you privately.'

Kitty wished she had not been caught out like this. Mrs O'Neill wore dainty boots, the latest pull-on hat and a dog-toothed patterned suit in brown and cream which hugged her waist and hips and made her look real smart. Kitty felt like a frump in her wellies and old winter coat. 'You'd best come in,' she said stiffly, releasing Ben's hand and leaving him with Teddy.

Without waiting for the other woman's response, she led

the way indoors, slipping off her wellies in the vestibule and carrying them into the empty kitchen.

'You're cross with me,' said Mrs O'Neill, following her in.

'Not really,' said Kitty, startled by her forthrightness. 'I've just had a fright and I wasn't expecting you.'

'I'm sorry about that. But I thought it best if I just came along. I went to see Celia and she told me about you and your sons.' She stared at Kitty from curious green eyes. 'John's never mentioned you.'

'Perhaps he didn't think me worth mentioning,' said Kitty.

'Oh no! I don't think it's that,' said Mrs O'Neill, smiling. 'May I sit down?'

'Sorry.' Kitty reddened. 'I should have taken you into the Smoking Room. It's more comfortable there.'

'This'll do fine.' The other woman seated herself. 'Perhaps I'd better explain that I'm not a widow. I have a husband and three children and it's due to my husband that I know John.'

'Why are you telling me this?' said Kitty awkwardly as she poked the slumbering fire so that the coal flared up.

'Because of the way you put the phone down. I thought, this woman is proud. She doesn't like asking for help but she's turned to John which means she must know him well enough to believe he would help her.'

Kitty stiffened. 'You're right. Although I don't know him that well.'

'That makes it even more interesting.' The other woman gazed expectantly at her but Kitty was more interested in hearing what Mrs O'Neill had to say about John. After a pause the other woman continued, 'Your son tells me you're in trouble.'

'Did he now?' Kitty was surprised. 'And did you tell him you were a friend of Mr McLeod's?'

'I told him I'd heard you were in trouble from Celia and that I was here to help. He said you've been threatened by someone called Charley, who sounds like he's trying to get a protection racket going. Celia filled in the gaps. She's seen him in action. It was then your son explained about John's involvement.'

Kitty took a deep breath, even so her voice trembled when she spoke. 'I'm not blaming John. How was he to know Charley would come here and threaten me with a knife and steal from me and then break my windows?'

'That bad! Poor you. Do let me help?' Her tone was so sympathetic that tears filled Kitty's eyes.

She looked away hurriedly and said unsteadily, 'I told myself I wasn't going to let him frighten me but then Ben played a stupid trick on me today and I was terrified that Charley had got to him. I was ready to give him anything as long as he left my children alone.'

'You really believe he might harm your sons?'

'I wouldn't put anything past him.' She rubbed her eyes with the back of a hand.

'You've thought of the police?'

'Yes. But—'

'You'd rather keep them out of this?'

Kitty nodded. 'Guests don't like disruptions. Especially if it involves the police. I just don't know what to do.

There's my uncle but he's no match for Charley and I can't involve the neighbours.'

'You don't think Charley would try and turn the screws on them?'

Kitty stared at her. 'I never thought of that – but he's only one man isn't he? I mean it's one thing threatening a woman without a man but he might be taking on more than he can chew if he tried threatening other people.'

'He might think of it, though. And he might think of enlisting other thugs like himself.'

'I don't know if he's got the brains,' said Kitty, her brows knitting. 'That would take organising.'

'Well, let's stop him how, just in case. We can't get in touch with John but we can enlist my husband's help. He has men he can call on. Unfortunately he won't be home from New York until tomorrow but as soon as he arrives I'll explain the situation to him.'

Kitty was dumbfounded. 'Why are you offering to help me like this?' she said in a low voice. 'Why should you and your husband want to get involved?'

Mrs O'Neill wriggled her nose and toyed with her gloves. 'John's a friend and the most he'll ever take from us is a bed for the night. I've no idea how you met but the fact that he hasn't mentioned you I find interesting. He's been here several times I believe?'

'Yes,' said Kitty. 'He did some work for me. I sort of offered him a permanent job but—'

'You'd really have him to stay despite the way he lives?'

Kitty smiled. 'I'd expect him to change his lifestyle. There would be no need for him to busk and go wandering if he had a permanent roof over his head.'

'If only you could get him to do that,' said Mrs O'Neill fervently. 'Daniel's been trying to get him to settle down for ages but he keeps saying he's happy as he is.' She rose to her feet. 'I'd best be going. I've left the girls with my maid, Hannah, and she isn't the most patient of people.'

'I should have given you a cup of tea,' said Kitty apologetically.

'It doesn't matter.' The other woman smiled. 'Come and have tea with us when the weather improves. In the meantime I won't forget to speak to Daniel but don't forget to lock all your doors and windows tonight.'

'I certainly won't,' said Kitty, returning her smile. She saw her visitor out, scarcely able to believe that soon her trouble with Charley would be a thing of the past. That was if the beautiful Mrs O'Neill's husband really could be depended on to help a perfect stranger. It almost seemed too good to be true.

Chapter Six

The rock came through the basement window just as Kitty arrived downstairs after seeing Ben to bed. It sent glass flying onto the linoleum and startled the cat out of its box.

'Blinking heck!' Teddy shot to his feet and the book slid from Mick's knee onto the floor. They stared at Kitty, wide-eyed as she reached for the poker and made for the area door. This could not be happening when she had believed it over. It was two days since she had spoken to Mrs O'Neill and they had not been disturbed by Charley in that time.

'No, Ma, it's dark out there,' hissed Teddy, grabbing hold of her arm. 'He might be waiting to get hold of you.'

Still clutching the poker, Kitty sank onto a chair feeling sick with apprehension. She stared at the curtains fluttering in the cold air coming through the hole. Swine! She could murder him for giving her a shock like that but thank God he had not chosen to break one of the guests' windows. But why hadn't he? And why hadn't Mr O'Neill done something about him? Perhaps his wife had been wrong about his willingness to get involved?

There came a scrabbling noise at the area door and

instinctively she rose to her feet. 'What's he up to?' whispered Mick.

'I'll have a gander out of the window,' muttered Teddy. But before he could do so there came a keening noise which caused the hairs to rise on the nape of his neck.

'What was that?' whispered Mick.

'Get out of my way,' said Kitty, gripping the poker tightly and heading for the door. Mick and Teddy followed close at her heels as she drew back the bolts.

A large bundle lay in a heap on the threshold but Kitty could see no one as she glanced outside and up through the area railings onto the pavement. The keening sound came again and she looked down at the bundle at her feet. It moved. She bent to have a closer look and her blood seemed to run cold. 'Help me, Mick,' she said, thrusting the poker at Teddy.

'What is it?' he asked.

Kitty's feelings threatened to choke her but she managed to gain control of her voice. 'It's Annie. Help me lift her.'

'What's he done to her?'

'Don't ask questions! Just lift!'

They managed to get their arms under her and to lift. Annie's eyes remained shut but that keening cry issued from her swollen lips again, unnerving them so much that they nearly dropped her. They shuffled over to the sofa and placed her down. 'Teddy, shoot those bolts,' ordered Kitty. 'Then the pair of you go and look in the yard for a piece of wood to board up the window.'

They vanished through the door which led to the back basement as Kitty gazed at her cousin, noting her bloodied face and scratches with a sick heart. She blinked back tears. The top buttons had been ripped from her coat which gaped open revealing the torn blouse beneath. Her stockings were laddered and there was blood and fluid smeared down her legs. A lump rose in Kitty's throat and she pressed her lips to her cousin's cheek before hurrying to fetch water and a cloth.

She knelt on the rug and dabbed gently at Annie's face. Her cousin's eyelids flickered open. 'It's OK, luv,' said Kitty. 'I've got you.'

'Kit!' Annie started up, clutching the front of Kitty's cardigan and gazing at her with wide frightened eyes. 'He-he-he-he,' she stammered.

Kitty dropped the towel and hugged her. 'Hush now, hush! It'll be all right.' That keening cry issued forth from Annie again and Kitty wanted to weep. 'You just hang on to me,' she said unsteadily. 'You're going to be all right.'

'He – he raped me,' gasped Annie, 'and I was saving meself for Jimmy.' She burst into uncontrollable weeping.

Kitty rocked her back and forth, wanting to scream out the truth about Jimmy and the woman he had gone off with but what would be the point? The truth would hurt Annie unbearably. She let her cousin cry and eventually she lifted her head. 'What am I going to do, Kit?' Her voice wobbled and her eyes brimmed with tears once more. 'What am I going to do? How can I tell Mam and Dad what that swine's done to me?'

'You have to tell them,' said Kitty.

'I can't! It'll upset them terrible.'

Kitty took a deep breath. 'I'll tell your mam.'

'No!'

'Yes, Annie. What if you have a baby?'

Annie started up. 'I'll kill meself if that happens.'

'Don't talk like that,' said Kitty, her own voice shaking.

'I will! I'll kill myself,' said Annie frantically, swaying backwards and forwards. 'I wish I could get him! He deserves to die for what he's done to me.' She began to sob again. 'I was going to go to Rhyl in summer to see Jimmy but he won't want me now.'

'Forget about Jimmy,' said Kitty. 'He left us remember.'

'So did the big fella. This is all his fault.'

'He wasn't to know this would happen,' protested Kitty. 'Listen, love. I'll see you home after I've made the supper drinks and speak to your mam.'

'I don't want to go home. I can't go home.'

'You have to! Your mam'll be worried about you.'

'I can't! I look a mess! I can't walk through the streets like this. I want to stay here with you. I'm frightened to go out. He might be there waiting.'

Kitty realised there could be some truth in that. 'OK. You can stay here. Go and have a wash and a lie-down upstairs. If your dad comes looking for you he can—'

'I'm not letting me dad see me like this! He might try and do something and that fella'd make mincemeat out of him. Dad's only little!'

'OK! OK! What'd you want me to do?'

Annie clutched at Kitty's cardigan again. 'Say I've been sick.'

Kitty smiled despite the desperate situation she felt them to be in. 'What do we blame? My cooking? Besides your face is a mess. It'll have to be something else.'

'Say I fell down the steps! That I've broken me leg!'

'Now you're getting carried away. You'd be—'

'Mrs Ryan!' The voice was male and caused the women to clutch each other. It came again. 'Mrs Ryan, I'm Daniel O'Neill. You've met my wife. Can you let me in?' It was an Irish voice. It had music in it and was like hearing a voice from heaven now she knew whom it belonged to.

'Hold on.' Kitty covered her cousin's legs with a towel and hurried towards the window. She glanced through the hole before going to the door and sliding back the bolts.

'I hope I didn't frighten you?' said the man outside.

She could barely see the face which showed faintly between a crop of curling dark hair and a navy blue fisherman's jumper. 'You did. But come in, Mr O'Neill. I'm glad to see you but I wish you'd come earlier. He got to my cousin.'

'I'm deeply sorry. He knew the back streets better than my men and now we've lost him, dammit!' He stepped inside wiping his feet on the coconut mat.

'You'll get him, though?' she said, unable to keep the fear out of her voice. Now she could see him more clearly she was in some way reminded of her dead husband Michael who had been dark-haired and of sturdy build when they had first met. He'd also had that Irish lilt to his voice.

'Sooner or later. If he tries to get back home we've got him,' said Mr O'Neill. 'The police might be afraid to walk the back alleys of Scottie Road but my men aren't.'

'And if he doesn't go back home?' insisted Kitty.

'We'll keep looking – but don't you worry we won't leave you and your family unprotected. I'll have someone watching this place.'

That relieved her mind. 'Thank you.'

He held out a hand. 'I wish we could have met under happier circumstances, Mrs Ryan.'

'Me too.' Kitty was reassured by the strength in his grip and was reminded of the big fella. 'Have you heard from Mr McLeod?' she asked impulsively.

'No. But my wife wrote to his uncle's address yesterday.'

'You think he'll have reached there? I thought maybe the weather might have delayed him.'

'Hopefully not. But John knows how to look after himself anyhow.' He seemed about to say something more but at that moment the inner door opened and Mick and Teddy entered carrying a sheet of plywood. Mr O'Neill nodded in their direction and left.

Kitty explained to the boys what he had said and they seemed relieved that at least someone was keeping a watch over them. 'I wonder who these men are helping him,' said Mick.

'Probably sailors,' said Teddy, hammering in a nail crookedly. 'Celia said the O'Neills own Green's shipping line.'

'You've met Celia?' asked Mick, surprised.

'Yeah! She came with Mrs O'Neill the other day. I think she was sorry to have missed you.' He changed the subject.

Kitty saw Annie to bed and did the supper drinks. When one of Annie's sisters called to see why she had not arrived home, she was told that Annie was not feeling so good and would be staying the night. Fortunately the young girl showed no interest in seeing her sister and went back home. Kitty made sure all the downstairs windows and doors were locked and went to bed. Not to sleep, though. She was too tense for that, worrying about her cousin and wondering what John McLeod would do when he received Mrs O'Neill's letter.

The next morning Kitty was thankful she had few guests because she determined to manage without Annie's help and left her cousin undisturbed, waiting until she had cleared away the breakfast dishes before going upstairs to her room. Annie was not there and after a quick search Kitty found her in another of the vacant guest rooms polishing the lino as if her life depended on it,

Before Kitty could speak Annie said, 'You don't need that bully boy to ruin things for yer, Kit, if things don't buck up soon you'll be going out of business. You should get the boys down the Pier Head touting for custom like Jimmy used to. Now he was a worker.'

'You should be resting,' said Kitty, distressed at the sight of her cousin's bruised and battered face.

'Can't rest.' Annie looked up at her from dark-circled eyes. 'I keep thinking.'

'Thinking what?'

'If that Mr O'Neill has found the swine yet.'

'There's a man outside keeping an eye on the place so I don't think he has. I'm sure he'll do his best, though.'

'What if he doesn't find him?'

Kitty was silent. She did not want to think about that.

'What about the big fella?' said Annie.

'What about him?'

'D'you think he'll come back?'

'I hope so.'

'And what then?'

Kitty stared at her wondering what she wanted her to say.

'Will he be staying here?' said Annie strongly. 'Because if he does I'll leave.'

'What d'you mean leave? You can't surely be blaming him for what happened to you?'

'Some of the blame has to be his. How would Charley have found us otherwise?'

It was on the tip of Kitty's tongue to tell her that Jimmy had told him where to find them but she did not have the heart. 'I don't know,' she said. 'And maybe the big fella won't come back. He's gone to try and make things up with his grandfather so maybe he'll stay up in Scotland.' She hesitated before adding, 'I don't want to lose you, Annie. You know how much I depend on you. I doubt I could find anyone prepared to work as hard as you do. Two girls couldn't do your work.'

'I'm sorry, Kit,' said Annie, getting to her feet with difficulty. 'But you've got me wrong. I want him to come back so I *can* leave. He's a big strong fella and not averse to getting his hands dirty. He could do some of my work and the boys could do the rest in their spare time until yer get really busy. Then you can take on a couple of girls, as well.'

'If you're not against him then why leave?' she asked, confused.

Annie sighed deeply. 'I can't stay here anymore. It'll be

a constant reminder of last night. I've been thinking if I'm
OK I'll go to London – see a bit of the world.'

'You'll be lonely, love.'

Annie's expression hardened. 'I don't care about that.
I want to be with strangers. I don't want people staring at
me, asking questions.'

'Who's going to do that? Nobody knows what happened
except us.'

'And I want to keep it like that! That's why I'd like to
stay here a few nights. If I go home while me face is like
this Mam'll have to know what happened and our crowd'll
soon hear about it then – yer know how they earwig. And
before yer know it, it'll be all over the neighbourhood.'

'All right, you can stay here but don't mention London
again.'

'I want to go to London. You write me a good character
reference and I should be able to get a job in an hotel there.'

Kitty shook her head.

'I've made up me mind,' said Annie and getting down
on her knees she began to polish the floor again as if her
survival depended on it.

The next few days passed slowly with no word from the
O'Neills but then on the Friday when Kitty was returning
from the market she saw a car parked in front of her hotel.
As she approached Mrs O'Neill got out.

'Have they found Charley?' asked Kitty eagerly.

'I'm afraid not, but Daniel reckons he's left town.
He hasn't been home and hasn't been seen in any of his
usual haunts.'

Kitty's face fell. 'Damn! I'd have liked him caught but

I'm sure your husband did his best. Thank him for me.'

'You can thank him yourself when you see him,' said Mrs O'Neill. 'I have a son, David. He's a bit of a loner and doesn't rate his sisters much as playmates. Bring your boys to tea this Sunday if you can manage it.'

'I'll manage it,' said Kitty, her pleasure showing. 'It'll be good to get away from here if only for a short while. We're slack at the moment so it's no problem.'

Mrs O'Neill smiled. 'I'll look forward to it. Tell Teddy the car's in need of a wash. I'll pay him.' She got into the car, beeped her horn and drove off.

When Kitty told Annie what Mrs O'Neill had said about Charley, her cousin swore and expressed once again her determination to go to London if she was OK. Neither of them wanted to think what would have to be done if Annie was pregnant.

The next few days were fraught. Knowing that Charley had not been caught, Kitty half-expected him to turn up despite Rebekah O'Neill's words of assurance. When Saturday arrived and there was still no sign of him, she began to look forward to visiting the O'Neills, in the hope she would soon learn more about John McLeod.

Chapter Seven

'Where's that bit of paper?' asked Kitty.

'What bit of paper?' Mick glanced up from his homework to where his mother was standing by the sideboard.

'The bit with Mrs O'Neill's telephone number on it. She didn't tell me her address and we've been invited to tea tomorrow.'

'All of us?' He rested on an elbow.

'All of us.'

He frowned. 'Why are we going there, Ma? Is it because they're friends of the big fella?'

'I suppose it is.' She looked under the runner on the sideboard, trying to ignore the edge to his voice. 'As well as that I think it's something to do with you being boys. She only has the one son and he's a bit of a loner.'

'How old is he?'

'She didn't say.' Kitty lifted a vase but the paper wasn't there and she leaned against the sideboard, feeling annoyed with herself for losing it. 'We won't be able to go if I can't find that paper.'

Mick hesitated. 'Celia will probably know the address if you can't find it.'

'That's good. You can go and ask her then, can't you?' She smiled at him.

He pulled a face. 'I don't have to go right now, do I?'

'No. Tomorrow morning'll do. There was something else I wanted you to do for me today.'

'What's that?' His voice was wary.

Kitty went over and stood behind him, placing her hands on his shoulders. 'You know how slack things are at the moment, love. I just wondered if you could go down the docks with the handcart like Jimmy used to and see if you can find some customers for us?'

His heart sank because he really did not want to do it. There were some right toughies down at the docks and he was not a fighter by nature. Still, he was luckier than some. At least he was being given the chance to make something of himself. It had been his gran who had insisted he accept the scholarship and do something with his life. It was only after her death that his mother started going on about them all working in the hotel full time. He knew all hell would break loose once he told her he had no intention of doing what she said, but for now he was going to keep quiet and appear willing to do what she asked. He closed his book. 'I suppose I could go if our Teddy'll come with me.'

'I'm sure he would.' She was pleased he had not argued even as she worried about him going down to the docks. He was not a pushy boy, which could be a disadvantage in certain circumstances. She only hoped that what he lacked in boldness Teddy would make up for.

*

The wheels of the cart rumbled over the cobbles past McIver's shipbrokers and the Walker's pub on the corner of Chapel Street and on under the overhead railway. As Mick came to the floating roadway where vehicles crowded in a line waiting to get on the luggage boat, he wished Teddy had stuck with him. His brother, though, had skipped off as they passed Fontenoy Street, saying he had a way of making money without him going down the Pier Head. Mick knew his mother would not be pleased by Teddy's actions, especially if they had anything to do with the engineering works in Fontenoy Street where they reconditioned engines and made engine parts. It was where Teddy would like to work when he left school, although he had not told their mother that but was biding his time like Mick. He became aware of the slap of water against the wall on his left and breathed in that smell of the sea which was so much a part of every Merseysider's existence. He came to Princes Parade and hurried in the direction of the customs and baggage sheds. Once through customs some people would catch a train at the Riverside station to destinations as far away as London and would see little of his Liverpool, but a fair number would be staying in the port for at least a few days. Pigeons flew up in front of him, only to land a few feet away, their tail feathers dragging and their heads bobbing. There seemed less of them than there used to be and he wondered if there was any truth in the tale Teddy had told him about men luring them to their doom and putting them in pies to sell.

Mick glanced at some of the hungry-looking youths who hung around the waterfront, as ready to pick a pocket as to be paid to carry a bag, and his heart sank. He had no illusions about the task before him. It wasn't going to be easy but at least it was a fine day and the choppy waters of the Mersey appeared navy blue instead of the familiar oily greeny-grey.

There were several liners anchored in the river and the tenders were having a busy time. His spirits lifted. Maybe things were on the up at last and the lean times would soon be behind them. He lowered the handles of the handcart to the ground and eased his fingers as he gazed ahead. Already there were several men and youths confronting those coming out of the sheds weighed down by baggage. He took hold of the handles again and broke into a trot.

Mick offered his services to several people. Some ignored him whilst others waved him away. Several times he was pushed aside by stronger and bigger males. He was starting to feel desperate when at last he managed to seize an opportunity by elbowing a smaller youth out of the way. 'Carry your luggage, madam?' he enquired of a dark-haired, olive-skinned woman wearing a peacock-blue coat and matching hat.

The woman gazed at him through a haze of smoke and waved a cheroot in its holder in the air. She had handsome dark eyes. 'That's very generous of you, young man, but I am being met.' She spoke with a foreign accent.

Mick stifled his disappointment because he had considered she would have been good for a tip and moved away. Even as he did so he heard her speaking to someone. Then she called, 'Young man! Young man, back here!'

He turned to see that the woman had now been joined

by a couple of men and another woman who was not so well dressed and much older. The woman in peacock-blue beckoned him.

'You have an honest face, young man. Do you know of an hotel that would suit this woman here?'

Mick could not believe his luck and said eagerly. 'Yes, madam. A very good clean hotel with an excellent cook.'

'For a shilling would you deliver this woman's luggage to that hotel and prepare them for her coming?'

Mick accepted with alacrity and wrote the Arcadia Hotel, Mount Pleasant, and drew a sketch map on a scrap of paper. He handed it to the woman in blue. She surprised him by taking his hand and gazing at it for at least half a minute before pressing a shilling onto his palm. She stared intently into his face and said in a deeply accented voice, 'There will be four women in your life whom you will love. There will be heartache but the right one will choose you. You will travel far over the water but do not worry, you will return.'

Mick had an urge to laugh but managed to keep his face straight. She patted his hand. 'Believe me. You will find comfort from what I say in the future. Now take this and that.' She pointed to the suitcase and large cloth bag at the older woman's feet.

'Thank you,' said Mick, feeling in a bit of daze as he picked up the suitcase and loaded it onto the cart. Odd, he thought, but at least he had managed to find one guest and in his pocket was an incredible shilling tip.

It was as Mick was panting his way up the Mount that he heard running footsteps behind him. Turning his head he saw Teddy. 'Give us a hand,' said Mick. 'Where did you get to? That engineering works?'

Teddy grinned and took hold of one of the cart handles. 'I might have dropped in there but not for long.'

'What have you been doing?'

'Firewood. I managed to get hold of some orange boxes – don't ask how – and I borrowed an axe from a mate of mine. We chopped them up and tied them in bundles. We've been selling them door to door. I've made a whole five bob! I'll give Ma four and keep a shilling meself. I worked hard to get that much.'

Kitty was pleased with their efforts. 'Let's hope this is the start of better days. And Teddy, I forgot to say earlier, Mrs O'Neill said you can clean her car tomorrow and she'll pay you.'

'That's a whizz!' he said, smiling happily. 'Things are looking up!'

'A strange thing happened, Ma,' put in Mick. 'The foreign woman who gave me the tip read my palm.'

'She what?' Kitty stared at him, amused.

'Honestly. She said that I'd cross the water but not to worry I would return.'

Teddy gave a laugh. 'You're going on the ferry, mate.'

Mick's smile was slight. 'I don't think she meant the ferry.'

'She was having you on,' said Teddy.

'Why should she?' protested Mick. 'I wasn't paying her.'

'Forget it,' said Kitty. 'It's not important. Think instead about getting the O'Neills' address tomorrow.'

It was then that Mick made up his mind not to say

anything about the four women he would love. They would only laugh. Whilst he – he felt sure the woman had meant every word she had said.

Church bells were ringing as Mick came out of the basement door to find Ben sitting on the area steps seemingly playing some imaginary game or other as he talked to himself. Kitty stood on the hotel doorstep in the sun reading a newspaper. 'I'm going now, Ma,' he called.

She lowered the newspaper. 'There's been an earthquake in America. It's killed hundreds of people.'

'Anything happening here?' he asked.

'They say women are afraid to go out at night. There's an outcry for a Banditry Bill to be passed to cope with the rising rate of motorised crime. Apparently bandits are driving into shop windows and stealing things.'

'That's bad. Will you be OK, Ma? You're not worried about being here with just Annie and Ben?'

She smiled and shook her head. 'It's broad daylight. You go on your message. I'll see you soon.'

Mick went on his way reassured.

The pet shop was shut and Mick didn't know what to do. He rattled the latch and the letter box and felt irritable. He had a hole in his shoe and had placed a bit of cardboard in it, but it had wrinkled up and the sole of his foot was sore. He had not told Ma because she would have worried about him needing new shoes.

A woman came out of the house next door wearing a pinnie and men's carpet slippers that had holes in the toes. 'They're out.'

Tell me the obvious, thought Mick. 'When will they be back?'

'Shouldn't be long.'

'Thanks.' He gazed in the shop window. The white pup with the black patch over its eye was still there, curled up in the straw fast asleep. A couple of pups had gone and he wished his mother was not so against having a dog. He tapped gently on the glass but the pup made no sign of having heard. He tapped harder and it cocked one of its ears. He tapped again.

'You trying to break our window?'

Mick turned and saw Celia, her mother and an old lady. Celia smiled and he imagined pressing a kiss against her mouth. Immediately his cheeks felt hot. Since they had discovered from the woman whose luggage he had collected that the lady in peacock-blue was a Spanish gypsy fortune teller, he had not been able to forget what she had said about women, and where as once he would not have taken much notice of girls in a sexual way he now found himself fascinated by them.

'He'll pay for it if he does,' said Celia's mother, turning a key in the door. 'Can't you see we're shut, boy.'

'I haven't come to buy,' said Mick hastily. 'I just want Mrs O'Neill's address. We're going to tea and Ma's lost it.'

Celia's mother sniffed and jerked her head in Celia's direction. 'Ask her.' She disappeared indoors.

Mick shrugged and became aware the old lady was watching him.

'Take no notice of her, lad,' she said. 'I don't know how my son ever fancied her. He could have done much better. I told him your old mother has rubbed shoulders with dukes and earls and they look just the same as us with no clothes on.'

'Gran!' A giggle escaped Celia. 'You'll be giving him the wrong idea!'

'No! I can see he's a man of the world,' said Celia's grandmother with a twinkle. 'I was a looker in my time, lad, and many a compliment I've had passed me by those with money.'

Mick grinned. She was quite gusty was the old girl and reminded him of his own gran in a peculiar way. 'Tell me about it?'

Celia groaned. 'Don't start her off!'

'In my young day I used to gamble, son. You've heard of *La Marguerite*!'

He shook his head.

'You've never heard of the greatest paddle steamer on the Mersey that sailed between Liverpool and the Menai Bridge!' She sounded incredulous. 'Some called her the Merseyssippi Gambler. You could play pontoon and twenty-one from dawn to dusk – as long as you were at sea.'

'Did you win much?'

'I kept me head above water.' She patted his arm. 'You look after my granddaughter. She's a good girl. Not prune-faced like that one in there.' She winked at him and went inside.

'Well!' said Celia, covering her eyes. 'I don't have the nerve now to look you in the face after that.'

'Don't be daft,' muttered Mick, flushing all over again. 'I didn't take any of that serious.'

She lowered her hand. 'No?'

'No. What I want is that address.'

'You're not coming in?'

'No. We're going to tea today at the O'Neills', so if you don't get a move on we won't be getting there.'

She pulled a face at him. 'You're always wanting something from me *and* you're always in a rush.'

'That's because I'm a busy person. Now if you don't mind – that address?'

Celia smiled and did as he asked.

The O'Neills' house was large with bay windows and was situated not far from Sefton Park and the Wavertree Playground. The Ryans had to ease themselves past the automobile parked in the drive to reach the front door.

'Ring the bell, Mick,' ordered Kitty.

He did as told, setting the ship's bell that hung on the wall clanging, but it was several minutes before dragging footsteps were heard and the door was slowly opened to reveal a grey-haired, bony-faced female in a maid's uniform.

'Are thee expected?' she demanded.

Kitty smiled. 'We've come to tea.'

The maid's sharp eyes roamed over them. 'Thou's three lads. They'll have muddy boots and dirty my clean floor. Best thee go round the back.' She made to close the door.

Kitty placed her foot hastily in the gap. 'We're not going round the back. We're guests! Please tell your mistress that Mrs Ryan and her boys are here.'

'It's all right. I know.' Mrs O'Neill came into view dressed in a rumpled tea gown and with her hair ruffled.

She was carrying a toddler. 'Hannah, give way and stop frightening them off.'

The maid sniffed. 'Thee'll rue the day, Missus Rebekah. Lads are the Devil's spawn.'

'Hush, woman! Or you'll be back in Gerard Street with that brother of yours quicker than you can say the Lord's Prayer.'

A quiver of distaste passed over the maid's face and without another word she whipped the caps from the boys' heads and hung them on a hatstand. 'I'll put on the kettle,' she said, and with a dragging step went up the hall.

Mrs O'Neill raised her eyes heavenwards. 'You'll have to excuse Hannah. She's getting on and had enough of kids when she was young, having had most of the responsibility for bringing up her brothers and sisters. Hang up your coats and come through.'

They were led into a large room overlooking a garden, where a small girl with dark hair which curled almost to her waist was sitting on a pouffe near the fire. She did not look up as they entered.

'Sit down,' said their hostess, waving them to a large, well-worn but comfortable-looking sofa. 'Unless, boys, you'd rather go outside?' Boldly Teddy mentioned cleaning the car and she immediately told him to get cloths and things from Hannah in the kitchen. Mick hurriedly accompanied him out, saying he would help.

Mrs O'Neill glanced at her daughter. 'Sarah, show Ben the den.' She turned back to Kitty and said ruefully, 'Davy's gone down to the docks with his father. They'll be back soon. Still I'm glad of this time alone with you so we can have a chat about John.' She placed the toddler in a playpen near the window and looked at the girl who had not moved from her perch on the pouffe. 'Sarah, did you hear me?'

The girl made no response and Ben leaned against Kitty's knee. They watched Mrs O'Neill go over to her daughter and kneel on the rug beside her. Kitty's heart ached as she realised that the daughter who had been stillborn would probably have been similar in age to this girl. Ben gave Kitty a speaking glance as Mrs O'Neill said in a low voice, 'This is bad behaviour. You've sulked long enough and if you don't behave it'll be a smack and bed for you, my girl. Now show some manners.'

Sarah's head turned and she stared at Kitty and Ben from beneath frowning dark brows. She had a softly rounded but determined face and eyes which appeared almost black. Her chubby figure was clad in a jade-coloured woollen frock and beige leggings. 'I don't like boys,' said Sarah. 'But I suppose now you're here I'll have to be nice to you.' She came over to Kitty and held out a hand. 'How do you do, Mrs Ryan.'

'Hello, Sarah.' Kitty shook the small soft white hand. 'Ben, say hello.'

'Hello.'

The two children gazed at each other measuringly. 'I'm seven in April. How old are you?' said Sarah.

'I'm seven *now*,' said Ben with a superior smile.

Sarah looked annoyed.

'Never mind how old you are,' said her mother firmly. 'You can take Ben into the garden. Then you can help Hannah bring in the tea things.'

With an audible sniff, which was a perfect imitation of the maid's, Sarah stalked out of the room with Ben hurrying after her.

Mrs O'Neill moved over to a walnut-veneered cabinet. 'She's getting a right little madam. Sherry, Mrs Ryan?'

'Call me Kitty. Yes please. You don't know what a treat this is.' She leaned back into cushions that yielded, and relaxed fully for the first time in days.

'You must call me Becky then. You have a busy life.'

'I'm understaffed but can't afford to take more people on. Fortunately or unfortunately, whichever way you like to look at it, we're not very busy at the moment. Now Annie's threatening to leave.'

'She's one of your maids?'

'She's my only full-time maid but she's also my cousin.' She hesitated before saying in a low voice. 'That swine Charley treated her terrible.'

Becky stared at Kitty with concern. 'Will she be all right?'

'We don't know yet.' She took the glass from her.

'I see.' Becky's brows puckered. 'That's terrible. I didn't realise it was as bad as that. If John knew he'd be furious. He would blame himself for a start, saying he should have foreseen what happened.' She seated herself in an easy chair.

'How could he have foreseen it,' said Kitty, thinking Becky must know John pretty well to know how he would feel.

'He's been blamed before for things that weren't his fault.'

'In what way?'

'His wife and daughter died in childbirth.'

'He had a daughter?' The words burst from Kitty. 'So did I once. She was born dead. My mother took her away from me and put her in a soapbox and had her buried,' she said rapidly.

'So you have something in common,' said Becky quietly. 'But how sad that you should lose your only daughter.' Kitty took a gulp of her sherry. 'My mother blamed my husband for her death and my being so ill afterwards. He blamed her saying she expected too much work from me.'

'Mothers must be the same wherever,' said Becky. 'It was Margaret's mother who blamed John. She wouldn't even allow him in the house. He came home from the war to be informed that his wife and daughter were dead and buried, and neither she nor his sister would take him in. He was crazed with grief. It was no wonder he couldn't settle to anything. And his grandfather's behaviour didn't help. That reminds me.' She got up, went over to the mantleshelf and picked up a letter which she brought over to Kitty. 'It's from up north but *not* in his uncle Donald's handwriting. It's typewritten. I'm dying of curiosity but Daniel's ordered me not to steam it open.' Her eyes contained a rueful gleam. 'It could be a solicitor's letter, don't you think? Perhaps his grandfather's died and left him all his money?'

'Maybe.' Kitty was still trying to take in all that she had just been told but her heart had gone out to John McLeod wherever he was. A daughter! He had fathered a daughter who had died.

A daughter! She had stopped dreaming of having a little girl to replace the one she had lost but now she began to think that maybe—

There came a scream, a crash and raised voices. A few seconds later Sarah bounced into the room, her face lit by a large grin. '*He's* got a mouse and has frightened Hannah into dropping the tea tray. Will he cop it?'

Kitty shot to her feet. 'A mouse! I don't believe it! I'll have him!'

Becky's eyes danced. 'Don't worry about it. There's not much that frightens Hannah. It's nice to know she has a weak spot.'

They moved out into the hall and could hear the sound of Hannah's curses issuing from the kitchen. 'Thee imp of Satan! Thou wrecker! Hell's fire'll claim thee, melad! Thou see if it don't! Get it, get it! Over in that corner. Thou's missed it. Thee'll have the strap for this or I'll have something to say! There it is! Thou bring it to me and I'll cut off its tail.'

'No!' shrilled Ben. 'No!'

They entered the kitchen to find Hannah standing gripping the table with one hand and brandishing a chopper with the other. Ben had his back to a wall and his hands clasped together with the tip of a quivering nose thrusting its way between two fingers.

Kitty said wrathfully, 'Ben, get that mouse out of here! Look at the trouble you've caused!' She turned to Becky. 'Who'd have boys! I'll pay for the crockery.'

'You will not! It was an accident.' She smiled at Ben. 'I suppose you bought it from the pet shop?'

He flashed her one of his most beguiling smiles. 'I didn't exac-er-ly buy it but when I've saved the money I'll give it them.'

'So thou confesses to being a thief now,' gasped Hannah, sitting down on a chair. 'Fire and brimstone'll rain down on thee, melad.'

'Oh, be quiet! He's going to pay for it. You heard him,' said Becky. 'Come, Ben, let's find a box. And Hannah, let's have some cheese for the mouse.' She left the kitchen with her arm around Ben's shoulders.

'He's not going to cop it!' Sarah's tone was disgusted. 'Mummy always lets Davy off with things, too. When I dropped a plate I was sent to bed.'

'Aye. But thou dropped it deliberately just to see what thy ma and pa would do,' sniffed Hannah. 'Thou's no angel, me girl.'

'He'll cop it when he gets home, don't you worry,' said Kitty, placing broken crockery on a corner of the kitchen table. 'Hannah, have you a brush and shovel and I'll get up the rest?'

The maid sniffed but her tone was warmer when she said, 'Thou's a guest. Missus Rebekah would have me if I let thee do such a thing. But thee can cut a sliver of cheese for that creature if thou wishes, because that I won't do.'

Kitty cut the smallest sliver of crumbly Cheshire and carried it into the sitting room on a piece of broken crockery. Sarah walked beside her asking what punishment Ben would get. Kitty told her that she had not made up her mind yet and wondered why the girl did not like her brother.

As soon as they entered the sitting room, Sarah seemed to overcome her thirst for Ben's punishment and knelt beside the biscuit tin which had once contained building blocks but was now the mouse's temporary home.

'Twitchy's only ever had breadcrumbs and a titchy bit of bacon rind,' said Ben as his mother placed the cheese in the tin. 'I didn't know what else to give him.'

'Mouse food, of course, silly,' said Sarah.

'You'll have to go to the pet shop and get some and own up to what you've done,' said Kitty severely.

Ben forced up his nose with a finger, groaned, then plonked his forehead on the rug.

The two mothers smiled and Sarah giggled. 'I've never been in a pet shop,' she said.

Ben lifted his head and grinned at her. 'Mick'll take us next Saturday. He knows the way.'

'Sorry, Ben, but Sarah can't go,' said Becky.

'Why not?' demanded the girl bouncing to her feet.

'We're going to Ireland.'

Sarah stamped her foot. 'Don't want to go! Don't like Uncle Shaun. He stamps around and frightens me.'

'You make it obvious you don't like him when you should be kind to him,' said Becky crossly. 'Honestly, Sarah, I'd leave you behind if I could!'

Kitty, who had decided she would like nothing better than to have a little girl to stay, said, 'Maybe Sarah would like to stay with us?'

There was silence as mother and daughter stared at each other and Kitty almost retracted her offer. Then Sarah said, 'Mummy, I'd like to stay.'

'No. It would be too much for Mrs Ryan,' said Becky firmly. 'She has an hotel to run.'

'Please, Mummy,' she pleaded. 'I won't be any trouble.'

'I'd like to have her,' said Kitty. 'Unless you're worried because of Charley?'

Becky cast Kitty a rueful glance. 'He was the last person on my mind. I really was thinking about you. Girls can be a handful, too, you know. But it would a godsend if you really meant it. Sarah hates the farm and as it is Siobhan's getting to be enough of a handful when there's animals around.'

'I can go then?' said Sarah.

'You can go.'

Sarah smiled happily and slipped a hand into Kitty's. 'Honestly, Mrs Ryan. I will be good.'

Kitty believed her and looked forward to having her company. She had forgotten that the following weekend was the one before horse racing began at Aintree.

Chapter Eight

Kitty was up to her eyes in work. There had been an influx of guests yesterday and more had arrived on the Irish boat early that morning. It lacked an hour to lunch time and Kitty was tired. Sarah was sharing her bed and she was a wriggler as well as a chatterbox; albeit an amusing chatterbox, but at two o'clock in the morning Kitty had been in no mood for laughter. Now the girl had reminded her of her promise and there was no way Kitty could see herself keeping it. She was all behind and still had shopping to do. She went into the kitchen and placed a breakfast tray on the draining board, noticing just how dead the potted hyacinth on the windowsill was and wondering where the big Scottie was now. She longed for him to return and for a moment dreamed of him being there with his arms around her.

There were footsteps behind her and she glanced over her shoulder, thinking for a second that her dream had turned into reality, but it was only Mick. Only, she thought, and smiled. 'Do me a favour, love, and take Sarah and Ben to the pet shop.'

Immediately his dark eyes took on a haunted expression. 'Do I have to?'

'Yes, you do,' she said crossly. 'Who else is there? Teddy's done a vanishing act and Annie's helping me with the late breakfasts.'

'Couldn't one of the cousins do it?'

'No! I've got them working upstairs. I did mean to take them myself but you'll have to do. At least you won't have to walk. Mrs O'Neill left money for the tram.'

'OK!' groaned Mick. 'But what do I do about our Ben pinching the mouse?'

'Just say sorry and pay for it. And I want you back here by three o'clock.' She poured herself a cup of tea. 'I'm going to need your help. The girls will have gone by then. I'll want Teddy as well. Someone's got to take hot water up to the guests' rooms. I wish he'd say where he's going when he disappears. He could be on the moon for all I know!' She sipped her tea whilst standing and wished it had been any other weekend but this that Sarah came to stay.

'You were mad having her,' said Mick as if reading her mind. 'She's taken over the place. There's dolls everywhere. And hair ribbons!' He pulled a pink one from his pocket and dropped it on the table. 'I found this in the lobby. She must have a hoard of them. And what about that doll's pram? Mr Jones almost fell over it last night.'

Kitty raised weary shoulders and let them drop. 'He was very understanding. He thought it was nice for me to have a little girl about the place.'

'As a change from us boys, you mean?'

'I wouldn't change you. But . . .' she murmured, half to herself, 'If my little girl had lived I could have dressed her in frilly things.'

Mick shook his head incomprehensibly. 'Having that kid here for the weekend's enough. Seven! And she's already planning on who she should marry.'

'Someone rich,' said Kitty, her eyes twinkling. 'I know.' She reached in a drawer and took out her purse.

Mick grinned, seeing the funny side of it now. 'And a lot older. She'd even thought of the big fella because he dragged her dad out of a burning car, but he's a bit too old and hasn't any money. Then she thought of me. Our Ben offered to marry her, but she said if he couldn't afford a mouse then he was too poor.'

'What did Ben say to that?'

'That he could get richer.'

'I'm glad he's got ambitions.' She handed him some money.

Mick was about to open his mouth and tell her about his ambitions when Annie entered.

'Men!' she exclaimed and dropped the tray on the table with a crash.

Mick took one look at her face and scarpered.

'What's wrong?' Kitty hurriedly checked that none of the crockery on the tray was broken.

'Mr Jones pinched my bottom!' Annie's sharp little face was indignant.

'He what?' Kitty could not believe it. Mr Jones was a guest of long standing who came and stayed at this time every year.

'He pinched my bottom!' repeated Annie, her eyes filling with tears. 'Is there something about me, Kit? Do I look different since that swine had his way with me? Mr

Jones has never done anything like this before. In fact I always thought him a bit of a love.'

'He is a love but he's just lost his wife! I'm not making excuses for him,' she added hastily. 'It could have just turned him funny, though. Shall I have a word with him?'

Annie rolled a napkin into a tight ball with restless fingers. 'No,' she muttered. 'I'll just keep out of his reach. I know you can't afford to lose his custom and he just might leave.'

'If he's upsetting you I'll tell him to go. I'm sure someone else'll turn up.'

Annie stared at her and shook her head. She squared her shoulders. 'No. If I'm going to stay in the hotel business as I'm still hoping, I'll have to learn to cope with difficult customers. Besides he's a good tipper and I could do with the money.'

'Are you sure?'

'I'm sure,' she said grimly.

Kitty wished Annie's period would come. She admired her cousin for the way she had coped so far and wondered how she would have felt about men if she had stood in Annie's shoes. How did a woman scrub a man's violation from her body and mind? There was no easy way. Good and evil left their mark for better and for worse.

The bell went in reception and Kitty went to answer it. She had given up locking the front door since the night before because she could not be answering the doorbell all the time and there were not enough front door keys to go round all the guests.

'Can I help—' The words died on her lips as the big fella removed his cap. She stared at him, thinking he looked more tired and thinner than last time she had seen him, but there was still that air about him that had attracted her, almost from the beginning.

'Hello, Kitty,' he said quietly, placing his rucksack on the floor. 'I came as soon as I could. How are you?'

'I'm OK.' She took a deep breath and moved to the chiffonier to give herself time to compose herself. She was glad of its support because her legs seemed to have turned to jelly. Her fingers trembled on the register and her voice quivered when she spoke, 'And you?'

'Fine. Worried about you, though. Did they get Charley?'

So he had received Becky's letter! Kitty cleared her throat. 'Mr O'Neill thinks his men have scared him off. We haven't seen hide nor tail of him. He thinks he's left Liverpool, but who knows?'

John nodded, looking grim-faced. 'Can you give me a room?'

Her expression must have shown her astonishment even before she spoke, 'You want a room here?'

He nodded, and rested an arm on the chiffonier. 'If that's all right with you?'

'Actually we're full up but—'

'I understand.' His expression was suddenly bleak and he bent and picked up his rucksack and turned away.

Kitty moved swiftly to the other side of the chiffonier and grabbed his arm. 'No, you don't understand! We *are* full up! I was going to say you can have Jimmy's old room and Annie can move in with me and Sarah, or go back to her mam's. I'll show you it. There's nothing fancy about it but if you're not fussy?'

He looked relieved and took her hand from his arm and lifted it to his lips. She felt peculiarly breathless and experienced a need to swallow. 'You'll have to work,' she said in a voice that was far from normal. 'I'm overworked and understaffed and—'

'You don't have to say anymore. I get the message.' He kissed her hand again and held it firmly, smiling down at her.

She did not know how long they stood just looking at each other. It could have been seconds or half an hour. Then the grandmother clock on the wall chimed and he released her hand. She felt like she had woken from a long sleep. Her tiredness had vanished.

'I've the market to go to and I'm running late,' she said rapidly. 'Will you come with me? I was going to take the sledge. It's in the shed outside. There's a lot I need.'

'I'll get it,' said John. 'I'll dump my gear in the kitchen.'

They were crossing the lobby when the vestibule door opened and Teddy came in. His clothes were filthy. There was a tear in a trouser leg and an oil smear across his left cheek.

Kitty groaned.

Teddy ignored her, only staring at John from unfriendly eyes. 'So *you're* back. We had a heap of trouble because of you.'

'That's enough!' Kitty frowned at her son, vexed with him for more than one reason. 'It's rude.'

Teddy's ears reddened and his face was set as he walked past them and slammed some coins on the top of the chiffonier. 'I earned some money. This is for you, Ma.'

'Thanks. But I'm never going to get those clothes clean by the look of them.'

'They won't go to waste,' muttered Teddy. 'I'll keep these for the yard. Jack said he can find me the odd job which'll stand me in good stead when I leave school.'

'I don't care what Jack says.' Kitty's voice was firm. 'I've told you there's a job for you here when you finish.'

'I like the work!' he cried, suddenly looking desperate. 'And I don't see you needing me here if Mr McLeod's back! Or will he up stakes and go off on his travels again like he did before?' His gaze veered to the man standing at Kitty's side.

'Don't push your luck, son,' said Kitty. 'Or I'll land you a clout. Hurry and get changed and you can help Annie keep an eye on things.'

Teddy's lips compressed and he turned and took the stairs two at a time, almost colliding with Annie as she came down.

'I thought I heard yer voice,' she said to John. 'I'm glad yer back. It means I can leave any time I want now.' And she sailed past them into the kitchen.

John stared at Kitty and raised an eyebrow. 'Annie's leaving?'

'She might be.' She took hold of his arm and hustled him towards the door not wanting him to get into conversation with her cousin right now. 'Let's go shopping. I told you I'm all behind.'

John resisted. 'What about the sledge you mentioned? And where's your coat and hat?'

Kitty pulled a face. 'I was forgetting. You get it while I fetch my coat. And don't waste time talking to Annie! I'll meet you out front.'

To Kitty's relief she found John leaning against the wrought-iron railings when she came up the basement steps, which meant he hadn't spoken to her cousin. He straightened as she approached. 'The kitchen door's sticking. I'll fix it for you later.'

'Thanks.' She was keyed up in case he started to ask about Charley and the reason for Annie leaving.

Sure as the tide came in on the Mersey, as they began to walk down the Mount, John said, 'Why is Annie leaving?'

Kitty had an answer ready. 'She wants to see a bit of the world so she's going to London.'

He looked surprised. 'I thought her a homebird.'

'She surprised me!' A sigh escaped her. 'I don't want her to go but she's got it into her head that she must.'

'You'll miss her.'

'I will.' She decided to change the subject before it got complicated. 'Did you see your grandfather?'

'I saw him.'

There was something in his voice that caused her to look up at him. 'So he's not dead.'

'No. My uncle is, though.'

'Your uncle! Oh, I am sorry.' She slipped her hand into the crook of his arm in an attempt to comfort.

He pressed her hand against his side. 'I'm still having trouble believing it. We hadn't seen each other in years but his letters meant a lot to me. He was a link with my grandmother.' There was sadness in John's face. 'I should have gone back to Scotland sooner and taken care of him. He never married and I think he looked upon me as the son he never had.'

'I'm sure your letters meant a lot to him, too,' she said softly.

'The solicitor said they did.' He paused. 'I intended writing to you.'

'Why didn't you?' It pleased her that he had at least thought about writing.

There was a shadow in his eyes. 'I started several times but the past got in the way. Seeing my grandfather raked up memories, painful memories. But worse than that, was that he didn't believe I'd made the journey to see him. He thought I was there purely because of Uncle Donald's death.'

'You told him the truth, though?'

'Yes! And I asked for his forgiveness although God knows I hadn't done anything that I was ashamed of where he was concerned! But it was a waste of time.'

'It's sad. But you tried and you couldn't do more than that.'

'I could have gone back and tried again but I'd had enough.' His expression changed. 'He was glad Uncle Donald was dead and didn't utter a word of sympathy,' he said harshly. 'I doubt I'll make the effort to see him again. Let's change the subject.'

She asked him about the journey and told him about her visit to the O'Neills' house, about Ben and his white mouse and about Sarah's comments, and was glad to see that he was amused. She was certain it was on the tip of his tongue to mention Charley again but by then they were at the hotel and she busied herself with making them some lunch. Afterwards, having found some tools in the outhouse, John set about planing a touch off the door, creating a heap of fragrant wood shavings. It was as if he had never been away, marvelled Kitty, as she got on with preparing the evening meal. It was served earlier on a Saturday because so many of the guests were going out to see a show, a play or a film.

The inner door opened and Mick, Ben and Sarah entered. 'Uncle John! What are you doing here?' cried the girl, dropping her doll and bouncing over to where he knelt on the floor. One of her plaits had come loose and as she flung her arms about his neck almost throwing him off balance, her long hair wrapped itself round his face.

'Careful!' He placed the plane on the tiles and removed hair from his mouth before hugging her.

Kitty felt warm inside, thinking it said something about this man that Sarah was pleased to see him, but from Mick's expression he obviously had mixed feelings about John's return. Ben, though, was delighted. He went over to John, his face beaming. 'Hello, Little John. We bought some proper mouse food. It's got maize, sunflower seeds and peanuts in it.'

'So you got your way, laddie,' drawled John. 'You want watching.'

Sarah said, '*I* wanted to buy a mouse to keep Ben's company but Mick wouldn't let me. He said we could end up snowing in them. What does he mean by that, Uncle John? How can it snow mice?'

John exchanged glances with Kitty. 'Ask your mother when she comes home,' he said.

But Sarah was nothing if not persistent and, resting against his knee, she asked, 'Is it the same as having two rabbits? Davy had rabbits and they had babies during the night but the daddy killed them.'

'Why?' asked Ben, wide-eyed.

'The buck, that's the daddy rabbit, should have been taken out as soon as we knew about the babies but we didn't know until my daddy came back from America.' She screwed up her face. 'I wonder why the daddy killed his own babies?'

'Perhaps he was jealous of them,' said Ben.

'I doubt rabbits feel jealousy,' said Kitty thoughtfully. 'They're not like human beings.'

'They act on instinct,' said John. 'It could have been that the buck was frightened when he smelt and felt something different moving in the straw in the dark. Perhaps he thought it was another buck and saw him as a threat to his mate.'

Mick cleared his throat. 'Did Ma tell you about the man who threatened her with a knife while you were away, Mr McLeod?'

Kitty tensed, her eyes on John's face. 'I knew about it. That's why I'm here,' he said without emotion.

'Are you going to stay forever?' asked Ben, looking pleased.

John said gravely, 'Forever's a long time.'

'I'd like you to stay a long time,' said Ben. 'He was a bad man.'

'I'll stay as long as I'm needed.'

'Who said you're needed?' The voice came from the doorway and their heads turned.

Kitty did not know whether to feel angry or sad as she looked at Teddy who was standing in the doorway looking blatantly hostile. 'I say he's needed,' she murmured. 'So get that chip off your shoulder and behave yourself.'

Teddy opened his mouth but she gave him a warning look and without another word he walked away. Mick glanced at her before following his brother.

There was a silence and Kitty made a move towards the door.

'You're best leaving them,' said John. 'You've said what you feel. Best to give them time to think about it now.'

She nodded, thinking she would have to fill him in on the Charley episode sooner or later. Maybe it would be best sooner. 'Ben, you take Sarah upstairs and feed that mouse,' she ordered. 'And no messing about. I need to finish these pies and get on with things.' She opened the door for them and ushered them out.

She did not speak immediately after the children had left, but brushed the top of a pie with a mixture of egg and milk. Her hands were amazingly steady considering how pent up her nerves were. She jumped when John spoke.

'How bad was it with Charley?' He picked up the plane and removed some wood shavings from the blades. 'I need to know what I'm being blamed for.'

She remembered suddenly what Becky had said about

him feeling responsible for the death of his wife and daughter. 'Don't get all guilty,' she said. 'Jimmy's as much to blame as you are for what happened.'

John's gaze slid over her face. 'Your brother-in-law? What's he got to do with this?' he said slowly.

'Charley knew Jimmy. He'd obviously spoken about me and this place. Charley said about me being a woman alone and needing protection.' She kept her voice light. 'Myrtle Drury had sacked him and he saw me as a way of making easy money. It wasn't as easy as he thought though because the boys and Annie came on the scene. I was frightened and angry but for me things could have been much worse. As it was I escaped with a scratch on my face and a few bruises.'

'The boys?'

'He didn't harm them, thank God! It was Ben who insisted we involved you. And Mick fell in with that.'

'Teddy?'

'He wanted us to fetch the police. I didn't want to.'

He nodded. 'So Daniel involved himself.'

She smiled. 'He frightened the life out of me and Annie, as if she hadn't already suffered enou—' The word tailed away and she moved to place the pies in one of the ovens. Her voice was muffled as she said, 'Let's forget about it for now. I have enough on my plate to think about at the moment.'

There was silence and she heard his footsteps going towards the back door.

'Could you give me a hand with this?' he said.

Relieved, she straightened up from the oven. 'With what?'

'Balance the door so I can screw it back on. Here, stand here.'

She did as he asked and his body was at her back, his arm brushing her hair with every forceful movement of the screwdriver. She was aware of an overwhelming desire to lean against him, to relax, but her nerves were as overstretched as a drumskin. She shivered in the draught from the open doorway and closed her eyes, willing him to do something. She wanted to feel his body warming hers.

'You can let go now.'

Her pent-up emotions threatened to explode. 'Is it OK now?' Her voice was strained.

He swung the door back and forth with no trouble. 'Satisfied?' There was an expression in his eyes that made her think he knew what he was doing by not touching her.

She nodded. 'A cup of tea?'

'Thanks.' He began to gather his tools together.

As they sat drinking tea he told her about having been caught in a blizzard in Argyllshire. 'I thought my last hour had come and then I thought of you.' His tone was serious.

Kitty froze with her cup halfway to her lips. 'And did it help?' she asked lightly.

John rested his elbows on the table and gazed into her eyes. 'What do you think? I'm here aren't I?'

There was a silence and again she waited for him to do something, but he made no move to touch her. She glanced at the clock and rose to take the casseroles out of one oven and the pies out of the next and determined to keep their relationship on a business-like footing. She wondered if she had dreamed him kissing her hand and that electric-like charge between them earlier. Perhaps she was reading more into what he said and did than there was. And yet before he had gone away he had kissed her. She was confused. 'Have you ever waited on table?' she asked.

'The odd time in cafes. I've done all kinds of things to earn a crust. I've no black trousers, though.'

She stared at him, not wanting him in the dining room wearing the faded corduroy trousers he had on. Then she remembered how he had appeared the first time she had seen him. 'Wear your kilt and they'll think they're getting something extra for their money,' she said positively. 'Come on upstairs now and I'll show you where you're sleeping and you can change.'

He followed her out of the room. 'What about Annie? Have you told her I'll be putting her out of her bedroom?'

'She wants you to stay. She'll fall in with whatever I say,' Kitty said shortly. 'Give it a week and most of our clientele will have left. It's the National on Friday. Then you can have that room where you put the trunk.'

'Are you going to tell me why Annie's suffered enough?'

She paused on the stairs and glanced round at him. She drew in a breath. 'I'd rather not. But if you have to know – that swine ruined her.'

His expression was suddenly steely and his eyes fixed on Kitty's face. 'And you want me to put her out of her room?' His voice seemed to catch somewhere in his throat.

'No!' She caught her lower lip between her teeth and

took a deep breath. 'But I have to put you somewhere and she can sleep with me.'

'Your bed's going to be crowded with Sarah in there as well. I could sleep in the kitchen.'

'On the tiled floor?' She shook her head. 'Annie won't mind. She'll feel safer with me, and even more so with you in the next room. As it is she's slept with me a couple of times since it happened.'

'Did he beat her, too?' She nodded and the skin round his jaw tightened. 'And he hurt you. I'd like to throttle him.'

'I'd like him nibbled to death by crabs,' she said lightly, 'but that's neither here nor there right now. We've meals to serve and I'd rather I never saw Charley again.'

He stared at her but remained silent and she carried on upstairs, knowing that John would dearly like Charley to return.

Kitty liked John in a kilt. She liked what she could see of his legs. There was strength in his legs. Poor Michael's legs had been white and limp like forced celery but the Scotsman's knees were muscular and, having been exposed to all kinds of weather, were the colour of fallen leaves in autumn. As she carried a tray into the dining room she imagined the chaos which would ensue if she gave in to temptation and fondled his knees.

She was being daft. She knew that, but at the back of her mind now lurked the fear that if Charley did return then there would be a fight between him and John, and whilst the logical, sensible part of her mind felt sure John could look after himself (after all he had beaten Charley once before), another part of her mind told her Charley was mean and sneaky and would not fight fair. A knife in the back was a very real thing. She shook herself mentally. Daft! She really was imagining herself in one of those gangster movies. This was Britain not America. She tilted her chin and put on a smile for the customers.

'Something tickled your sense of humour, good lady?' asked Mr Jones. He had a mop of silver hair and baby-blue eyes and try as she might Kitty could not dislike him, but he reminded her of Annie. She wondered where her cousin was because she had not seen her for the last hour.

'Just something one of my sons said,' she lied smoothly.

'The youngest one's a handful and no mistake,' he said, chuckling.

What had Ben been up to, she wondered, but did not probe. Instead she asked Mr Jones what his plans were for that evening and was told he was going to the Pavilion to see a variety show. She moved on to the next guest.

'Who's your new man and what happened to the other?' asked Mrs Mahoney, rapping her stick on the floor. She was from the Irish Free State and booked in regularly for the horse racing at Aintree. 'Family, wasn't he?'

'Jimmy's gone to work in Rhyl,' said Kitty. 'How's your family, Mrs Mahoney?'

'Don't change the subject, girlie!' Her sharp eyes stared covertly at John. 'Is he one of the family, too?'

'Not exactly.' Kitty glanced at the Scotsman who was serving at the next table. As if aware of her gaze he looked up and smiled before carrying on with what he was doing. Kitty's responding smile lingered as she felt a moment of happiness.

'Soon will be I shouldn't wonder,' grunted the old woman. 'Strong looking fella. He'll keep those boys of yours in order and no mistake.'

Kitty made no comment, only smiling before hurrying into the kitchen to heat milk for the custard.

John entered shortly after her, carrying a plate. 'There's a man complaining he doesn't like onion. I was tempted to tell him he's lucky to be able to afford to have a meal put in front of him but—'

'You resisted.'

He smiled. 'I was diplomatic. I offered to remove the onion but he said he wanted something completely different. Insisted the onion contaminates the gravy.'

'Ask him would he like an omelette. Got to keep the punters happy. Also is there anything else he doesn't like? You can guarantee the complainers always have more than one thing they'll complain about.'

'I can believe it. He had that kind of face.'

As John left the kitchen he almost collided with Annie on her way in. 'Sorry,' she said.

'Think nothing of it,' he murmured and walked on.

Kitty glanced up. 'Where've you been? I was worried. Your Mo and Barb have gone off and we're all rushing round like maniacs!' She stared at Annie. 'You look awful! Putting up your hair like that makes your face look drawn. I mean the frock's nice but – why are you wearing that frock? It's one of your good ones, isn't it?'

'Yes! I'm going out with Mr Jones,' she said with a hint of defiance.

Kitty could not believe it. 'Why?' she demanded. 'He's old enough to be your grandfather. Why?' she repeated with a sense of helplessness.

'If he's old enough to be my grandfather then he'll pop off the quicker if I marry him,' said Annie defiantly.

'Marry him! You're never!'

'I might.'

Kitty shook her head and stirred the custard vigorously. 'You've run daft. I know the feeling, sweetie. I've felt like that. Like your whole world is falling apart. But just stick with it and things'll work out. Not like you wanted them to but something else'll turn up.'

'It's easy for you to say,' said Annie sniffily. 'You've got the man you want here. I wanted Jimmy and I'll never get him now. As well as that I'm feeling sick and me stomach and head aches.'

'Then you shouldn't be going out,' retorted Kitty. 'Get an apron on and do some work. I need seventeen bowls.'

'But I've told Mr Jones I'll go out with him,' wailed Annie, now looking unsure of herself.

'Just do some work here first, then go out with him – but keep him in his place. And by the way, you're sleeping with me tonight. The big fella's having your room.'

'Is he now? Perhaps I should go home? Then perhaps I shouldn't. Mam'll want to know why.' Annie looked torn by indecision.

'Put your apron on,' ordered Kitty. 'You can sleep with me I said.'

'Perhaps, it's just as well I should,' said Annie, her face brightening unexpectedly. 'You never know.' She flushed as she looked at Kitty, then put on an apron and got out the bowls without another word.

'Thank God that's over,' said Kitty, pulling a chair up to the fire and resting her stockinged feet on the brass fender.

'Am I having help cleaning the shoes in the morning? More guests mean extra work,' said Teddy, looking at her. 'It makes no difference to our Mick doing the fires.'

John glanced up from a book of *Grimm's Fairy Tales* which belonged to Sarah. She was sitting on his knee dressed for bed in a flower-sprigged nightdress and pink dressing gown, cuddling both a rag doll and a golliwog. 'I'll help you.'

For a moment Teddy was lost for words, then he muttered, 'I'd rather our Mick. You could do the fires.'

'I'm no good with grates. Ask me to get a fire going in the open and I can manage it but I'm hopeless indoors. I'm good with boots.' He wriggled his stockinged feet, seemingly unaware of a hole in both toes, and smiled blandly at Teddy before continuing with the story of Hansel and Gretel.

Teddy glowered and half-opened his mouth, but before he could speak Kitty said, 'That reminds me. I'll have to get the sweep. I noticed some soot on the hearth in the Smoking Room. If more comes down it'll make a heck of a mess.'

'I'll go and see him after school on Monday if you like?' said Mick.

'Can I go with you?' asked Sarah sleepily.

'No,' said Mick shortly. 'You'll be back home by then.'

'Can't you go tomorrow?'

'Sunday's a day of rest.'

'For some,' murmured Kitty, yawning. She would have to take Sarah and Ben to bed soon. It must be well past the girl's normal bedtime. She felt a moment's guilt at having spent so little time with her. Then she thought of Annie. How was she getting on with Mr Jones? She glanced at the clock on the mantlepiece and wondered at Annie's cryptic statement about the sleeping arrangements. Did her cousin really think John would come creeping into her bedroom with Sarah there? She smiled wryly and pictured it before letting her mind drift for a while. A cinder dropping in the grate roused her and she forced herself to her feet. 'Sarah, Ben, time for bed. Mick, Teddy, could you put the kettles on and make the guests' supper drinks?'

The boys groaned, but they did as they were told. John closed the book and rose with Sarah in his arms. Kitty removed her feet from the fender and held out a hand to Ben. He protested for a moment but then went with her. She thought how nice this was and wished they could be one big happy family.

'A nightcap?' asked Kitty, and without waiting for John's reply, she turned a bucket upside down and stood on it.

'You shouldn't be standing on that.' He put away the last cup and came over to her.

She turned with the bottle of whiskey in her hand. 'I thought you might like a drink?'

He lifted her down from the bucket but kept his hands on her waist. 'OK. But just the one. I might sleep too heavy otherwise, and I have to be up early if I'm to keep up with Teddy.'

'You'll probably have to wake him. Why did you do it?' She gave him a quizzical stare.

'Do what?'

'Volunteer yourself! You won't get round him that way.'

He smiled, removed the bottle from her hand and placed it on the table before putting his arms round her from behind. She closed her eyes and leaned against him. At last it had happened. 'I like cleaning boots, and shoes for that matter,' he murmured against her hair. 'Especially nice new ones. I've had boots fall apart on me and had to go barefoot. You get to appreciate a decent boot at a time like that.'

'I'm sure you do.' She was shocked to hear he had gone barefooted. 'How far do you think you've walked in your life?'

'Too far to reckon. I'd like to marry you, Kitty.'

Her heart seemed to jump into her throat. 'A bit sudden isn't it?' she said gruffly.

'You need a man about the place.'

'I know. But you and marriage. It means—'

'I know what it means.'

She could not think what to say. Her womanly instincts said marry him and be held like this more often. She imagined his being passionate with her in bed – thought of a baby daughter, of freezing winter nights and warming her cold feet on him. But did he love her? He hadn't said so. He could be a wife beater for all she knew! He'd want to be the boss. She felt a moment's panic. Her first marriage had not been like most normal arrangements because for most of the time she had ruled the roost. 'I don't know if it would be sensible,' she said slowly.

'Sensible!' He laughed. 'I thought I was being sensible.' She turned in his arms and faced him. 'I don't know.'

'What don't you know?' He looked puzzled.

'I don't know if it'll work!' Her voice rose on the last word because now she remembered her sons. 'What about the boys?'

His lips twisted. 'I haven't forgotten them.'

'But I had for a moment! Mick and Teddy aren't going to like it.'

They stared at each other and she felt suddenly desperate. She wanted to marry him.

'Forget I mentioned it,' he said, and lifted her off her feet and kissed her long and deep.

When her feet eventually touched the ground again she went over to the table and unscrewed the top of the whiskey bottle. She put a couple of tots into two glasses and handed him one. To her own she added a dash of water, before downing it in one go and walking unsteadily out of the kitchen.

Chapter Nine

'We've got to do something,' said Teddy, lifting his eyes from his scrutiny of the Grand National runners on the page of the *Sporting Life* which one of the guests had left behind. He rolled over on the floor and gazed up at the nicotine-stained ceiling whilst puffing on a cigarette.

'Such as what?' said Mick, gazing through the Smoking Room window and thinking their mother would have a fit if she could see Teddy.

'I don't know. It's you that's supposed to be the brains of the family. Think of something!'

'I thought the Irish great-uncles would be of some use but they seem to like him,' murmured Mick, noticing the girl who had stopped outside their hotel. '"Big strong fella just what your mammy needs!"' He mimicked his great-uncle Kevin. 'And you can't deny that, Teddy. The big fella is just what Ma needs. Neither of us want to work here after we've finished school. I hate it! Especially when it's bursting at the seams like it is now.'

'I know! But we'd still have to live here and I don't want him bossing me around. So what do we do?' said Teddy.

'Don't ask me,' muttered Mick. Opening the door, he

went outside, glad that Annie, who had been a lot more cheerful this week, had gone out for a few hours, taking her goofy sisters with her. For once he and his brothers had the place to themselves. Ben was upstairs in the attic but most of the guests had gone to the races and were not back yet. Kitty and the big fella had also gone to Aintree with the O'Neills. He thought about how excited Kitty had looked and he realised how seldom she had a day out. Even so, he felt certain it was not only going out that had made her look like she had picked out the winner for the National.

He stood on the step, his hands in his trouser pockets, and stared at the girl coming towards him. He had been right. It was Celia. The black hat had put him off the scent because he had never seen her wear one before and it made her appear older. She was carrying a puppy. His puppy! The one that favoured a black eye patch.

'Hi!' he said and walked towards her.

'Hello, Mick.' Her smile revealed how unsure of herself she was in this different setting. She wore a brown coat which made her look thinner and which somehow did not go with the hat. He realised close up she had been crying.

'What's up?' he said gently.

Immediately her eyes filled with tears. 'Me gran's dead and she's left only enough money to bury herself. Me mam's furious.' Her voice trembled. 'I had to get out. She was screeching right, left and centre and she had a man there taking away the animals. I only just about managed to save Nelson. I've brought him for you.' She held the puppy out to him.

Mick stared at her in astonishment and took the dog

from her and automatically began to stroke it. Nelson
turned his head and licked his hand. Mick's mind began to
race frantically in search of a way he could keep the dog
and pacify his mother at the same time.

'He likes you,' said Celia, managing a watery smile.

'I like him,' he said simply. 'Are you coming in?'

'Will your ma mind?' she said anxiously.

'Of course not! Besides she's not back from the races
yet.' He led the way indoors. 'Want a cup of tea?'

'Love one.'

He led her into the warm kitchen, which was redolent
with the smell of roasting mutton and baking. Nelson's
head went this way and that and he struggled to get down.
'I'll have to put him in the yard,' said Mick. 'Ma'll go mad
if I let him loose in here.'

'Perhaps I shouldn't have brought him after all,' said
Celia doubtfully. 'But I knew how much you wanted him
and they'd probably have drowned him.'

'No! It's OK! It's just that Ma has a thing about dogs
and mess. My gran was the same.' He opened the back
door and placed the puppy in the yard. Nelson started to
sniff around.

'He'll be all right,' said Celia confidently. 'Feed him on
bread and milk and little scraps and he'll cope.'

Mick felt sure Nelson would, but his main worry was
where to put him until he had a chance to explain to Kitty
how useful a dog could be. Perhaps he could hide him in
the outhouse? It was far enough away from the hotel for
any noises not to penetrate the kitchen. He put some milk
on a saucer and put it outside.

He had just made tea when Teddy sauntered into the
room. He nodded in Celia's direction and said to his
brother, 'Everything OK?'

'Celia's lost her gran.'

He grinned. 'Where did she lose her?'

Mick frowned. 'She's upset, dope. They've got no
money and her ma's had to close the pet shop.'

'That's tough luck,' said Teddy sympathetically.

Celia swallowed. 'We're both going to have to find jobs.
I didn't realise it but Mam's got herself into debt again. I
don't know what to do! I wondered if you'd heard anything
from Little John. He can calm her down like no one else
can.'

Teddy's eyes gleamed. 'Funny you should say that.
He's working here. As soon as he comes in we'll tell him
about your trouble.'

Celia stared at him. 'Working here! But why?'

'He's after me ma that's why,' he said impatiently.

'You mean—?'

'It looks like wedding bells,' said Mick gloomily. 'You
can see it in the way they look at each other.'

Teddy pulled a face. 'You think they'd be too old for
all that soppy stuff but they're goo-goo eyed about each
other.'

'You mean they're in love!' exclaimed Celia, her eyes
unexpectedly bright. Mick and Teddy said nothing but she
did not seem to notice. Then her expression altered. 'Oh
lor'! This changes things. I can't ask him to speak to me
mam now. Yours wouldn't like it.'

Teddy exchanged glances with Mick before smiling at

Celia. 'Ma wouldn't mind. A good Christian woman is our ma. Although she doesn't have time to get to church she'd help anyone in trouble. Why don't you send yours round here? She could have a job. We could be getting rushed off our feet more often now the O'Neills are going to advertise our hotel on their ships.'

Celia looked at Mick. 'You really think your ma would give her a job?'

'I'm not saying anything,' he said, scowling at Teddy.

'Sure she will,' said his brother, pulling out a chair. 'Sit down, Celia.'

She sat, gazing about her. 'Is it all as nice as this?'

'What? The kitchen?' said Mick, going over to the back door and opening it to check the puppy was all right. It was sniffing the drainpipe.

She grinned. 'No, the hotel. I've never been in one before.'

'You're not missing much. I'd rather have a proper home.'

'Oh I don't know. Gran always said it's people that make a house a home.' Her eyes filled with tears and Mick said hastily, 'Don't cry,' handing her the nearest thing to hand which happened to be a tea towel.

Celia looked at the size of it and laughed. 'I don't know why I'm crying. She had as happy a life as anyone could, she always said.'

'She was nice.' Mick smiled and Celia returned his smile.

Teddy stared at the pair of them. 'Perhaps Celia would like to see over the place?'

She turned her smile on him. 'I'd love it.'

'Not the guests' bedrooms, though,' said Mick swiftly. 'Ma wouldn't allow that.'

Teddy nodded and held out a hand to Celia but Mick brushed it away. 'After she's finished her tea I'll show her around.'

Teddy grinned. 'OK, big brother. I think I'll slip round to the engineering works if I'm not needed here. Ma'll be back soon, don't forget. See you later.'

There was silence after Teddy had gone. Mick made the tea before picking up a knife and removing a cloth from one of the square baking tins on the table. He knew his mother had been up at four that morning to get a headstart on the day and saw that she had made bakewell tart. His mouth watered and then, with a spurt of irritation, he remembered that guests came first and replaced the cloth. 'Jam buttie?' he asked, going over to one of the bread crocks.

'Thanks,' said Celia. 'Who does the cooking?'

'Ma. She does most things with Annie and our help. At the moment we have her two younger sisters helping as well, but they're hopeless.'

'And Little John. What does he do?'

Mick considered as he sliced bread. 'You could say a bit of everything. I'll give him that he's prepared to help Ma where and when she asks him,' he said grudgingly.

'You don't like him.' Celia stared at him and, after a moment's hesitation, added, 'I suppose it's natural.'

He frowned. 'What do you mean it's natural?'

'An older man in the house. You're jealous.'

'I'm not jealous!' He slapped plum jam on the bread.

'I did have a father once, you know, and an uncle living here.'

Celia continued to stare at him and he felt discomforted. He handed her the buttie on a plate. 'I'm not jealous,' he repeated, and bit into the bread.

'If you say so.'

'What's that supposed to mean?' he said with his mouth full and a glint in his eye.

'What I said. If you say so it must be true.'

Mick swallowed. 'It is true. I just don't think Ma needs a husband. A man around the place – yes, I can accept that. Me and Teddy aren't strong enough to do some of the things he can but why does she have to marry him?'

'Has she said she's marrying him?'

He shook his head.

'Then why—?'

'Because,' he said vehemently, 'it's as I said before, it's the way they look at each other when they think none of us are watching. It makes me feel . . .' He searched for words and then wondered why he was telling Celia all this when he didn't have to. 'Let's forget them,' he muttered. 'Drink your tea and I'll show you round the place. That's if you still want to see it, and you think it's all right to leave Nelson alone in the yard?'

'I do want to see it,' she said hastily. 'As for Nelson, the way you talk about your ma, it might be a good idea if you tell her Nelson'll make a good guard dog when he's bigger. He could chase off any other Charleys that might come round.'

Mick grinned. 'I suppose it's worth a try.'

'Nothing ventured, nothing gained,' said Celia.

He showed her the main rooms downstairs and the bathroom on the first floor. 'Ma'd like one on every floor and washbasins in all the rooms with hot and cold running water. It's her dream.'

'It's lovely!'

'What?' Mick blinked at Celia.

She smiled and folded her arms across her budding chest. 'You are lucky. It must be really interesting having different people coming and going. Where do they come from?'

Mick had never considered himself lucky in that way. Lucky in having food and clothes and shoes on his feet, yeah! But not—

He saw she was waiting for an answer. 'America, Ireland, Scotland, Wales, Holland, Sweden, Norway. My grandfather was a Norwegian whaler and we have relatives there that we've never met. Although Ma sends a card at Christmas and her Norwegian aunt sends her one back.' He waved a hand. 'People from all over the place! England included!' He grinned, feeling unexpectedly better about living in the hotel.

'Lovely,' she repeated quietly. 'I like people. I'm going to miss the shop. We used to have sailors coming in selling us parrots and monkeys before the Depression and there was a good trade for them then. Ma used to chase me out. I reckon now it was so she could flirt with the men. I don't think I'll tell her Little John's here.'

Mick stared at her. She seemed quite different all of a sudden. Before he lost his nerve he leaned forward and kissed her. It was a clumsy kiss and almost missed its mark but she did not seem to mind. Only when she stepped back from him did he see that her cheeks were rose-petal pink.

'I'd better go,' she said with an unexpectedly mature air.

'Why?'

Celia hesitated. 'I'd just better.' She leaned forward, kissed his cheek and fled.

Kitty hurried upstairs, with John dogging her footsteps, and into her bedroom. He followed her in, closing the door behind him. She whirled and they stared at each other. Her bones felt as if they were melting. 'There isn't time,' she said, withdrawing a couple of hat pins and removing her hat. 'Some of the guests are already home and they'll be wanting their dinner.'

'Not even time for one kiss,' he murmured, reaching for her.

She dropped her hat on the bed and went into his arms. 'Only one,' she said firmly.

They kissed as if they had not met for a month instead of having spent most of the day in each other's company. She had enjoyed herself immensely. The crowds had been huge and although the Prince of Wales had disappointed by not being at the races, the Princess Royal had looked lovely in a fur-trimmed coat and a chic little hat. Mr Churchill had worn a snappy grey trilby and carried what must have been the largest binoculars on the course. An Irish horse tipped by the uncles had won the race, so it looked like Ben would not have to worry about her not giving him sweetie money for weeks, because the uncles had bet a

whole shilling each way on Kellesboro Lad for each of the
boys. Daniel and Rebekah had been good company and
John had amused. Although some of his remarks had been
slightly barbed and aimed at the nobs, that was probably
down to the poverty he had experienced in his wanderings.

Poverty! Kitty might have discovered there was a life
for her besides work, but she only had to wander some of
the back slums in the 'pool to come face to face with the
degradation which lack of work and money could cause.
She was not about to forget she had a hotel to run just
because she wanted the big fella to make mad passionate
love to her. It was something they had not done – yet.
'John, let me go,' she muttered against his mouth.

'I don't want to let you go.' He lifted and flung her
on the bed and dropped beside her. 'We're lying on my
working frock,' she whispered, hoping none of the boys
were in their bedroom and that Annie would not choose
this moment to come in.

'Sod your frock,' he said, dragging her against him.
'Marry me now, Kit. I want you and it's no use your saying
you don't feel the same way.'

'I do, I do,' she said softly. 'But you haven't been back
a week – and what about the boys?'

He groaned and was silent a moment before saying,
'Teddy resents me being here as things are. So what's
going to be different?'

'We'll be married. You'll be here for ever.'

'That's what I want to be.' He gazed into her eyes and
his hand caressed her breast. 'Say yes. Everything'll be all
right, sweetheart.'

She was silent, considering the life he had led. 'Are you sure you really want to stay for the rest of your life? If you upped and left because, maybe, you're not used to being in one place,' she said in a rush, 'I wouldn't like it very much.'

'Trust me. This is where I want to be.' His face loomed close and he kissed her again.

There was a knock on the door and instantly she pushed him away and rose swiftly from the bed. 'Who is it?' she called.

'It's me, Annie. I've taken the meat out and put the vegetables on. Will you be doing the gravy?'

'Yes. I'm just changing. I'll be down in a minute.'

'OK.'

There was the sound of retreating footsteps and Kitty glanced at John. 'I'll have to get ready.'

He sat back against the pillows and smiled. 'When we get married we'll have to buy a longer bed.'

She shook her head at him. 'Never mind that now. If we don't get cracking there won't be any money for a bed. Out please.'

'Seeing as how you said please I'll go.' He stood, hugged her in passing, and left the room.

'Everything OK, Annie?' asked Kitty, reaching for her pinafore when she entered the kitchen.

'Don't ask,' muttered her cousin, not looking up from stirring soup. 'Our Mo has walked out and taken our Barb with her. She dropped a plate and when I told her off she had the nerve to say she couldn't work with me. Jobs as hard to find as gold dust and she's flung in the towel! I ask

you, Kit, where's her brains? Mam'll have a fit. I mean
our Barb would have gone anyway. She's too young to be
working all hours but our Mo is just a lazy madam.'

'Damn!' said Kitty, rubbing her nose with the back of
her hand. 'Where are Mick and Teddy?'

'Mick's seeing to the fires and Teddy's carrying the hot
water up. They're good lads. Although I had to speak to
Mick a bit sharp-like. He seemed in a bit of a dream.'

Kitty was silent, wondering if it was John's presence
which was having that effect on her eldest son. She took
out the cornflour.

Annie glanced at her. 'He'll be OK. I believe boys go
through it as well as girls at that age.' Kitty stared at her
uncomprehendingly. 'The growing up-like, Kit! He'll
come round to the big fella and you getting married. You
are getting married?'

Kitty hesitated. 'We haven't known each other long. It's
a big decision, Annie.'

'How long d'yer need at your age?' said her cousin
scornfully. 'I was ready to marry Mr Jones just to have a
father for the baby and to get away from everything, but
thank God I don't need to now.' Annie's period had come
the evening she had gone to the Pivvy with the old man. 'I
know the big fella's got no money but he's strong and, give
him his due, he'll work.'

'I wish you weren't going, Annie. I could up your wages
a little. Even more so if we stay busy.'

Annie shook her head. 'Ta, but I've made up me mind.
You give me a good reference and I reckon I'll have no
trouble finding work in London.'

Kitty hoped Annie was right, for her cousin's sake, but comforted herself with the thought that if Annie was wrong she would be back in her old job before too long.

John entered and Kitty asked him to cut bread to go with the soup and serve the first course with Annie. He nodded and they all got on with what they were doing. The boys came in and for the next hour or so they were all rushed off their feet.

It was only later, when the kitchen was silent for a few minutes, that Kitty became aware of a dog yelping, but she ignored the sound. It was only when she went into the yard to put something in the dustbin that she realised the noise was coming from the outhouse. She hesitated a moment before making her way down the darkened yard.

She did not open the door straightaway but stood listening, thinking that it did not sound like a very big dog. She inched the door open and immediately a damp nose thrust its way into the opening and against her leg, its owner emitting short sharp yelps. It did not look very fierce but she had never had a dog and closed the door quickly before running up the yard.

She burst into the kitchen to find John and the boys there. Annie had gone to her mother's to see what she had to say about Mo quitting, and the Irish great-uncles who might have spent this time with them had gone to the Irish centre up the road to celebrate with their winnings. 'Whose is it?' she demanded.

'Mine,' said Mick, before anyone else could ask what *it* was. On the defensive he stood next to the ovens. 'I know what you're going to say, Ma, but I couldn't say no.' He spoke rapidly. 'Celia brought him, you see, and he'd have been drowned if she hadn't.'

'Celia's been here?' said John.

Mick nodded. 'Her gran died and her ma's getting rid of the animals because there's no money. She said something about her ma getting into debt again.'

John groaned. 'She'd manage without the drink.'

'Celia said they'd both have to find jobs,' said Teddy, his eyes gleaming. 'We said they could work here.'

Seeing the expression on Kitty's face, Mick said swiftly, 'And Celia said she wasn't going to mention it to her ma.' He glanced at his brother. 'You haven't met her. She'd turn milk sour. She's not like Celia.'

Kitty glanced at John. 'You didn't know anything about this?'

'I know as much as you do. I haven't had time to go round there yet.'

'So what do we do?'

'About what exactly?' he said cautiously.

'About the dog down the yard! That has to come first because it's here now! I've told Mick in the past – no dogs!'

'But, Ma, he'd make a good guard dog,' said Mick. 'Think, if Charley ever came back Nelson could rip the pants off him.'

'Nelson!' Kitty shook her head as if in disbelief. 'He was one of England's greatest heros. That little thing out there couldn't scare anyone! And you know how I feel about dogs indoors. I've heard they leave hairs everywhere and I can't be doing with that, Mick. And don't say it can stay in the outhouse. It can't. It'll yowl the place down.'

'I'll make sure he doesn't leave hairs. As for him being little. He's only a pup. He'll grow! And I'll look after him. Feed him and take him walks and that,' said Mick earnestly. 'An-and I'll make him a kennel.'

'You make him a kennel!' Again Kitty shook her head in disbelief. 'I thought you told me you weren't good at woodwork.'

'I could help him,' said John. 'I think Mick's got a point. A dog in the yard keeping a watch on our rear makes me feel happier. Even if he couldn't rip the pants off anyone, his barking would warn us if there was an intruder.'

Kitty stared at him and thought of his being knifed in the back. Ben said sleepily, 'I like dogs.'

'I'm on Ma's side,' said Teddy. 'It'll want to come into the house – and what about the cat?'

'Thanks, brother!' Mick scowled at him. 'But haven't you forgotten the cat lives indoors – and that leaves hairs sometimes.'

'It kills mice, too,' said Kitty, dismissing his remarks. 'It's useful.'

'I think we should give Nelson a chance,' said John.

'Isn't that up to Ma?' said Teddy.

'She asked me for my opinion so I'm giving it. I think that's only right if we're going to get married.'

Kitty drew in her breath sharply. 'John, not now!'

'Why not now?' He reached out and took her hand. 'I think they realise that it's on the cards.'

'But I haven't said yes!'

'But you will,' he said.

Mick stared at them wanting to say, you don't have to

marry him, but John supporting him over Nelson had put him in an awkward position, so all he said was, 'What about money? You hasn't got any.'

'Show sense, Ma!' urged Teddy. 'Give him the old heave-o!'

Kitty looked at her two sons, trying to understand exactly how they were feeling. 'You mean – throw him out on the streets penniless?' There was a quiver in her voice.

'It's where he came from,' said Teddy promptly. 'But I suppose you could give him some wages before he goes.'

'I'm not saying throw him out,' said Mick. 'He's a good worker for a busker.'

'Thanks a lot,' said John sardonically.

They ignored him.

'I can't have him working and living here without marrying him for much longer,' said Kitty, trying to sound as if this marriage was a purely sensible arrangement. 'People'll talk. If Mr McLeod is to stay I'll marry him. Money isn't everything.'

Ben lifted his head from the table. 'Little John's got money,' he said with a yawn.

They all stared at him. 'Sarah listens at doors. She told me,' he said.

'Is it true?' demanded Teddy of John.

John's gaze washed over his face. 'I'm tempted to say it's none of your business but I'll give you the benefit of the doubt that your interest is because of your concern for your mother not yourself.'

'Why didn't you tell me?' said Kitty, wondering if Sarah could have made a mistake.

'Ach! I planned to! Anyhow it isn't a lot of money,' he said, a faint smile softening the lines of his face.

'How much is it?' said Mick, experiencing a peculiar relief. He'd seen a film only a short while ago about a man who'd been a prince in disguise. Not that the big fella could be a prince. 'I mean approximately?' he added hastily. 'I'm Ma's eldest son and – and I think it is my business.'

'You mean you stand in place of her father?' said John woodenly.

Mick thought about that and nodded.

'You're her son, though, and under age,' said John promptly. 'And I think you've got a cheek asking but I'll tell you this much, I plan to invest some of it in this hotel. I think my uncle Donald would have approved of that. Fortunately he never married and had sons.' He paused. 'Can we eat now? I'm starved.' He moved away from the table and opened the oven. 'And hadn't you better see to that pup? It's probably hungry.'

Kitty felt as if she was in a dream as she followed him over. 'Do you really mean it about putting money into the hotel?'

'I wouldn't have asked you to marry me if I couldn't bring something to the marriage. I would hate being dependant on you. The giving should never be one-sided.'

'I suppose not.' She took the casserole from him. 'You sit down. You shouldn't be doing this.'

'Why not? I've been waiting on tables all week.'

'It's different now.'

'You mean because I've got money I can now sit down and be waited on?' A twinkle lurked in the depths of his eyes.

'No! Your money makes a difference, of course, because it means I won't worry about making ends meet so much. I meant you can sit down and be waited on because you're off duty now. Besides this is my domain.' She stretched up and kissed his cheek. 'Now sit.'

John did as he was told. He smiled at Ben. 'I'll know never to tell you any secrets, laddie. Are you going to come to the wedding, then?'

'Can I bring my mouse?'

'Why not?' John rested his elbows on the table. 'The more the merrier. Just keep it under control.'

Teddy said, 'I suppose me and Mick'll have to be at the wedding?'

'Your mother'll want you there,' said John, obviously full of pep. 'Pity you weren't girls, though. You could have worn flowers in your hair and come as bridesmaids.'

'That's not funny,' said Teddy, glowering at him. 'I've a good mind not to go.'

John's smile faded and he leaned across the table to the boy and said quietly, 'What you said earlier about me being chucked out wasn't funny either. I'm telling you now, Teddy, that your staying away would make no difference to me but it would to your mother. Make the best of the situation and with a bit of luck we can both keep her happy.'

Teddy's ears went red. If he had not been so hungry, he would have got up and walked out, but he decided a dignified silence was what the situation called for. Hopefully his mother would think he was sickening for something and be sorry.

But Kitty did not seem to notice anything different at all. She was full of wedding plans, talking across the table to John and ignoring the boys until it was time for the guests' bed drinks and then it was, 'Put the kettles on, Mick. And you, Teddy, take our Ben up to bed.' Teddy could have spit.

The next week was no different, although come Sunday his mother insisted they went to the Anglican Presbyterian church up the Mount to hear the banns being read. Normally Teddy avoided church like the plague, but there was no escape this time with the big fella watching him in a way that seemed to freeze the marrow in his bones. Mick was no help. He had accepted the wedding would take place even though he was not completely happy about it, because he could not see what they could do to stop it. Besides, Mick's time was taken up with Nelson and plans to build a kennel. Teddy considered going in search of Jimmy but he had decided the sooner he started saving up for a motorbike the better. One day he thought darkly, his ma and that Scottie would be sorry. Off he'd whizz into the blue yonder without telling them where he was going.

John and Kitty went to visit Celia and her mother but the girl was out and they were not made welcome by Mrs McDonald who told them domestic service was something she could never do. She had found herself a job and she would thank them to keep their noses out of her business. Kitty was relieved. The last thing she wanted to do was to take on a maid with a drink problem but she had felt she had to make the offer to please John.

A new maid, Hetty, was taken on. She was a distant cousin of Annie's but not half as good a worker. Although she was better than Mo, who had taken up sewing as a way of making a living just like her mother.

The hotel was given a swift spring clean. A new double bed was delivered from Page's furniture store, and John, and a man they hired for the job, painted the outside of the hotel primrose and cream. The wedding was to take place on the Saturday after Easter, the last one in April. The day Everton were to play Manchester City at Wembley for the FA Cup.

'It's a daft day for a wedding,' muttered Teddy, striving to catch sight of his reflection in the mirror that stood on the chest of drawers as he and Mick fastened their ties. 'I just might have wanted to spend me money on a ticket for the blue train to London.'

'Ma wouldn't have let you go,' said Mick, narrowing his eyes and thinking he looked quite handsome. He combed his dark hair again but there was a tuft which would not stay down. He smiled at his reflection, considering that it was a pity Celia wasn't coming to the wedding. Mrs O'Neill was to be matron of honour and the thought of her brought a flush to his cheeks. She was very pretty and teased him and somehow did not appear to be as old as his mother. Annie had been asked to be a bridesmaid but had said she'd rather not thanks very much. Weddings made her cry. She would stay behind making sure everything was OK for the breakfast afterwards. Then the first Saturday in May she would be off to London.

Mick put away his comb. 'Where's our Ben?'

'Probably with Sarah. Ma made sure he was ready an hour ago.'

'I've warned him not to bring that blinkin' mouse,' said Mick.

A smile darted across Teddy's face. 'So's Ma but *he* says the big fella said—'

'It was a joke! Shall we go in and see if Ma's ready?'

'I suppose so.' Teddy dragged on his suit jacket and followed his brother out.

Ben was sitting on Kitty's bed alongside Sarah who wore a dress full of frills and lace. Becky was fluffing out Kitty's newly cut hair beneath a small-brimmed and beribboned hat tilted over one eye, which she wore with a peach georgette two-piece and beige and black court shoes. She looked so unlike their mother that Mick and Teddy sat on the bed, dumbstruck.

'Well?' said Becky, smiling at them. 'Aren't you proud of your mum? Doesn't she look lovely.'

'Lovely,' echoed Mick, blushing. He had a sinking feeling in his stomach. His mam was all dressed up like a dog's dinner for the big fella and never again would he feel the same coming into this bedroom. It would be *his* and hers, and he would be an intruder. He glanced at his brother who had said nothing so far.

'She's all right for her age,' mumbled Teddy and lowered his head staring at his new black shoes.

'All right!' exclaimed Becky, her green eyes widening. 'She does you credit does your hard-working mama. The cream I had to rub into those hands of hers to soften them.'

'Don't rub it in.' A wry smile curved Kitty's mouth but

it faded as she stared at her boys. She caught her lower lip between her teeth and for a moment her love for them threatened to overwhelm her and she had to struggle against tears. Eventually, in a voice not the least bit like her own, she managed to say, 'He's a good man. There's no need for you to be scared of him.'

Teddy's head shot up and he looked defiant. 'I'm not scared of him!'

'Good,' said Kitty, bending to kiss the top of his head.

He pulled away. 'You'll mess up me hair.'

She turned to Mick and there was a pleading expression in her blue eyes. He held out a hand and she grasped it. 'It'll be OK, Ma.' They both knew they were not talking about the wedding.

'I'm sure it will,' she whispered.

Tears shone in her eyes as she looked at Ben who grinned and said, 'What are you crying for?'

'Because she's happy,' said Becky, planting a kiss on his cheek before turning to Teddy. 'At last you get to have a ride in my car. So let's be having you, boys. I've got to get you to church then come back for Kitty and your Uncle Fred.'

They all trooped out. 'Bye,' said Kitty in a forlorn voice, feeling as if she was saying a real goodbye to them. Her relationship with them was bound to be different from now on. She squared her shoulders and told herself not to get maudlin. This was supposed to be a happy day.

Kitty went downstairs and into the dining room where she, Annie and Hetty had reorganised the tables after the guests' breakfasts that morning. John had stayed with the O'Neills. Annie was fussing about the one-tier wedding cake, which had been made by a friend of her mother's who had trained as a confectioner. It was Annie's family's present to the happy couple and Kitty appreciated it all the more because she knew the struggle they had to make ends meet.

'Everything OK, Annie?' she said.

Her cousin glanced her way. 'Everything'll be fine as long as that Hetty doesn't go touching things. Yer look nice, Kit.'

'Thanks.' She took a deep breath. 'I hope he thinks so.'

'Well, he's seen yer at your worst in the kitchen first thing in the morning, so he's got no shocks coming.'

'I've brushed my hair by then and don't look like a wild woman.' Kitty went over to the huge oak sideboard which had come from the house in Crown Street and gazed in the mirror hanging on the wall above it. She was nervous. Was she doing the right thing? Would John and Teddy learn to get on or would they be daggers drawn for ever after? 'I hope he likes my hair like this,' she murmured.

'It's pretty . . . all wispy-like. It makes you look younger. I wish mine was that colour instead of this ginger. I suppose he'll have had his hair cut too.'

'Mr O'Neill was taking him to his barber.' She sighed. 'Where's your dad?'

'In the Smoking Room having a last cigarette. He's nervous as a cat on a hot brick. He doesn't like being in the limelight.'

'I know. But who else could I ask? Besides he did it once for me before.'

'He was younger then. I think having all us girls and the Depression has done for him.'

Kitty idly ran a finger over the sideboard. 'We were all younger then. You were only a tot and ma was still alive and Michael . . .' Her voice trailed away, remembering that other wedding day and so much hoped for.

'Don't let's forget Jimmy,' said Annie with a fixed smile. 'He was around then and the whole world seemed a nicer place.'

'The war changed everything.' Kitty felt melancholy. Poor Annie!

Her cousin shook her arm. 'Come out of it! If it weren't for the war yer wouldn't be standing here dressed up to the nines getting married again! There's the door – go and find me dad – and be happy!'

Kitty nodded and smiled and left her. Be happy! The words ran in her head as she met her uncle in the lobby. Be happy! she thought as she climbed into Becky's car. Be happy! The phrase re-echoed in her mind as she walked down the aisle and glimpsed her boys sitting alongside Annie's sisters – and wasn't that Celia she had glimpsed back there. Who'd told her to come?

Kitty came to a halt besides John and she *was* happy as he slid his ring onto her finger, despite knowing that nobody can live happily ever after. There would be highs and lows, disagreements, strained atmospheres, but where there was love, not that he had ever mentioned the word, there would be making up and, hopefully, a daughter.

Chapter Ten

John closed and locked the hotel bedroom door – a room which had a washbasin and hot and cold running water. Kitty switched on the light and divested herself of her hat and jacket before going over to the basin and turning the hot tap on and off and on again. She washed her face and hands, dreaming of the day when she could install such luxury in the Arcadia. She wondered idly whether Myrtle's hotel in Rhyl was fitted out in such a way, but she did not think about her old enemy for long, because her husband said, 'Come here, woman,' and pulled her into his arms.

'Let me dry my face first!' There was amused pleasure in her voice.

'I've waited long enough,' he said, and his mouth came down over hers in such a way that it proved to her that this was the moment he had been waiting for all day.

She knew how he felt. It was wonderful to get away from people, including the boys, to be just the two of them. Not that they had not enjoyed themselves so far, taking in the pleasures of Blackpool's Central Pier before going on to the fair; once they discovered that neither of them had ever been to a fun fair in their lives before. They had acted like a couple of juveniles, riding on the bobby horses and swings. He had tried to win her a prize on the rifle range and she had thrown rings on the hoopla stall, both of them without success but nevertheless they had enjoyed being part of the happy, bustling crowd. Never before had she felt so carefree and wished the feeling could last for ever, but they only had one night in Blackpool and tomorrow it would be back to work.

John carried her over to the bed and they kissed a little longer before, by unspoken agreement, they began to undress. As she struggled with the fastenings on her new corset, he said, 'Want some help with that?'

She smiled. 'Please. But be careful. My savings are tucked inside.'

He laughed. 'I suppose it's as safe a place as any.'

'Ma always thought so . . . and talking about money, love, I wondered—'

'I don't want to talk about money.' He flung the corset on the floor and his hazel eyes were questioning as he knelt on the floor in front of her to cup her breasts and kiss them. She folded her arms around his head and crushed him against her, overwhelmed by her emotions. It seemed an age since a man had roused her in such a way and she sighed with pleasure. He lifted her in his arms, laying her in the centre of the bed, and gazed down at her for several minutes before leaving her to switch off the light. When he came back he rammed her body against his, causing excitement to soar inside her until she realised he still had his pyjama bottoms on. She couldn't understand it. There was she panting for him one might say, but it appeared he didn't feel so hot about her. Yet – yet he must do, because

she could feel him hard against her through the fabric. He
began to kiss her in a way that made her think he was going
to swallow her up and his hands were all over her body.
After what seemed at least ten minutes of such behaviour
she was so pent up waiting for them to unite that her teeth
began to chatter, which was something they did when she
became too emotional.

'What is it? Are you cold?' His voice sounded raw.

She shook her head, wanting to cry out, 'Do something!'
But the next moment he was turning away from her and her
mind was screaming out, 'You've made a mistake, Kitty.
This man doesn't want you after all. He's a tease.'

Then he was back again and within seconds they had
merged into one and were galloping away to a panting
finish that left her gasping, but not particularly with
pleasure. 'What have you done?' She almost choked on
the words.

John did not answer immediately because he was out of
bed and at the sink, running water. 'I was protecting you.'

'You used something!' She sank back on the bed
wanting to drum her heels against it. 'Why?' she cried.

'I don't want you getting pregnant.'

Kitty felt stunned. 'But it's wrong to use such things,'
she stammered. 'Where did you learn about them? During
the war? I suppose you went with – with whores and that's
how—'

He turned on her and said harshly, 'I thought you knew
me better than that! I learnt about them when I was doing
medicine. I told you I don't want you getting pregnant.'

'You – you don't want a child?' Here was something

she had not taken into consideration in her daydreams. He was silent as he came and sat beside her and suddenly she realised the truth. 'You're scared I'll die! Because your first wife died you think—'

'If it happened I couldn't bear it.' His lips brushed the edge of her eyebrow and he held her so tightly she could scarcely breathe.

'Ease up,' she gasped as relief flooded through her. He might never have said he loved her but he must care for her a lot. She placed a hand on his shoulder and gazed up into the shadowy contours of his face. 'I've given birth four times and I'm still here.'

'And you told me you lost a baby! You work so *hard*, Kit, and you're not as young as you were.'

'Tell me something I don't know,' she said in a frustrated voice. 'I might be getting on but I'm strong.'

He stared down at her and touched her cheek. 'We never think it can happen to us.'

Kitty's eyes were suddenly damp as her emotions see-sawed again. 'You must have loved her very much.'

There was a silence before he said, 'I didn't want Margaret to die because of something I'd done.'

'It's a risk people who love each other take,' she whispered. 'A child to carry the seed of what we are into the next generation.'

This time he was silent a lot longer and he moved away from her before saying, 'It's a risk I won't take. Goodnight, Kit.' He switched off the light, got into bed and turned his back on her.

She wanted to weep. To cry out, 'But I want your baby!

I want your daughter!' Instead she did neither of those
things but lay back and began to think. It was her mother
who had taught her that sometimes acceptance was the
only way to cope with disappointment, but she had also
shown her that with enough determination some setbacks
can be overcome.

When the McLeods returned to Liverpool, it was to
discover that Annie had already packed her brand new
suitcase and was about to leave a city that was cock-a-
hoop over Everton winning the FA Cup.

'Couldn't you stay just a week longer until I can train
someone else to take your place?' pleaded Kitty.

'Sorry, Kit.' Annie refused to meet her eyes and set her
pointed little chin. 'If I do that then I might never leave.
I've got to go now. You just keep yer eye on Hetty, that's
all. Relative or not, I wouldn't trust her as far as I could
throw her.'

'She's not a worker that's for sure,' sighed Kitty.

'At least yer've got the big fella but yer can't expect him
to make beds and empty the pots.' She added indignantly,
'That little madam downright refused to do the pots and
threatened to leave! They're all the same these young ones.
They don't want to dirty their hands with domestic work
anymore. Factory and shop work is what they're after.
Some of them are real bolshie.'

'I'll ask the boys,' said Kitty, who was in no mood for
an argument with Hetty of the sallow skin and limpid dark
eyes. In the meantime she would draw up a work roster
and tell everyone just what was expected of them.

It was Teddy she approached first after they had finished

supper the following evening. 'Me empty the chamber pots!' Teddy's expression was one of distaste. 'I have the shoes to do, Ma. I can't fit that in. Ask Mick.'

'Mick wouldn't have the time,' put in John, who was reading the newspaper. 'He has further to go to school than you and he has to give the dog a run before he leaves. You'll have to do it until your mother finds a new maid.'

'I still don't see why it should be me,' argued Teddy. 'It's time our Ben helped out.'

John leaned across the table towards him. 'The slop bucket would be too heavy for him. Don't argue. Just accept you have to do it for the moment.'

Teddy stared at him sullenly, wishing one of his brothers was there so he could have had a go at him, but Ben was in bed and Mick had taken Nelson for a walk. 'What about Celia?' he muttered. 'She was looking for a job.'

'She has a job,' said John.

Kitty glanced at him. 'You didn't tell me.'

'I only found out today. When I took those posters Mick did to Green's shipping office. Becky found it for her.'

'Where is it?'

'Rodney Street. It's with a Dr Galloway.'

'I know Dr Galloway,' said Kitty in surprise, smoothing the sheet of paper on the table in front of her. 'He attended Michael in his last illness. He's a widower and was in the Liverpool Scottish during the war.'

'He also has a daughter who's a bit of an invalid, according to Daniel. The doctor wanted someone young and cheerful who had a bit of nous about them to be company for her. One who wasn't too proud to help out in general about the place. But what clinched it for Celia was that Dr Galloway remembered her father, Andy, who was in the medical corps with the Liverpool Scottish.'

'That was useful,' murmured Kitty. 'It's as they say. It's not always what you know but who you know.'

'I wonder if our Mick knows she's working there,' said Teddy.

Kitty and John stared at him and he flushed, saying belligerently, 'He is friendly with her! She did bring him Nelson.'

John nodded. 'You're right. They have become friends but there's nothing wrong with that.'

'As long as that's all it is,' said Kitty, getting to her feet and beginning to clear the table. 'He's too young to be forming attachments.'

She looked at Teddy. 'Right, son, you'll do the pots then?'

'I suppose I've no choice,' he muttered and getting up he walked out of the room.

Kitty stared after him. 'I wish I hadn't had to ask him.'

'It won't do him any harm for a short while. Perhaps Mick can do it at the weekends, give Teddy a break,' said John.

She nodded. 'I hope Teddy's wrong about Mick and Celia.'

'I wouldn't worry about them. Attachments at that age come and go. Say nothing about it and it probably won't turn into anything.'

Kitty piled crockery on a tray. 'I hope you're right. I met Michael at Celia's age and ended up marrying him.'

'Would you have, though, if there hadn't been a war?' He opened the door for her.

She paused with one foot on the bottom step and flashed him a teasing smile. 'Probably. He was a bit of a charmer and had a fascinating Irish accent. I'm a sucker for an accent. What about you? You were only young when you married Margaret.'

'She was verra pretty,' he said, putting on his Scots accent, which came and went according to his mood and to whether he was wearing his kilt or not. 'I married her for her face and carried her photo with me everywhere. I used to take it out and show it to the other blokes and boast about how pretty she was. After a while, though, I had to look at it to remind me that I really did have a wife. I'd stare at her picture, trying to work out what she was really like underneath because I barely knew her.' He took the tray from Kitty. 'When I was wounded she came out to see me. She stayed for a while, having volunteered for the Red Cross. Then she realised she was having the baby and came home.' He paused and his eyes were sombre. 'I never saw her again – never visited her and the baby's grave. I was too wracked by guilt for that.'

'Did you get to know Margaret? Did you really love her?' said Kitty in a low voice.

'I told myself I did. It made her death more bearable somehow.'

Kitty stared at him, trying to work out what he meant by more bearable if he loved her. Surely a death was easier to cope with if you didn't love the person? But then perhaps a lack of love made the guilt worse? One thing was sure, she no longer felt jealous of Margaret. Instead she experienced a sort of grief for John's dead wife and baby girl whose lives had been cut off so tragically, just like Michael's and her own daughter's. 'If I was a Catholic,' she said abruptly, 'I'd want a mass said for Margaret and your baby. Did she have a name?'

'I didn't hang round long enough to find out.' He shrugged. 'Now it's too late – and besides does it matter anymore?' He carried on up the steps and she followed slowly, trying to see a way forward so they could have their own little girl.

The next few weeks passed swiftly and if it had not been for Teddy's obvious resentment towards John, Hetty's habit of disappearing just when she was needed, being overworked and her longing for a daughter, Kitty could have been happy.

Elsewhere in the world there was trouble and unrest. In America a tornado wreaked havoc. In India Gandhi was fasting and drawing attention to that continent's dissatisfaction with British rule. Whilst in Germany people were burning books and parading tanks, troops and bombs. The actions of the Germans bothered her more than anything. She just would not be able to bear it if there was another war.

Kitty glanced across at her husband, who was peeling potatoes, and wondered what he made of events in Germany, but she did not ask him because she did not want to trigger any nightmares about the Great War. It was at such times he was vulnerable, and she wanted a strong man. So she kept silent, just as she did when he went out without saying where he was going. She did not want him to feel caged, just in case he suddenly took off and went wandering again because he missed his freedom.

Hetty's disappearances were a different matter. 'I wonder where that girl is? I'd give her the push if I had the time to train someone else,' she muttered.

'You definitely need another maid.' John lifted his head from his task, his long gold-tipped eyelashes sweeping up as he gazed at Kitty.

She nodded and said abruptly, 'Becky offered me Hannah for a week. They're going on a Mediterranean cruise – supposed to be a working trip – and apparently Hannah hates the thought of going and staying with her brother in Gerard Street even for a week.'

'Take Becky up on the offer. At least Hannah's a worker.'

The kitchen door opened and both their heads turned, expecting to see Hetty, but it was Mick and he had on his best jacket. 'I'm going out, Ma.'

'Where?'

He lifted shoulders which had broadened somewhat in the last few weeks. 'Just out.'

'Where?' she repeated. 'I like to know where you're going. There's been too many reports in the papers lately about bandits and people being held up.'

Mick grinned. 'They'd have to be desperate to hold me up!'

'Some people are desperate,' said John, dropping a potato in water.

The boy glanced in his direction and muttered, 'I don't have to be told that. I haven't forgotten Charley or him pinching Ma's money.'

'There's no need to mention Charley,' said Kitty firmly.

'Sorry.' Mick shrugged again. 'Anyway, I don't know why you should be worrying about me when our Teddy's been out all day and you haven't gone looking for him.' It was Saturday.

'He'll be at that engineering yard.' Her brows knitted and she felt dissatisfied all over again with Teddy's fascination with engines. She would have preferred him to be doing something else with his free time but knew that there was no way of stopping him going to the yard without keeping a watch on him twenty-four hours a day.

'You don't know that for sure,' said Mick.

'Then where else could he be, smartie pants?' murmured John. 'Come up with a good answer or I'll give you a clip round the ear for arguing with your mother.'

Kitty and Mick stared at him and he stared back. 'I mean it.'

Mick swallowed. 'All right! He probably is at the yard but he could be down at the Cassie. He goes fishing there sometimes with his mates.'

John glanced at Kitty. 'What and where is the Cassie?'

'It's the Cast Iron Shore, out Dingle way,' Mick answered for her.

'You get the train from Central to St Michael's station and walk down to the shore. You need to watch the tides, though. There's sandbanks and the water comes sweeping in really fast,' added Kitty.

'Do you fish?' John asked Mick.

Mick shook his head. 'I never learnt. Can I go now?'

John nodded. 'Be in by nine at the latest. It's your turn for the supper drinks.'

Kitty turned to her husband as her son disappeared through the doorway. 'You let him go without us finding out where he was going or who he's meeting.'

'I think you can trust Mick,' said John, placing his knife on the table and putting an arm around her.

'You surprise me.' She rested her head against his chest 'I thought you were against him.'

'Only against him giving you cheek. Teddy bothers me much more. He always has since the day I set eyes on him. And Mick's right. We do only have Teddy's word for it that he's at that yard.'

Kitty was about to say, a little indignantly, that her son's word was good enough for her when the back door opened and Teddy entered.

'I'm not late!' he said before they could speak.

'You're filthy, though, and you stink of petrol!' cried Kitty.

'It's what we use to get the oil off our hands. It can't be helped,' said Teddy.

She frowned. 'That's no excuse. You shouldn't be round at that yard. I presume that is where you've been?'

'Where else?' he said, going over to the sink.

'The Cassie,' said John, picking up the potato knife.

Teddy cast him a quick look, then lowered his eyes to the sink. 'That's for Sundays. I prefer being at the yard whenever I get the chance.'

'It beats working here, you mean,' said John.

Teddy shot him another glance. 'It's real man's work,

not like what you're doing.' The words were out before he could recall them.

Kitty looked at her husband and saw that the muscles of his face had gone rigid. She felt a tinge of fear. She acted swiftly and went over to Teddy. She nudged him in the ribs and hissed, 'Don't let me hear you speak to the big fella like that again. I won't let you round that yard if you're going to come home giving cheek.'

Teddy acted like he had not heard her but his ears had gone red. He dried his hands and hurried out of the kitchen, whistling under his breath.

John threw the potato knife on the table and said grimly, 'I wondered how long it would take.'

'He shouldn't have said it.'

'No, he shouldn't have because I won't forget it.'

She slipped a hand in his arm. 'He's only a boy. I'm sure he didn't mean it.'

'He's old enough to have some manners – and he did mean it'

Kitty knew that John was right. 'I did tell him that if he speaks to you like that again it'll be the end of his going to the yard.'

'I hope you meant it.'

She hesitated. 'As long as he believes I meant it that's what really matters.'

John shook his head. 'Oh no, it isn't! You've got to mean it! I'm telling you now if he speaks to me like that again I'll show him how much of a man I am.' He removed her hand from his arm. 'I'll go and check the fires.'

Damn and blast, thought Kitty, staring at the half-peeled

potatoes on the table. He was right! But surely he must realise how difficult it was for her? If she carried out her threat, Teddy would be even more sulky and awkward than he was already. She just hoped he would have some sense and keep his mouth shut or she could see there was going to be real trouble between the two of them, much sooner than she had thought. How she wished they could be more tolerant of each other and find a common interest. Football or something!

At that moment Hetty entered the kitchen. 'Where the hell have you been?' demanded Kitty, speaking more strongly than she would normally. 'I'm not paying you to skive off when you feel like it.'

'It's me 'ands,' said the maid, looking at her from eyes which were so dark one couldn't ever really tell what she was thinking. 'They get real sore in and out of water. I went and got meself some cream. I didn't think yer'd mind.'

'But I do mind when it's on my time,' said Kitty sharply. When did she have time to worry about *her* hands? 'Now get on with the vegetables and be quick about it.' She considered once more how she really could do with someone who had a bit of nous about them. If only she could have managed with just the boys' help she would have done so.

Mick climbed into bed, settled himself on his back and gazed up at the ceiling. Teddy crawled in beside him, poking him with his elbow. 'Move up! You're taking up all the room.'

Mick shifted a few inches. 'That suit you?'

Teddy grunted. 'If I had my way I'd have me own bed a thousand miles from here,' he said loudly.

'Shhh! You'll wake Ben, What's up with you?'

'I'm fed up of this place. I'm fed up *of him*! Ma's threatened to stop me going round the yard!' His voice rose. 'She'd have never done such a thing before she married him.'

'She wanted to know where I was going and who I was going with,' said Mick.

'And?'

'I didn't tell them.' Mick smiled into the darkness.

There was a short silence. 'Did *he* say anything to you for not telling them?' asked Teddy.

Mick hesitated and turned on his side and said in a muffled voice, 'Nothing I took much notice of but I think we need to be careful what we say.'

'I'll say what I like!' said Teddy fiercely. Mick was silent. 'You're scared of him,' taunted his brother. 'I'm not scared.'

'More fool you,' muttered Mick, sitting up abruptly and staring down at him. 'A backhander from the big fella could knock you to Kingdom Come.'

Teddy lay back, his hands behind his head. 'I don't think he's that tough. I as good as called him a cissy and he didn't say a word.'

'Was that when Ma threatened you?'

'Yep.'

'That's why she did it then. She's worried he might hit you.'

'Naw! She's always worried about us. And so she should be!' said Teddy with some heat.

'She's probably worried more now. What if he did hit us?' And what if Kitty defended them? The big fella might just land her a wallop. They all knew he could be violent if roused because he'd broken Charley's nose. Mick felt sick at the thought of his mother being hurt. 'We've got to think twice, Teddy,' he said, pulling the covers up over a body which now felt cold.

'You're yella.'

'No, I'm not,' said Mick, firing up and aiming a punch at his brother. They wrestled on the bed causing it to creak while each sought to get the upper hand.

The door opened and John stood there. 'What's going on?' His voice sounded stern.

'We were just messing about,' said Mick hastily. 'Sorry.'

'Get to sleep. You've got to be up early in the morning.' He closed the door.

'Phew! I thought we were for it then,' said Teddy, flopping back against the pillows.

'I thought you weren't scared of him,' said Mick sotto voce.

Teddy made no reply, only rolling onto his side away from his brother and thinking about what he would do to the big fella if he ever grew to his size.

Kitty glanced at John as he slid into bed next to her. She had strained her ears in an attempt to hear what was being said in the next room but had only been able to catch the murmur of their voices. She wanted to ask if he had hit them but did not want to put him on the defensive. After this afternoon she wanted more than ever for John and the boys to like each other and to share in male interests like proper fathers and sons did when they had the spare time. She wanted it as much as she wanted a daughter.

'Where were we?' her husband murmured, pulling her against him and beginning to make love to her. Immediately she realised he was not using a sheath and thought with a soaring hope that surely he must be aware of it and had changed his mind. Perhaps now he wanted a child of his own. She pressed her hand against his spine, urging him on to a climax, but the next moment he was out of bed and she knew her opportunity to make a daughter had gone.

Afterwards she lay flat on her back, feeling low-spirited and weepy, wishing that her husband was not so strong where some things were concerned. She might never have a daughter and she had so set her heart on one that she found it difficult to mentally go back to the state of acceptance that had been hers before she met him. She cried out to God to give her what she wanted. Then she turned over, thinking she had to get some sleep. Tomorrow would be another busy day and she had to telephone Becky about Hannah first thing. She felt a need to have an older woman around.

Chapter Eleven

'"Fight the good fight with all thy might",' bellowed Hannah, scrubbing the front step with vigour. She had arrived a few days ago and was obviously enjoying herself.

'Are you all right doing that, Hannah?' asked Kitty from the doorway. She was a bit concerned about the old woman getting down on her knees because of her complaints about rheumatism, but ever since Becky had dropped her off, the maid had not stopped working and had gone through the hotel like a dose of salts. According to Mick she had called Hetty a lazy trollop. The younger woman had been furious, saying that either the old biddy apologised or she would leave. Kitty had said bluntly that perhaps there was something in what that old biddy said. For once Hetty had showed signs of wanting to please Kitty. She had apologised, adding that she did her best but it wasn't the kind of work she was used to. Kitty had almost said, 'What work are you used to exactly? If you're used to work at all.'

'Don't thee be worrying about me, missus,' said Hannah, shifting on a piece of old matting and wiping her brow so that water dripped from the scrubbing brush all down her arm. 'Thee worry about them boys of thine. Straight to hell they'll go if thou don'ts get them up to the meeting house. I saw one of them with a girl. And as for that trollop inside, she's meeting someone as well. A shifty-eyed fella and up to no good I'll be bound. I know his sort.'

'You mean you saw Mick with a girl?' asked Kitty, ignoring the rest.

'That's the eldest lad?' She nodded. 'They were going in one of them palaces of sin, holding hands and looking for all the world like May and June.'

Celia! thought Kitty, and went in search of John. She found him in the basement totalling figures in a ledger.

She came up on him from behind and wrapped her arms about his neck. 'John, we've got to do something. Mick's walking out with Celia. They've been seen going into a picture house.'

'Is that all?' He kissed the back of her hand before removing it.

Kitty went and sat where she could see his face. 'Don't you think it's enough for me to worry about?' she said wryly. 'I think he's too young to be taking girls to the pictures.' She suddenly noticed that Nelson was lying on the floor at John's feet and was distracted. The dog had lifted its head from its front paws and was gazing at her. It had the most comical face and she could not help smiling. 'What's that dog doing here?'

Her husband looked slightly discomforted. 'Dogs like company and I offered to take him for a walk when I've balanced these figures.'

She sighed. 'He'll bring in fleas and isn't he supposed to be guarding our rear in case Charley turns up?'

'You can't expect Nelson to stay out there all the time.' John bent and patted the dog's head. 'As for him having fleas, Mick's dunked him in that old hip bath in the yard and drowned all his fleas.'

'How can he be sure of that? Has he been all over him with a fine-tooth comb?' She stared at Nelson and the dog shifted forward on its belly and licked her shoe. She patted his head, thinking that as long as he didn't go upstairs it was all right for him to come indoors – but she would have to be firm. 'Do you think you should have a talk with Mick?'

'About fleas?'

Her eyes twinkled. 'No, silly! About how babies are made and controlling himself. What if the pair of them think themselves in love and get carried away?'

He shook his head and said firmly, 'I'm not doing it. We'd both be embarrassed and it would put him off me completely.'

She pulled a face. 'Surely things aren't that bad between you?'

'He's scared of me and Teddy's not scared enough. A little healthy fear is a good thing but embarrassment and lack of trust is something else. Mick's a decent lad. He's not going to do anything he shouldn't. Besides Celia's got a sensible head on her shoulders and she worked in a pet shop. She'll know something about the birds and bees. You're just being an overprotective mama.'

She wrinkled her nose. 'I can't help it.' She brushed away Nelson's head from her shoe and went and sat on John's knee. She put her arms about his neck. 'How come you know so much about mothers and sons when you lost your own so young?'

He kissed her throat where the pulse beat before resting his cheek on her arm. 'Because I had an overprotective mama myself. I slept with her until I was seven. Except when my father came home. Then I was kicked out. I remember the first time it happened I raised a helluva fuss. He hit me with a slipper and I yelled the place down.'

'What did he do to you then?'

'He locked me in a cupboard but that only made me yell more.' He grinned at the memory.

'And?'

'They argued outside the door that long I fell asleep.'

'Your mother spoilt you,' she said, smiling and shaking her head at him.

He did not argue but rubbed his nose against hers. 'Father wanted to send me to boarding school but she was dead against it. She died the summer before I was due to go. It messed up all his plans. He'd expected mother to have made the arrangements but she hadn't. He was in the Far East and couldn't get home so I stayed with my sister, which we both hated. She was more like an elderly aunt and friendly with Margaret's mother. Not that I noticed Margaret in those days. Then Gran offered to have me and you know the rest.'

Kitty drew away from him and rested against his arm. 'I know bits. It must have been a lot different to Liverpool.'

'That's an understatement,' he said gravely. 'Like the streets are playgrounds for city kids, the mountains and the lochs were mine. I fished, I rambled.'

'You never thought of staying when your uncle Donald left you his money?'

'Not for long.' He drew her back against him and nibbled her earlobe. 'There was Grandfather, remember. I did think of finishing my training.'

'Why didn't you?'

'Perhaps I'd seen enough pain and suffering in my life. Besides I'd met you.' He kissed her and she thrilled to the touch of his mouth on hers. She forgot everything as that kiss lengthened and deepened. Then he opened her blouse and pressed his face against her breasts. She undid his shirt and slipped a hand inside, dragging out his vest and shirt.

'No,' he muttered. 'I have to get these figures done.'

'Please,' she whispered, kissing his mouth, his eyelids, his throat.

He kissed her hard before pushing her away. 'Let's go upstairs. We might be seen here and that wouldn't be good for our reputation.' There was a mocking gleam in his eyes.

Her hopes and her desire for him soared. Perhaps this time passion might carry him away? But it didn't, and she wondered again if it ever would.

Kitty was just fastening on her stockings when she heard footsteps outside the door. There was something furtive about the sound and John's questioning eyes met hers. He must have felt the need for silence as much as she did because he put a finger over his mouth. They waited for a knock which did not come. The door handle turned slowly but they had locked the door. The next moment they heard footsteps hurrying away.

John was across the floor in seconds and Kitty followed

him. They crept along the tiny landing and gazed over the bannister.

'Did you see who it was?' she whispered.

'Hetty! What on earth was she doing up here?'

'I suppose she could have had a message for me?'

'Your guess is as good as mine. But it was deathly quiet down there when we came up.'

'We'd best go and look anyway,' said Kitty.

They went downstairs and found Hetty polishing the newel post at the bottom of the stairs. She did not speak or look up as they passed but rubbed the wood harder with a duster. They checked the Smoking Room but it was empty, so they went outside and asked Hannah if anyone had come or gone whilst she was there. Her answer was in the negative.

'I reckon we'd better keep a watch on dear Hetty's movements in future,' murmured John as they went into the kitchen. He beat a tattoo on the table with his fingernails. 'I could be wronging the girl but I reckon you're best wearing your corset at all times.'

Her mouth turned up at the corners. 'Even in bed?'

A smile flicked over his face. 'You can put it under the mattress. It should be safe enough there.'

She remembered what Hannah had said about seeing Hetty with a shifty-looking bloke and told him about it. 'We'll definitely have to keep our eyes open for him,' said John.

'Do we tell the boys? They could be a help.'

'And have them behaving like Sexton Blake and his cronies? Let's wait and see how things go.'

'But we can't be everywhere!' she protested. Mick's sensible and Teddy's not that bad either. 'Have you ever thought about how you and he have a common interest?' she added, going off at a tangent.

'And what would that be?'

'Fishing.'

He grinned. 'Kitty, what has that to do with what we're talking about?'

'Nothing, I suppose. I'd just like you both to be a bit more friendly.'

'I'll remember it. Now let's get on with some work.'

Mick and Celia came out of the picture house, arm in arm. 'The way Bela Lugosi rushed around carrying a coffin under his arm was hilarious,' he said with a grin. 'I'm glad they reissued the film. I was only a kid the first time it came round.'

'He was horrible,' Celia said, giving a shudder. 'Those terrible staring eyes! No wonder kids aren't allowed in to see it.'

'I told you we could pass for sixteen.'

'OK! So we both look older than we are,' said Celia, letting go of his arm. 'But we lied, Mick! And I kept waiting for a hand to clap me on the shoulder and throw me out.'

'We didn't lie,' protested Mick, hurrying her along Lime Street. 'The doorman didn't ask us how old we were so we didn't have to.'

'OK, OK!' said Celia. 'You're right and I'm wrong, but it's so easy to get into the habit of lying. Ma does it all the time so that I don't know when she's telling the truth and when she isn't. Where did you tell your ma you were going?'

'I didn't tell her anything but I'm supposed to be back by nine.'

'You're not going to make it.' Celia glanced both ways as they crossed the road. It was a fine evening and people were window shopping without any danger of the little money in their pockets being spent. She paused on the pavement in front of the Adelphi. 'Look, if you're late your ma'll get annoyed and might get really awkward. We'll split here and I'll make me own way. Nothing's going to happen to me in broad daylight.'

'No,' said Mick, frowning. 'I'm already late. So what does it matter if it's ten minutes or half an hour.' It did matter of course, but he was not going to admit it.

'Let's run then.'

They raced all the way to Rodney Street, almost colliding with a couple standing not far from the Georgian-style house where Dr Galloway and his daughter lived.

'Did you see who that was?' whispered Mick as they halted at the bottom of the steps. 'I hope she didn't recognise me, but we were past quick, weren't we?'

'I didn't look at them,' said Celia, uninterested. 'Anyway I'd best go in. Miss Geraldine hasn't been well. She's got this cough that's real persistent. I think the doctor should get her away to the country or the seaside for a long spell.' She sighed.

Mick stared up at Celia where she stood on the step so her face was on level with his. 'You think she's really sick?' He looked concerned. There had been a boy at his school who'd had a persistent cough and he had died.

Celia gnawed on her lower lip. 'I hope not. But her dad's a doctor so he should be able to do something, shouldn't he?'

He nodded. She smiled. 'There's something I overheard that you'd like because you're real ghoulish.'

'Go on,' he urged.

'There's supposed to be a secret passage going from beneath the workhouse on the Mount under Brownlow Hill to the infirmary and university.' Her voice was solemn. 'In the old days, when paupers with no family died their bodies were smuggled out that way to be experimented on for the advancement of medical science.'

A shiver raced down Mick's spine and he said with a delighted smile, 'It could be true! Weren't there body-snatchers up in Scotland years ago? They came unstuck when they started pinching them out of graves and people kicked up a fuss. Spooky!'

'I knew you'd like it.' She smiled. 'I'll see you tomorrow.'

Mick glanced around, kissed her quick, and then ran as if his life depended on it. His chest was heaving when he entered the kitchen.

'You're late,' said John, turning from the range.

'Where's Ma?' gasped Mick.

'Putting her feet up. I said you're late.' John's expression was uncompromising. 'A good half hour! Your mother'll want to know where you've been. I suppose you've an excuse?'

Mick realised he should have thought one up. But then

why should he make up excuses? he thought resentfully. He did not like telling lies but neither did he want to tell the truth, so he kept silent, going over to the gas refrigerator and taking out a jug. He began to pour milk into cups. The big fella had already put on the kettles.

'The silent treatment,' murmured John. 'I suppose you haven't seen Hetty on your travels?'

Mick was startled and stared at him dumbly. How could he know that? Or perhaps he didn't? Whatever, he'd better keep his mouth shut. If he confessed to having seen Hetty up Rodney Street his stepfather might put two and two together and stop him seeing Celia.

'Am I to take this further silence as a yes or as a no?' said John, slamming a hand down on the table so that the milk in the cups splashed up and Mick jumped out of his skin.

'Yes, I mean no. I – I mean – I did see her. She was with some bloke.'

'What was he like this bloke?'

'Er – I didn't look that close. Though I think he had big ears.'

'That description'll get us far,' said John with gentle sarcasm. 'Were they behaving like sweethearts?'

The question took Mick completely by surprise. 'Erm, I – er, no!' he said positively. 'In fact I think they were arguing.'

'People who love each other argue.'

Oh, smart! thought Mick. 'What do you want me to say?' His voice rose. 'They weren't kissing and cuddling so they weren't acting like sweethearts in my book.'

'Keep your voice down or you'll have your mother up here.'

Mick lost control. 'I don't care! I'd like Ma up here! She wouldn't let you bully me! Anyhow what's wrong with Het—'

John clamped a hand over Mick's mouth and rammed him against him. The youth gasped with shock and tried to wriggle free but he was completely helpless. 'Now listen to me – would you recognise the bloke again? Nod or shake your head.' Mick managed to nod his head. 'Good,' said his stepfather, releasing him.

'You shouldn't have done that,' said Mick, seething with rage and frustration at being rendered helpless.

'Why, what'll you do, Mick?'

Mick was silent.

'Take it as a warning that I won't have any impudence from you, laddie. And listen, I don't want what we've said in here to go further than these four walls.'

'Why. Because Ma'll know what a bully you are then?'

John looked bored. 'How old are you?'

'You know how old I am,' Mick said sulkily.

'And you've been seeing Celia, haven't you? So why don't you start behaving like the man you'd like to be. Your mother has enough on her plate without worrying about our differences.'

Mick went sick. 'I suppose you're going to stop us from seeing each other?'

'Ach, no! I'm sure your friendship with Celia is harmless.'

Friendship! Harmless! Did he really believe that? Mick felt like telling him that he loved Celia! Only he felt sure his stepfather would mock him because he couldn't possibly understand the powerful feelings that surged through his body whenever he so much as brushed against Celia. 'Thanks,' he said stiffly.

'That's OK. The kettles are starting to boil. Do you want a hand?'

The sudden change in his stepfather's manner threw Mick off balance. 'Er, no thanks. I'll manage.'

John left him alone.

As Mick spooned cocoa and made tea he found himself reliving that suffocating moment when his stepfather had seemed intent on squeezing the life out of him. It had been frightening but Mick made up his mind that he was definitely not going whingeing to his mother. But what had all that been about Hetty?

Mick was still puzzling over it the next morning when he saw Big Ears standing at reception. He would not have stood out in a crowd but for those ears. Mick thought of going over and asking did he want to see Hetty but the vestibule door opened and the O'Neills entered.

'Hello, Michael,' said Becky, flashing her lovely smile at him.

He blushed. She was the only person who ever called him by his full name. 'Good afternoon, Mrs O'Neill. Ma's about somewhere. I'll go and fetch her, shall I?'

'In a minute. How's Hannah been?'

Mick couldn't prevent a grimace.

'That bad?' she said sympathetically.

'No,' he said hastily. 'Ma said the place has never been so clean. Us boys, though, are going to hell.'

She shook her head and said ruefully, 'She really is the limit.'

'Hello, Micky.' Sarah slipped her hand into his. 'How's life been treating you these days?' It was a phrase her father often used and sounded strange issuing from one so young.

'OK! How was the trip?'

Mick never got to hear because at that moment Kitty and John arrived on the scene and he was ordered to go and make tea and bring it down to the basement.

Mick did as he was told, lingering only for a few moments to listen to what the O'Neills had to say about the cruise. To his disappointment they were discussing tomorrow's foundation stone laying ceremony for the Roman Catholic cathedral on Brownlow Hill. He slipped away, fastening a lead to Nelson's collar he went to meet Celia.

He had just arrived outside St Luke's Church in Leece Street when she came running, her hair flying behind her. 'I'm sorry I'm late,' she gasped, 'but we've had a burglary and the house has been in an uproar. All the silver's been stolen.'

Mick felt quite excited. 'Has the doctor had the police?'

'Of course he has! I had a job getting away. My room was searched and they kept asking me questions,' she said indignantly. 'They don't seem to have a clue, though, how it happened. There's no sign of a break-in. Miss Geraldine's real upset and had one of her coughing bouts.' She took a breath. 'What's the world coming to, Mick? A day doesn't go by when you can't read of a burglary or a smash-and-grab somewhere in the country.'

'It's the Depression,' he said, taking her hand. 'That's what the big fella said . . . and talking about him, he knows about us.'

Celia stared at him, wide-eyed. 'What did he say? Did you get into trouble?'

'He asked me about Hetty and really went on about recognising the big-eared bloke. He got rough but I took it on the chin.' He squared his shoulders. 'He's not going to stop us from seeing each other.'

'You stood up to him?'

'I had to – for you.' He squeezed her hand and she smiled, and the rest of the world was forgotten by both of them.

'There's been a burglary,' shouted Ben, erupting into the basement through the area doorway, clutching a ball to his chest.

Kitty glanced up from the sheet she was darning and her eyes met her husband's. 'Where?' asked John.

'Rodney Street. I heard Mr McFarlane and Mr Rubenstein talking. It was three masked men and they took the silver.' Ben's eyes were shining. 'I wish I had a magnifying glass. I could go and look for clues.'

'You mean someone saw them?' asked Kitty, surprised.

'Must have.' He stared at John. 'Have you got a magnifying glass?'

'No, Ben.' He put down the periodical he was reading and got to his feet. 'I think I'll take a breath of fresh air.'

'You're going to have a nose about,' said Ben, raising himself up on his toes and down again. 'Can I come?'

Kitty put aside her sewing, her eyes on John's face.

'Maybe I should take a turn upstairs? Hetty's supposed to be keeping her eye on things but I doubt she's expecting burglars. Besides it's time I was doing something about supper. Mick and Teddy should be in soon.'

John nodded and went outside, followed by Ben. The first person they saw was the dentist from next door who John had already discovered had done his training in Edinburgh. He was standing on his front step smoking a pipe. 'They say there's been a burglary.' He pointed his pipe in the direction of Rodney Street.

'Three masked men I believe,' said John. 'Which house was it?'

'Doctor Galloway's place. Took every penny, so I heard, and even the Sunday joint out of the larder.'

John said, 'Is that so?' They talked for a moment about the burglary and then to Ben's disappointment changed the subject and began to talk about Edinburgh.

He listened for a moment before wandering away to take a look at the Galloway's house and parked himself on the kerb opposite. He rolled his ball in the gutter, watching for any suspicious characters but nobody who looked the least bit exciting passed by. After a while he returned to the hotel where there was a Sunday stillness about the place. He went down into the area and he bounced his ball against the wall, thinking it would be fun to tail someone like the hero had done in the film he had seen last week.

Several guests came along, some ignored Ben but several spoke kindly to him, asking had he seen the streets decorated for the ceremony tomorrow. Teddy came bounding down the Mount and went through the front door without showing any sign of having seen his brother. Ben heard him say sorry to someone and the next moment a man came out of the hotel doorway, carrying a bag. Ben looked at him and his interest was caught as the man looked furtively about him.

Carefully Ben crept up the steps, pausing to peer through the railings before emerging onto the pavement and following him. The boy enjoyed himself, darting behind lamp posts and hiding in shop doorways whenever the man paused to change the bag from one hand to the other. He followed him all the way to a back entry not far from Scottie Road. Ben did not hang around waiting when the man went inside one of the yards but ran all the way home for his tea.

A spate of burglaries in the area was reported in the *Liverpool Echo* during the next few weeks. Then it went quiet for a while, maybe because people stopped being so trusting and locked their doors and windows. Celia told Mick that so far the police had had no luck in finding the doctor's silver.

'It's really upset Miss Geraldine and he's thinking of taking her away for a fortnight in August. She wants me to go with them.'

Mick stared at her with a sinking heart. 'Do you have to go? I'm going to miss you terribly.'

She squeezed his hand. 'I'll miss you, too, but Miss Geraldine needs me.'

'I need you,' he said. 'I wish you could come and work for us.'

Her expression was wistful. 'I wish I could but if your ma had really wanted me she'd have asked. Besides I'm really fond of Miss Geraldine and I wouldn't like to let her down.'

Mick supposed she was right. His mother had never expressed a wish to employ Celia even when she could have done so. They carried on walking Nelson round Princes Park in the warm sunshine, discussing whether to see Ginger Rogers and Fred Astaire or Laurel and Hardy next week.

Someone else who had been enjoying the sunshine that Sunday afternoon was Teddy. With the arrival of summer they were not so busy at the hotel as people took off to the country or the seaside, so both boys had a bit more leisure. He was down at the Cast Iron Shore, sitting on a rock with his mate Bert. They were fishing with hook and line, using bite-size chunks of cod's head as bait. On the foreshore was a group of men playing pontoon, and he and Bert were supposedly keeping an eye out for any sign of the police.

Teddy glanced in the direction of the road which ran up to the railway station. The golf links were on one side and further up on the other was St Michael's cast iron church, from which the Cassie got its name. His eyes fixed on a tall figure striding along the road and he shot to his feet, almost dropping his line. 'Damn and bloody blast!'

'What's up?' said Bert.

'It's the big fella! What the hell's he doing here? If Ma's sent him to check up on me I'll go mad!' He felt a twitch on his line and swiftly gathered it in. There was a small fluke on the end. He unhooked it carefully and threw it back and rebaited his hook.

'He'll probably go away once he sees yer all right,' said Bert placidly.

'You don't know him! He's just out to spoil me fun,' said Teddy, grinding his teeth.

'So what are yer goin' to do? D'yer wanna hide?' suggested Bert.

'What? Hide from him! You must be joking! I'm not scared and we're only fishing, aren't we?'

'And keeping an eye out for the rozzers.'

'He doesn't have to know that,' said Teddy scornfully. 'Anyway watch your line. If we keep looking at the river he mightn't notice me.'

But John had already recognised his stepson's unruly dark head set on a neck that was still boyishly slender. He approached the rock where the two youths sat. 'Caught anything?'

'A couple of little fluke and crabs,' answered Bert, disarmed by the tall fella's smile. 'We threw them back. Me ma would have laughed at me if I'd taken them home for tea.'

John climbed onto the rock beside them, despite Teddy's glowering expression, and held his face up to the sun and the sea breeze. 'Not a bad spot.'

'It's a good spot,' said Bert earnestly. 'Do you fish, mista?'

'I did when I was younger. My uncle had a rowing boat and we'd go out where the water was real deep sometimes.'

Bert sighed. 'It'd be good having a boat.'

'It was good.' John lowered his gaze and watched Teddy throw out his line further. 'You don't have a rod.'

'Does it look like I have a rod?' said Teddy sullenly.

John's eyes narrowed. 'It was a statement, laddie, not a question, and don't be impudent. Do you enjoy fishing?'

Teddy nodded, unsmiling.

John got to his feet. 'Stay out of mischief and make sure you're home for tea on time.' He got down from the rock and began to stroll along the water's edge.

Teddy stared doggedly in the direction of Rock Ferry on the other side of the Mersey, wishing the big fella to Kingdom Come, and thinking of a few things he'd like to say to him if he had the nerve. He was so caught up in his own thoughts that it was not until he heard the squealing of brakes and the shouts of men did he realise the rozzers had arrived. 'Hell!' he cried, staring over his shoulder at the uniformed figures spilling on to the beach.

The gambling school had broken up and men were running here, there and everywhere in an attempt to escape arrest. Several shot past him and splashed into the sea. One shouted, 'What happened to yer, lad? Last time we pay yous to keep a decko out for us.'

'Sorry,' said Teddy, much too late because the man had gone, and much too late to realise that his stepfather was in earshot.

'Does this happen often?' demanded John.

'They wouldn't play here if it happened often,' muttered Teddy, not looking at him.

'But it happens and you keep a watch out for them. How long before you start gambling? How long before you're carted off in a Black Maria? How would that make your ma feel?'

Teddy was silent, hating John for saying such things in front of his mate.

'I'll answer for you,' said John. 'She'd hate it. We'll wait until things calm down and then we'll go home.'

'I don't want to go home,' protested Teddy.

'You're going home.' John's expression was uncompromising as he parked himself on the edge of the rock and watched the melee taking place on the foreshore.

Teddy seethed, thinking, one day, one day he'd get his own back.

Chapter Twelve

Teddy had dozed off but something woke him. A dim light filtered through a gap in the curtains and he lay there wondering what time it was. He had gone to bed early, tired out with fresh air and temper. He yawned and glanced in Mick's direction but his brother was asleep and so was Ben. He lay for a while, thinking over the day's events, and his anger boiled over again. *I won't be able to show me face for a while down on the Cassie*, he thought. The pool of gamblers would be back after a few weeks but they wouldn't ask him to be a lookout again. He'd lost a way of making money and it was all down to his ma marrying that Scottie. What wouldn't he like to do to him? Boiling oil was too good. He let his lurid imagination run away with him and conjured up images which included giant spiders and the rack.

He was just turning over to grab a bit more shut-eye when he realised he could hear voices and recognised one of them as Hetty's. Puzzled, he tumbled out of bed, feeling as if he had hardly slept at all, and padded over to the window. It was darker than he expected and the street lamps were still on. A man and a woman entered Hunt's Hotel on the opposite side of the road but the woman was definitely not Hetty. He realised it was still Sunday and not Monday morning as he had thought.

He went back to bed, convinced he had imagined the voice. He'd only just settled himself when he heard a smothered giggle and the noise of a drawer opening in his mother's bedroom. It was enough to get him out of bed again and into a pair of trousers. He opened the bedroom door slowly and squinted through the narrow gap. He was just in time to see the back of Hetty and a man going downstairs.

Teddy closed the door quietly and crept to the bend in the stairs. He peered over the bannister and could see the maid and the man on the landing below. He had Kitty's bunch of keys and was opening one of the guest rooms.

'I'll see yer later at Morry's place,' whispered Hetty. 'I'm going off now.'

The man nodded and slid inside the room. Excitement almost choked Teddy. Here was the thief who had been burgling the neighbourhood and *he*, Edward Ryan, had spotted him. Perhaps there was a reward for his capture? What to do? The last thing he wanted was to enlist the big fella's help.

The man came out of the guest room and went into the next. Teddy crept further down the stairs but had to shrink back as the man came out onto the landing once more and headed downstairs. Teddy followed swiftly. From the second stairway he watched the man go over to the top of the first flight of stairs and stand there a second before walking back and unlocking another door. It was obvious to Teddy that the thief knew which rooms were occupied and which were not, and that had to be down to Hetty.

Teddy decided there was only one thing for it. He would have to trail the man. He was debating whether to risk going upstairs for his shoes when the man came out and went downstairs.

Teddy followed in a rush, scared of losing him. In his haste he slipped on the stairs and, despite all his efforts to save himself, slithered to the bottom. He landed in the lobby with most of the breath knocked out of him. The man glanced at him and dropped the keys on the chiffonier, rushing for the front door.

'Stop thief!' gasped Teddy, scrambling to his feet and staggering towards the kitchen. 'Help! Help!'

The kitchen door opened. 'What on earth's going on?' demanded Kitty.

'There's been a burglar upstairs, Ma. He's just escaped. We'll have to go after him,' cried Teddy.

Kitty hurried towards him as John appeared in the kitchen doorway. 'What's going on?'

'Teddy says there's been a burglary.' She put an arm round her son. 'Are you all right? You look a bit dazed.'

'I fell downstairs. I wanted to catch him.'

John said in exasperated tones, 'Typical! It's Sexton Blake as I said.'

'Love, show a bit of sympathy,' said Kitty, smoothing back Teddy's hair. As her eyes went from her husband to her son's face, she was remembering the atmosphere when they had arrived home earlier that day. She had longed to ask what else had gone wrong between them but her instincts had told her it would be a mistake.

'I'm OK, Ma.' Teddy scowled and pulled away from her. 'We have to go after him!'

'You're not going anywhere,' said John.

The Smoking Room door opened. 'What's all the commotion?' asked a bedding salesman from Lancashire.

'Nothing,' said Kitty, pinning on a smile.

The man puffed on a cigar. 'The lad looks poorly.'

Teddy forced a smile. Having grown up with the knowledge that guests had to be protected from unpleasantness at all times, he knew the procedure. 'I'm fine.'

'Yer don't look it, lad.'

'I've got naturally pale skin,' lied Teddy.

'This is getting us nowhere,' muttered John, and headed for the front door.

'Something else wrong?' said the salesman.

Kitty smiled. 'It's my son's pet mouse. It's escaped.'

'Oh dear! Don't tell the ladies.' The man vanished inside the Smoking Room.

'Do you think you can catch him?' whispered Kitty, hurrying after John and followed by Teddy. 'I wonder what he got away with?'

'It must only be small stuff. He wasn't carrying anything,' said Teddy.

'Small stuff can be valuable.' John stood on the pavement looking about him. 'If I knew what he looked like I might be able to do something. You should have come and told us as soon as you suspected something, Teddy.'

Resentment sparked in the youth's eyes. 'I couldn't risk

it! I can tell you that he has big ears and carroty hair and Hetty's in cahoots with him.'

Kitty and John exchanged looks. 'So we were right,' he murmured. 'I wonder if she's gone straight home.'

'She's gone somewhere called Morry's,' said Teddy.

'That saves a trip to her house straightaway.' John smiled. 'Morry's, Morry's,' he murmured. 'Sounds familiar.'

'Shouldn't we call the police?' said Kitty. 'We can't keep this from the guests.'

'Let me and Teddy have a walk down the Mount first and see if we can spot him,' said John. 'Come on, lad.'

Teddy would have liked to refuse. He could have made the excuse that he only had slippers on but he did not want to miss out on anything so he did his best to keep up with John's long stride. With a certain reluctance, he asked, 'How did you know Hetty was involved?'

'She was snooping around upstairs a few weeks ago. Can you see anyone who looks like the man?'

Teddy stood in Ranelagh Place, watching the people coming and going. He shook his head. 'He must really have legged it.'

'He would with you shouting thief!'

Teddy's ears went red and he turned and padded away from John, wishing he had not told him about Hetty and Morry's. The big fella could have been on his way to Hetty's house by now and he and his ma could have gone to the police station. He would have been a bit of a hero bringing such information.

Kitty was waiting for them at the front door. 'You didn't catch him then,' she said in a low voice.

'No sign,' said John.

'We'd best go the police station then,' said Teddy.

'We?' said John, his eyebrows shooting up. 'You're not going anywhere, me lad. You can get to bed.'

Teddy opened his mouth to argue but Kitty said, 'John's right. You had that fall. You're best in bed.'

'But I don't want to go to bed,' shouted Teddy. 'I'll miss all the excitement and it was me that told you about the thief!'

'You've had enough excitement,' said John. 'Don't argue and get up them stairs.'

Teddy opened his mouth but Kitty gave him a warning look and, almost in tears with rage and disappointment, he stomped up the stairs.

Kitty turned to John whose face was screwed up in concentration. 'I'll have to tell the guests, love.'

His eyes met hers and he smiled. 'Leave it as long as you can. This Morry that Teddy mentioned. I'm sure I've heard the name before, up Scottie Road way. I've a feeling he owns a pawnshop. Why don't you just wait for the guests to discover the thefts? If they're only small valuables they mightn't notice they're missing until the morning.'

That's wishful thinking, thought Kitty, but kept her mouth shut.

'I'll go and take a decko at the place. I might just catch up with them.' added John.

'You'll be careful?' she said, instantly worried.

'I'll be careful.' He kissed her lightly and went off down the road.

Kitty closed the door behind him and hurried into

the kitchen to make the supper drinks which were now extremely late. She was surprised no one had come looking for her to complain. She took them in, having decided that she would wait until the thefts were discovered and take matters from there. She was glad that there was only a few guests and, feeling guilty at keeping quiet, she served the drinks swiftly before going upstairs to the attic to check on Teddy.

She was about to open the door when she was suddenly aware of movement and whispering inside. The next moment the door opened and all three boys came out.

'And where do you think you're going?' she hissed, folding her arms across her chest.

'To catch the burglar!' piped up Ben, his eyes bright. 'I know where he is.'

'Big mouth,' groaned Teddy and poked him with his elbow.

'Don't do that,' said Kitty automatically and fixed her stare on her youngest son. 'How do you know?'

Ben pressed his lips firmly together but Mick said excitedly, 'Ma, you've got to let us go. Ben followed Big Ears the day Dr Galloway was burgled!'

'I see,' she said, giving Ben a severe look. 'What have I told you, me lad, about wandering off?'

'It was only a game,' he said with a sigh.

'Thieving isn't a game,' she said strongly. 'Have you all forgotten Charley?'

They exchanged looks and shook their heads.

'There you are then! Anyway, there's no need for you to go playing heroes down Scottie Road. Ah, that surprised you didn't it?' she said as they all started. She allowed herself a triumphant smile. 'But you don't know that the big fella has a good idea where this Morry's place might be and he's gone there.'

Their faces fell. 'He's always spoiling our fun,' growled Teddy.

Kitty frowned at him. 'Do I have to repeat this isn't a game?'

'Then why has the big fella gone there?' demanded Mick. 'He should have informed the police instead of charging off himself.'

Teddy nodded. 'Mick's right. What if they bash the big fella over the head and they get away?'

'They're not going to bash him over the head,' said Ben with a positive jerk of the head. 'He's too big.'

'The bigger they are the harder they fall,' murmured Teddy, gazing at his mother.

'OK!' said Kitty, giving in to her fear. 'We'll go to the police with the information, just in case.'

Her sons exchanged looks and Mick said, 'I suppose it's better than being sent back to bed.' And they crowded round her as she went downstairs.

'Someone should stay and hold the fort,' she whispered as she pulled on a jacket and looked at Mick.

'Awww! Don't be mean, Ma,' he protested. 'The burglars have gone and this place isn't going to run away.'

She relented and they left the hotel, closing the door quietly behind them.

Everything happened much quicker than Kitty expected because they had not gone far when they met a policeman on his beat. She explained what had happened and in no time at all they were at the police station and she was giving a statement. A police car was dispatched to Morry's place and they were allowed home.

There were a couple of irate guests for her to soothe when she arrived back but the news that the identity of the thieves was known, and that it was likely that their property would soon be recovered, helped her in her task. She saw the boys to bed and then sat waiting for John to arrive home.

It was one-thirty in the morning before her husband returned. Kitty made toast and cocoa and did not ask any questions until they were both settled on the sofa in front of the fire.

'Well? Did they catch them?'

'Red-handed.' John's teeth crunched into a slice of toast. 'The police have suspected for some time that Morry's might have been acting as a fence for stolen goods but had never been able to trace anything to him. I had a lecture on taking the law into my own hands, but as they arrived before I'd done much, I didn't take any notice.' He smiled at her and pulled her against his shoulder. 'Everything's been recovered and the police'll be here in the morning to sort everything out.'

'Well, I hope they do it discreetly,' murmured Kitty, pleased by the news but wondering just what her husband had done for the cause of justice in the pawnshop.

'I did manage to bring something away with me.' He placed his cup on the floor and drew from his pocket the locket which had belonged to her mother.

Kitty's eyes widened and the fact that Hetty had stolen from her somehow made the whole thing worse. 'The bitch! I should have got rid of Hetty ages ago but with her being sort of family I gave her more second chances than I should have.'

'You've got rid of her now and it's Teddy you have to thank for that.' He pulled a face.

'You'll give him a few words of praise,' she said lightly.

'He went about it all wrong,' he said.

She looked at him. 'Fair's fair, love. If it wasn't for him, as you've just said.'

'OK!' He rested his head against the back of the sofa. 'I'm thinking it was a good job you had your money in your corset.'

'Me too.' She smiled and added, 'Fasten my locket on for me.'

John did so, kissing the back of her neck before easing her against his shoulder and undoing her blouse and slipping his hand inside. 'You're going to have to get a new maid.'

'Hannah!' said Kitty, closing her eyes and enjoying his touch. 'I trust her.'

'But she's Becky's maid! You can't just snaffle her.'

She sat up abruptly. 'Ah, but I know Becky only took her on because she felt sorry for her and they don't really hit it off. Besides, Becky wants someone younger.'

'We could do with someone younger. How about offering Celia the job?'

Kitty turned her head and stared at him. 'Are you mad? Hannah's experienced and she's a hard worker.'

'Celia's young and a worker too.'

'Her and Mick are like May and June! I have it from Hannah's lips.'

'Take the two of them on then. I bet Hannah won't let Celia get away with canoodling with Mick on the stairs.'

Kitty half smiled, imagining what the elderly maid might say if she caught the two young ones kissing. She felt young herself tonight and remembered a film she'd seen a few weeks ago with Maurice Chevalier and Jeanette MacDonald called *Love Me Tonight*. 'I'm wide-awake,' she said.

'Me too.' He glanced at the clock, which stood at two, and pushed her against the cushions, kissing her. Relief, excitement and exhilaration filled them with exuberance not caution.

Afterwards as she lay in bed, Kitty thought they had never made love like it. Lovely! It had been lovely! And if they hadn't made a baby during it, then surely they never would.

Chapter Thirteen

Kitty was sitting in the O'Neills' garden a couple of evenings later. Sarah was out of earshot, pushing her youngest sister Siobhan on the swing, whilst Rebekah's eldest, David, and Ben, were playing in the tree house built in the branches of the old oak that shaded Kitty and Becky from the sun. It was an idyllic setting and for a moment Kitty thought how lovely it would be to have a garden and more time to relax, but the thought passed. For too long her ambition had been making the Arcadia the best hotel of its kind in Liverpool.

'Of course you can have Hannah,' said Becky with a grin. 'Your need is greater than mine. I'll give that servant bureau on Mount Pleasant a visit, I'm sure they'll be able to find me someone pretty quickly. I pity Celia, though, if she does agree to work for you. Hannah gave me a rough time with the boys years ago. Although, if I'm honest, she's mellowed a bit since then.' She began to tell Kitty something of her youth but the tale was cut short when Siobhan fell off the swing and her screams caused them to wince. Both women rushed to pick her up but Kitty reached her first and soothed her whilst Sarah looked on.

'Sarah pushed too hard,' wailed her sister who, despite

her tear-stained face, still managed to look like an angel with fair curls and brown eyes.

'I didn't! You're just a crybaby,' said Sarah, sticking out her tongue.

Becky slapped her. Sarah pressed her lips firmly together and flounced away to climb the rope ladder to the tree house. Her mother called her to get down but was ignored.

'Be thankful, Kitty, you don't have daughters,' said Becky, shaking her head at Sarah and taking her youngest into her arms. 'They can be right cats and real secretive. Boys are much more open.'

Kitty did not doubt it but it did not put her off wanting a daughter. If she could manage three boys she could cope with one girl. If only! She had her fingers crossed and was praying for a baby girl.

With Hannah promised for the following week, Kitty's next task was to find out if Celia would leave the Galloways and come and work in the hotel. She decided to give her eldest son the task of asking her.

Mick concealed his delight over Kitty's proposal extremely well. He'd had some idea of what was coming because Ben had told him what he had overheard whilst up the O'Neills' tree. Ben was not at all pleased about the elderly maid joining them because he had not forgiven her for threatening to cut off Twitchy's tail, but the mouse's fate was the last thing on Mick's mind that summer afternoon in 1933. 'I'll ask Celia, Ma. But you do know she's got kind of fond of the Galloways.'

Kitty smiled. 'I'm sure you'll be able to persuade her.'

Mick was sure of that as well, and went in search of his love. He found Celia brushing the steps outside Dr Galloway's house. She seemed to be in a dream and appeared not to have noticed him. 'Hiya!' he said, waving a hand in front of her face.

She blinked and slowly a smile replaced her rather sombre expression. 'What are you doing here?'

'I've a message for you.' He paused for effect, although he was almost bursting with the news. 'Ma wants you to come and work for us.'

Celia could scarcely believe it. 'Say that again?'

Mick repeated the words. 'Well, what d'you think? You'll come won't you?' he said eagerly.

She rested her chin on the end of the broom handle and did not speak for several moments. 'I don't think I can,' she said slowly.

Mick could not believe it. 'What do you mean you don't think you can? Of course you can,' he protested. 'It'll be better than your working here. Remember what you said months ago about it being really interesting working in an hotel?'

'I haven't forgotten.' Celia lifted her head and began to sweep dust towards the gutter. 'But Miss Geraldine coughed up blood this morning. It was awful to see her suffering. She clung to me hand – and afterwards told me how fond of me she was and how lovely it was to have someone young about the place. She's only twenty-two, you know.'

He stared at her with a sinking heart. 'You'd be best getting out of that job, Cessy. I'm surprised the doctor hasn't got her into the consumption hospital on the corner if she's that bad.'

Some of the colour faded from the girl's face. 'I know what you're thinking but you could be wrong. Sometimes people bring up blood through just straining. It doesn't say it's – it's *that*. Anyway, I've told you, he's going to take her away and I'm going with her.'

'You're mad,' said Mick, worried. 'If she was family I could understand your staying with her and taking a risk but she isn't. Just think, Cessy, if you came to work for Ma we could see more of each other.'

'I know that and it'd be lovely,' said Celia. 'But I'd be letting Miss Geraldine and the doctor down. He's an awfully nice man, saying thank you for every little thing you do for him. He doesn't deserve this to happen to him. The cook says he's a gem of a master and it's true.'

'But what about us?' said Mick, getting annoyed.

'What about us?' she said, smiling, as she went to fetch the shovel. 'We can still go on seeing each other. I'll still be here only a few minutes away.'

'I know that, but . . .' He frowned and kicked at the dust in the gutter, deeply disappointed.

'Don't do that!' she said, brushing the dust off his shoe and onto the shovel with the rest.

'Sorry! It's just that I thought you'd want to come. To be with me above anyone else! But now it looks like you prefer the Galloways' company to mine.'

'That's not what I said!' Celia was startled by his vehemence because Mick was not one to get angry normally. 'And will you keep your voice down. I don't want them hearing you.'

'Perhaps you'd rather I didn't speak at all,' he muttered, kicking the edge of the kerb.

'Don't be daft! It's just that I'm working right now and the housekeeper could get funny if she caught me talking to you.'

'I'll go then.' His voice was positively cross.

She started to feel annoyed with him. 'You do that. Some of us have work to do. We can't just come and go when we please because our ma's the boss.'

Mick considered the time he had been awake that morning, taking up water and emptying chamber pots, and his annoyance got the better of him. 'That's a rotten thing to say and you know it! Ma keeps our noses to the grindstone!'

Celia knew that was true but she was not prepared to take back what she had said. Why couldn't he see her side of things? Half of her wanted to accept his mother's offer but half of her was touched by Miss Geraldine's need of her.

'Goodbye then,' he said stiffly.

'Goodbye.' Celia did not look up as he walked away. *He'll be back*, she thought.

Mick found Kitty hanging out of one of the front bedrooms, watering a window box filled with geraniums and French marigolds. 'She doesn't want the job,' he shouted up to her.

'She doesn't!' Kitty was surprised. 'Why on earth not?'

'She prefers Miss Geraldine and the doctor to us.' There

was a tiny choke in his voice and he disappeared quickly inside before his mother could start asking questions.

He found Teddy in the kitchen eating jam bread. 'What's the matter with your face?' asked Teddy.

Mick was not going to say anything but suddenly all his anger and hurt came spurting out.

Teddy stared at him and then grinned. 'You're daft! What do you want to be getting all serious about Celia for? Girls take your money and you've got little enough as it is with still being at school.'

Mick was startled. He had not begrudged a penny he had spent on Celia because he had considered her company worth it, but now he realised just how true Teddy's words were.

'Forget her,' said Teddy, biting into the slice of bread and jam. 'And come rowing with us tomorrow.'

'Rowing!' exclaimed Mick. 'I didn't know you could row.'

Teddy looked slightly discomforted. 'Our stepfather can. And Ma thinks it'd be nice for him to teach me. You never know. It just might come in useful one day.'

Mick forgot Celia for the moment. 'I thought you didn't like him.'

'I don't. But I've got to try and get on with him for Ma's sake. He actually thanked me for spotting Hetty and her boyfriend and gave me a bob.' He smiled at the memory.

'Lucky you,' said Mick. 'D'you think he'll mind me going rowing, as well?'

'I don't see why he should. I bet it'll be lovely on the lake in Sefton Park.'

Mick imagined floating on cool refreshing water and his sore young heart was momentarily soothed.

'What do you think all that was about?' asked Kitty, turning to John who was oiling a squeaky wardrobe door in the room behind her.

John shook his head. 'I'm surprised she turned it down.'

'Me too. Perhaps she's already cooling off.' She frowned. 'I don't know whether to be glad or sorry.' John was silent. She stared at him. 'What do you think about it?'

'They're young. They'll fancy themselves in love time and again before they're much older.'

'Was it like that for you?' She remembered how Michael had been the only sweetheart she'd had as a young girl, despite many a flirtation with milk and butcher boys who had called at the house in Crown Street.

'I was a bit older than Mick when I started getting interested,' he said as he put down the oil can. 'My grandparents kept me on a tight rein. It wasn't until I got to Edinburgh that I had the chance to take a girl out.' He put an arm round Kitty. 'Thinking about love and all that, how are you feeling?' His voice was gruff.

She looked up at him in surprise. 'About what in particular?'

'About the other night.' His anxious eyes gazed into hers. 'I'm sorry, Kit.'

'That's OK.' She rested her head against his chest. 'It happened and there's nothing we can do about it.'

'It was a stupid thing to do.'

Kitty smiled. 'There's no use worrying about it. At the

moment I've other things to think about. Summer's not our busiest time but if we do get busy I can send the linen out to be laundered.'

'It's a pity Annie ever left,' said John gloomily.

Kitty agreed but knew there was no chance of her cousin returning. She had written to say she had found a position in a small London hotel and was building a new life for herself. So for now, thought Kitty, they would have to manage with Hannah and the boys. If she was to have a child, of course, she would have to think again.

The day after Hannah took up her position as all-purpose maid, Ben sought Kitty out before school, obviously suffering from some great anxiety. 'Ma, you won't let Hannah clean our bedroom, will you?'

Kitty stared down at him. 'Why not?'

'She'll find Twitchy and cut his tail off,' he whispered.

Kitty suppressed a smile. 'I'll see to it, son. Don't you worry.'

'You'll keep your eye on her?'

She agreed to keep her eye on her.

Kitty meant what she said but the joy of having Hannah working for her was that, unlike Hetty, there was no need to check that she was working. Despite complaining occasionally of rheumatic twinges, Hannah knew what she was about – although she had a strong will and a habit of saying exactly what she thought in a mixture of Quaker-style thees and thous and Scouse. This had been known to take the guests by surprise at times, as it often did Kitty.

The maid had not been in the hotel a fortnight when she said to Kitty's face, 'Thou needs someone like me around because thee'll never save them lads elseways. The Lord sent me because he knows yer too soft with them.'

'No, I'm not,' protested Kitty, who was feeling low and weepy because her period had come.

The maid smiled in a grim knowing way and, picking up the cat, she limped out of the kitchen with it. 'I'll be up the stairs if thee wants me.'

Kitty turned to John who was eating a late breakfast. 'I'm not soft with them,' she said crossly.

'You wanted her here,' he said with a smile, dipping bread into an egg. 'And I'm glad she is because you don't have to work so hard – but what I'd dearly like to know is what she wants with the cat. She hates animals.'

Kitty gazed at him and then shot off after Hannah, catching up with her just as the maid was about to mount the stairs to the attics. 'Not up there, Hannah!'

'I've started so I'll finish,' said the maid, and lifting the wriggling, growling cat in her arms, she threw it up the stairs.

'No!' yelled Kitty and almost fell over her feet in a rush to beat the cat to the top. She threw herself forward, stretched out an arm and grabbed its tail. The cat's head twisted and a rumble sounded in its throat. 'Don't you growl at me! You know you're not allowed up here,' she said crossly.

'Yer's daft talking to dumb creatures,' said Hannah.

'And you're impertinent.' Kitty came downstairs, clutching the cat. 'And cruel. You know Ben loves that mouse.'

'Mice is vermin. They's dirty creatures.'

'Twitchy's a tame mouse and God created him just as much as He created you and me.'

Hannah sniffed, turning her back on Kitty, and limped along the landing, vanishing into one of the bedrooms. Kitty smiled, knowing she was the victor, and went downstairs, carrying the cat. She told John what had happened and he seemed to enjoy the tale, although he added, 'She's right, Kit. Mice are vermin and make dirt.'

'I know that. But she goes to extremes.'

'That's due to her background. She grew up in filthy surroundings. Becky's aunt told me. There's enough diseases today without cures but it was worse when she was a girl. You don't hear of many cases of cholera or of typhus but Hannah'll remember some. Dirt is the enemy and anything that can spread it has to be destroyed.' Almost without a pause he added, 'I was talking to Dr Galloway the other day.'

'About disease or Celia?'

Their eyes met and she could see that he was concerned. John hesitated. 'As it happens both. We were discussing his daughter. She's consumptive, Kit, and because I'm Celia's godfather he asked me did I think he should ask her to leave.'

'Oh, poor man,' said Kitty, sitting down. 'Is it terribly serious?'

'It's in the early stages and she'll be starting treatment soon. But he wants to take her on holiday first to a cottage in Cornwall. All that clean air will be good for her but the problem is whether it's good for Celia. The girl wants to go and he knows precautions need to be taken to protect her.'

'Has he explained the situation to Celia?'

John nodded. 'She knows she needs to wear a mask and how important it is to have a spittoon handy. He says she's a sensible girl.'

'What does her mother say?'

'They don't see much of each other and I doubt she'd be interested,' he said grimly. 'She's taken up with some bloke, according to Celia, and is hardly ever in when the girl goes there.'

'Then I wouldn't interfere,' said Kitty, torn between admiration for Celia's courageous loyalty to the Galloways and relief that Mick was no longer seeing her.

'You're probably right,' said John. 'It would have created difficulties.'

Kitty could guess at what they might be. If he lost the girl her job he would feel honour bound to find her another. And however sorry she herself felt for Celia, she was unsure about the rightness of offering her a job at the Arcadia again. Consumption was infectious and so unpredictable. It could strike down the strong as well as the weak and kill rapidly. Yet she had known people to survive for years and some to be cured, but the last thing she felt able to do was to put guests, or her family, at risk. She only hoped that Mick had definitely got over what he felt for Celia and would not be tempted to see her again.

Mick's heart was still sore when he thought of Celia but he had no intention of taking up with her again. He missed her but he filled up his hours outside of school as much as he could. When he had calmed down and thought logically

about what Celia had said, it did not make him feel any
better. Her actions were those of a considerate person but
he had wanted her to consider him before the needs of her
employer. It seemed a natural thing to expect if you believed
someone was in love with you. He decided that she could
not have been in love with him at all and perhaps what he
had felt for her was calf love. He dismissed her from his
mind if not his heart, and took interest in other things.

Chapter Fourteen

Summer had gone and the dingy leaves had fluttered down from the trees in the gardens and parks in the city, leaving the branches looking forlorn and naked. Choking fog concealed the river and the old buildings around Mount Pleasant took on the semblance of something out of a horror movie. Most Liverpudlians went about their business against the mournful background of fog horns on the Mersey but some were imprisoned in their homes not daring to go out because the fog was a killer for anyone with 'a chest'. John was out though, and Kitty was worried.

She gripped the sink waiting for the dizziness to pass. Despite the pleasure she felt about her condition, she wondered how much longer she would be able to keep it from her husband. It was obvious to her that he was restless. He had suffered nightmares lately and there was also the matter of Teddy giving him cheek only a few days ago. The mood of optimism she had felt during the summer concerning Teddy's and John's relationship had vanished, only to be replaced by a moody pessimism. Things had got even worse since John had punished her son by not allowing him to go round to the engineering works. Instead Teddy had had to stay in the kitchen for a whole Saturday, peeling vegetables and washing dishes. It had not gone down well and now he did not speak to his stepfather if he could help it. Instead, he went round looking like he had a hobgoblin sitting on his shoulder all the time because Kitty was still insisting that he worked in the hotel when he left school, which would be any time now. She just hoped they'd all be able to dredge up some Christmas cheer from somewhere.

She tried to pull back her shoulders and lift her head, remembering there were others much worse off than her. Poor Dr Galloway was suffering. His daughter had wasted away from galloping consumption three weeks after she had returned from holiday. It had been such a shock and Kitty could scarcely bear thinking about what he must be going through.

Think a few happy thoughts, she told herself. *Think of the miracle of new life growing inside you against all the odds.* John had been so careful but it had happened and she could still hardly believe it. This morning she was convinced she had felt the baby quickening inside her. Sooner or later she was going to have to tell him, but not yet. If he did not run away from the stark truth about her being pregnant, he just might fuss over her and insist she take things easy, and she had no time for that. Christmas was coming and although they were closing down over the festive season, people were still flooding into town from Wales and Lancashire and staying a couple of nights to shop and see a film or a show. Then they were gone and although she had taken on a couple of part-timers it still involved more work for her.

'Hast thou a pain?'

'What?' Slowly Kitty turned to face Hannah.

'Thee hasn't been thyself lately.' The maid's eyes were concerned.

'I'm fine!' Kitty braced her shoulders and tilted her chin.

'Thee looks peaky if thee asks me.'

'Nobody's asking thee!' cried Kitty, and to her horror her eyes filled with tears. 'Just – just come and help me lift this pan.'

'I'm glad thee's showing some sense by not lifting it on thy own.' Hannah's normally austere expression was gentle as she brushed Kitty's hand aside and lifted the pan. 'There's no need to cry, missus. I'm here to help thee but the sooner thou tells that man of thine what's up with thee the better.'

Kitty blinked back tears and sniffed, giving a good imitation of Hannah. 'I don't know what you're talking about!'

The maid smiled grimly. 'Just because I'm an old maid doesn't say I don't know nuthin'.'

Kitty saw there was no use in pretending anymore. 'I want this baby,' she said fiercely.

The maid sniffed. 'I suppose he doesn't though, and that's why thee hasn't told him. Thou's a fool.' Hannah's voice had softened. 'If thee goes on slaving away thou'll miscarry and that could finish thee off and where will that leave all thy menfolk?'

'Ever cheerful,' said Kitty, feeling a chill at her heart as she gazed at her maid from beneath drooping eyelids.

'Yous have to face facts. Tell him. Babbies can't be hidden for ever.'

Not for ever, but perhaps a bit longer. She had to pick her time, she thought.

Two days later Kitty fainted clean away whilst queuing up in the market. She was standing next to a Christmas tree at the time and fell into it. On regaining consciousness she was aware of the hard stone floor, a rich resinous pine-like smell and needles sticking into her palm. The stallholder, Mr Green, informed her that her husband had been sent for and insisted she sat and wait for him. He pressed her into a chair and handed her a cup of tea. It was sweet and she sipped it slowly, feeling stupid and irritable and, if the truth be known, worried. It was the first time she had ever fainted in her life.

John arrived and he sat back on his haunches in front of her. 'What happened?' There was a furrow between his chestnut brows and an anxious expression in his eyes.

She had almost decided to tell him the truth but now she changed her mind and lied effortlessly. 'I went dizzy. It must be my age or hunger.'

'What's your age got to do with it?'

'I'm thirty-seven, John!' She smiled. 'Women of my age do have fainting fits.' She stared at him, willing him to get her meaning. He returned her stare but said nothing and she lowered her eyes and sighed. 'I'll probably get middle-age spread and you won't love me anymore.'

He laughed then. 'I don't believe it! It's more likely due to your working so hard. Or you could be anaemic and need a tonic. You should see Galloway, Kit.'

'Doctors cost money!' She concealed her alarm by smiling up at the stallholder and handing her empty cup to him. She thanked him for looking after her.

'No trouble, luv. As long as yer didn't hurt yerself when yer fell against that tree.'

Kitty gazed at the tree which had a couple of crushed and bent branches. 'I'll buy it,' she decided. 'The boys'll enjoy decorating it.'

'Yer don't have to,' protested Mr Green but she could see her offer had pleased him so she insisted, and ordered John to take possession of the fir tree.

'You must be feeling better,' he drawled. 'Giving your orders.'

'I do feel better.' She paid the stallholder, who wrapped old newspaper about the tree roots and and handed it to John. She picked up her basket and slipped her free hand into her husband's arm and squeezed it. 'You mustn't worry about me. I'll be fine,' she said.

'You still look pale.' His gaze travelled slowly over her face. 'You'll do as you're told and go and see Galloway. Go soon.' She protested but John was not having any. 'You'll go if I have to drag you there by your hair,' he commanded.

'All right, I'll go!' She saw nothing for it but to do as he said.

They set the Christmas tree up in the Smoking Room. It was not often that Kitty was able to entertain her own friends or relatives but on Boxing Day she had invited the O'Neills for dinner before they went off to Ireland for the New Year, and she planned having Annie's family for Hogmanay.

When the boys arrived home from school she handed scissors, glue and sheets of tinsel and coloured paper over and told them to get cracking. She dug out the box of candle holders and glass baubles they'd had for years and placed new candles in the holders. Several guests arrived on the scene and Kitty hurried into the kitchen to finish the preparations for dinner, leaving two of them helping the boys. At last she felt there was a real spirit of Christmas in the air and she began to enjoy herself, despite the fact that at the back of her mind she was wondering what to say to Dr Galloway when she saw him.

On the morning of her appointment Kitty washed from head to toe and put on her Sunday best. She was still undecided as to what to tell him when she arrived at the surgery. Perhaps she should just say she wanted a tonic? That she was feeling run down? It was true enough.

It was not until the door was opened by Celia that Kitty had a moment's disquiet. With so much on her mind she had forgotten John's god-daughter was working for the doctor. Then she asked herself what was she worrying about? The girl wasn't to know why she was here. Celia smiled shyly, wished her a good morning and showed her to the waiting room.

Kitty thanked her and gazed about the room. There was only one other person there, whom she did not recognise, so she picked up a copy of *Good Housekeeping* and sat down. She realised she was a bag of nerves. It was a long time since she had been to the surgery. The boys were blessedly healthy, although all had suffered measles and chickenpox and Mick had had mumps. If they cut themselves or got the odd bump or cold, she dealt with it herself using concoctions passed on to her by her mother who'd had a fear of doctors and hospitals.

Kitty opened the magazine and flicked over a page. Her eyes caught the words *The Children's Charter. An explanation of the Children's and Young Persons Act of 1933.* She had heard of the Act, of course, and so read with interest, taking note of the hours a child under twelve could be employed, which meant not more than two hours on Sundays or school days. Those hours could not be during school hours or before six in the morning or after eight at night. She thought of Teddy who would soon be officially on her payroll.

The door opened and the other woman left the waiting room. Kitty read on. There was a conflict of opinions between the House of Lords and Commons over the birching of young boys. The Commons were against, the Lords for. Kitty mused on the issue and decided that there could be no hard and fast rule. She hated the thought of any child being beaten but crime was on the increase and that included juvenile crime and it needed to be dealt with.

Celia popped her head round the door. 'Dr Galloway will see you now.'

Kitty was shown upstairs and into a room overlooking the street. Her legs felt shaky. Perhaps he would say she really was going through the change of life? Or worst that she had something seriously wrong with her?

The doctor was seated at a desk, writing. He lifted his head as she entered and his strained expression disappeared in a smile. Immediately her nervousness vanished and she stopped thinking of herself. This man had lost a child and could put a brave face on it, so what was her problem in comparison? He had the gentlest of grey eyes and a warm smile. 'Good morning,' he said.

'Good morning, Doctor.'

'Please sit down. I won't keep you a moment.'

She sat and waited, thinking not for the first time how terrible it must be to lose your only child. He finished writing and leaned forward, clasping his hands on the sheet of pink blotting paper on the desk. 'What can I do for you, Mrs McLeod? It's not often I get to see you in here.'

She took a deep breath. 'I'd like a tonic. I think I'm a bit run down. I – I fainted in the market.'

Dr Galloway got to his feet. 'Let's have a look at you.'

Kitty was alarmed. 'You mean you'd like to look at my tongue?' she babbled and stuck it out.

'Very nice,' he murmured. 'But—'

'My eyes then.' She opened her eyes wide.

'Mrs McLeod, please!' He smiled but his expression was thoughtful when he took her wrist and held it for a few moments. 'Why don't you tell me what's bothering you?' he said gently.

'You won't tell my husband?' She could hear the anxiety in her voice and could have kicked herself for it. 'What you tell me will be strictly confidential.' His voice was grave. 'Doctors take an oath about that sort of thing, Mrs McLeod.'

'I know that but—' She hesitated. 'I'm having a baby and my husband's not going to like it.'

Dr Galloway did not show the surprise she expected.

'Up on the couch with you,' he said. 'I am sure you know what you're talking about but let's make certain.'

A few minutes later he was confirming her diagnosis and advising her to be confined at the new maternity hospital in Oxford Street. She had never been in hospital before and had caught some of her mother's prejudices, but perhaps the new hospital would be different. She remembered the Princess Royal coming to lay the foundation stone when the hotels on the Mount had been decorated in her honour and the pavements lined with Girl Guides. Perhaps she would not have lost her little girl if she had gone into hospital then?

The doctor went over to the sink whilst she adjusted her clothing. Then he sat behind his desk and told her to sit down. 'Sometimes Mr McLeod and I have a yarn,' he murmured. 'He's led an interesting life and it's a pity he never finished his training after the war.'

Kitty nodded, remembering that the doctor had served in the Liverpool Scottish Regiment. 'I suppose you discuss the war.'

'Sometimes. Interestingly your husband and I met Captain Chavasse. A brave man. You know of him, of course?'

'Yes.' *Who didn't in Liverpool*, she thought. The captain had been a doctor and worked in the port before the war. He had won two Victoria Crosses and saved numerous lives at the cost of his own. His father had been a Bishop of Liverpool and was principal founder of the Anglican Cathedral. He had lost another son on the Somme. Such loss was a terrible burden to bear for any parent. 'Sad,' she understated.

'Hard to lose a child at any time,' said Dr Galloway, looking drawn. 'Fortunately the bishop has another two sons and twin daughters. I had only the one and it is a great grief to me to have lost her. You're worried about Mr McLeod's reaction to your pregnancy. Well, don't be, my dear. He's been given a second chance at making something of his life because of his marriage to you and that can only be good for him.' Kitty was touched. 'Naturally he will worry about you,' continued the doctor. 'But I'm certain he will be pleased about the baby. Children are a blessing. I'll give you an iron tonic and arrange about the hospital. You must eat well and make sure you have plenty of rest. If you do that I'm sure you'll have no problems. Come and see me again in two months' time and we'll have a little chat.'

Kitty saw there was nothing more to be said. She thanked him and paid his fee on the way out. Celia held the door open for her and impulsively Kitty asked how she was.

'Why do you ask?' said Celia, two bright spots of colour appearing on her freckled cheeks.

'I just wondered. I know how fond of Dr Galloway's daughter you were.'

The girl looked relieved. 'It was sad. Really sad! That's why I'm staying on with the doctor. He says he likes to see a young face about the place. He's having me trained to be a receptionist.'

'I'm sure you'll do well, Celia,' said Kitty sincerely.

'Thanks very much,' said the girl, beaming at her. 'And I hope you have a happy Christmas, Mrs McLeod. And all the family.' She hesitated. 'You'll give my best wishes to Mick?'

'I will,' said Kitty.

'Well?' demanded John, taking both her hands as she entered the kitchen. It was with a sense of shock she realised he was shaking and immediately she was concerned about him.

'I'm very well thank you.' Her tone was confident. 'He's given me a tonic and told me I must look after myself because I'm not getting any younger.'

The worried lines about John's eyes did not ease. 'So he said everything was all right?'

'Would I be smiling if he hadn't?' She twinkled at him.

He lifted one of her hands and kissed it. 'But if you faint again you'll go straight back there.'

'Of course I will.' She told herself she would tell him in the New Year. The last thing she wanted was him fussing about her all over Christmas, insisting that she rest. Rest at the moment was the last thing she could do.

'You know the doctor's going away for Christmas,' said John.

'He didn't say.'

'Well, he is. Which means Celia will be stuck with her mother and her fancy man, unless—'

Kitty caught on quickly. 'Unless we ask her to do a couple of weeks' work here, you mean?'

'You could do with some extra help.'

Kitty hesitated, wondering whether Mick would like the idea. Should she ask him? Was it necessary? He hadn't mentioned the girl in months, although she had sent her best wishes to him. She really *could do* with extra help and it would only be for two weeks.

'I don't know what to say,' said Celia, shifting her gaze from Kitty's face to polish the doctor's brass plate with more than her customary vigour.

'Do you want a day to think about it?'

'Perhaps that would be best.' She rubbed her cheek absently on her outstretched arm. 'What does—? Have you—? Would I live in for the two weeks?' she asked with a rush.

'There's a small guest room you can have. We're never full at this time of year. When is Dr Galloway leaving for Scotland?'

'The day after tomorrow. He's going by the night express. He's going to see his brother.'

'Let me know by tomorrow then whether you'd like to come.'

'Rightio. And thanks Mrs Ry – Mrs McLeod for thinking about me,' said the girl, squeezing the duster between her hands and smiling. 'I'll think about it.'

Kitty said, 'I'm sure we can make you feel at home – and you can have Christmas Day off to go and see your mother.'

'Thanks.'

Kitty turned for home but she had not got far when Celia came dashing after her. 'I've thought. I'll come,' said the girl.

'Fine,' said Kitty. 'See you Saturday then.'

Celia nodded, thanked her again and ran back up the street.

That girl smiles with her whole heart, thought Kitty, and decided that perhaps she had better mention what she had done to Mick. She got her opportunity later when they were alone in the Smoking Room.

'It looks lovely, doesn't it?' said Mick as he gazed at the candlelit and tinsel-bedecked tree.

'Lovely,' echoed Kitty, glancing at it before breaking a large lump of coal with the poker. She watched tiny jets of flame set alight the gas that hissed from fissures and thought with half her mind what a gift from God fire was. 'By the way, son, I've asked Celia if she would like to come and work for us for a couple of weeks. Dr Galloway's going to be away and I could do with some extra help. I've been feeling tired lately.'

Mick said casually, 'If you want her to come let her come. It doesn't make any difference to me.'

Oh, doesn't it! she thought, not deceived. 'That's OK then.' She smiled. 'The poor girl's upset. We'll have to do our best to cheer her up.'

Mick nodded and went out of the room whistling.

Celia arrived the day before Christmas Eve. 'Last shopping day before Christmas,' said Kitty to those gathered in the kitchen. 'We can flop after today. Make Sunday a real day of rest, but now there's still work to do. Celia, would you empty the ashtrays in the Smoking Room and give the place a thorough going over. Then go on to the dining room. Hannah's started on the bedrooms. You can help her upstairs after you've finished downstairs.'

'Can I put a note on the Smoking Room chimney ledge, Ma?' asked Ben.

'Why?' asked Mick, slipping Nelson a bit of sausage and not looking in Celia's direction. 'You've already put one up the chimney in the front basement.'

'I'm worried in case it got burnt up,' said Ben anxiously. 'You know that chimney's funny.'

'I'm sure Father Christmas read it first,' said Kitty soothingly, getting her shopping baskets. She glanced at John. 'Are you coming? It'll be the last time for three days and I need your strong right arm.'

He looked up from the letter he had received that morning and said starkly, 'My brother's dead! Died a few months ago. Now apparently his daughter's coming to England and wants to meet me.'

She put her hand on his shoulder. 'Do I offer you my condolences? You didn't really know him, did you?'

He shook his head. 'The letter was sent to my sister. She sent it to Uncle Donald and the solicitor's sent it on. You'll remember I wrote to him about us getting married.'

'She didn't know your uncle was dead?'

'Apparently not, although we did inform her. She's enclosed a covering letter to him but there's no address on it. It seems she's moved.' He turned the letter over and shrugged.

'She doesn't want you to get in touch,' said Kitty positively.

'Seems like it.' He rustled the letter between his fingers and his expression was rueful. 'There's something really strange here, Kit. How is this for timing? My brother's daughter's ship—'

'You mean your niece,' she said helpfully.

'My niece,' he said obediently. 'Her ship's due to dock in Liverpool today.'

'I don't believe it!'

He raised three fingers. 'Scouts' honour!'

She groaned. 'What d'you want to do?'

'I suppose I should find out what time it's due in. It's not often a distant member of my family turns up out of the blue.'

'We'll have to put her up,' she said starkly.

He nodded. 'You were going to have a rest.'

'I don't think we've got much of a choice. We have to offer. She's family.' Suddenly it all seemed too much and she sank onto a chair, still clutching the shopping baskets. 'Gosh, I wish Annie was here.'

John took the baskets from her. 'You *are* tired if you feel like that. Perhaps I shouldn't ask Nancy to stay.'

'Don't be daft!' Kitty forced a smile. 'It's only one person. Hannah won't be going anywhere for Christmas and Celia will be around on Boxing Day. But do I put off the O'Neills? And what about presents? Do we buy her a present?'

'I'll see to that.' He helped her to her feet. 'If I had my way I'd leave you here but you know what you want to buy. Let's get it done. I can telephone Canadian Pacific from the Post Office and find out from them when the ship's in.'

He glanced at his stepson. 'Mick, I've made up the bills for those two sisters and that husband and wife. See you hand them over and get their money. No going out until it's done, d'you hear?'

'I hear,' said Mick with a sigh. 'But it's all right for this evening, isn't it?'

'What's this evening?'

'We were all going to see *King of the Jungle* with Buster Crabbe, as well as Laurel and Hardy. You said it was your treat.'

'Did I?'

Ben looked at John anxiously. 'Yes, you did!'

'I'd forgotten. We'll have to see, laddie.' He smiled and hustled Kitty out of the kitchen.

Mick and Ben exchanged glances. 'We'll have to see, laddie!' Mick mimicked John's voice and scowled. 'Which probably means no now he's got this woman arriving.'

Ben slipped a hand into his brother's. 'We could still go. You can take us.'

'He was treating us and I've spent all my money with it being Christmas. I wish I hadn't bought him those Marcella Whiffs now,' said Mick moodily. John smoked only occasionally but when he did it was cigars or cheroots.

'Perhaps Teddy'll have some money,' said Ben.

'And perhaps he won't.'

'So what do we do?' insisted Ben. 'I want to see those films. I've heard they're real good.'

'I'll have to think,' said Mick, wishing Teddy hadn't gone off to the yard but his brother had finished with school now and desperately wanted Laystall's to take him on without his mother knowing.

The bell in reception sounded and Mick went out. It was the married couple. He put on a smile and handed them their bill. He took their money and helped them outside with their suitcase and parcels before wishing them a pleasant and safe journey home. Then he placed the money

in his mother's cash box and put that in the cupboard of the
chiffonier and locked it. He slipped the key in his trouser
pocket. When the two sisters arrived downstairs he helped
carry their luggage to the station and received a tip.

As he re-entered the Arcadia he considered that if it
hadn't been for the big fella's relative arriving they would
have almost had the place to themselves. He thought of
Celia for a moment and experienced a familiar ache,
which had eased during the time he had avoided her, but
which was now making itself felt once more. He decided
he would carry on avoiding her whatever his mother and
stepfather might think.

They reappeared an hour later but John only lingered to
dump the shopping in the kitchen before going out again.
'Make us a cup of tea, love,' said Kitty.

Mick put on the kettle. 'What's happening, Ma? Is his
niece coming to stay?'

'Probably.' She yawned. 'We'll eat in the dining room.
Put a couple of tables together. I was going to do shepherd's
pie but it'll have to be something a bit more fancy now.'

'Your shepherd's pie's nice,' said Ben, leaning against
her knee. 'Ma, what about the pictures? Will we be able
to go?'

She put an arm around him and rested her cheek against
his hair. 'I don't think so. Not if we've got a visitor.'

'She might like to come.'

Kitty smiled. 'To see *King of the Jungle*? I doubt it,
son.' She got to her feet and began to unpack the shopping.

John arrived back a few hours later in a taxi with a woman
whose black coat was made less severe by the addition of a

red hat, gloves and scarf. She had a round smiling face and
her hair was brown with a few silver strands. 'Kit, this is
my niece Nancy Higson,' said John, smiling.

'Hello, Kitty!' Nancy held out a hand. 'It seems
ridiculous that I'm his niece, doesn't it? It's good to meet
you and real nice of you to offer to put me up. As I've got
nobody left now Pop's gone I thought I'd make the trip.'

Kitty returned Nancy's infectious smile. 'You're
welcome. Is your husband—?'

'Dead. Damn war.' She smiled at the boys. 'These
yours? I never had any kids myself. It was a real grief to
me but there it is.'

Kitty introduced Mick and Ben who shook hands
politely. She told Mick to ask Celia to make tea and bring
in the sandwiches and cakes and to tell her that when she
had finished could she ask Hannah to make up another
bed. Reluctantly Mick went to do as he was told.

He found Celia in the bedroom vacated by the sisters
from Todmorton. 'Ma wants you to make tea for four and
bring in some cakes.'

'OK.' Celia did not look up but carried on polishing the
tallboy.

'Now,' said Mick loudly.

She dropped the duster on the floor and brushed past
him with her nose in the air.

Mick felt a little better. He had not forgotten what she
had said about his getting away with things because his
mother was the boss.

When he arrived downstairs Ben was hanging around in
the hall with Teddy, who had a smear of oil across his chin.

Ben pounced on Mick. 'What are we going to do about the pictures?'

'I don't see how there's anything we can do. Unless—' He glanced at Teddy. 'How much have you got?'

'Sixpence. I've spent up . . . bought Ma some chocs in a rather nice box.'

'That's it then.' Mick sighed as he emptied his pockets and gazed at his threppence tip and the key on the palm of his hand. 'We haven't got enough.'

'Perhaps Ma would give us the extra?' said Ben, scuffing his feet against the bottom of the chiffonier.

Mick shook his head. 'She's too busy with the visitor to be bothered about us going the pictures.'

'So that means we don't go and all because of his blinking relatives,' muttered Teddy, looking fed up.

'One relative,' said Mick, fingering the key now back in his pocket. 'There's money in the cash box.'

His brothers stared at him. 'We could borrow five shillings,' said Teddy. 'If we go now we'll make first house and we won't really be missed 'cos we'll be back for dinner.'

Mick hesitated. 'I didn't mean—'

'Then why say it?' demanded Teddy. 'We can pay it back can't we?'

'Yep, but – I'm not so sure if we should take money without asking.'

'You want to see the film, don't you?' hissed Teddy. 'And they're taking no notice of us.'

'Of course!' Before he could change his mind Mick went over to the chiffonier.

He was just putting the box back when Celia came out of the Smoking Room. They started at each other and he felt himself flushing. He shut and locked the cupboard door swiftly and, without looking at her again, joined his brothers and left the hotel.

The boys enjoyed the films but they had no sooner come through the front door than John came out of the dining room and confronted them. 'Have you three been to the pictures?'

'Yes! Is there anything wrong with that?' said Mick. 'We're not late for dinner.'

'No, you're not late for dinner but we couldn't find the key to the cash box and we wanted to get some drink but had no money because we had spent up.'

Mick reddened and took the key from his pocket. 'Sorry. I didn't think.'

John smiled. 'That's OK. You'd all best get changed.'

The brothers were halfway upstairs when Mick remembered about the money he had taken and wished it was his mother who had asked for the key. He hurried downstairs to find John counting the money. His stepfather did not look up as Mick placed a hand on the edge of the chiffonier, feeling dreadfully nervous. Celia came along the passageway, carrying a laden tray. Mick cleared his throat. 'I borrowed five shillings,' he said huskily.

John looked up. 'Borrowed?'

'Yes! Borrowed!' Mick was aware that Celia had paused in front of the dining-room door. 'Ben really wanted to see that film and we didn't have enough money.'

'You should have asked.'

Mick's face went red. 'I know! But you were busy and so was Ma. It was difficult.'

'I'm sure it was.'

'It was!' Mick's voice had risen. He was convinced his stepfather was being sarcastic at his expense. 'It's not as if I was stealing! I mean I wouldn't have done it if you'd still been taking us to the flicks.'

'You've no cause to blame me,' said John mildly. 'What was I supposed to do, Mick, dump my niece to please you?'

'No! But – hell! You could have thought of giving us the money. It's not often you give us anything.'

'It isn't is it? Do you believe I should?'

'No, well! I don't know if you've got any of that money left that your uncle left you. You could be hard up again for all I know.'

John looked amused. 'Forget it, Mick. And forget the five shillings.'

'No! I'll pay it back. It's Ma's money after all. This is her hotel,' said Mick crossly, and turning away he ran upstairs.

As he changed he wondered at his temerity in saying what he had. Would there be repercussions?

Mick avoided looking John's way as he entered the dining room but was conscious of him nevertheless. Somehow this evening his stepfather's presence seemed to fill the room as he amused his niece and wife with tales of his travels. Mick wondered at him and felt a reluctant admiration, considering how he would have been ashamed to have admitted to tramping the length of Britain and busking in its streets, but the women hung on John's every word.

Mick decided to admit to his mother about borrowing the money and managed to gain her attention for a few moments when the table was being cleared.

She shook her head at him. 'You should have asked.'

'That's what *he* said.'

'*He?*'

'The big fella!'

Kitty sighed. 'Why can't you call him Dad?'

'Because he's not my dad.' Mick frowned. 'Anyway I'll work the debt off.'

'Did you tell your stepfather that?'

'He said I could keep the five bob but I didn't think it was his to give. This is your hotel, Ma.'

She stared at him. 'You didn't say that to him, did you?' Colour rose in Mick's cheeks and he was silent. 'You did! Oh Mick,' she groaned. 'How could you be so thoughtless? He has his pride you know, and he's put money into this hotel.'

'I'm sorry!' His tone was stiff. 'I thought I was speaking the truth.'

'What does it matter whether you were speaking the truth or not? It's his feelings that matter.' She clicked her tongue against her teeth. 'I feel real cross with you. Now go away!' She shooed him with her hands and he had no option but to leave.

Mick walked out of the room. It was seldom his mother got angry with him and he felt a surge of emotion and an unmanly desire to burst into tears. It wasn't his fault if the big fella couldn't take the truth. He should have kept his promise and taken them to the pictures, even if it meant insisting that the women went too. He was really fed up and not at all in the mood for company.

He went upstairs and sat in the cold bedroom, contemplating leaving home as soon as he left school. He had thought of doing something to do with calligraphy. He wouldn't mind drawing maps or signs for shops but how did he go about that? He supposed he could find out.

There came a tap on the door. 'Who is it?'

'Celia. Can I have a word?'

He was so relieved that it was not the big fella he sprang off the bed and opened the door. 'One word or two or three?' he said jocularly.

'I wondered if this would help?' She held out an envelope.

He stretched out a hand and took it and felt coins through the paper. He handed it back. 'Thanks but no thanks. I can't take your money. And you shouldn't eavesdrop.'

'Why can't you take my money?'

'I don't take money from girls.'

'You take it from your mother.'

'That's different. I earn it and I'll pay it back the same way. Anyway what made you change your mind about working here?'

She leaned against the wall. 'It's only for two weeks and it beats going home.'

'So you're not permanent.'

'I said I was only here for two weeks, didn't I?'

He smiled. 'So you did. So I'd best make good use of you.

I'll have a cup of tea and you can bring it up here.' He closed the door and was aware of an unexpected sense of wellbeing. Perhaps Christmas wasn't going to be so bad after all.

Chapter Fifteen

'Wow-wee!' exclaimed Ben, leaping off the bed and causing sweets, fruit, a jigsaw, a printing set and several toy soldiers to slide to the floor. He pranced around the tricycle wrapped in brown paper which stood on the linoleum before tearing off the paper and chanting, 'A bike, a bike, I've got a bike!'

'Shut up, Ben,' groaned Mick but Teddy sat up and rubbed his eyes. 'He has. He's got a bike!'

'What!' Mick lifted drooping eyelids. He watched Ben a moment before exchanging looks with Teddy, who said in disgust. 'Spoilt! He's spoilt rotten. We never got a present anywhere near as good as that!'

'You can have a go on it,' said Ben generously. 'As long as you don't break it and get off when I tell you.' He glanced anxiously at Teddy. 'Aren't you going to open your present?'

'What present? Father Christmas doesn't visit us,' said Teddy.

'There's something on your bed!'

Teddy and Mick both peered through the grey morning light and saw that Ben was right. There were four parcels. One was long and narrow and lay alongside a small square one on Teddy's side of the bed. The other two were rectangular and oblong and were on Mick's side. They reached out and untied labels which read *Love Ma and Dad.* They pulled faces at each other and tore off green tissue paper. Teddy's presents were a rod, reel and the rest of the paraphernalia needed to go fishing. Mick's were a box of calligraphy pens, nibs, bottles of different coloured ink and a good quality drawing pad.

'Damn!' said Teddy savagely.

'Ditto,' said Mick, gently fingering a nib. 'The big fella must have helped pay for these. Ma wouldn't have had the money and she wouldn't have known what to choose and where to go for them either.'

'Yeah! We'll have to bloody thank him.' drawled Teddy.

'You can send him a letter up the chimney,' said Ben who had only caught part of the conversation.

Mick smiled but said nothing, only lying flat on his back with the box of pens clutched to his chest.

'You're a dope,' said Teddy, grinning at Ben. 'Father Christmas isn't going to have time to collect a billion letters. He'll be beddy-byes at the North Pole by now. Besides it's Ma and the big fella who bought you the bike and us these things.' He slid from beneath the covers and shivered as he stood on the cold linoleum. 'Let's see you ride it then.'

Ben did not need telling twice. He climbed onto the tricycle and ding-a-linged the bell before pushing the pedals with his bare feet. He narrowly avoiding crashing into a chest of drawers.

Teddy laughed. 'Here let me have a go?'

'Not yet,' said Ben, straightening the handlebars.

'I can show you how.'

'No! It's mine.'

Teddy seized the handlebars and Ben yelled, 'Let go!' and attempted to push his hand away.

'Leave him alone, Ted, or you'll have Ma and the big fella in,' said Mick. 'Play with your fishing rod.'

'It's not a toy.' Teddy frowned but picked up the box with the reel in and began to read the instruction leaflet inside.

He had attached the reel to the rod and had almost finished threading line through the rod's metal hoops when Kitty popped her head round the door. 'Everybody happy?' She brought in a pitcher of steaming water.

Ben climbed down from the tricycle and threw his arms round her waist. 'Thanks, Ma!' He pressed his head against her stomach. 'It's a beautiful bike.'

'Careful! You don't want to—' She stopped abruptly and smoothed his ruffled hair before moving away to pour the water into the bowl in the washstand. She looked at her elder sons. 'And what about you two? Are you happy?'

'Yeah, fine,' said Teddy. 'Thanks, Ma.' He waved the fishing rod, which wobbled at its narrow end.

'And you, Mick?'

He flushed, 'I never expected such a good present. You shouldn't have spent so much money.'

'But you're pleased with it?' she said anxiously.

'Of course! I can't wait to use them. Thanks, Ma.'

'You won't forget to thank—'

'Dad,' muttered Teddy.

She glanced at him. 'Would it be so difficult to say?'

He was silent. Mick said, 'Does he want us to call him Dad?'

'I thought it would be nice,' said Kitty, sitting sideways on the bed. 'It would make us sound like a proper family.'

'Couldn't we call him Pops?' asked Ben, climbing back on the tricycle. 'A girl at school calls her dad Pops.'

'But he's not our dad,' said Mick.

There was a silence and Kitty felt frustrated.

'I'm going to call him Pops,' said Ben and rode between the beds twice. 'I'll say "Thanks, Pops, for my bike".'

'You can! You're younger,' muttered Mick. 'You don't remember Dad the same as I do.'

There was another silence which was broken by the sound of footsteps. John knocked on the open door before entering.

'Thanks, Pops, for my bike,' said Ben, missing John's toes by half an inch as he rode past him.

'Yeah, thanks for the present,' said Teddy, and his smile flashed briefly.

'Thanks,' said Mick, hugging his knees. 'It's – it's just what I would have chosen myself – if I'd had the money.'

'Glad you're all happy.' John slipped his hands in his trouser pockets and smiled. 'Shall we all go down for breakfast? You've ten minutes to have a quick lick and get dressed. Hannah and your mother have been up for the last hour. Food's ready and Nancy's waiting.'

'What about Celia?' asked Mick.

'I went with her late last night to her mother's,' said John. 'She'll be back tomorrow morning.'

'So you don't have to worry about her,' said Kitty, although she was worried herself after what she'd seen and heard of the woman, but a girl owed a duty to her mother. 'Now move yourselves or we'll eat yours.'

'One of my earliest memories before we went to Canada,' said Nancy, spreading Tate and Lyle's golden syrup on a slice of toast and smiling round at the family, 'was of pushing a dolly's pram along the front at Brighton after dinner on Christmas afternoon. It was before the war, of course, when women used to wear those huge hats with feathers and flowers, and skirts down to their ankles.'

'Mother often used to take me into Brighton,' said John. 'And we always had to look at the Royal Pavilion. It was like something out of the *National Geographic* with its onion-shaped domes and ornamental plaster work. I never forgot what it looked like all my years away. I didn't realise until I returned there that Mother was crazy about Prinny and anything Regency.'

'Who's Prinny?' asked Kitty, enjoying this new insight into her husband's past.

'The Prince Regent, of course,' said Nancy, signalling Hannah to fill her teacup.

'King George IV to be,' explained John. 'Queen Victoria's uncle. He spent a fortune on the Pavilion and was in debt for thousands of pounds. During the war part of it was used as a hospital for Indian soldiers. It had nine kitchens so it could cater for the tastes of the different castes.'

'I didn't know that!' said Nancy.

'Why should you?' said John, glancing at Kitty and

smiling before giving his attention once more to his niece. 'You were a Canadian by then.'

Nancy sighed. 'It seems a long time ago in some ways and yet in another it's like yesterday. I must see the Pavilion when I visit your sister. I should also visit Great-Grandfather.'

'It's a long journey and you could be wasting your time,' said John.

'We'll see.' She dabbed at the corners of her mouth with a napkin. 'Now where's the nearest Presbyterian church? Can't miss going on Christmas Day.'

The whole family went to church leaving a goose and a leg of pork flanked by potatoes and shallots sizzling in the ovens.

Hannah had been ordered to take the rest of the day off but she said she would be back to serve supper as she would have had enough of her family by then.

To Kitty's relief the remainder of the day after dinner was restful. They talked about Christmases past over nuts and drinks. Ben rode his tricycle up and down the Mount whilst Teddy tried to get the hang of casting properly. Mick practised different lettering with his pens in a corner of the Smoking Room, which was fragrant with the scent of John's cigar and the perfume of the women.

'This time last year I never thought I'd spend Christmas Day like this,' said Nancy as she mounted the stairs for bed. 'I've really enjoyed it and I thank you for your hospitality from the bottom of my heart.' She beamed round at them all.

'You're welcome,' said Kitty, giving her a hug and

hoping that Boxing Day would pass off as well as this day had done.

It was Hannah who opened the door to the O'Neills. Sarah stood on the doorstep alongside her brother David.

'Hello, Hannah,' said Sarah, removing her coat and untying her new cherry-red bonnet and handing them to the maid. 'Do you like my new frock?' She did a twirl and the buttercup-yellow, wool-linen skirts fanned out above her knees. She had slimmed down a little in the last months and her long dark hair had been cut in a more modern style so the ends curled about her neck and on her cheeks.

'Thou's getting more above thyself than ever,' said Hannah, giving a sniff. 'I don't doubt that sooner or later thee'll fall flat on thy face.'

Sarah pulled a face but on hearing Kitty's and Mick's voices she brushed past the maid and skipped to meet them.

'You look pretty,' said Kitty, a hand going to her belly as she thought dreamily of how she would dress her daughter when she was born.

'I do, don't I?' Sarah chuckled and did another twirl with her eyes on Mick's face. 'What do you think?'

'I think we should put you in a box and give you away as a Christmas present.' He grinned.

She spluttered, 'I don't look like a doll! I'm too big. Siobhan's like a doll. She has lace on her frock and knickers to match.'

'You shouldn't mention unmentionables in mixed company,' said her brother coming up behind her. David

O'Neill was dark and good-looking like his father and almost three years older than his sister.

'You've mentioned them,' said Sarah.

'That's different. I'm only correcting you.'

'You two aren't squabbling again!' exclaimed Becky, coming up behind them. 'How many times have I told you not to in company?'

'It wasn't really a squabble,' said Kitty, smiling. She asked if they'd had a nice Christmas before ushering the whole family into the dining room where Kitty, Hannah and Celia had laid out a buffet.

John introduced Nancy to the O'Neills and it was not long before everyone was eating and drinking. Both maids had been asked to join them earlier and Celia did so, but Hannah departed to the kitchen with an 'I know my place'.

Nancy's gregarious nature made for conversation which was interesting and friendly and all joined in. There were a few difficult moments and they came when she asked Daniel what on earth the Free State of Ireland was thinking of leaving the British Commonwealth? Daniel spoke of real independence and of the Irish having been a race apart long before the Dark Ages. It was different with Canada, which was populated with people of mainly British descent. She saw his point but said it was a pity that they couldn't all stay linked to each other like a family. John reminded them that the Scots were a race apart too, and that although part of the British Isles, some felt strongly about being independent from England.

'Now come on,' said Kitty indignantly, who had only listened so far. 'We all need each other and we're all a bit of a mixture. I'm half English and Norwegian, Becky's English and Irish, and you, John, are part English as well as Scots. As for you, Daniel, you live in England and your children have English blood running in their veins. You also have cousins who were born in Liverpool. Let's have peace between us.'

'I'm sorry.' Daniel smiled at her and she remembered how he had tried to get rid of Charley for her. 'I always get overheated when I talk politics. Shall we drink to all our countries? That they'll never fire a shot in anger against each other.'

'Here, here!' said Nancy, and clinked her glass against his. She turned her face to the young ones. 'And what about them? Isn't it time we played some games? It feels like we've been sitting and talking for ages. Perhaps we could have some music? Musical chairs maybe, Kitty? It's what I played when I was a girl.'

'If you like.' Kitty glanced at John. 'Where's your fiddle?'

'I'll get it.'

The elder boys were ordered to set up the chairs in two rows back to back and when John returned, the strains of *I Love a Lassie* filled the room. Nancy and Becky urged the children up and round the chairs. The younger ones ran or skipped. Celia had Siobhan by the hand and was encouraging her. Mick and Teddy strolled around, which wasn't on, thought Kitty. For the smaller ones to enjoy it everyone had to appear to be eager to take part.

She moved away from the fireplace and nudged the boys in the back. 'Make an effort,' she murmured.

'Do we have to?' said Teddy. At that moment the music stopped.

'Come on, Mick,' called Becky. 'I'll race you to that end chair.'

'And I'll race you to the other,' said Kitty to Teddy, deciding that she would make sure he got there first, but she had not reckoned on his playing the fool. He dropped on to his hands and knees and crawled along like a snail and she found herself still in the game.

'Come on, Ma,' said Mick, grinning. 'You've got to give it your best.' So she did.

After musical chairs they played Oranges and Lemons, and then Farmer's in his Den. It was as she was playing Ring-a-Ring-a-Roses with the girls she came over faint. Fortunately Becky saw her going and seized her arm, propping her up with a shoulder so she did not sink to the floor.

The music stopped and John came over, looking angry.

'I'm all right,' said Kitty, feeling sick and worried by the expression on his face. 'It's all the prancing about. I just went dizzy.'

'I don't believe it. It's normal for you to prance about without going faint all the time. I'm going to have something to say to Galloway when he comes back.'

'No, John! It's nothing to worry about. It's just that I'm—' The words stuck in her throat.

'Having a baby?' said Becky helpfully.

'Yes,' whispered Kitty, watching John's face register shock. 'I didn't tell her,' she added. 'Honestly, love.'

'I guessed,' said Becky swiftly.

John took hold of Kitty's arm and sat her down. 'Don't move,' he said. His expression was hard and uncompromising.

She did as she was told, sitting bolt upright as he went over to the children. She could not hear what he was saying to them but could only watch as they dispersed. She was still feeling light-headed and peculiar and longed for her bed but she sat on the chair as if glued to it, not wanting to make John angrier. She continued to watch him as he picked up his violin. Daniel went over and spoke to him before going and pouring out a couple of drinks. John left the room and Daniel came over to her with a glass of sherry.

'You all right now?' he said, giving her a smile which was somehow reassuring.

She nodded, still unable to make the effort to speak. She just wanted everyone to go. Becky and Mick had got some board games out and the young ones were now playing quietly.

Becky came over to Kitty. 'Another half hour and we'd best be getting home. It's well past Siobhan's bedtime,' she said.

Kitty nodded and reached out a hand to her. 'Thanks for asking no questions.'

'No need. I'm sure John'll be pleased once he gets over the shock.'

Kitty was silent, wondering if he would. She could only hope.

Three quarters of an hour later and the O'Neills had left. Three hours later and the household was asleep, with the exception of Kitty and John who lay silently side by side in their large bed – but it was not a comfortable silence. As of yet he had asked no questions about her pregnancy and so she had not volunteered any answers. She was waiting for him to go first, but the minutes ticked by and still he was silent. She wondered how to put her deepest feelings about the baby into words but it proved beyond her. She was too tired, too anxious. Eventually she drifted into sleep with the pleasure she felt over the baby still unexpressed.

Chapter Sixteen

John put the suitcases up on the luggage rack, stepped back and smiled down at Nancy. 'Have a good journey.'

'Thanks!' She sighed at she looked up at him. 'I am gonna miss you all.'

'You'll be seeing us again.' He wanted her to go, go.

'That's true!' Her face brightened and she reached up and kissed his cheek. 'You take care of yourself and Kitty and I'll see you in a month's time. Now that I've found you I don't want to lose touch.'

'I think I speak for both of us when I say we don't want to lose touch with you either.' At least that was the truth.

'Will I give your regards to Aunt Emily?'

'If you like.' He could not have cared less. Being reminded of his sister reminded him of Margaret and he did not want to think about Margaret.

She shook her head. 'It's sad you don't keep in touch.'

'It was her choice. She's never approved of me.' He squeezed her hand. 'Anyway I'd best go now. Enjoy your time down in Brighton.'

He left her and stood on the platform watching the train steam out and wondering whether he should have told her about the baby. She would have been pleased.

He was the last male McLeod in direct descent from his great-grandfather. Suddenly he realised that he might have a son one day to carry on his line. Some of his anxiety and anger dispersed to be replaced by a joyous expectancy and he hurried home, needing to see Kitty and talk about the baby. It was something they had not done yet.

As John walked up Mount Pleasant he marvelled afresh at how different his life was to what it had been a year ago. Then, he had lived for the moment with no thought to changing his ways, although he had become something of a philosopher. Being alone and travelling the country gave a man not only time to think about the big issues of life and death but also to see how people dealt with them, and he knew that there were things he had been avoiding.

He could have settled in Liverpool years ago when he had met up with Daniel again and been offered a job with Green's, but he had not wanted anyone depending on him to be in the same place, at the same time, day in day out. There had still been that something inside him which caused such commitment to horrify him. Sooner or later he might let them down.

Then he had met Kitty and there had been something about her that had interested him. Perhaps it was the unusualness of that first meeting? Then had come the second and the realisation of a physical attraction. She had looked less serious, less the mother. After that it had seemed fated that they should meet a third time. He grinned as he remembered her throwing the fish at Mr Potter. It had soon become obvious to him that she was a woman who could not only stick up for herself but seemed prepared to

fight his corner. Here was a woman who was capable of
reaching out and providing him with the necessary inner-
strength that he lacked. She had made him feel that he
could be a new man, but he had not been quite ready to
be made over then. There had been those older sons of
hers at that awkward age between boy and man. They
were straining at their mother's apron strings but they had
not yet broken loose and their emotions were a mixture of
dependancy and protectiveness towards her. Of course that
was down to them having no father. Then he had left for
Scotland – to please her if he was honest, but also because
he was still unsure whether he could live up to what he
believed she would expect of him. Then Uncle Donald
had died leaving him five hundred pounds, his grandfather
had rejected him, and Becky's letter had arrived with the
news of Charley. It was enough for him. Kitty was vulnerable and needed a man's strength. She needed him. He
had forgotten his fears and taken the chance of his life, but
then hadn't Shakespeare said, 'There is a tide in the affairs
of men which taken at the flood leads on to fortune'? And
his Kitty was worth her weight in gold. But he had lain
himself open to fear all over again when he married her
because once he began to live with her he could not bear
to live without her.

He came to the Arcadia and ran up the steps. He
exchanged the time of day with one of the guests on her way
out to the sales before going in search of Kitty. He found her
upstairs stripping Nancy's bed. 'You OK?' he asked.

'Why shouldn't I be?' Kitty bristled slightly. 'I'm past
being sick and all that.'

'Fine.' He hesitated, wanting to say so much but scared of saying the wrong thing. He had made his feelings clear about having a child and it was obvious that was why she had kept quiet about her condition. He still could not understand how it happened but it had, so he had to look after her as best he could. 'I didn't mean for Nancy to stay so long,' he said awkwardly, wanting to take her into his arms but aware she was cross with him.

'It doesn't matter.' She struggled to fold the heavy blanket.

He took it from her. 'You shouldn't be doing this.'

'Don't be daft,' she said shortly. 'I'm not an invalid, but we're going to have to replace Celia. She'll be going back to the doctor's in a couple of days.'

'Anything you want,' he said. 'Get two new maids if you like. I think we can afford it.'

'You're forgetting Teddy,' said Kitty. 'We're going to have to pay him.' She glanced across the bed at John. 'Have you seen anything of him today?'

'He did the shoes.' John was not interested in Teddy at that moment. He was keyed up to talk about the baby.

'It's just that I thought I'd teach him how to cook. Make a chef out of him. He's always been interested in food,' said Kitty.

'Sod Teddy!' exploded John. 'When is the baby due?'

Kitty had been waiting for this moment since Boxing Day. It seemed incredible that he had waited so long. She lowered her eyes. 'Sometime in May.'

He could scarcely believe it. 'So soon! Good God!'

She turned on him. 'Yes, so soon! I've felt it moving

inside me. I'm sorry things didn't work out the way you planned and now we've got another mouth to feed and will need even more help when it comes, but there it is! You can't have your fun and not pay for it.'

He stared at her. 'You can't believe I'm not willing! It's you I didn't want to have to pay! It's you I don't want to suffer!' He reached out and covered her hand with his. 'You must know that.'

Her anger died. 'That's what I tried to tell myself but the last few weeks I haven't been so sure. Dr Galloway wants me to go into hospital. Will you still be here when I come out?'

John stared at her in disbelief. How could she think . . .? He felt angry and pulled on her arm so that she fell on the bed. He scrambled across it and lifting her, pressed her against him. 'I'll never leave you,' he said hoarsely. 'I love you, Kit, honestly I do. I'll never let you down if I live to be a hundred.'

She rested her cheek against his shoulder and for a moment could not have spoken to save her life. Then she cleared her throat. 'I must have been crazy to think you would. Put it down to my condition.'

He hugged her tightly. 'We'll have to tell the boys so they'll understand the changes that'll have to take place. You'll have to rest more, Kit. I was going to mention it to Mick the day after Boxing Day but I couldn't bring myself to. Now they all need to know. They can't go on expecting you to do so much. I wish Celia would stay. I thought she might because of Mick but—'

'I think her and Mick's feelings have changed. They

seem to get on OK but they're definitely not May and June. Teddy'll be a help.'

'Perhaps,' he said.

She lifted her head and looked at him. 'What d'you mean perhaps?'

He frowned. 'His heart's not in it. You know that, and there's jobs that you can't really expect him to do. Can you see him sweeping the carpets, changing beds or polishing?'

'I told you – I'm going to teach him to cook,' she said earnestly. 'I can't be doing it all when the baby comes.'

John was still doubtful. 'Cooking's a skill, Kit. I can't see Teddy in the role.'

She tilted her chin, not prepared to surrender her plan. 'Are you sure you're not just saying that because you don't want him around all day?'

'I don't because he'll have a face like a wet week and will get on my nerves,' he said frankly. 'But it's not just that.'

'That's all right then,' she said brightly. 'I think he'll make a good cook. He likes food and that'll help him to learn. After all, why have I worked so hard to keep this place going if it wasn't to provide jobs for him and Mick? Their place is here,' she insisted.

John let it go, not wanting to upset her in her condition. 'When will we tell the boys about the baby?'

'It might as well be today,' she said. 'We could tell Mick, and leave him to tell the others.'

'You're having a baby?' Mick's eyes went from Kitty to John. He was not sure with which one of them he felt most annoyed. He had thought them too old for that kind of thing and was embarrassed.

'I know it's come as a bit of a shock,' said Kitty, wondering why she had given no thought to how the boys would feel.

A bit! thought Mick. That was an understatement!

'You'll tell the other two for us?' said John.

'If you want me to.' Mick could not wait to see what Teddy had to say about it all.

Without another word he went in search of his brother. He found him under a lamp post in Pleasant Street with a group of youths and girls.

'Can I have a word, Ted?' said Mick.

His brother looked up. 'Can't it wait?'

'I'd rather it was now.'

Teddy came over to him. 'What's up?'

'Ma's having a baby,' said Mick in a low voice.

Teddy was silent and it was obvious to Mick that he was completely taken aback. 'I never thought about that happening,' said Teddy. 'The big fella's really got his feet under our table for life now. I'll see you later.' Teddy walked away.

'Is that all you've got to say?' yelled Mick.

His brother waved a hand without looking back. 'Later!'

Mick felt irritated, wanting to discuss the matter. A baby meant nappies and smells and his mother even busier than she was now.

He bumped into Celia in the lobby and blurted out. 'Ma's having a baby.'

Celia's mouth fell open. 'She's going to have her hands full!'

'I know. I wish Gran was still alive. I don't know how we're all going to cope. Can you see Hannah being any use?'

Celia eyelashes flickered involuntarily as their eyes met and she said bluntly, 'Would you like me to stay?'

He was unsure how to take that question. He felt there was more behind it than staying because of the baby. 'I'm sure Ma would like you to stay,' he said carefully.

'But not you?' There were two patches of colour on her cheeks.

'I'm not the boss,' he responded, considering how he still felt something for Celia, although he was not sure what. 'Ask Ma.'

'I don't think I'll bother. I'm not that keen on babies anyway,' she said and walked on upstairs.

Mick thought how he would never understand girls.

'You do realise,' said Teddy when he and Mick were in bed, 'that Ma's going to be busier than ever when the baby comes?'

'Of course I do, nit! And Celia almost said she'd stay, but I think she wanted me to say I wanted it and I'm not sure I do.'

'You should have said yeah for Ma. You should have sweet-talked her.'

That comment annoyed Mick. 'Since when have you been an expert on girls?'

'I'm not. But one of the fellas said that girls like all that soppy stuff they hear in films. You know the sort of thing!

You tell them that they mean the earth to you and you can't live without them.'

'I thought I couldn't once,' said Mick, and was silent, remembering.

'I hope I never feel like that,' said Teddy seriously. 'I just want that job permanent at Laystall's – and a motorbike.'

Mick was glad to be distracted from his thoughts. 'You've got a hope. I heard Ma talking to Mrs O'Neill about turning you into a chef.'

'A what!'

'You know what a chef is!'

'I know, I know! It's a bloody cook! I'm not having it,' said Teddy with a hint of desperation. 'I'll – I'll run away first rather than be stuck in that kitchen all day doing women's work.'

'Don't be daft. You'd worry Ma silly.' Mick said absently. 'The person we need is Annie. She was the best.'

'Yeah, but I don't know where she is exactly,' said Teddy gloomily.

'She's in London,' murmured Mick.

'I thought it was Rhyl. That's where Jimmy is and you know she had a pash on him.'

'It's London I tell you! Ma had a Christmas card from her.'

Teddy scowled. 'I don't know why Ma can't just hire another maid. Another two in fact!'

'She won't take just anyone on since Hetty let her down, and none of Aunt Jane's lot want to work here. They want to work in shops. I think it's going to be down to us. I don't know why she bothered letting me have an education,' he said, feeling depressed.

'Damn daft,' muttered Teddy. 'I'm not having it, Mick. I can't be doing women's work.'

Mick yawned. 'I bet you're not the only one who isn't happy. I bet the big fella's really cock-a-hoop with the idea of having you around all day.' He turned his back on his brother and pulled the covers over his head.

Teddy's jaw set. 'I'm not going to be able to stand it, Mick. I'm going to have to do something.'

His brother made no reply, so Teddy slid down the bed and began to make plans.

Chapter Seventeen

'Is Teddy here?' asked Kitty, popping her head round the boys' bedroom door a few days later.

Mick paused in the act of taking off his school tie. 'Isn't he in the kitchen?'

'You haven't seen him on your travels?'

He shook his head. 'I thought he was helping you in the kitchen.'

'No. I've just come from there,' she said patiently. 'He's not in the dining room either or anywhere else and he better hadn't be in the coal cellar. I've told him no more scuttles. He's got to keep his hands clean.'

'I know,' muttered Mick. 'He's not to clean shoes, either, or empty chamber pots.'

'*You* don't empty chamber pots!' She made it sound like an accusation. 'And Ben's doing his bit now so I don't know what you've got to complain about.' She hesitated before adding, 'John went round to Laystall's yard this morning and they said Teddy hadn't been there today, but he had been there yesterday.'

Mick lowered his gaze. 'It's where he wants to work.'

'It's not where I want him to work,' said Kitty crossly, and sat down abruptly on one of the beds. 'He's been missing all day and he hasn't come back yet. He's an ungrateful wretch! There's boys who'd give their eye teeth for a nice comfy job indoors on a day like this! Don't you agree?' He said nothing. 'You don't agree?' she added.

'He loves engines!' blurted out Mick. 'You know that, Ma! And it's not as if they won't give him a job round at the yard. They will! If you're not careful you'll drive him away.'

'What d'you mean by that?' It was John standing in the doorway.

'It was just something he said.' Mick shrugged and began to take books out of his satchel. 'He was probably only joking. Can I get on with my work now? I've my big exams this year.'

'Let's in on the joke,' said John.

Mick hesitated and John seized him by the back of his collar and lifted him off his feet. 'I can understand your loyalty to your brother,' he said against his ear. 'But I will not have your mother upset! Now tell me what you know.'

'John, put him down!' cried Kitty, jumping to her feet.

Her husband ignored her whilst Mick scrabbled at his collar. 'He said something about running away,' he gasped.

John lowered him to the ground. 'Did he have a place in mind?'

'He didn't say. He was just fed up.'

'We all get fed up! Now think! Where could he be?'

'I don't know!' Mick could not think straight with John glaring at him.

'Dammit!' John thumped the end of the bed. 'Think, Mick!'

'I don't know!' yelled Mick. 'He doesn't tell me everything. He has mates, you know. Go and ask his mates. He could be at one of their houses.'

'Names and addresses,' said John, picking up Mick's pencil from a chest of drawers.

Mick found a sheet of paper in his satchel and wrote down a couple of names and addresses but he did not know exactly where all his brother's mates lived. John snatched the paper from him and strode out of the bedroom.

Kitty sank onto the bed and Mick sat next to her. 'I didn't realise he wanted it that much,' she said woodenly. 'I didn't know he was so unhappy.'

'That's because you don't hear things you don't want to hear, Ma!' His tone was earnest. 'You love this place. How would you feel if someone took it away from you? You'd be miserable wouldn't you?'

Kitty remembered how she had felt when Jimmy had asked her to marry him and run the Arcadia alongside her and how determined she had been to hold on to what was hers. John had never asked that of her. He just did what he felt needed doing without question.

'See!' exclaimed Mick when she made no answer. 'You'd hate it! I'd like to do something with signwriting or commercial art.'

'But – but I'd like one of you working here,' she said.

'There's always Ben.'

She protested. 'He's not even eight! I need more help than he can give. It's not fair, Mick. One of you'll have to work here.' And on those words she got up and walked out.

John came in an hour later on his own.

'You haven't found him?' said Kitty, whirling round as he entered the kitchen.

'No. But when I do I'm going to kill him for getting you worked up like this,' he said grimly.

'Me too, although . . .'

'Although what?'

'Nothing! I'm not going to say. Perhaps I was wrong to try and force him.'

'He should be damn grateful he's got a home like this,' muttered John, picking up the flour sifter and putting it down again. 'There's thousands who would leap at the chance of doing the job he's been asked. Thousands who go to bed hungry because they have no jobs to go to!'

Suddenly Kitty sagged against the table. 'Hunger! That's what'll bring him home. You know how he loves his stomach. He couldn't have bought food because he was talking at Christmas about not having any money. He can't have got far, John. He'll come home soon.'

'And I'll leather him when he does.' He put an arm about her, pulled her against him and kissed the top of her head. 'Now you stop worrying.'

It was useless to tell Kitty to stop worrying and when Teddy had not come home by midnight, despite John's insistence that she stay behind, she went with him to scour the neighbouring streets, the city centre and as far as the Pier Head, but they did not find him,

They went to bed but Kitty could not sleep. She was

visualising Teddy bruised and bloody in a gutter or drowned in the Mersey. She was up earlier than her usual hour and John rose with her. He lighted fires and polished boots, and after a quick breakfast he went out and visited Teddy's mates again.

It was a while before he thought of calling at the yard a second time. A different worker informed him that Teddy had hitched a ride on one of the work's lorries going to Wolverhampton where they had another engineering works.

'Wolverhampton! What's he doing in Wolverhampton?' cried Kitty when she was told. 'We don't know anyone there!'

'I doubt Teddy considered that,' said John, stuffing a change of clothing into a rucksack. 'I wonder what he was thinking, though. He's not stupid and he's sure to know we'll go looking for him. Anyway I'm going to find him and when I do, Kit—'

'Just bring him safely home,' she said, watching her husband and wondering if he was glad to be going travelling again.

He kissed her and left.

John did not find Teddy in Wolverhampton but he got news of him. 'A little Scouse lad,' said a driver. 'You've missed him, mate. Cadged a lift to London. We have another works there.'

'Where exactly?'

'Edgware.' The man wiped his hands on an oily rag. 'Determined little sod. Seemed to know exactly where he was going. Said he had a relative in the Smoke he needed to see urgently. A matter of life and death. As it was he slept under a tarpaulin as he couldn't go until this morning.'

John wondered if he was right in what he was thinking about Teddy's destination. 'Is there anyone going south who can give me a lift?'

The man jerked a thumb. 'You're in luck, mate. Billy over there will be drawing out any minute. Say I sent yer.'

John thanked him and was soon on his way.

It was dark by the time the lorry reached London but nobody there could tell John anything about a small wiry Scouse lad. It seemed John had come to a full stop. After thinking for a few moments he went in search of something to eat, choosing a place that had a telephone, and ordered some food and drink before asking could he put a call through to Liverpool. He spoke to Becky and then ate while he waited for a return call.

Annie sat with a smile on her pointy little face, watching Teddy devour mince and potatoes like a ravenous beast. 'When did you last eat?'

'Dunno!' He lifted his head. 'You're a good 'un, Annie.'

'I'm daft is what yer mean. I know what the missus would say if she found yer in here.'

Teddy glanced around the small, sparse kitchen and shivered. It was not very warm but it was much colder outside. 'Never mind what she says. You've got to come home. Ma needs you. She's going to have a baby.'

'A baby! So that's what this is all about?' Annie looked thoughtful. 'But why couldn't she have just written to me?'

'She thinks you don't want to come home but looking at this place I think you would. It's not as homey as ours.'

Suddenly she sat down opposite him and rested her elbows on the table. 'I don't deny it, Teddy. I've been real homesick but it was difficult finding a place and this was the best I could get. It isn't even what I'd call a proper hotel, more like your guest house, but I just haven't had the money to get me home. She's a real skinflint is the mistress.'

'Ma would probably give you more money because she'll want some help with the baby and wouldn't that come under special duties?'

Her face brightened. 'So it would. But I can't help thinking, Teddy Ryan, there's more to your being here than meets the eye. It's a puzzle to me how you got here. What was Kit thinking about sending you?' He had appeared on the doorstep only an hour ago and had not given her one word of explanation. Fortunately she had opened the door herself and, swiftly overcoming her initial shock, had ushered him into the kitchen. He had asked for food and she had given up her own dinner because she had felt so emotional at seeing someone from home.

'I'll get us to Liverpool,' said Teddy confidently. 'I got here on me own. I'm sure I can get us back.'

She looked at him doubtfully. 'I can't go just like that. She might dock me wages and I'll be left with nothing.'

'We don't need money.'

'She owes me! I'm not going without it,' she said stubbornly.

'Ma'll make it up to you. Honestly, Annie, she will.

Now she's married to the big fella we have more money. Honestly you should have seen our Christmas presents!'

'Well, I'm glad about that but even so—'

'Annie, you've got to come home,' he said urgently. 'Ma wants to turn me into a cook and I can't bear it. She doesn't know I'm here. I ran away. You were my best bet for persuading her to change her mind.'

Her expression was dismayed. 'You shouldn't have done that! Kit'll be worried sick.'

'She'll feel a lot better if you come home,' said Teddy persuasively. 'This place isn't good enough for you, Annie, and our place hasn't been the same since you left.'

'Don't soft-soap me,' said Annie. 'Anyway, I never said I wouldn't come, just that I couldn't come right away.'

'Tomorrow?' he said.

'I'll think about it. You'd best sleep in my room. I'll sneak you up the back stairs. In fact you'd best go up before she comes home. She's gone to play bridge with some of her cronies. It's freezing up there but I'll give you the oven shelf wrapped in newspaper to put in. If you keep your clothes on and snuggle right down you'll soon warm up.'

He smiled at her. 'I am tired. Thanks, Annie. You're real good.'

'Hummph,' she said. 'Drink that tea and let's get you upstairs.'

It was half an hour later that there was a *rat-a-tat* on the door. Annie hurried to answer it, thinking that her mistress had forgotten her key again and muttering the little speech she had prepared, only to receive another shock when she saw John standing on the doorstep. 'You were quick,' she said. 'How did yer know he was here?'

'A guess,' said John grimly. 'Can I come in?'

She nodded and led the way into the kitchen and then stood as if on guard. 'I've sent him to bed. He was cold, hungry and tired out.' said Annie.

'He deserves to be the way he's worried Kitty sick. Wait till I get my hands on him. He'll be sorry,' said John, glancing around him.

'I'm not surprised yer feel like that,' said Annie. 'But he didn't come here for nothing. He says he wants me to come home. That Kitty needs me.'

'She does,' said John, his expression easing. He leaned against the table and folded his arms across his broad chest. 'Is there any chance of it, Annie? If there is then I mightn't skin the hide off him.'

Annie's eyes shone. 'Oh, I said to him I'd come but I feel so much better with it coming from you.'

He smiled. 'I'm glad you feel like that. Kit'll be made up.'

'I've missed her,' said Annie, putting on the kettle. 'We worked as a team, not like this one here. And tight-fisted!' She rolled her eyes. 'I can't begin to tell yer the way she cuts corners! And the meals – she can't cook for toffee!'

'Did Teddy tell you Kit was trying to turn him into a chef?'

'He did and I couldn't believe it! He'd never have her nice light touch with pastry! Her shortcrust melts in the mouth. She'd lose custom.'

'You tell her that.' John straightened. 'Don't bother with tea, Annie. I've drank at least six cups already this evening.

I'll be back in the morning but don't tell Teddy I've been, I want to surprise him.' He squeezed her shoulder and left.

Annie slept the other end of the bed to Teddy. It was not as comfortable as it might have been but at least it was only for the one night. *Come morning*, she thought happily, *I'll be on my way back to dear ol' Liverpool.*

Teddy travelled back to the Pool in more style than he had to London, by train. He tried to act in a cowed fashion after receiving a tongue lashing from John, but he was cock-a-hoop because he had achieved what he had set out to and his hopes were high that his mother would no longer insist on him being a cook. He dared not hope just yet that she would let him have his way and work in the yard.

No sooner did they set foot inside the hotel than Kitty and Annie fell into each other's arms. 'Oh Kit, it's lovely to be home. You can't imagine how lonely I've been.' Annie's eyes shone with a luminous brightness.

'It's lovely to have you back. I've really missed you.' Only now, seeing her cousin's familiar little face, did Kitty realise how well they had worked together in the past. Hannah might be a good worker but she wasn't kin and could not talk about the happy times when Kitty's mother was alive. She really was delighted to have Annie back and she knew whom she had to thank.

Kitty turned and looked at Teddy who was to all outward appearances repentant. 'I should give you the back of my hand,' she said. 'Why couldn't you have written to Annie?'

'But it wouldn't have got me anywhere,' he said earnestly. 'At least my way you sat up and took notice.'

'It wasn't kind, and I've a good mind to say that you still have to stick it out here but John says he doesn't think he can put up with your miserable face round the place day in, day out. So you can go and work in your smelly old engine yard but don't come moaning to me in a year's time saying you hate it.'

Teddy's ears went red and his eyes shone. He made to throw his arms round Kitty but she drew back. 'No, I'm still cross with you. So beat it before I change my mind.'

He repeated for the fourth time, 'Sorry, Ma.'

'OK. Get out,' she said severely, but inside she rejoiced that he was home safely. That was all that mattered.

Teddy rushed out of the kitchen and went in search of Mick to tell him his good news.

Chapter Eighteen

With Annie's return Kitty's life became easier. Her one worry had been that Hannah might turn awkward but Annie seemed able to cope with the older woman's grumpiness. She was not so pleased about having to share a bedroom with her, but as the only other option was to go and live at home again where she would be sharing with two of her sisters she decided to stay put. As for Hannah, she grudgingly admitted that Annie was not a bad little worker. Kitty began to allow herself a few dreams once more. With two such good workers and her plan for Mick to work full time at the Arcadia when he left school, together with a couple of extra girls when they were particularly busy, as well as herself and John, and Teddy and Ben doing their little bit, she decided she should be able to cope with running the hotel and looking after the baby.

She allowed John to cosset her, putting her feet up any odd moment she had and accepting cushions for her back. She used the time to knit tiny pink matinee coats and bootees. John made some comment about the colour but she barely took it in. She was too wrapped up in dreaming of the day she would push a pram down the road with her curly-haired daughter in a frilly bonnet inside it.

Nancy returned at the end of January, bringing with her the news that Aunt Emily was a shrew but at least she was performing a kind act in providing a home for an orphan girl who had recently lost her grandmother. In return this Jeannie, for that was her name, helped with the housework and cooked the meals.

'How old is she?' asked Kitty, her fingers stilling on the knitting needles.

'Fifteen – sixteen. Her father was killed in the war. Lovely looking girl and competent with it. She knows exactly how to handle Aunt Emily, which isn't easy. She's a demanding woman.'

'She always was from what I remember,' said John, passing her another scone. 'We've got some news.'

'Oh!' Nancy gazed expectantly at him and Kitty.

'You tell her, Kit,' said John, smiling at his wife.

She twinkled back at him, loving him madly. 'I'm having a baby. A little McLeod.'

Nancy's face lighted up. 'But that's wonderful! When?'

'May.'

'But that's only three months away!'

Kitty nodded. 'It'll be on us before we know it.'

'You'll have your work cut out,' said Nancy thoughtfully. 'You're not so young. You'll have to take care of yourself.'

'I'll make sure she takes it easy,' said John, his expression revealing a touch of anxiety as he looked at his wife.

Kitty pulled a face at him. 'I'll be OK! I know the drill. And I can't be sitting every minute twiddling my thumbs. It'd drive me mad.'

'You'll do as you're told,' he said firmly.

Nancy's eyes went from Kitty's face to John's. 'Would it help if I stuck around?' She bent to give Nelson a morsel of scone.

They both stared down at her flushed profile. 'But haven't you got to go back to Canada?' said Kitty, wondering what Nancy meant by 'sticking around'.

Nancy sat back in the chair. 'I'm not saying I'll stay forever, but who have I got to go back to, really? Mother died three years back and father's dead now. I have a few friends and of course there's George's brothers and sisters but they won't really miss me. They have their own families taking up their time. My apartment's only rented. I have a small regular income and shares in George's family's timber business which pay me a yearly dividend. So you don't have to worry that I'd be a financial burden on you.'

'We weren't thinking of that,' said John hastily. 'We'd love you to stay, wouldn't we, Kit?'

'Love it,' said Kit obediently, despite certain reservations.

A smile broke out over Nancy's round eager-to-please face. 'I'd stay on the same terms as any other of your regular guests but help out when you needed me. You'd give me a lot of pleasure in allowing me to do that.'

'You've made it so we can't say no,' said John lightly. 'Isn't that true, Kit?'

She agreed but wondered exactly how long Nancy would stay. Come National week she would need her room, but she decided she would worry about that when the time came.

In the meantime, life went on pretty much as it had done, except now Teddy was happy. Mick was working with his school books, determined to do well in his exams despite Kitty telling him there was no need to work so hard. There was one sad day for Ben when he found Twitchy dead in his cage. Kitty and her youngest son had a ceremony and buried the mouse in one of the window boxes, and it was not long before Ben found consolation in his tricycle and the company of Nelson.

Grand National week arrived with its usual flood of guests and Kitty had difficulty working out where to put them all. There was a French couple whom John was able to converse with, having picked up some of the language during the war. A group of young people, full of the joys of spring and looking for a good time, agreed to share with complete strangers for just a couple of nights because every hotel and guest house in the city was full. It was rumoured that houseowners near the race course were even renting out tents in their gardens, and getting good money for them. Kitty divided a few of her larger rooms with blankets hung over a length of string to provide her youthful guests with some semblance of privacy. Some slept on the floor, but they all seemed happy enough and, although noisy, they were polite when John asked them to keep the sound down.

To Annie's and Kitty's relief, Mr Jones had not booked with them that year but Mrs Mahoney had turned up as usual and this time she had one of her nephews in tow. Her wrinkled face showed satisfaction when she saw Kitty's increased girth. 'So you married him, girlie,' she said, ramming her walking stick on the floor and staring at her from eyes which appeared not as bright as they used to be. 'I'm glad to see you had some sense and I hope he'll always be good to you.'

'He is good to me,' said Kitty and showed the old lady to her room, promising a cup of tea would be brought up to her.

By the morning of the big race Kitty was worn out but the last thing she wanted was John insisting that she stayed at home. She kept a smile pinned to her face as she dressed in one of the new maternity smocks that Aunt Jane had made for her and chattered to him about how much she was looking forward to the day out.

It was a mistake and she realised it pretty swiftly when they had to park the car some distance away and needed to walk the rest. They arrived at the crowded race course with Kitty desperate for the lavatory. Her condition caused some of those waiting in the queue to allow her to go in front of them but no sooner had she found John, the O'Neills and Nancy, and had watched the first race, than she wanted to go again. She saw little of the other races and it was a relief when it was time to leave. She looked forward to relaxing in front of the fire after the evening meal was served.

But there was to be little relaxing that evening. No sooner had she settled herself with her feet up on the stool which John had put solicitously close, than Annie came flying downstairs.

'Kit! Something terrible's happened!'

'Not the boys?' she said immediately, dropping the

newspaper and pushing herself out of her chair.

'Sit down,' ordered John, who was already on his feet. 'I'll see to it. What is it?' he asked Annie.

'It's Mrs Mahoney,' she said breathlessly, resting both hands on the back of a chair. 'Her bell was ringing away so I went up to her room.' She paused for a swift intake of air. 'And there she was flat out on the floor. Her face is a funny colour. I think she's dead!'

Kitty's heart sank. 'We'll have to get the doctor!'

Annie said, 'Mrs Higson's gone for Dr Galloway. I told her where he lived.'

'Good ol' Nancy,' said John, looking relieved. 'You stay here with Kit, Annie. I'll go and have a look at the old girl.' He hurried out.

'Perhaps she's not dead,' said Kitty hopefully. 'Guests don't like it when people die on the premises. Neither do I! It causes problems. Poor Mrs Mahoney!' She was struck by a thought. 'I wonder if we should find a priest? And where's that nephew of hers?'

'He went out with Jimmy's great-uncles,' said Annie, clasping her hands and bobbing about, unable to keep still. 'Should I go and find him?'

'Don't be daft,' said Kitty. 'Where'll you look? He could be in any ol' pub. Sit down and keep still. You're making me nervous.'

'Perhaps I should go upstairs and see what's happening?'

'You can stay here with me! I hope the rest of the guests stay out till midnight. Or if any do come home early perhaps we can get her out without anyone seeing!'

'We could put her in that big trunk that's still up there!'

Annie giggled. Then covered her mouth. 'Sorry,' she said in a muffled voice. 'But I'm all of a doo-dah.'

There was a scrabbling noise at the area door and they both jumped. Annie's mood was catching and Kitty felt slightly hysterical. Knock, knock, who's there? she almost said. Then they heard Mick's voice and Nelson's sharp little bark.

The door opened and youth and terrier entered. Mick stared at them. 'What's up with you two? You look like you're ready to burst.'

Annie snorted and covered her mouth again.

Kitty took a deep steadying breath. 'Something terrible's happened. Mrs Mahoney's dead upstairs.'

'And we're wondering how to get the body out without any of the guests seeing it,' said Annie on a choke.

'It's not funny,' said Kitty severely. 'Poor old lady.'

'At least she had a good day at the races,' said Mick, opening the back door and setting Nelson free in the yard with the mutton bone left over from that evening's meal.

'That's true,' said Kitty, feeling a little better. She got to her feet having decided she had to know what was going on upstairs. The other two followed her.

They found Nancy and Dr Galloway in the lobby. John was just coming downstairs. 'She's dead all right,' he said. 'Where's Hannah? She can help sort out the mess.'

'Shush!' hissed Kitty. 'We don't want everybody to know.'

'There's nobody here,' said John in a low voice.

'How do you know? There could be someone behind the Smoking Room door,' she whispered. 'The guests don't like dead bodies. It would be better for us if she could have died on the way to the hospital.'

'Perhaps I could see the body?' said Dr Galloway in a restrained voice.

Kitty drew herself up in as dignified a manner as possible. 'Of course.'

'I'll lead the way,' said John.

Kitty went to follow them but her husband said, 'Not you, Kit. We don't want you getting upset in your condition. Make a pot of tea, love.'

She stared at his broad back, thinking that this time last year it would have been her duty as hotel owner to go with the doctor. She felt relegated to a lower order. 'Tea!' she muttered. 'Yes, I'll make tea!'

'A good idea,' called the doctor. 'This probably won't take long.'

It didn't and soon Nancy, Kitty, John and Mick were sitting in the kitchen drinking tea. The doctor had gone to ring for an ambulance from his house, saying that he understood their problem and it did not matter to him where the old woman died. He would be back to escort her to the hospital and would state that she had died in the ambulance. He'd square it with the attendants.

'What a nice man,' said Nancy, her short plump fingers cradling a cup. 'Really helpful! Such sad eyes, though. Is he married?'

'A widower,' said Kitty. 'He lost his daughter not so long ago. He's the doctor that Celia works for. You remember Celia?'

'The freckled-faced girl who was here at Christmas?'

'She hasn't got that many freckles,' muttered Mick, frowning. 'Cousin Monica has more.'

'The sun's kisses! That's what Ma called them,' said Nancy. 'I suppose he has a family.'

'He lost a couple of brothers in the war but he does have one in Scotland and a sister, as well,' said John, winking at Kitty.

Her earlier irritation vanished and she winked back. They had little time and privacy to themselves so if it was possible to do a little matchmaking, then why not? Nancy would be good for the doctor. She was kind, capable and full of life. It would be great having her living close by, but not right on top of them.

Dr Galloway returned ten minutes later saying the ambulance would be there in a jiffy. He was thanked and handed a cup of tea.

'We wondered if you'd like to join us for supper tomorrow?' said John. 'Most folk'll have gone by then and we'll have the place almost to ourselves.'

The doctor hesitated. 'I'm not very good company I'm afraid. Since Geraldine went . . .' His voice trailed off.

'We understand,' said Kitty gently. 'But come all the same. It's not good for you to be on your own so much.' She knew he spent most evenings alone because Celia had told her. 'John can entertain us with his fiddle.' She reached a hand up to her husband and he took and clasped it in his own.

'You're very kind,' said the doctor. 'But—'

'You must come,' said Nancy, leaning towards him. 'We really do understand. We've all lost someone we loved.'

Doctor Galloway's sad eyes met hers and registered a response. 'I'll come then but don't expect me to be the life and soul of the party.'

'Your presence'll be enough,' she said, returning his smile.

Kitty refrained from giving John a triumphant nudge in the ribs.

Much to Kitty's relief the ambulance came before any of the other guests or Mrs Mahoney's nephew returned. When he did arrive, he seemed unable to accept that his aunt had died of a stroke. 'But she was indestructible,' he kept saying. 'Are you sure now it is herself that's dead and not someone pretending to be her?'

'Absolutely sure,' said John gravely whilst Kitty struggled to keep her face straight. 'I'm sorry there was no time to get a priest.'

'Not to worry about that,' said the nephew, shaking his head and swaying slightly. 'She'll bang that cane of hers on the ol' pearly gates and St Peter'll have to let her in. I suppose I'll have to get a priest, though, and she'll have to go home. The family'll all be wanting to make sure that she's gone. It'll be a grand wake we'll be having before we plant her under the turf and have the will read for sure.' He left them and went unsteadily up the stairs.

John put his arm around his wife and they slowly followed in the nephew's footsteps. It had been a long day, thought Kitty, glad of her husband's shoulder to lean on. She thought of Mrs Mahoney, of death, of birth, of life and of how one needed to make the most of every moment because you never knew the minute. She hoped something

would come of inviting Dr Galloway to supper, but she
was glad it was not tonight. She hoped there would not be
another day like today for a long time. At least not until her
daughter was born. After that she felt certain she would be
able to cope with anything.

Chapter Nineteen

'Have you seen this, Kit? The Post Office has been criticised for taking on more women,' said Annie, reading from a sheet of the *Liverpool Echo* that the fish had come wrapped in. 'And on the same page it says that there are eighteen hundred to two thousand deserted wives dependent on the ratepayers!' She laboriously read out the information. 'And that doesn't include those living apart from their husband by mutual consent! It says there's too much casual wedlock.' She looked up. 'It makes you think, doesn't it, that married women should be allowed to work? Although with the way the job situation is I suppose it can only make it worse.' She realised that Kitty was taking no notice of what she was saying but appeared to be staring intently at the wall. 'Are you OK?'

'I think my waters are leaking,' said Kitty, her forehead knitting. 'I haven't got any pain but – oh!'

'You think this is it? Oh heck! What should I do?' Annie's voice held a note of panic. 'Should I go and get the big fella? Or should I get Hannah?'

Kitty was determined to keep calm as she faced her cousin, but she was now starting to feel fraught. 'John's gone to the docks. Where's Nancy?'

'She went out.'

'She's got no right to go out! She's supposed to be keeping an eye on me! Dr Galloway said I was to go into hospital but now it's come to it I don't know if I want to!' Her fingers trembled as she gripped the edge of the table. 'People die in hospitals.'

'Perhaps you shouldn't go then?' said Annie, alarmed. It wasn't like her cousin to talk in such a way. Perhaps she'd had a premonition? 'Should I get Mam?'

'I don't know.' Kitty put a hand to her head. 'I'd better go and change and find a bag and stuff some things in it. I might just walk up there.'

Annie looked at her as if she had gone completely doolally. 'Perhaps you should just sit down and take it easy.'

'I don't want to sit down,' cried Kitty and sallied forth into the lobby like a ship in full sail.

Annie followed her.

Nancy was standing at the chiffonier arranging flowers. She looked at Kitty and dropped a carnation. 'Are you OK?'

'I'm glad you're back. I am going to have a baby,' said Kitty distinctly and began to climb the stairs.

'Of course you are, Kit dear,' said Nancy hastily, exchanging glances with Annie. 'You'd best get off to the hospital right away.' She left the flowers and hurried after Kitty.

Annie followed and whispered to Nancy, 'She's acting strange. She said she doesn't want to go the hospital. She thinks she's going to die.'

Nancy said in alarm, 'She has to go to the hospital. She can't have the baby here!'

'I think she's changed her mind now because she said she's going to walk, but she could still change it back again.'

Nancy bit her lip and caught hold of Kitty's arm, bringing her to a halt on the first landing. 'Listen, Kit dear! Malcolm says everything is beautifully hygienic in the maternity hospital. No septicaemia and trained midwives there to look after you.'

'I know.' Kitty's smile flashed briefly and she pulled her arm out of Nancy's hold and carried on upstairs. Nancy had started calling Dr Galloway Malcolm in the last week.

Nancy and Annie followed her and Hannah, who had been sweeping the bedrooms, came out of one of the rooms and called, 'Hast thee started, missus?'

'Her waters have broken,' said Annie, leaning over the bannister rail. 'You'd better start praying.'

'Is she going the hospital?' Hannah left the Ewbank and hurried after them.

'I shall walk to the hospital,' said Kitty, sitting down on the stairs abruptly and taking several deep breaths.

Nancy squeezed in beside her. 'But what if the baby starts coming on the way? Perhaps we should get an ambulance?'

Kitty shook her head. 'It's not going to come yet, believe me.' She rose to her feet and went on up the flight of stairs, packed a bag with those things she deemed necessary, and set out for the hospital with Nancy.

Kitty laboured for the rest of the day whilst a fraught John walked the surrounding streets accompanied by Nelson. Every time he came to the hospital he would go inside and enquire after his wife, but it was not until half past midnight that Kitty gave birth to a nine-pound boy.

As they held up her screaming baby she could not believe he was her son. Her emotions were all in confusion and the darkness of the depression that suddenly overshadowed her outstripped the tearing and searing pain she had endured. She turned her face away and stared unseeingly at a far wall. The baby could not be a boy. It was a girl, all through her pregnancy it had been a girl.

When John came to see her that evening she lay against the pillows not even attempting to put on a bright face for him. His happiness was obvious. It shone in his eyes.

'A McLeod laddie to achieve the things I never achieved. Thanks, darling Kit! You can't imagine how I feel at this moment. He's all that I could wish for.'

He's not what I wished for, she thought bitterly. There was a sensation in her chest which felt like a lump of sandstone had lodged there.

'I'll work! I'll slave! I'll do anything so he can have his chance,' said her husband, lifting her hands to his lips and smothering them in kisses. 'You'll see. One day you'll be proud of our son.'

She wished he would go away. She only wanted to be left alone, but no one was going to allow that. She had to breastfeed her baby and it was as much as she could bear to touch him, only by pretending could she do that.

He could not be a boy. She had prayed for a girl and God would not have let her down. The baby was a girl, she told herself. She did not want a boy.

Two weeks later Kitty and her baby came home to the Arcadia. He was to be called after his father, so John said, but Kitty had made no response. Even when Ben arrived home from school and went down the sunlit yard where the baby lay in his pram and immediately declared, 'We've got a real Little John now,' she could not bring herself to accept his words.

Ben gazed down at the face almost concealed by a pink bonnet, glanced at her and said in disgust, 'What's he wearing that for? Pink's for girls.'

'That's what I told your mother,' said a grim-faced Annie, who was unpegging nappies from the line. 'But she said she knitted it for him so he's got to wear it.' She shot Kitty a worried glance.

'He looks daft.' Ben pursed his lips. 'When's he going to be big enough for me to play with?'

'You'll be working by the time he's your age,' said Annie. 'Anyhow, don't you go wishing his life away. He's a luv'ly baby. Let's enjoy him.' She unfastened the ribbons on the bonnet and eased it off. 'There now, beautiful boy,' she said.

Hannah, at the other end of the line, sniffed. 'Pity it was another lad. The missus wanted a girl.'

Ben said swiftly, 'You won't cut off his tail like you were going to my mouse, Hannah. Ma wouldn't let you.' He looked at his mother but she made no response.

'Of course she wouldn't,' said Annie, chuckling. 'He's

a lovely, healthy baby and that's the main thing. And good! There hasn't been a whimper out of him all afternoon.'

'Thee waits till he gets to bed,' said Hannah morosely. 'He'll wake us up soon enough demanding attention like all his sex.'

'It's got nothing to do with sex,' said Annie loftily. 'I've got five sisters and I can tell you they made demands on Ma all right. I remember our—'

'I don't want to know,' said Hannah cutting in ruthlessly. 'Thee's besotted. I don't know why thee don't find a man of thy own and breed. Then we'd all have a bit of peace.'

'Because I'm a one-man woman that's why,' countered Annie. 'But he went away and—'

'Didn't want thee, did he?'

'That's enough, Hannah,' said Kitty, some memory from the past stirring her to defend her cousin. 'It's time the vegetables were prepared. And Annie,' she turned to her cousin, 'perhaps you could go and get me some Nestle's condensed milk and a couple of feeding bottles and teats. I'm not going to have the time to feed this baby myself the way I did the others.'

'I'll feed him for you,' said Annie eagerly, and hurried indoors.

That suited Kitty down to the ground. All she wanted to do now was to get back to work and ignore the baby. But he could not be ignored. When Mick came home he said the baby had his mother's eyes.

'He's like the big fella, too,' said Annie who, having followed the instructions on the tin of milk carefully, was now doing her best to persuade the baby to take to the rubber teat by holding him against her breast in her best surrogate mother fashion, but he was baulking at it.

'Figures,' said Mick and disappeared upstairs to revise for his next exam.

Teddy's reaction was a bit different to Mick's. He gave the baby a cursory glance and said to Ben, 'He's a threat to you, mate. You won't be the baby in the family anymore, so there'll be no more spoiling, shrimp.' He then went off to change his clothes.

Ben gazed down at the baby but could not see how he could be a threat. He was so tiny in comparison with him and, besides, his mother did not seem to be giving him any more attention than she did the cat. He went out to ride his tricycle, practising whistling, which he had just managed to master.

It was a couple of weeks before John realised that Annie was bottle-feeding little John. The baby seldom woke in the night and Kitty breast-fed him first thing in the morning and last thing at night when he was around. There was another thing that was bothering John about the baby. He had put off saying anything because he knew she was disappointed, but now something had to be done. He wasted no more time seeking her out.

He found her in reception where she was making out menus for the following week. 'Why is Annie bottle-feeding the baby?'

'It's better for me,' said Kitty shortly, not looking up.

'But what about him? It isn't better for him, Kit,' he said in a hard voice. 'What's up with you? You can't say you haven't any breast milk. I know you have.'

Her head lifted. There were dark circles beneath her eyes because even though the baby slept through the night, she did not. 'It tires me out feeding him,' she said.

His chestnut brows came together. 'How does it do that? If you're feeding him you're sitting down. Feeding him makes you rest, Kit. He needs the goodness that's in your milk. It makes him stronger to fight disease. And besides bottle-fed babies can end up with upset tummies.'

'Annie knows to boil the bottles and teats.' She lowered her head again and carried on writing, but her insides were tying themselves in knots.

John made an exasperated noise and wrenched the fountain pen out of her hand. 'That's beside the point. And while I'm at it, will you stop putting pink bonnets on him! I know you'd have liked a girl but he's a boy and I won't have you making a cissie out of him. Is that clear, Kit?'

'Perfectly clear.' She stared at him, wanting to throw herself in his arms, cry against his shoulder and be comforted but the thought that he had managed to give Margaret a daughter and not her held her back. He had failed her.

'Good.' His expression softened and his eyes searched her face, coming to rest on the unhappy droop of her mouth. 'Kit, I think it's time I took over more of the running of this place.'

A shock rippled through her. 'No! My mother left it to *me. To me! Her daughter!*' Her voice trembled. 'I can manage perfectly well!'

'No, you can't,' insisted John. 'You're overtiring yourself. I've watched you at work for over a year now and

I think it's time I promoted myself from general dogsbody to manager while you put in more time being a mother.'

'I don't want to put in more time being a mother,' she yelled, flinging the menu cards on the floor. 'This is my place not yours! That baby! He's yours! Why don't you look after him and I – and I . . .' Her voice broke and she brushed past him and ran out of the hotel.

She did not stop running until she came to St John's Gardens behind St George's Hall. There she sank onto a seat near the memorial statue to the Liverpool King's Regiment, horrified with the way she had behaved. She did not know what to do. She felt as if her mind and body were encased in a desolation so intense that it was as if she had been bereaved. He would have her locked away. There was something unnatural about a mother who did not want to love her own baby. Love. How could she love it when she longed for that dream baby which had shared her life for the last nine months. How?

After a while she dragged herself to her feet and turned to make her way home. It was then she saw John sitting on a bench a few yards away. He stood and came towards her, stopping a foot or so in front of her. He looked so unhappy that unexpectedly Kitty's eyes filled with tears and there was a tightness in her chest which made it hard for her to breathe. She held a tentative hand out to him, which he grasped and pulled through his arm. Neither of them spoke on that walk back to the hotel but she no longer felt so alone.

The menu cards were still scattered on the floor and she withdrew her arm and picked them up. He went into the kitchen and by the time she followed he had poured out two cups of tea and was sipping his. She sat and looked at him. 'I'm sorry,' she whispered.

He nodded. 'Are you feeling better now?'

'Better than I was.'

'Good. Drink your tea.'

She did so, relieved that he had not turned down her apology or gone on about her caring for the baby. He only seemed concerned about her wellbeing.

The bell rang in reception and John left the kitchen. Kitty went over to the sink and washed the cups, gazing out of the window as she did so. Annie was sitting on a chair in the sun, nursing the baby. She was singing a lullaby and suddenly Kitty frowned. What was Annie thinking of? She went outside and called, 'You'll spoil him. Put him in the pram.'

'You can't spoil a baby with love,' said Annie with a hint of defiance. 'You should try it yerself.'

Kitty felt a spurt of anger. How dare Annie, who had never had a child, tell her how to look after her own baby!

Kitty walked down the yard. 'Too much mother-love can restrict a child's development. Mothers can be overprotective so children have trouble in developing confidence by trying things out for themselves.' She stared at Annie. 'I read that in the *Echo*.'

'He's only a baby,' said Annie, shaking her head and looking worried. 'A baby! It's not his fault he's not a girl.'

Kitty's eyes glinted. 'I know that! There's a pot of tea in the kitchen so go and pour yourself one. Then go and brush the stairs.'

Annie opened her mouth but Kitty said, 'Go, please!'

Her cousin put the baby back in the pram and Kitty sat in the chair she had vacated and held her face up to the sun. Little John whimpered but she ignored him. The whimper became a grizzle and the grizzle a cry. She stood and went over to the pram and shook it. For a moment he stopped crying but she could hear him sucking the back of his hand. She lowered the hood, lifted him out and immediately he turned his head and butted her breast rooting with an open mouth. For a moment she was undecided then she began to unbutton her blouse.

Once again she sat in the sun struggling with her resentment, grief and sense of failure. Why God? Why couldn't he have been a little girl? So many of her neighbours and acquaintances had said how nice it would have been for her to have a little girl for a change. A daughter who could understand and share the feminine things of life, but it wasn't to be.

Her son tugged on her nipple and she looked down at him. A baby! *He's only a baby*, she thought, recalling Annie's words.

'I know it's not your fault you're not a girl,' she said aloud. 'I know!'

He looked up at her. His eyelashes had uncurled themselves and were long, luxurious and tipped with gold like his father's. She thought of John's pleasure in him and of how he would have forgone that pleasure because he had not wanted to risk her life. Her eyes filled with tears. She closed her eyelids on them, trying to force them back, but they trickled over and down her cheeks. She thought about how it would have been for him and her boys if she had died, and life was suddenly very sweet.

Slowly she began to relax, aware that the only noises penetrating the sunny yard were those of the suckling baby and a pigeon cooing under the eaves. The dream daughter faded and the reality of the child in her arms took over. At least she knew how to handle boys.

John found them there half an hour later and thought at first Kitty had dozed off. The baby's head nestled against her shoulder and a strand of his silky nut brown hair was curled round one of her fingers. He thought he had never seen such a beautiful sight and his heart swelled with emotion. Then Kitty's eyelashes fluttered open and for a moment his love and pride of possession was spoilt by fear. Then she smiled and he dared to kiss her.

When he lifted his mouth from hers, she said quietly, 'I can't feed him all the time, John. I can't give up everything just to look after him.'

He was still a moment and she waited with her breath catching in her throat. 'Just give him what you gave your other sons. That's all I ask,' he said.

She nodded and their lips met again. Then, with her carrying the baby, they went up the yard. Once inside the hotel, she changed the baby's nappy before settling him back in his pram. Then she went and finished the menus.

Chapter Twenty

Everything in Kitty's life did not become smooth sailing just because she had found it in her heart to accept her husband's dictate and deal positively with her disappointment. She was less tired, though, because almost immediately John made several changes. He had had a telephone installed, hired a couple of girls fresh from school to come in daily and he bought a Maple washing machine. He also told Kitty that it was wrong of her to expect Mick to work in the hotel after he had finished school.

The latter was the biggest surprise. 'Why?' she said. 'He knows the ropes. He'll be a big help.'

John leaned over the chiffonier towards her and said, 'I know you want him here, Kit, but stop trying to control his life. Let go of the reins. It would be a waste of his talents if he took over what I presume was Jimmy's role in the hotel. The lad's had a grammar-school education. Let him do his own choosing or he might resent your actions in later life.'

She was shocked by his words. She only wanted Mick to be secure and not have to worry about getting the sack from another employer.

As soon as her eldest son arrived home she spoke to him but did not immediately say what John had said. Instead she asked Mick what he thought of working in the hotel as a full-time job.

There was a pause before he answered. 'I know it's what you want, Ma, but it's not what I want.'

She kept her voice brisk. 'What do you want?'

'I'd like to do something with my calligraphy, but exactly what I don't know.'

'What is there?'

He shrugged. 'I could write signs for shops and things and there's illuminated addresses but it's not what you'd call secure work and I'm young and inexperienced. Probably the most sensible thing would be to get a job as a clerk in an office.'

'A shipping office?' she said with a stir of interest.

'Maybe. Although I did see an advertisement a few weeks ago for the Customs and Excise, so I wrote after a job there. It would be pretty secure, I'm sure. They told me to apply again when I was seventeen.' He hesitated. 'Perhaps I could work here until my next birthday?'

A smile broke over her face and she squeezed his arm. 'That's fine with me. You're talking now like someone who's got their head screwed on right. Have a break. Take Nelson for a walk. He's been barking like mad since he heard your voice.'

With Mick working with them for the moment and more help about the place, John suggested they might have a few days away. Maybe August when business was slack. Nancy was still with them, although for how long they did not know. She and Malcolm Galloway were seeing more of each other, but John doubted she would be leaving them just yet.

'Where were you thinking of going?' asked Kitty. 'Blackpool? Llandudno?'

'Scotland.' He said the word almost casually, pulling her against his shoulder and kissing the corner of her mouth. 'I haven't told you before but Uncle Donald left me his cottage near Oban.'

'A cottage!' She immediately had visions of a thatched roof and roses round the door, of a garden full of hollyhocks and tall daisies. Her head twisted on the pillow and she tried to see his face in the dark. 'Why didn't you tell me?'

'Because it's not up to much. There's no mains water or sewage. No gas, no electricity! It's oil lamps, rainwater and an outside privy. But it would probably do us for a change for a few days and I'm sure the boys would enjoy it. There's good walking and there's the loch for fishing.'

Kitty's pretty picture vanished and her heart sank. 'What about cooking?'

'There's the fire and an oven.' He added rapidly, 'I know it sounds primitive, Kit. That's because it is. But it's beautiful country and if we went it would mean I could go and see my grandfather.'

'Your grandfather?' she said carefully.

'Hmmm!' He kissed the corner of her mouth again. 'I thought I'd take little John to see him.'

There was a pause whilst she thought that one over. 'I see,' she said. 'Couldn't you just go up there with him on your own?'

'You can't be serious. He's a baby! I couldn't cope with him on my own. I need you!'

'But it sounds such hard work!'

'You won't have to do any housework.' He hugged her closer and kissed her full on the mouth. 'There's only two rooms and a scullery. It'll be almost like camping out. The boys'll enjoy it.'

Kitty thought, *If he says the boys'll enjoy it once more I'll scream.* 'I thought this holiday was for me,' she said.

'It is! It'll be a change for you.'

A change from hard work to harder work, she thought. 'Am I allowed to think about it?'

'Of course! August is a few weeks away yet. See how you feel after the tunnel opening. You might be glad of a bit of peace and quiet in the country by then.'

The opening of the Mersey tunnel was only a week away. The King and Queen were coming to do the honours and there was to be a Grand Parade with a cast of thousands. Liverpool was going to be bursting at the seams.

Maybe John was right, thought Kitty, as she stood wedged among the crowd watching the procession. It was warm and sticky and it felt as if the whole city had turned out. There were floats and people on horseback dressed in fancy dress and a lot of flag waving. It made one feel proud. The actual opening of the tunnel was no different. Thousands and thousands of people lined up to see the royal couple arrive in front of the tunnel entrance at the bottom of St John's Lane. The sun blazed and Kitty longed for a cool breeze and no people.

Mick had excused himself and taken Nelson to Prince's Park where he met a couple of friends and lazed all day. Teddy would have gone fishing at the Cassie but Becky

O'Neill, who was determined to be one of the first to drive through the tunnel, had asked him to join her and David in the car. Kitty thought how little John – or Jack, as he was starting to be called to prevent confusion – had no idea of the importance of the personage he was looking at as his father held him high in the air as George V performed his momentous task. In future years, she thought, he would be able to say he had been there on that important day for Merseyside.

Afterwards, when family, friends and guests were still eating a celebratory buffet inside the hotel, Kitty was outside in the yard. She had just fed the baby, and was placing him in his pram and enjoying the quiet, when she heard Ben and Sarah coming down the yard. Her son was saying that he had found it more exciting watching the motorists revving up to be the first through the tunnel than seeing the King actually open it. Kitty smiled, thinking how they had all cheered Becky on despite her not having been the first in line.

'I prefer the ferry to cars,' said Sarah, taking a sucked bullseye out of her mouth to look at its changed colour. She sat alongside Ben on the pile of bricks taken from the Potters' trunk.

'You're only saying that because your ma took our Teddy instead of you,' said Ben, his arm round Nelson's neck.

'It's true,' said Sarah, widening her eyes. 'I like the sea wind in my face, not horrible petrol fumes. Besides, what about the men on the luggage boats? They won't have as much work now and'll probably lose their jobs.'

'That's progress, Teddy says. Like having an inside lavatory instead of an outdoor one.'

'We have an outside privy on the farm in Ireland.' Sarah wrinkled her fastidious nose. 'It has flowers growing round the door but it smells inside. If there's a war and we go there I'm going to hate it because I can never go to the toilet when I go there and Mummy gets all cross.'

'Why should there be a war?' said Ben, fondling Nelson's ears. 'I haven't heard there's going to be a war.'

'It's the Germans.' She pulled off her ribbon, which had slipped down her shining hair, and twisted it round a couple of fingers. 'They've marched their big boots in somewhere. Daddy says it's made everyone nervous.'

'We won them last time,' said Ben comfortingly. 'And if they start fighting again our men'll shoot them all and they'll be sorry. Shall we go and take Nelson for a walk now? I want to show you where Green-toothed Ginny's ghost lives.'

They got up, smiled at Kitty and left the yard by the rear door.

Kitty closed the door after them and walked slowly up the yard. She sat on the pile of bricks, not wanting to think about the disturbances in Austria which had almost resulted in civil war. Instead she considered it was times like this, when Becky brought Sarah and Siobhan to the hotel, that she grieved for what might have been. The pretty frocks and ribbons she could have bought and enjoyed dressing a daughter in. She realised with a start how big a part the buying and dressing up had played in her dreams, but she knew there was more to having a daughter than that.

She said as much to John that night in bed. He pulled her into his arms and murmured against her ear, 'If it's buying pretty clothes you're missing, buy some for yourself. Not too many mind, but I like you looking nice and too often I only see you in an apron or a nightgown.' He paused. 'Now about that trip to Scotland . . .?'

She had almost forgotten about going north of the border. 'How far is it?'

'About three hundreds miles.'

She was dismayed. 'How are we going to get there?'

'The O'Neills are going cruising again. They said we could borrow the car.'

'You can drive?'

'I drove a field ambulance during the war.'

'But three hundred miles,' she said, appalled. 'And with a baby. What about nappies and changes of clothes for him? What about all the washing? I'll never manage.'

He hesitated before hugging her tightly and saying, 'Of course you will. You're a very capable woman.'

'Not that capable,' said Kitty. 'And what if it rains when we're there? I've heard it rains a lot in Scotland. I'll never get things dry.'

He pulled away from her and his eyes looked very dark. 'Who says it's going to rain? The weather can be lovely up there.'

She hesitated, but no, she couldn't cope with it. 'Lovely or not, I think it's a daft idea to take a baby all that way when there's not even running water when we get there!'

'There'll be plenty if it rains,' he retorted, laying on his stomach with his head on his arms.

'Very funny,' said Kitty. 'Why don't you just write to your grandfather and tell him about Jack?'

'It's not the same,' he said in a muffled voice. 'He needs to see him to believe in him. If Jack's to go to medical school he'll have to have help. Grandfather's got money and if he doesn't want to leave it to me, I'd like him to leave it to my son.'

Kitty lay on her stomach and brought her face close up to John's. 'You're doing what you told me not to do with Mick. You're planning his life for him. He mightn't want to be a doctor,' she said emphatically.

'Why should he not?' His tone was huffy.

'He just mightn't.'

'And he might! Don't argue with me, Kit. I know more about what men want than you do.'

'He's only a baby,' she said, exasperated.

'And Grandfather's an old man. He could die tomorrow!'

'It'll be a waste of time going up there then.'

He pushed himself up on his knees, dragging the covers with him. 'You just don't want to go.'

She turned on her side and looked up at him. 'I don't want to go,' she said sweetly. 'A rest is what I need. A rest! I'd come back from what you plan half-dead. Leave it till Jack's potty trained and then we'll go.'

'It could be too late,' he said harshly. 'Haven't you listened to a word I've said, Kit?'

Kit did not answer, having made up her mind it was no use arguing with him. She rolled onto her other side and closed her eyes.

'If he dies before he gets to see Jack it'll be your fault,' said John, pulling the covers off her as he lay down.

Kitty did not move or say anything. The covers were flung back over her and she smiled. 'See what the morning brings,' she said, thinking that perhaps if she bought a couple of dozen more nappies and extra nightgowns and buster suits she might manage if it poured with rain. But bang went the couple of new frocks she had intended buying.

Incredibly, Nancy chose the next day to tell them that Malcolm had asked her to marry him. 'He wants the wedding immediately. Will you give me away, John?' Her chubby face was pink with emotion.

John glanced at Kitty, almost as if to say, you willed this! 'Of course he will,' she said, concealing her relief. 'Will you have the wedding breakfast here?'

'Only a small one,' said Nancy hastily. 'We don't want a big fuss. Just a simple ceremony with family and a few friends. We thought we'd go up to Scotland for a week's honeymoon.'

'Where in Scotland?' said John woodenly. 'You wouldn't be going anywhere near Grandfather's?'

'She couldn't take the baby,' said Kitty, her tongue in her cheek. 'Not on their honeymoon.'

John looked at his wife and there was a glint in his eyes. 'Don't be daft! As if I'd suggest such a thing.'

'What is this?' asked Nancy, looking bewildered.

'Just a thought,' said Kitty. 'Were you planning on visiting your great-grandfather?'

Nancy looked dubious. 'I have thought of it in the past as you know – but next week? I'm not sure what Malcolm's planned.' Her face brightened. 'If I get the chance I'll go. I could tell him about you and John being married and little Jack.'

Perfect, thought Kitty, and relinquished all thought of a holiday with only the teeniest of regrets. There were other things more important.

Maybe next year?

Chapter Twenty-One

But the following August Kitty had other things on her mind. 'There's something not right with Annie,' she mused, unwrapping sandwiches and gazing at John who was stretched out on a towel in navy blue bathing drawers.

'She seems all right to me.' He groaned as Jack plonked a damp sandy bottom on his bare thigh.

'You don't know her the way I do.'

'Bite!' exclaimed Jack, bouncing on his father's leg and opening his mouth like a fledgling. He was fifteen months old.

Kitty tore a bite-size morsel from the cold mutton sandwich and popped it in his mouth. She smiled as he chewed solemnly, remembering how he had looked when they had set out on the ferry that morning. He had worn yellow linette shorts and a white cellular blouse and had looked a picture.

'What do you think's wrong with her?' asked John.

Kitty looked to where Ben was splashing at the water's edge and said vaguely, 'I could be wrong but I think she's broody – and it's all down to her sister getting married. I remember she was a bit that way out last year when Nancy got married.'

John sat up and eased Jack's damp bottom off his leg and onto the towel. 'We don't want Annie getting married.'

'I know! And isn't that selfish of us? The trouble is she's always said that she's a one-man woman and that one man is Jimmy.'

'So what's the problem?' said John, reaching for a sandwich. 'She can't have Jimmy so it looks like she's going to stay on the shelf. Which suits us fine because we don't want to lose her.'

'That sounds all right,' murmured Kitty. 'But I hate the thought of her being that unhappy she goes into a decline. She hardly ever takes time off and when she does she never seems to go anywhere. Perhaps she could do with a little holiday? Go to Blackpool or Morecambe with one of her sisters. It would probably do her good and she'd settle down happily afterwards.'

'I'm surprised you dare mention the word holiday.' John fixed her with a steely look.

Kitty pulled a face at him and gave her son another morsel of food. 'It takes enough organising coming to New Brighton for a few hours so imagine what I'd have to do to make a three-hundred-mile trip? And what would be the use, love, if your grandfather refuses to see you?' She tried to sound reasonable because they had already aired this issue several times. 'You heard what Nancy said when she came back last year. He's become a recluse. He won't open the door to anyone, not even the minister or the doctor.'

John said nothing but he did not look convinced.

'Maybe next year, love,' she continued. 'Jack'll be

potty-trained then and he'll be talking more and will be far more interesting to an old man.'

'Stop making excuses,' said John, biting savagely into another sandwich and chewing forcefully. 'The trouble with your reasoning is that you keep forgetting Grandfather's in his nineties and could die any minute.'

'He's lasted this long,' murmured Kitty, reaching for the bottle of homemade lemonade. 'And if Jack's meant to have his money then he'll get it. Your grandfather has to leave it somewhere. You have written to him and I sent a letter at the beginning of this year with a photograph of Jack.'

'And we heard nothing back.'

'He's a stubborn old man. You've admitted that yourself.' Kitty thought it sounded like he was also senile but she kept that thought to herself and changed the subject. 'About Annie – shall I tell her to take a few days off?'

'Why ask me?' said John, stretching himself out on the towel again. 'It's you that makes all the decisions.'

That's not fair, she almost said but decided to let it go. After all he was not insisting they went to Scotland and neither had he spoken against Annie having a break, so she had got her own way twice.

'Have a holiday?' Annie looked at Kitty as if she had run mad. 'I've never had a holiday. What d'yer want me to go on a holiday for?' She sounded put out.

'You need a holiday,' insisted Kitty, shaking her head at her. 'You haven't been yourself lately. It shows in the way you've just spoken to me. Go and paddle in the sea and enjoy all the fun of the fair. Get right away from Liverpool. It'll do you good.'

For a moment she thought Annie was going to turn down her suggestion flat but her elfin face suddenly brightened and she said, 'Perhaps I will. I'll let yer know tomorrer for definite. Yer can always get our Monica to give yer a hand with it being the school holidays. She's not a bad little worker.'

The following morning Annie came downstairs with a small cardboard suitcase. She was dressed in a saxe blue afternoon frock, which she had bought from Lewis's during their eighty-second birthday sale and she looked very different to her usual self. 'I'm going, Kit, and I'll be back in a couple of days. Whether that'll be for good or not I don't know.' Her mouth was set determinedly.

'What's that supposed to mean?' asked Kitty, feeling slightly alarmed and wondering if her idea was going to backfire on her. 'Where are you going?'

'Ask no questions and yer'll get told no lies,' said Annie, tilting her chin. 'I'll tell yer when I come back.' Without another word she departed.

'She's being real mysterious,' said Ben, dipping a finger of toast in the yolk of a boiled egg and holding it out to Jack who nearly took his fingers off as he bit it. Ben grinned. His younger brother's greed amused him greatly.

'I wonder why?' murmured Kitty. There had been something in the way Annie had spoken that reminded her of someone.

'She's entitled to her privacy,' said John.

'There it is again!' cried Kitty, puckering her brow as

she sank onto a chair. 'There's something on the edge of me mind but I can't think what it is.'

'If it's important it'll come back to you,' said her husband, folding the newspaper and getting up.

She agreed and went to fetch her shopping baskets, leaving Ben to look after Jack.

The next day, to Kitty's surprise, Annie arrived back home and appeared to be in a worse state than when she had left. Her face was pale and she looked visibly shaken.

'What is it? What's up with you?' asked Kitty, taking hold of her cousin's shoulder and pressing her into a chair.

'I saw him!' Annie looked up at her with stark terror in her eyes.

'Saw who?'

'Charley!' She swallowed noisily. 'He was walking along the prom eating candyfloss just like a normal person! He leered at me and I panicked, even though there were crowds of people about. I ran, Kit! I ran I was that scared!' The words came pouring out. 'I hid meself as best I could in the crowd and when I knew I'd lost him I went in a cafe and had a cuppa tea, but I was shaking that much I decided to come home. I couldn't cope with the thought I might bump into him again.'

'Where was this?'

'Rhyl! I went to see if I could find Jimmy. I've been that lonely lately, Kit. I thought, I can't go on like this. I've got to know if I do still love him and I can only know that by seeing him. And then I saw that monster and I thought is God playing some trick on me? I looked for Jimmy and

I found that swine and I ran. I'm ashamed of meself. I shouldn't have let him see I was scared but I am and I'm still shook up.'

Kitty squeezed her shoulder reassuringly. 'You behaved like most women would in the circumstances – but I'm glad we know where he is now. You're safe here so stop worrying.' She moved away from Annie and took a bottle of Scotch from the shelf. She poured a little into a glass and handed it to Annie. 'Drink this. It'll calm you down a bit. I'll just go and have a word with the big fella.'

She found John in conversation with one of the guests in the Smoking Room. She did not interrupt immediately but saw to the fire, catching snippets of their talk which seemed to be about Mussolini and Hitler and some pact or other. She sought an opening and stepped neatly in. The next moment her husband was excusing himself. Outside in the lobby she told him about Charley.

John swore softly. 'We'll have to do something.'

'Such as what?'

It was like a shutter coming down over his face and he shrugged. 'I don't know. I'll go and see Daniel. He might have some ideas.'

She decided not to ask any questions. She wanted Charley dealt with and she didn't particularly care how her husband did it, but she was concerned about his safety. 'You'll be careful?'

He smiled and kissed her. 'You worry about Annie.'

Kitty returned to the kitchen and found Annie had been joined by Hannah and her sister Monica. 'What's going on?' asked the old woman, resting her hands on the table.

'This one here's been drinking. Drink's not good for thee. It can make thee behave wild.'

'Dutch courage,' said Monica, her dark eyes as bright and inquisitive as a robin's as she looked at her eldest sister. 'What's up with our Annie boozing at this hour of the day?'

'Yer can both mind yer own business,' said Annie sharply, ramming the glass down on the table. 'Get on with some work both of yer! There's vegetables to be done, I don't doubt.'

'Done, Miss Bossyboots,' said Hannah with satisfaction. 'We's don't hang about whether thee's here or not.'

Kitty hid a smile. 'You can put them on to boil,' she said. 'Monica, go and see if Jack's all right, love. He's playing in the yard.' She turned to Annie. 'We'll talk in the basement.'

'The big fella's gone to see Mr O'Neill,' she said as soon as they were sitting down.

Annie sighed with relief. 'What d'you think they'll do to him?'

'I didn't ask but I think we can stop worrying. They'll find him.'

Annie's expression changed. 'Kit, what if Charley comes here? Yer know – he – he's seen me and knows where I live. He just might . . .' Her voice tailed off and there was fear in her face.

'Don't be stupid,' said Kitty sharply. 'Why should he? He's left us alone all this time. There's no reason why he should.'

'He's seen me and he's a bad 'un. He likes people being

frightened of him.' She laced her fingers tightly together. 'I'm scared, Kit. I'm scared.'

Kitty rose from her chair and put an arm round her shoulders. 'You're not to be scared. The men'll find him and when they do he'll be sorry he ever started with us!'

'How'll they find him? I never thought – but where'll he start looking?'

'Hotels.'

Annie stared at her. 'That was how I was going to find Jimmy. But of course Charley could be there on holiday. It'd be funny if the big fella bumped into Jimmy.'

'Very funny,' said Kitty, her mouth unexpectedly dry. 'But let's not be thinking about that. I'll have to go up and sort out tonight's meal. You stay here and have a rest.'

'No!' Annie jumped to her feet and slipped a hand through Kitty's arm. 'I'm coming with you. I don't want to be left on my own.'

'There's nothing to be scared of Kitty sought to reassure her. 'It's different now to last time. We have the telephone – and Nelson.'

'He could cut the wires and slit Nelson's throat!'

'You've been watching too many films,' said Kitty, but she saw that Annie would not be reassured and said no more.

They had finished washing the dishes after the evening meal but still no word had come from John, and Kitty was getting restless. She wanted to know what was going on. As if on cue, the telephone rang in the lobby and she ran to answer it.

'John, where are you?'

'It's not John. It's me!' Becky's voice came over the line. 'The men have gone to Rhyl by ship. I was told not to ring you until they'd sailed and then Sarah played up, so I've only been able to get to the phone now.'

'The idiot! I've been on pins. Did he think I'd try and stop him or something?' cried Kitty.

'Don't ask me to try and explain the ways of men. It's real *Adventure* comic stuff. I'm just following orders. How's Annie?'

'Scared out of her wits. She's worrying in case Charley turns up here.'

Becky said quietly, 'I bet they haven't thought of that.'

'I didn't until she mentioned it and now I'm all on edge. I've got me rolling pin handy and Nelson's on guard. If there looks like being any real trouble I'll phone the police, little as I like the idea.'

Becky said a few comforting words and then rang off.

Kitty returned to the kitchen and told Annie and the boys what was happening.

'So we've just got to sit tight,' said Teddy.

'It looks like it,' said Kitty in a voice far more cheerful than she felt. She was realising just how much she had come to rely on having John's protective presence around but she did not mention to the boys the possibility of Charley turning up at the hotel. She did not want them playing the hero and getting hurt. 'There's no need for you to stay up,' she told them. 'You both have work in the morning and we'll be coming up soon.'

'Forget it, Ma,' they both said.

But when ten-thirty came and all was quiet they went to bed. Kitty, Annie and Hannah stayed down a bit longer clearing away, emptying ashtrays and setting the tables for breakfast. It was then Nelson began to bark.

The colour drained from Annie's face and for a moment Kitty thought she was going to faint. She gripped her cousin's hand and continued to hold it as she picked up her rolling pin and went over to the back door and listened. She could hear a voice trying to calm the dog. She recognised it immediately and, handing the rolling pin to Annie, drew back the bolts.

Jimmy almost fell into the kitchen and only prevented himself from hitting the floor by clinging to the doorjamb whilst Nelson snapped at his heels. Kitty called the dog to her but he was that excited he ignored her. She seized his collar and dragged him under the table. He lay there, a growl still rumbling in his throat.

Jimmy whispered his thanks and she realised that his face was bruised and battered and one of the sleeves of his jacket had been torn away from the stitching at the shoulder.

'It's – it's Jimmy!' cried Annie. 'Oh God, what's happened to you?' She took hold of his arm and helped him to a chair.

Kitty ordered Hannah to put the kettle on while she went in search of her medicine box. 'What has happened to you?' she said.

Jimmy attempted to focus on her face from swollen eyes. 'You told me that if I was ever in trouble . . .' he said unsteadily.

'I remember,' said Kitty grimly, wiping blood from the corner of his mouth whilst Annie stood behind him with both her hands gripping the back of his chair.

'I got into a fight with Charley. Myrtle's dead!' He looked completely dazed.

'Myrtle!' Kitty's hands stilled. 'How?'

He swallowed. 'She had a gun.'

'She had a gun?' Kitty found herself repeating the words as if somehow that would make them sound more real. 'Good God, what for?' She stepped back and stared down at him, feeling a mixture of anger and fear. 'What have you done?' she whispered.

Jimmy's head lifted. 'It wasn't me!' he cried. 'She was threatening me and Charley with it. We were fighting because he'd boasted about what he had done to – to you and Annie. I saw red and I just wanted to beat him into pulp.'

'You did that for me?' said Annie, clutching at his shoulder.

Jimmy screamed. 'Don't do that! He's done something to me shoulder. Dislocated it or something. I don't know how I managed to drive here. Honestly, Kit, it was like something out of a George Raft film. She could have killed me.'

'The wages of sin are death,' said Hannah, causing them all to jump. She fixed sharp eyes on Jimmy. 'What evil hast thou done, me lad?'

'Not now, Hannah!' snapped Kitty, filled with a sense of unreality. 'Just make the tea.'

Annie had moved into a position where she could

see Jimmy's face. Her own was extremely pale. 'What's Myrtle Drury to do with you?' she asked him.

'I worked for her in her hotel.' He closed his eyes in obvious pain.

'And Charley?' she said.

Jimmy opened his eyes again. 'She'd long given him the push but he had a habit of turning up now and again and causing trouble.' He freed a heavy sigh. 'Annie, can you get me ciggies out of me jacket pocket? I'm desperate for a smoke.'

She scurried to do his bidding, watched by a scowling Hannah who muttered, 'Thou's daft, girl. Buzzing around after him like a blue-bummed fly. No good'll come of it.'

Annie ignored her and placed a cigarette in Jimmy's mouth. He drew smoke into his lungs and closed his eyes again.

Kitty pulled up a chair and sat close to him so their knees almost touched. She wanted to watch every change of his expression. 'Who killed Myrtle? And where's Charley?'

Jimmy moved the cigarette with his tongue to the corner of his mouth. 'It was Charley. He was trying to get the gun away from her when it went off. It was bloody awful. One minute she was all movement and the next limp like a sandbag with all the sand emptied out of it. I was scared out of me wits. There was Myrtle dead and Charley with the gun. I skedaddled fast.'

'So you don't know whether he got away?' said Kitty.

'Oh, he got away all right. He wasn't far behind me.' He inhaled deeply, closing his eyes. 'But I beat him to Myrtle's car.' He opened his eyes again. 'God! It's a nightmare! I was a damn fool to get involved with her.'

'I warned you,' said Kitty tartly. 'But you thought you knew her better.'

'I should have listened. Nothing turned out the way I expected.'

There was a silence. No marriage then, thought Kitty in passing, and framed her next question. 'Charley? The police? Do you think they'll come here?'

Jimmy forced his drooping eyelids up again. 'The staff know I'm a Liverpudlian and a few know I worked in a hotel here before going to Rhyl. The police could come. I don't know about Charley.'

Her heart sank. She would have dearly loved to know where that man was. 'You got here in a car you said.'

'I parked it well away from the hotel.' His gaze met hers. 'Give me that much nous, Kit.'

'They'll know you've come to Liverpool, though, when they trace it,' said Annie, her face looking more pinched than ever.

'I'm sorry. I couldn't think of anywhere else to go.' He slumped lower in the chair.

Kitty was silent. For the moment she could not think what to say or do next. She was glad when Hannah handed round cups of tea. Then the old woman sat and fixed her with her sharp eyes and said, 'The man needs the doctor. Missus Nancy's man'll see to him. He might even put him up. Then if the scuffers come we can tell them he's not here. Don't have to tell untruths.'

Kitty's sagging shoulders lifted. 'You're right, Hannah! Trust you to show us what to do. We'll take him out the back way and hope no one sees us. Will you be all right on your own?'

Hannah gave her a look. 'The good Lord'll keep me under his wing.' She nodded sagely. 'Thee just get rid of him before he goes giving our place a bad name.'

Kitty and Annie lifted a reluctant-to-move Jimmy to his feet and helped him over to the back door and outside. It had begun to rain and the pavement glistened in the light of the street lamps as they made their way by a devious route to the Galloways' in Rodney Street. The women's heels rang on the pavement, seeming to give off a hollow sound, and Kitty's imagination started to play tricks with her so that she could have sworn they were being followed. It was a relief when they came to the doctor's house.

It seemed an age before anyone responded to the ring of the bell and it was Celia who opened the door to peer through the gloom at them. 'Is that you, Mrs McLeod? Is somebody ill? That's not Mick, is it?' She sounded anxious as she gazed at Jimmy's slumped figure between the two women.

'No, it's my brother-in-law,' whispered Kitty. 'Go and wake the doctor. It's an emergency. And tell your mistress I'd like to see her, as well.'

'He would have come out to you if you'd rang,' said Celia, glancing over her shoulder at Annie and the muffled figure before ushering them indoors.

No sooner had Kitty left with Annie and Jimmy than Mick and Teddy entered the kitchen. 'Where's Ma?' asked Mick, glancing round. 'We heard Nelson barking.'

'They's gone to the doctor's with a wounded man,' said Hannah with relish. She brandished a blood smeared wad of cotton wool under his nose. 'Myrtle Drury's got her just desserts and good riddance I say.'

The brothers exchanged glances and there were matching gleams of excitement in their eyes. 'You'd better tell us the whole story, Hannah,' said Teddy. 'Whose door have you been listening outside now?'

'Don't yous be giving me cheek,' said the maid, bristling. 'I heard it in this kitchen and saw him with me own eyes. And that Charley's done murder and's on the loose again. He's got a gun.'

Both brothers sat down and Mick's hand strayed towards Nelson as he came out from under the table. 'Go on, Hannah,' said Mick, his expression sober now. 'Tell us the whole story.'

For a moment she looked like she was going to get on her high horse and refuse but then she began. She had only just started when Nelson suddenly shot from beneath Mick's hand and over to the back door, barking for all he was worth. Suddenly, the door was pushed open and a man stood there. Nelson went for his ankles, seizing a mouthful of trouser, only to be picked up and flung outside and the door shut on him.

'Talk of the devil.' The words must have come from Mick's subconscious because he was not aware of thinking them. All he knew was that the man he had never seen before but had heard described often enough did not seem to be carrying a weapon. Despite a sinking feeling in the pit of his stomach over the way Nelson had been treated – as if he was nothing more than a bothersome fly – he was relieved to see no gun.

'Where is he?' demanded Charley, his fair hair standing out from his head like a barbed-wire halo. There was a bruise on a cheekbone and one side of his jaw was swollen. His hot eyes fixed on Teddy. 'You! Where is he and where's your Ma?'

'Who are we talking about?' said Teddy, trying to keep his fear under control as his hands reached for the table behind him, seeking Kitty's rolling pin, which he felt sure he had seen a few minutes earlier.

Charley's mouth twisted in an ugly grimace. 'Don't play games, kid. Yer know who I'm talking about. Jimmy! He's got nowhere else to go. Tell me and I won't harm yer.'

'We don't know! We haven't seen him since he left,' said Teddy with convincing honesty.

'Yer lying,' yelled Charley and charged forward, his hand raised.

'The wages of sin are death,' cried Hannah, lunging forward as if she had never had rheumatism in her life. Reaching up, she seized hold of his outstretched arm with both hands.

'Gerroff, yer stupid ol' woman,' said Charley, trying to shake her away. He took his eyes off Teddy and Mick.

In that split second Teddy managed to find the rolling pin. He had no intention of getting close enough to Charley to grapple with him but instead flung the rolling pin at him. 'Bloody bullseye!' he crowed as it caught Charley on the temple. The man staggered and the brothers moved swiftly and concertedly, ramming him in the stomach and chest with their shoulders. His knees buckled and, like a flattened concertina, he sank to the floor.

Hannah picked up the rolling pin and hit him on the head. 'Just to make sure,' she said.

Mick and Teddy sat on Charley. 'Out cold,' said Mick, giving a great sigh of relief.

'Do we phone the police?' said Teddy.

Mick looked at Hannah. 'Was Jimmy here?'

She nodded. 'I thinks we should tie him up and wait and see what thy ma says when she comes back,' she said. Then she carried on telling her tale which had been interrupted.

Kitty was at that moment paying attention to what Malcolm Galloway had to say. She'd told him that Jimmy had been playing football and that was how he had come by his injuries and she was full up and couldn't put him up herself. Husband and wife had accepted her story without demur. 'His collarbone's dislocated,' said Malcolm. 'I've had a go at trying to manipulate it back but he's in too much pain, so I've given him something to make him sleep. He wants to see you before he goes off, Kitty, so spare a minute.' He smiled at her.

Kitty thanked him and hurried upstairs to find Jimmy in bed, looking like he had been dealt a second knockout blow. Annie slipped out of the room as she went in.

'Annie's just been telling me about your husband and baby,' blurted out Jimmy as soon as Kitty entered. 'You didn't waste any time.'

She stared at him coolly. After all she had done for him his remark was more than she could take. 'He wanted to protect me from Charley, which was more than you did! Isn't it time you stopped thinking of yourself and thought about others? Annie for instance! It was your fault Charley found us and raped her. She was saving herself for you and what did she end up with? Nothing!' Before he could say anything she left the room.

Kitty found Annie downstairs and, after thanking Nancy and Malcolm again for their help, the cousins left. Kitty longed for her bed with John in it. The last thing she expected to find was Charley on her kitchen floor with Mick and Teddy in attendance.

A bright-eyed Hannah was sitting on a chair, drinking a cup of cocoa and regaling the boys with the fate that waited Charley after he'd met the hangman. Immediately Kitty asked Annie to get the older woman to bed and to keep her quiet. For a moment she did not think Annie had heard her because her cousin was staring down at Charley as if she had seen her horse pass the winning post at Aintree. Then she turned with a huge grin on her face and went out with her arm linked through Hannah's.

After they had gone, Mick, who with Teddy's help had tied the still unconscious Charley up in so many knots with the clothesline that he was trussed up like a Christmas turkey, asked, 'Do we get the police?'

Kitty did not bother to think about it before shaking her head. 'He'll tell them about Jimmy and they'll hang around here, hoping he'll turn up. We don't want that. It won't do our reputation any good and it won't do Jimmy any good. We've got to get rid of Charley.' Her mouth set determinedly.

Mick and Teddy looked at her, apprehension written clearly on their faces. 'You don't mean—'

'What?' She laughed. 'Not the river, boys. The basement

until John comes home. It won't be easy getting him down there – we'll have to drag him into the yard and take him down the back area steps, but . . .'

Their faces brightened. 'We'll manage. You go to bed, Ma. We'll wake you if anything else happens.'

She nodded, glad to leave them to it, and crept upstairs, hoping there would be no more disturbances that night.

Kitty woke to broad daylight and John sitting on the side of the bed. She sat up and clutched him. 'When did you get back? Do you know Myrtle's been killed and that Charley's in the basement?'

'Not anymore he isn't,' he said, pressing his lips against her hair and hugging her. 'It seems I was where the excitement wasn't at. I should have stayed here instead of rushing off. Still we've got rid of Charley.'

'What? Where is he?' she said, startled.

'On a ship heading for China a bit worse for wear.'

She could hardly take it in and blinked at him. 'Why China? And hell!' she exclaimed, catching sight of the clock. 'What about the guests' breakfasts? I must have slept through the alarm.'

John smiled. 'Relax. All seen to. As for China there's a lot of sea between here and there if he doesn't behave himself. We couldn't have him shooting his mouth off about Jimmy and his connection with you and Annie and this hotel.'

She stared at him. 'Do you know about Jimmy?'

'Naturally. He's gone too.' He said the words very casually.

Kitty was not deceived by his tone. She remembered

that first time she had mentioned Jimmy to him and how he had spoken as if he suspected there was something between them. 'You couldn't have done so much already. Where's he gone?'

He kissed her. 'It's surprising how much you can do if you don't go to bed and you've got the means. He's on his way to Ireland on one of Green's ships. Relax.'

She tried to do as he said but it was not easy. Especially when the police arrived just after lunch asking if she had seen anything of a Jimmy Ryan who had once worked for her. She answered in the negative and so did everyone else and eventually, after a few days, the police went away.

The Myrtle Drury murder was a five-day wonder – when no one was arrested for the killing, it was pushed to the back of people's minds.

Kitty and Annie heard nothing from Jimmy until Christmas, when cards arrived in an unknown hand. He was living in County Cork with his uncles and an aunt who was a schoolteacher. She had taken it upon herself to teach him to read and write.

Kitty wrote a brief friendly letter back and from then on stuck to cards on his birthday and at Christmas. Annie, though, sent a monthly letter telling him all the news. She told of Mick working in the Custom House and of the family's trip to Scotland the following year having to be cancelled because Jack and Ben caught the mumps, of Nancy Galloway having a baby boy and of the rumours that all Myrtle Drury's property and money had gone to a cousin in Manchester. Everyone said he was a much nicer person than she had ever been, and he had a nice homely wife.

Annie began to receive regular letters from Jimmy and after a while she had a holiday in Ireland. She came home full of dreams and plans and asked for a raise. There was something she was saving up for which she was very mysterious about.

'We're going to lose her,' said Kitty over breakfast the morning the newspapers were telling of German planes bombing Guernica in Spain.

Sure enough, a few months later Jimmy proposed marriage, and in the spring of 1938 Kitty and the whole family took a ship to Ireland to see the best worker she had ever had become Mrs Jimmy Ryan, owner of the Arcadia boarding house in the town of Kinsale on the west coast of Ireland, bought with money lent to them by the Irish great-uncles.

Chapter Twenty-Two

'Thy ma'll catch thee a clout if thee don't stop doing that,' said Hannah, resting a hand on the area railings.

Ben, arched over his half-brother's back, flashed her one of his sweetest smiles. Despite his twelve years he still possessed that charm which could soften the hardest of hearts. 'Ma won't mind and it's keeping Jack out of her hair.'

'Let's go, Benny! Let's go,' demanded his half-brother, bouncing up and down on the saddle.

'Thou just make sure thee don't let him crash, or the big fella will skin thee alive,' said Hannah.

Ben eased his grip on the brakes from his position on the back crossbar but jammed them on again when he heard his name being called. He glanced over his shoulder and saw Nancy crossing the road.

'Is your Pops in?' she called, waving an envelope. 'I've a letter for him.'

'Yep! Go straight in.' Ben released the brakes and the tricycle coasted down the Mount.

'Isn't that dangerous?' shouted Nancy, but the boys did not appear to hear.

'Thee's talking to thyself, missus,' said Hannah. 'Lads'll

take no notice until they have an accident and even then some are daft enough to do the same thing over again. Thou's right to keep thy boy away from them.' There was a dry inflection in her voice.

Nancy flushed. 'It's not because I fear their influence. It's just that Alastair's too young to play with Jack.' She wondered why she was making excuses to this scraggy old maid and brushing past her went into the lobby where she found Kitty wielding a heavy vacuum cleaner.

'Shouldn't the maid be doing that?' shouted Nancy.

'What?' Kitty switched off the machine and looked at her.

'I said shouldn't one of the maids be doing that?'

'Hannah doesn't like machinery and I haven't any outside help today. Cup of tea?'

'That would be nice. Where's John?'

'Upstairs putting up a shelf. Do you want him?'

'I've a letter for him from Brighton,' said Nancy solemnly.

Kitty was amused. Since Nancy had become a mother she possessed an air of self-importance. 'Go up. He's on the first floor.'

She went into the kitchen wondering why John's sister was writing to him. Perhaps the news last week that Germany had invaded Austria had made her want to heal the breach between them? Fear of war made some people act differently. Poland and Czechoslovakia had rushed troops to their borders, fearing invasion, and the British and French governments had both spoken about German actions but so far they had done nothing. Nobody wanted another war but as John said, 'Give this fella Hitler an inch and he'll take a mile.' She was living in fear that at any moment the situation would escalate into a full-blown war and Mick and Teddy would have to fight. She busied herself, trying not to think of the horrors which might be in store for them if war came.

There was a sound at the door and Nancy and John entered. 'What's up?' Kitty pushed a mug across the table towards her husband who looked stunned.

'Emily's dead.'

'Dead and buried!' Nancy sounded disgruntled. 'Remember me telling you about that girl Jeannie? Apparently she arranged the funeral and didn't think to ask us if we wanted to go—'

'That's not true,' said John, lifting his head. 'She says in her letter she thought it a bit much expecting us to make the long journey in the bad weather.'

'That sounds sensible to me. That it then?' said Kitty.

There was a pause and John's eyes met hers across the table. She knew then there was more but he did not want to mention it in front of Nancy. 'Nothing important,' he said. 'She mentioned some family photographs and letters.'

She nodded. 'They'll be nice to have.'

He agreed and there was a silence. Kitty wondered what it was he did not want to say in front of his niece.

Nancy cleared her throat. 'I've something to tell you.'

They both looked at her expectantly and saw that she was upset. 'We'll be leaving you, John and Kitty dears. Malcolm doesn't like the way things are going in Europe and if there's going to be air raids, like some are saying in the newspapers, then he wants Alastair out of it. We're going to Canada.'

Kitty was dumbfounded. 'I thought you were here for life!'

John was silent and Nancy reached out to both of them and covered their hands. 'I can see it's come as a real shock to you. I'm going to miss you both terribly – and the boys, of course. You've all come to mean so much to me.'

'I'll miss you,' said Kitty, and she meant it. Nancy could be a bit of a fusspot but it had been good for John to have someone of his own family close by, and Malcolm being married to Nancy had strengthened the men's friendship.

John said in a vague tone, 'There mightn't be a war, you know.'

'I hope there isn't,' said Nancy in a shaky voice. 'But the decision's made and our passage booked. All that's left to be done is the awful job of deciding what to take and what not to take. And of course, I'll have to tell Celia she's out of a job.'

Kitty responded immediately. 'Send her here. I'm sure I can make good use of her.'

Nancy smiled. 'I was hoping you'd say that. I'm sorry for the girl to tell you the truth. That mother of hers leads her a terrible life and now she's not well she's even more demanding. Celia had to stop sleeping in, you know.'

'I didn't know,' said Kitty with a sigh. 'But Celia's a good girl and has a strong sense of duty. She would do what's right by her mother.'

'That's true,' said Nancy, getting to her feet and giving

John a glance. 'I'll be going then but I'll see you again before we leave. Bye, John.'

'Bye, Nance!' He spoke in a tone of voice which told the listener he was not paying attention.

Kitty felt like giving him a poke because she could see Nancy was hurt. Instead she saw Nancy to the door, saying in a soothing voice that the news of his sister's death had shocked him more than she would have believed. Nancy agreed.

Kitty returned to the kitchen and sat next to her husband. 'Well, what is it?'

He looked at her from eyes which appeared kind of shell-shocked. 'She wants to come here.'

'Who?'

'Jeannie.' He eased his throat. 'You're not going to believe this, Kit. I can hardly believe it myself, but she says she's my daughter.'

Kitty stared at him, unable to speak for several seconds. 'But your daughter's dead! Unless you had another? No!' Kitty dismissed that thought immediately. He wouldn't have. Her head was suddenly full of bubbling thoughts.

'She says Margaret's mother lied to her,' he said earnestly. 'Told her I'd been killed in the war.'

'But that's cruel!' said Kitty.

'You're forgetting she blamed me for Margaret's death.' There was a bitter note in his voice.

Kitty thought about that, imagined the mother with her only child dead and a living baby in her arms. Oh, she could easily picture the scene and feel the anguish of that mother. 'What do you want to do?' she said. 'Do you want to see her?'

He stared at her. 'A girl, Kit. A daughter!' His voice was unsteady. 'What do you think?'

She met his eyes and knew what he was thinking and she felt a stir of pleasurable excitement before a blast of sensible thinking blew it away. 'We don't know her! We don't know if she'll fit in! She mightn't like us.'

He looked taken aback. 'Why shouldn't she like us? Or do you think it's me she won't like? After all I didn't stick round long enough to visit her grave. If I had then I'd have known she wasn't dead and I'd have been around for her.'

And your life would have been completely different, thought Kitty. *We'd have never met.* She covered his hand with hers. 'I didn't mean she wouldn't like you. You're kind, you're good-looking, you're strong,' she said, boosting his ego. 'And you weren't to blame. Why shouldn't she like you? Does she know her granny lied to you?'

'I don't know. No, she can't. Who'd have told her?'

They were both silent a moment. Then Kitty said, 'How did she find out you were her father and that you were still alive?'

'By accident. A photograph she found in Emily's bedroom when she was clearing things out. It was a wedding photograph of Margaret and me.' He squeezed Kitty's hand tightly. 'Jeannie had never seen a photograph of me but she had one of her mother as a bride on her own. She had no idea her father was Emily's brother but my sister had written the information and the date of the wedding on the back of the photograph. Jeannie says in her letter she can scarcely believe it. Couldn't understand why her grandmother should lie to her. That she wants to meet me. Do I say come?'

There was a silence and Kitty knew this was a crucial moment in their lives. What if Jeannie proved a disappointment to that ideal they both carried in their heads? They knew so little about her, but then wasn't the best way of finding out more about her to meet her? 'Tell her to come,' said Kitty and leaning forward she kissed his cheek. 'And don't look so worried. I'm sure everything will be fine.'

John nodded but did not look convinced. 'Will you tell the boys?'

She hesitated, then made a decision. 'Let's meet her first. After all she might not want to stay.'

So it was settled. John wrote to the girl claiming to be his daughter and almost by return of post he received an answer saying she would be arriving Saturday.

They looked at each other. It was the start of the busiest week of their year.

'We have to squeeze her in somewhere,' said John, running a hand over hair which showed a few silver threads.

'What about the box room?' said Kitty.

'It's a mess and there's no bed.' He frowned.

'It's the best I can do,' she said firmly. 'She can have Jack's new one. He can squeeze in with Ben.'

'OK. I'll sort it out,' he muttered and walked out of the kitchen before Kitty could say anything else.

If she had not known already how worked up he was about Jeannie's coming, she would have realised it the next day. His nightmares returned, which told Kitty just how much he was worried about the past and what Jeannie would think of him. Kitty could only hope that once Jeannie arrived he would be able to find some peace of mind.

On Saturday morning they made an early dash to the market for food and John surprised her by buying an armful of flowers from one of the shawlies outside St John's market. 'I thought it'd be nice if you could put some in Jeannie's room,' he said.

Strangely she was reminded of that time he had given her the white hyacinth and she felt a momentary pang of jealousy. 'I'll fit it in somehow,' she murmured, thinking how she was already up to her eyes in work.

Not for the first time she wished she had not been so magnanimous in allowing Mick and Teddy to choose the jobs they wanted. But at least Ben was old enough to help her now and he was good with Jack as well. Maybe in a year or two, if there wasn't a war, they would be able to afford to put hot and cold running water in some of the bedrooms and that would be less work.

It was three o'clock when John told her he was off to meet Jeannie's train. They had decided earlier it would be best if just he and Jack went to this first meeting. 'How do I look?' he said.

She picked a thread of white cotton from the lapel of his best jacket and thought he looked a treat. It was not often John dressed up and she thought the girl would have to be mad not to appreciate him. 'You'll do,' she murmured and pushed him out of the door.

John stood by the hissing locomotive with Jack on his shoulders whispering in his ear. They had arrived too early and John was keyed up with waiting. What would she be like? He knew she was tall and fair but it was her personality he was interested in. Was she kind? Would she believe that if he had known she was alive he would have lived a different life? He took out Uncle Donald's watch and checked the time. He realised it was later than he thought and loped up the platform with Jack clinging on tightly and protesting that he had wanted to stay longer to look at the engine.

'Later, son,' gasped John, wondering why he had given in to the urge to bring Jack with him, but he knew why really. He was his son, his only son and Jeannie's half-brother.

The London train had steamed in and was disgorging passengers. John's hazel eyes scanned faces and then he saw her. It had to be her! She was so like Margaret it came as a shock. For a moment he wondered if he had made a mistake in being so keen to have her stay with them. What would Kitty think when she saw her?

'Jeannie!' he shouted.

Her head turned in the direction of his voice and she hurried towards him. She tilted her head to take in the full height of him with Jack on his shoulders. 'You look so like the old photograph it's uncanny!' Her voice was low and husky. She held out a hand.

'You're like your mother.' He gripped her hand and gazed at her in wonder. She had a lovely face with smooth skin and a perfectly straight nose with nostrils that flared delicately. He found the reality of her being here amazing. Miraculous! He could only stare and try and take in that she was truly his daughter. He cleared his throat. 'I'm so pleased to see you, Jeannie.'

'I'm glad to be here.' Her eyes looked suspiciously damp and they continued to stare at each other.

Jack tweaked his father's hair. 'Now she's come can we go and see the engines?'

John took a deep breath. 'This is my son Jack, your half-brother. Say hello to your sister, Jack.'

'Only if we can go and see the engine,' said his son, wrapping his arms tightly about his neck.

'That's cheeky.' John slapped his leg lightly. 'We'll come back tomorrow and see the engines.'

'But you promised I could see them now,' protested Jack, rubbing his thigh.

'I did not.'

'You said later.'

'I meant tomorrow,' said John exasperated, thinking he could do without an argument with his son right now but Jack had such a strong will. 'Jeannie will be wanting a cup of tea.'

'Who wants a boring old cup of tea?' said Jack, and smiled down at the woman who couldn't possibly be his sister because she was far too old. She wore a plain velour-brimmed hat on her chestnut hair and was dressed in a shabby navy blue dress and jacket, which did not look anywhere near as good as that worn by his mother, but she was smiling up at him in a way that was somehow encouraging. 'Perhaps you like engines?' he said hopefully.

'As a matter of fact, I do.'

Jack bounced on his father's shoulders. 'There ye'are, Pops.'

John smiled at his daughter. 'You don't have to be polite. You can be honest and say you hate them.'

'I am being honest!' She strode alongside him lugging her suitcase. 'I like mechanical things and going fast.'

'You'd like Teddy's motorbike,' called down Jack. 'He helps make engines for cars and aeroplanes.'

Jeannie looked at John with a question in her eyes. 'Is Teddy one of your stepsons?'

'Aye. Beware of him, though. He's a bit of a daredevil, so don't be persuaded to get on that motorbike of his.' He softened his words with another smile and reached out a hand. 'Here, give me that suitcase.'

She handed it over. 'There are two others, aren't there?'

'Yes, Mick and Ben. Mick's twenty. Ben's twelve. Both nice lads. Kitty, my wife—' He hesitated.

'Yes?' She looked at him with an expression in her eyes that took him completely by surprise and gave him such a thrill that he forgot what he was going to say.

'You're like your great-grandmother,' he said instead. 'I mean my grandmother not Margaret's grandmother. Not so much in looks but that expression was pure Gran.'

Jeannie's expression was wistful. 'I'm sorry I never got to meet her but Great-Grandfather's still alive, isn't he?'

'I haven't heard anything different.'

'Maybe I – we could go and see him one day?'

'Maybe,' said John, making up his mind there and then that they would. 'But right now we'll have a quick look at the engine. That's if you don't mind?' he said.

'I said I didn't mind.' She enchanted him with her smile again. 'As long as you don't think your wife will mind us being a little late.'

'No, Kitty won't mind,' he lied, certain that his wife would be on pins waiting to see what Jeannie was like. He felt a moment's unease, wondering how Kitty would feel when he presented her with this beautiful stranger. She was after all the spitting image of his first wife and Kitty knew exactly how he had felt about her. For a moment he wished he had kept his mouth shut, but it was too late now.

'She's here and I reckon she's gonna be trouble,' wheezed Hannah, planting herself down on the bed and watching Kitty dithering over where to put the glass vase of daffodils. There was little space in the box room and the roof slanted almost to the floor on one side.

'Why should she be trouble?' said Kitty, setting the vase on a chair and sitting beside Hannah. She had been sorting out rooms and greeting people most of the day and would have liked nothing better than to put her feet up.

'She's got the looks of a Delilah and thou knows what happened to Samson,' said Hannah.

'She chopped his hair off.' Kitty yawned, wondering what the maid was on about.

'Aye, but it wasn't just that,' said Hannah with a grim smile. 'He was led into wicked ways and lost his strength.'

Kitty smiled wearily. It had been a mistake to sit down because it made her realise how tired she was. If it hadn't been for Hannah nattering on, she could have easily dozed off up here where it was quiet. She wished she didn't have to go downstairs and face John's daughter. Now the moment was almost here she felt on edge because Hannah made her sound like a femme fatale. She wondered what the boys would make of her. What had John made of her? Perhaps he needed rescuing?

'Thou needs to be on thy guard when thee comes face to face with evil,' said Hannah darkly. 'A beautiful woman can be a snare to a man.'

'You're getting carried away,' said Kitty, getting to her feet. 'You should know better than to go by outer appearances, Hannah. Come on, let's go down and hopefully I'll find out just how wrong you are.'

John and Jeannie were in the kitchen where he was making tea. 'There you are, Kit,' he said, to all outward appearances thoroughly calm and in command of the situation. 'Meet Jeannie. Jeannie, my wife.'

'How do you do?' said Kitty, stretching out a hand and thinking Hannah was right, *Here comes trouble. She is beautiful.*

'I'm very well, thank you.' Jeannie's voice was well modulated and her manner confident. 'It's kind of you to have me here.'

'Our pleasure.' Kitty's tone was polite. 'How long are you planning on staying?'

'She's only just arrived! Give her a chance,' rebuked John.

Kitty bit her lip and said in a smiling voice. 'Sorry, Jeannie. I didn't mean anything by it. I confess I'm nervous. It's not every day a husband's daughter turns up out of the blue. Your letter gave us quite a shock.'

'I'm sorry. Finding out about my father was a shock to me, too.' She glanced up at him and smiled.

The look that John gave her caused Kitty a different kind of shock. 'I'm sure it must have been,' said Kitty abruptly. 'Do sit down. You do have proof of who you are, don't you?'

Immediately they both looked at her and the girl sat on a chair as if her legs could no longer support her. Her right foot twisted round one of the front legs of the chair as if to anchor her there. *Not so confident*, thought Kitty, feeling relieved.

'What do you mean?' said John.

'What I said!' Kitty returned his stare. 'How do we know she's telling the truth, John? Has she proof?'

John looked at her dumbly.

'Don't look at me like that, love,' she said, deliberately keeping her voice low. 'You're too trusting. We don't know this girl from Adam. She just writes claiming to be your daughter and you believe her without questions.'

'She's the spitting image of Margaret. I know she's my daughter,' said John, looking at her bewildered and gripping Jeannie's shoulder.

For a moment Kitty could not think what to say because his words had taken her breath away. Any jealousy she might have felt for his first wife had been short-lived. She was dead and gone but if this girl was so like her she was going to be a constant reminder to John of that tragic first wife, and what would that mean to their lives?

'I have proof,' said Jeannie, whose cheeks had paled. She reached for her handbag and from its depths took out an envelope and handed it to John. 'Your wife's right. You should have asked for identification. I have a cousin who's very like me.'

Clever! She's agreeing with me, thought Kitty, surprised into admiration. She watched John take out the contents of the envelope. He looked at them before silently handing them over to Kitty. There was a wedding photograph and a birth certificate, both of which were proof enough even for Kitty. She accepted the inevitable. 'Welcome to the family,' she said, handing the envelope back to Jeannie and standing up. 'I'll show you to your room. You'll be wanting to freshen up before meeting anyone else.'

'Thanks,' said Jeannie, looking at her father who nodded. She rose and they followed Kitty out of the kitchen.

'It's not very big,' said Kitty, leaning against the chest of drawers and letting her gaze wander round the room to take in the single bed, chair, washstand and Jack's dismantled cot. 'Sorry about the cot but it comes in handy when the odd guest brings a baby.'

'It's fine.' Jeannie placed the suitcase John had carried upstairs on the bed. He'd had to leave them and see to some luggage that needed collecting. 'It's not much smaller than the one I had at Aunt Emily's.'

'If you're still here next week I'll be able to give you a bigger room, only space is at a premium this week. Your father explained, did he?'

'About the horse racing? Yes. He said you were very busy. If there's anything I can do to help just let me know. I'm good about the house.' Her hazel eyes met Kitty's squarely.

The offer was unexpected and Kitty was unsure how to respond. Did the girl mean it or was she just being polite? 'I'll bear it in mind,' she said, adding, 'What did you do in Brighton? John never said whether you worked or just looked after his sister.'

'I did both. Aunt Emily lived on what her husband had left her, which had depreciated. She'd also made some bad investments which meant I had to earn my own living.'

'And how did you do that?'

'I worked in an hotel.' She smiled. 'Quite a coincidence, isn't it?'

Kitty could scarcely believe it. 'Does your father know?'

'He didn't ask. I suppose he didn't think about it.'

'I suppose with your looks and manner you were a receptionist?'

'That's right. Aunt Emily got me the job. The proprietor was a friend of hers and she wanted someone keeping their eye on me.'

'Why?' said Kitty bluntly.

'My looks.' Her mouth twisted. 'First Granny and then Aunt Emily worried about someone running off with me. It drove me crazy. You can understand why I wanted to meet my father once I knew who he was. He'd done it hadn't he? He'd managed to escape them both and live a free life.'

Kitty stared at her, puzzled. 'But not for the reason you're getting at. They didn't want him. It seems to me both your granny and aunt cared about you.'

'Oh, they did! I'm not complaining about that. It could be overpowering, though. They were overprotective and demanding at the same time. If I'd known my father was alive earlier I would have left. Perhaps that's what they were scared of?'

'Perhaps,' said Kitty, uncertain what to make of Jeannie. She seemed so sure of herself. Yet could any girl be that confident at twenty?

'I really wanted to meet him,' said Jeannie, almost to herself. 'You can't imagine what it's like never having known either of your parents and then suddenly discovering one of them's alive. I had this wonderful feeling of being found. I wasn't alone anymore! Up north I had a father!' She sank onto the bed and her eyes met Kitty's. 'I don't expect you to understand and I do realise that you mightn't want me here.'

Kitty moved away from the chest of drawers, placed the vase of daffodils on the floor and sat on the chair. 'I don't want trouble.'

'And you think I'll cause trouble?' A laugh fell from Jeannie's lips and she kicked off her shoes. 'It's the last thing I have in mind!'

'I'm sure it is but that doesn't say it won't happen. You're a lovely looking girl.'

Unexpectedly Jeannie's face showed strain. 'I've known a lot of women not like me but Gran always said beauty was only skin deep.' She curled her feet under her on the bed.

'Skin deep or not it's what attracts the men,' said Kitty, leaning forward. 'I'd feel happier if you were married. I'll admit to being surprised nobody has snapped you up.'

A mischievous expression flitted across Jeannie's face.

'I've had eleven proposals of marriage but I turned them all down.'

'Why?' Kitty was truly interested.

'Most were in love with my face. A couple made the effort to try and get to know me but neither of them matched up to the picture of the man in my head.'

'Your dead father,' said Kitty.

Jeannie stared at her. 'How did you know?'

'My own father died at sea when I was seven. I never knew him well enough for the picture I had of him to get spoilt. He was blond and strong with far-seeing blue eyes, and he lived what I thought was a life of adventure.' She paused. 'You see now why I think you could cause trouble. I know what it is to dream.' She stood up. 'I'll leave you to have a rest. We don't eat until eight-thirty, after the guests have had their meal. Your father and I will be busy until then. The family rooms are up here and down in the basement. Make yourself comfortable downstairs if you want. I'll see you later.'

She was at the door when Jeannie said, 'You're very honest. But thanks for welcoming me into the family. Believe it or not, it's what I've been looking for all my life. I don't want to cause trouble.'

'Don't do it then,' said Kitty, smiling at her before closing the door.

As she went downstairs she was remembering how during the Depression steamers had advertised a pound a day cruises to Norway. She remembered dreaming for days of sailing away to meet her father's side of the family. It had been out of the question, of course, and so remained only a dream. Part of her admired Jeannie for seeking out her father but another part of her was on her guard.

She squared her shoulders and decided she had coped with Jeannie the best she could in the circumstances. John might not think so but then he was a man. She and Jeannie were going to have to work things out differently between them. As for the boys' reaction to her, that was still something that had to be faced and Kitty prepared herself to watch her two elder sons be smitten.

Chapter Twenty-Three

Teddy entered the kitchen having arrived home astride the love of his life, a second-hand ex-TT 250cc Rudge motorbike which he had parked in the yard. He had grown in the last few years but was still shorter than he would have liked. To compensate for his lack of inches and to make himself look older, he was growing a moustache. 'Did she turn up?' He glanced at his mother who stood by the table making dumplings as if in a dream.

'Yes,' said Kitty, stirring herself to take a couple of large casseroles out of the oven.

'What's she like? How old is she?'

'Twenty. And you have to be nice to her – as is only right for someone who's John's daughter.'

Teddy blinked. 'You're joking!'

'Do I look like I'm joking?'

He stared at her and thought he had not seen her looking so stony-serious since she'd had Jack. 'You mean the big fella's really got a daughter?'

'How many times do I have to say it?'

'But how?' he demanded. 'I mean – I thought he only had one daughter and she died when she was a baby.'

'That's the one. Get her to tell you the story. It's quite

moving. Her grandmother told her that John was dead.'

'It sounds unbelievable.'

'It's true.' She sighed.

'What's up, Ma?' He went over to her and put an arm round her shoulders. 'Is she that bad?'

'Bad? No, I'm sure she isn't.' She looked into his face and thought how Irish-looking he was with his dark hair and sensitive face. What would he make of the girl and what would she think of him? Kitty had had first place in her boys' affections for so long that it caused her pain knowing that one day she would lose that position. For a moment she allowed her cheek to rest against his shoulder. 'It takes some accepting,' she said. 'It's knocked me for six.'

'How did the big fella take it?'

'He's over the moon. To be expected, I suppose.' She straightened and another sigh escaped her as she moved away from him.

Teddy toyed with his fledgling moustache and said thoughtfully, 'This makes you a stepmother like in Cinderella.'

Kitty pulled a face. 'I'm glad you missed out the word *wicked*.'

He grinned. 'It's a good job we're not girls.' He struck a pose. 'Sorry, Cinders, but you cannot go to the ball tonight. You've got our socks to darn and the kitchen floor to scrub.'

'I don't darn socks,' said a female voice unfamiliar to his ears.

Teddy turned with his hands in his pockets and froze as

Jeannie's heels tip-tapped on the tiled floor towards him. 'I'm Jeannie McLeod. Which one are you?'

'Teddy Ryan.' He took the hand she offered and gripped it like a drowning man would a lifebelt, terribly conscious that in high heels she was at least four inches taller than him. 'Er, welcome – to Liverpool. I hope you enjoy your stay.'

'Thanks. You're the one with the motorbike.'

'Er, yes. Who told you?' He glanced at his mother but she was putting the casseroles back in the oven.

'Jack. Our half-brother.' Jeannie's smile was warm. 'He said you make engines.'

Teddy took a deep breath and tried to relax muscles which seemed to have gone into a coma. 'Engine parts.'

'You like your work?' She sat on a spindle-backed chair.

That's better, thought Teddy, leaning against the table and looking down into eyes which caused sensations similar to those issued by the shock machine at a funfair. 'Love it. D-do you work?'

'Would you believe, in an hotel?'

Teddy glanced at his mother. 'Did you know that, Ma? It's perfect, isn't it? She'll be able to help you.'

'I didn't say I was staying,' said Jeannie, frowning. 'Although, I read up on Liverpool in the library before I came. It's had strong trading links with America for years in tobacco and cotton and—'

'Don't mention slaves,' said a loud voice behind her. 'They're well gone and they never were that important to the economy of the port. It was cotton that was king. Still is important and so's tobacco and a helluva lot of other commodities.'

Teddy could have hit his elder brother who was standing in the doorway. Mick was tall, dark, good-looking and oozed confidence. 'Hello. You must be Jeannie,' he said as he strolled towards her. Following on his heels came Ben and Jack with Nelson.

'She's my sister,' said Jack, trotting to keep up. 'You didn't know that did you, Ben? Pops told me she's my sister.' He gave his brother a superior smile.

'Sister?' Mick stared at Jeannie.

'Half-sister.' It was Teddy who answered. 'She was the baby who died but it was all a lie.'

'How come?' asked Mick.

'The grandmother lied,' said Teddy.

'I've proof,' said Jeannie hastily.

Mick looked down at her as he held her hand and Teddy swore inwardly. What chance had he with his brother around?

John entered the kitchen. 'So you've all met,' he said.

'Only just.' With obvious reluctance Mick freed Jeannie's hand.

'I haven't introduced meself,' said Ben, poking Mick in the ribs with his elbow and looking up at Jeannie. He liked lovely things and she was one of the most beautiful women he had ever set eyes on.

Mick said, 'This is Ben, my bad-mannered brother. He can be trouble so watch him.'

Ben smiled at her like an angel. 'I've never had a sister before. Hiya!'

'You did have a sister,' said Kitty in sharp tones. 'She never breathed but she was your sister for all that.'

'I didn't know that,' piped up Jack. 'When did it happen?'

'Before you were born,' said Teddy, glancing at his mother and stabbing at a guess what was riding her. His gaze slid to John who was staring at Kitty.

'You can't expect the boys to remember her the same as you, Kit,' he said reasonably.

Kitty stiffened. She knew he was trying his best to comfort her but his words were no comfort at all. How could he understand how she felt about her dead little girl anymore? His daughter had come back to life. She eased some air past the constriction in her throat and said, 'I know that. Anyway, they can all get out my kitchen. I've work to do. Mick, Teddy, get changed. You'll be needed to wait on table soon.'

Both looked at her face and came to attention. 'Right, Ma!' They hurried out of the room.

Jack and Ben went after them. 'Stepsister,' hissed Ben. 'Can you believe it?'

Teddy still found it difficult. He did not know how a stepbrother was supposed to feel towards a stepsister but he definitely did not feel brotherly towards her. He seldom took an interest in girls, preferring his mates and his motorbike, but now his equilibrium was disturbed; his breathing was all peculiar and his body felt as if it might float away.

'What do you make of her?' he asked Mick as they went upstairs. Girls seemed to like his brother and he had taken out at least a dozen in the past two years.

'Gorgeous! But you won't be allowed near her.' Mick took the top two stairs in one stride and stood aside to let one of the guests past. His brothers squashed themselves against the wall and all said, 'Good evening.' After the guest had passed Teddy caught up with Mick.

'What d'you mean?' he demanded.

'The big fella,' said Mick. 'You don't think he's going to let you touch her. Probably try and keep her away from me, too, for that matter. You know what some fathers are like with their daughters.'

'Davy O'Neill says it's terrible having sisters,' said Ben, flicking back a hank of flaxen hair which had fallen into his eyes. 'Especially one like Sarah who won't do as he tells her and thinks she's as good as a boy.'

'You can't compare Jeannie with Sarah O'Neill,' said Mick, starting up the flight of stairs to the attics. 'She's not like an ordinary girl.'

'She's like that girl in the nursery rhyme. "When she's good, she's very, very good, and when she's bad, she's horrid." Siobhan's like the other one,' said Ben. '"Sugar and spice and all things nice."'

'Who bloody well cares about the O'Neills!' said Teddy, exasperated. 'How *are* we supposed to behave towards Jeannie?'

'Ma was funny before,' said Ben.

Teddy closed his eyes tightly and groaned. 'You're getting off the subject.'

'She's upset,' said Mick. 'Here's this beautiful girl come on the scene, who turns out to be the big fella's daughter. She's bound to be funny about it.'

'She wasn't laughing,' panted Jack, struggling to keep up with his big brothers.

'Funny peculiar, not ha-ha,' said Ben, hoisting him up the last step.

'She wasn't expecting a daughter,' said Teddy moodily.

'She's not her daughter,' said Ben.

'Exactly,' said Mick, turning the handle of their bedroom door. 'And that's what's upsetting her.'

There was a silence in the kitchen after the boys had gone and, needing to match her actions to her words, Kitty put on the saucepans of potatoes and carrots and turnips before going into the dining room where she found Hannah.

'She's upset thee.' The old woman peered at Kitty from beneath overgrown greying eyebrows. 'Give her the boot.'

'You've been listening at keyholes,' said Kitty, straightening a knife. 'And she didn't upset me. I upset myself. Where's Monica? There's no napkins on this table.'

'She's seeing to the fire in the Smoking Room. Plenty of them in there. All waiting for their dinnas.'

'They'll be fed. But be nice to them; I can't right now. I've got a terrible headache.' Kitty rubbed the area above her right eye.

'Miss Esther used to get terrible headaches at thy age.'

'My age!' Kitty frowned at her and winced. 'There's nothing wrong with my age. I'm active. I've got me health.'

'Thou's getting wrinkles.'

'I am not!' Kitty went over to the mirror above the sideboard and gazed at her reflection. Lord! She did have wrinkles! Only faint and not many but they were starting. She felt depressed and a nerve throbbed behind her eye. She tried to smile but it was too much of an effort. *Damn that girl*, she thought. *He's not going to be able to stop himself comparing her with me. Margaret has never grown old in his memory and now he has her daughter.* She closed her eyes a moment wishing she could get that thought out of her mind but it was impossible.

There were footsteps and her eyelids flicked open. Reflected in the mirror was Jeannie, looking nervously defiant. 'Father explained. I didn't know you had a daughter who died. I'm not trying to take her place,' she said.

'You haven't.' Kitty forced back her shoulders and ran a finger over her eyebrows. 'Just don't stand too close to me. You make me feel old.'

The eyes so like John's widened. 'You're not old! Jack's only four.'

There was a logic there somewhere and it made Kitty smile. 'That's twice you've said the right thing.'

Jeannie heaved a sigh of relief. 'I like your sons.'

'Three ticks in your favour now,' Kitty's voice was grave. 'Anything else you want to say?'

'I just want to get to know my father,' pleaded Jeannie.

'Natural in the circumstances but that does mean getting to know us, too,' said Kitty, turning to face her.

'I know that,' said Jeannie hastily. 'I want to know you and Teddy – and Mick – and Ben and Jack.'

Kitty nodded. 'Let's see how we go then. Where's John?' The word father still stuck in her throat.

'He's in the kitchen. He's put on the soup. Is there anything I can do to help?'

'Not this evening.' Kitty did not want to spend time thinking what job to give the girl. Unless? She stared at her. The dress was a bit shabby but who was going to notice with that face. 'You could go into the Smoking Room and mix with people. See if they want anything. Explain you're your father's daughter without going into details.'

Jeannie hesitated before agreeing and leaving the room.

'Thou was soft with her,' said Hannah, giving one of her sniffs.

Kitty ignored her and went to face her husband.

John was stirring the soup as if it was made of mortar and she could not read his expression. 'I've been as nice to her as I can,' she said bluntly. 'I've told her to go and mix with people. She could be an asset.'

'I suppose you were right not taking her word for it,' he said, not appearing to have heard her.

'I thought she'd bewitched you. She's so pretty. It makes me wonder why she's not married.'

'She's only young. But it worries me.' He placed the ladle on the table.

'Worries you? Why?' Kitty lowered the light under the vegetables.

'How long before there's a line of blokes queuing up at the door?' he said, frowning. 'She'll be gone in a flash before I've got to know her.'

Kitty had not thought of that. 'You really think so?'

'Well, you've just said it, haven't you? You thought she should be married. She probably isn't because she's under age and Emily kept a strict watch over her. I'll have to do the same.' He ran a hand over his hair. 'I should have gone and checked that grave.'

'The past is the past and you can't change it,' said Kitty

impatiently. 'I don't think she's going to rush off anywhere. She wants to get to know you and I'm sure as her father she'll respect what you have to say.'

'I hope so.'

'I'm sure so,' said Kitty, glancing at him and wishing he would not get himself worked up about a girl who was a stranger, whether she was his daughter or not. 'Why else is she here?' she added. 'She's missed having a father all her life and now she wants to make up for it. I don't blame her. At her age I would have jumped at having a father like you.'

He reddened and looked gratified. 'You're different about her now,' he said, sounding surprised.

'I've had a few minutes to think. I, at least, knew my father for a short while. I wish I'd known him longer.'

The muscles of his face relaxed and he reached out and pulled her into his arms. 'So you don't mind her staying?' His voice was muffled against her hair.

'It depends how long. She hasn't said it's for keeps.' Kitty relaxed against him. 'Let's wait and see, love. She seems a pleasant enough girl. Maybe she takes after her father.'

'Or her paternal grandmother,' he said, hugging her tightly. 'I feel like celebrating. Let's have a party.'

She pulled away from him. 'When?'

'We'll talk about it over supper. Now we'd better get down to work or the boys'll be here and we won't have anything ready.'

Teddy opened the gate-legged table in the basement and Mick, who had been standing ready with a linen tablecloth, spread it over the table top. Ben took a handful of cutlery from a drawer and proceeded to set places, whilst Jack in his pyjamas played with a couple of cars on the rug. Then Teddy and Mick left the room to appear again ten minutes later with trays of food.

Jeannie had watched their activities in silent wonder but now she spoke, 'Do you always do this, Teddy?'

'Normally,' he said, flushing to the tips of his ears. 'Ma's always been busy with the hotel so we've had to muck in. It's not that we're cissies.'

She nodded and a fall of her shiny chestnut hair brushed a cheek. 'I understand. It's a family business so you all have to help.'

'That's right,' said Mick, pulling out a chair and indicating she sit down. 'Ma would have liked us in it full time but Teddy and I had other ideas. That's why she went a bit potty at the mention of our dead sister. She thinks a girl would have stuck with the business, unlike us.'

'She's never said that,' said Teddy, dragging Jack up from the floor and seating him on a chair, whilst all the time keeping his eyes on Jeannie's face.

'No, but it makes sense. Running a hotel is like running an ordinary household except on a larger scale,' said Mick, seating himself next to Jeannie.

Teddy wished he had got there first but took a seat opposite his stepsister. 'You can start eating,' he said. 'When we're busy Ma and the big fella tell us to get on with it whilst it's hot.'

'There's no soup,' said Ben, picking up his knife and fork.

'That's because it all went.' Mick flashed Jeannie a smiling sidelong glance. 'That's something you'll have to get used to if you decide to stay. Guests come first and we have what's left over.'

She nodded. 'I can cope with that. This smells good.' She gazed across the table at Teddy. 'Is that what you call my father – the big fella?'

'Yeah! Dad kinda stuck in our throats.' His eyes met hers across the table. 'Me and Mick remember our dad, you see.'

'That would make a difference. I didn't know either of my parents.'

Ben said, 'I remember Dad. He wasn't a bit like Pops. What'll you call Ma?' His clear blue eyes fixed on Jeannie's face.

'I haven't thought about it. I'm only just getting used to the thought of having a father.'

'It's incredible,' said Mick.

'What d'you think of him?' said Ben, addressing Jeannie.

'You shouldn't ask that.' mumbled Teddy. 'She's only just met him. Eat your dinner.'

There was almost complete silence whilst they ate. When they had finished Mick said, 'I remember the first time I set eyes on the big fella. It was when you were hanging from that spike, Ted.'

'Shut up,' said Teddy, without looking up.

'What spike?' asked Jeannie, her eyes going from one to the other.

'A railing spike in Roscoe Gardens. He had it stuck up

his trouser leg and couldn't get down.' Mick grinned.

Teddy scowled. 'I was only a kid.'

'You were thirteen and nearly lost—'

'Shut up!' Teddy leaned across the table and rapped Mick across the knuckles with his fork.

'I wasn't going to tell her,' hissed Mick, pushing back his chair and getting to his feet. 'You want to learn—'

'What's going on?' asked John, entering the basement.

Immediately Mick sat down. 'Nothing,' he said.

'We were just going to get the pudding,' informed Teddy, reaching across the table and taking Jeannie's plate.

'That was good. Tell your mother it was good,' she said, smiling up at him.

Teddy flushed to his ears.

John frowned at him. 'Get upstairs with those dishes and help your mother with the puddings. There's something we want to talk to you about in a minute.'

'Something nice,' said Jack, sleepily.

'I'll tell you when your mother gets here.'

'A party!' exclaimed Teddy, and groaned. He didn't shine at parties.

'Aye! A party,' repeated John, smiling. 'But you don't have to be there if you don't want to. It's to celebrate Jeannie being here with us.'

'I didn't say I didn't want to be there,' said Teddy.

'No, he didn't,' said Kitty, cuddling Jack who was falling asleep. 'Stop jumping on him, John. The trouble is we're all too tired to think about a party. It's been a hectic day. Decide when we're going to have this party and then let's get to bed.'

'We'll have it next Saturday. Most of the guests will have gone by then and those that haven't can join in. We'll ask the O'Neills and Nancy and Malcolm, your Aunt Jane and her girls and some of the neighbours.'

'You don't have to do this for me,' said Jeannie abruptly, resting back in her chair and staring at her father.

'Why not?' he said. 'I want to show you off.'

'It'll be fun,' said Mick, his eyes gleaming. 'We haven't had a party since – I can't remember last.'

'Since before Jack was born,' said Teddy. 'But perhaps Jeannie doesn't like the idea. She mightn't be a party person.'

Jeannie shrugged her slender shoulders. 'I don't mind parties but I don't want to be on show.'

'It doesn't matter what you want,' said Kitty kindly. 'You're bound to be even if you were ugly as sin, because you're a new face. But we'll give it for the Galloways as well, because they're leaving for Canada.'

'Why?' asked Ben.

'It doesn't matter why,' said Kitty, not wanting to talk about the possibility of there being a war. 'And at least one good thing will come from it. Celia's coming back to work for me.'

'Who's Celia?' asked Jeannie.

'An old flame of Mick's,' said Teddy, grinning at his elder brother.

'Never mind Celia,' said John crossly. 'I'd been hoping to persuade Malcolm to go fishing in Scotland this summer and to take Jack and Jeannie with me.'

'Well, that's off,' said Kitty promptly. 'But as for the party – it's definitely on?'

'Definitely,' said John firmly.

So it was settled. There was going to be a party.

Chapter Twenty-Four

The hotel was quiet after a hectic week and Kitty was in the Smoking Room with Ben and Jack attempting to make the place look festive on John's orders. He had gone off with Jeannie, determined to reward her for helping out during the past few days. She had willingly acted as general dogsbody by answering the telephone and taking a turn in reception, as well as carrying trays up to bedrooms and being a listening ear to some of the elderly guests. Mick had said he admired her patience with them. To which she had replied she'd had plenty of practice, having being brought up by her grandmother before living with an elderly aunt for four years.

Her actions had convinced John that here was the daughter that Kitty had been looking for and he had said so to her in bed that morning. She had retorted that it was early days and not to count his chickens.

'Don't you put her off staying,' John had warned. 'She's an asset to the place.'

'I've said that myself,' murmured Kitty. 'But we've only known her a week and it takes much longer than that to know if someone's going to fit in.' It was not true, of course. Kitty was used to making snap judgements in her line of business but she was not ready to be rushed into taking Jeannie into her heart.

'Ma, where should I hang these?' said Ben, holding up several inflated balloons.

Kitty blinked at him from her perch on the stepladder. 'I'll find somewhere in a minute. We'll need more than them, though.'

'I'll blow some up,' said Jack, dropping the Christmas garland she was pinning up and reaching for a balloon.

'You're a pest!' Kitty's tone was exasperated as she watched the garland detach itself from the wall.

'We need more help,' said Ben.

As if on cue there came a knock on the door. 'Come in,' said Kitty, hoping that Mick or Teddy had managed to get home early but it was neither of her sons. It was Celia.

'Mrs McLeod, Hannah wants to know if you want the ham out the oven?' she said, poking her head round the door.

'I should think so.' She smiled at the girl whom Nancy had lent her for the day. 'How have you been, love? You look a bit peaky.'

'I'm OK,' said Celia. Her freckles seemed to stand out in her pale face as she leaned against the doorjamb. 'Just don't get enough sleep that's all. Cough, cough! That's Ma all the time. I've told her to see a doctor but she won't. Stubborn, that's what she is.'

'It's probably the weather.'

Celia shrugged. 'It doesn't help, but she's smoking like a chimney. I tell her she'll smoke herself to death but she won't listen.' She made to go but Kitty called her back. 'Come and help me with these decorations. Mick and

Teddy could have done them better but by the time they're home it'll be too late.'

'I thought you might have had Miss McLeod helping you,' said Celia, picking up the end of a garland.

There was an inflection in her voice which caused Kitty to give her a second glance. 'Jeannie's gone shopping with her father. They haven't had much time on their own since her arrival.'

'It was a real turn up for the book, wasn't it?' marvelled Celia. 'I mean one minute you all thought she was dead. The next minute she's here. Wouldn't it be lovely if people really did come alive again?'

'It could cause problems,' said Kitty, mounting the stepladder. 'Especially if you'd picked up the insurance or you'd remarried.' Her eyes twinkled down at Celia. 'They say in heaven there's no marriage or giving in marriage.' Kitty drove home a drawing pin and descended the ladder. 'Did Mrs Galloway mention about coming to work for me permanent, Celia?'

'She did. But . . .' The girl hesitated before adding, 'I wasn't sure if you'd still want me with the big fella's daughter working here.'

'She mightn't stay,' said Kittly lightly. 'And even if she did I'd have room for you. You're a good worker.'

Celia flushed. 'Thanks, Mrs McLeod. I really appreciate you saying that.'

'It's true. Here grab the end of this, then I suppose you'd better go and tell Hannah to take that meat out. And, Celia, I expect you to be at the party tonight. Come and enjoy yourself. You're only young once.'

'I'd like that,' said Celia, visibly relaxing. 'I don't get a chance to get out much with Ma.'

'I haven't got a thing to wear,' said Kitty as she opened the wardrobe door clad only in her underwear.

'I don't believe that for one minute,' said John, knotting his tie. 'You bought a new frock for Christmas. Can't you wear that?'

'I suppose so.' Kitty sighed, thinking not so long ago he would not have bothered with his tie but would have taken time out for a bit of loving at such a moment. Did it have anything to do with him comparing her to Jeannie? She removed the Christmas frock from the wardrobe and held it against her. It was damson-coloured taffeta and the swirling skirts had panels of lace.

'I bought Jeannie a couple of frocks,' said John, glancing her way. 'I thought she needed them. She should look smart if she's going to be working here.'

'If,' murmured Kitty, not looking at him.

John's expression darkened and he came over to her. 'What's that supposed to mean?'

She looked at him squarely. '*If* she's going to be working here. She hasn't said she's definitely staying to me.'

'Have you asked her?'

'I don't see it as my place to ask her,' said Kitty, slipping the frock over her head. 'I thought that would be up to you.'

'Wrong! And you know it,' said John. 'Why are you being so awkward if you agree she's an asset to the place?'

Kitty was silent. If he couldn't see why then she wasn't going to explain.

'Is it that you're jealous because of the attention I've been giving her?' He rested his hands on her shoulders and stroked her neck with the balls of his thumbs.

Her head shot up. 'Jealous! Me! Of course not! It's just that I don't want you pressurising the girl into doing something she mightn't want to.'

'You tried to pressurise the boys into working here.'

'And you told me I was wrong!'

'That was because their hearts weren't in it. It's different with Jeannie. She likes it here *and* she's a girl, which means you could teach her all you know. You'd be good at that, Kit.' He kissed the nape of her neck.

She relaxed against him. 'You're trying to soft-soap me.'

'What if I am? It's important to me that you accept her. After all, I've tried to be a father to your sons. You should make an effort to be a mother to my daughter.'

'I wondered when you'd say something like that,' murmured Kitty, and the confusion she felt when thinking about her sons and his daughter caused her to move away from him to stare at her reflection in the mirror. 'Jeannie's twenty, John. She doesn't need a mother.'

'How do you know?' He followed her over. 'I bet there's times when you miss your mother and you're over forty.'

Her eyes met his in the mirror. 'Jeannie's never had a mother to miss.'

'She needs an older woman's guidance.'

'I'm not so sure.' She frowned as she tweaked one of the lace sleeves so its folds fell better. 'From what she said to me she was fed up of older women telling her what to do. I reckon it's more likely she wants the company of young people.' She paused, thinking of Mick taking Jeannie to see Errol Flynn on Monday night. She'd known he was besotted despite his casual attitude towards the girl. 'Besides it was different with you and the boys.'

'In what way?' demanded John.

Kitty gnawed on the inside of her cheek and then burst out.

'The boys were younger when you came to live here. It was different. They knew what having a father was. I don't know what Jeannie expects of me.'

'Don't worry about what she expects. Think of what I expect! Make her feel wanted and at home. Behave as you do towards the boys.'

A small laugh escaped her. 'That's the trouble – I can't! I've known them all my life! They're part of me!'

His mouth tightened and she knew she had hurt him. 'And Jeannie's part of me, so you'd better try and make her feel wanted or there'll be trouble,' he said roughly.

She turned and stared at him, unable to believe that he should threaten her. Despite his size, he had never bullied or belittled her. 'I mean that,' he said, shrugging on his jacket and taking up his violin case before leaving the room.

Kitty sank onto the bed knowing that she had tried to do what John said, up to a point. The difficulty was that she was certain that the last thing Jeannie wanted was her bossing and loving her as she did them. Did John behave exactly the same towards the elder three as he did to Jack? No. Still she supposed she could try and behave like a mother – but not until after the party.

*

'She really is lovely looking,' murmured Becky, accepting a glass of sherry from Kitty.

The room was filling up and there was a babble of noise and the tinkle of glasses and laughter – some of it coming from the centre of the room were John stood with Jeannie, Malcolm and the young doctor who was taking over his practice. Sarah and Davy O'Neill's gathering was noisy too, and included Ben, Monica and Mick whose eyes constantly strayed to that other group.

'Lovely,' said Kitty, her eyes on her stepdaughter. 'But she assures me that her granny told her that beauty is only skin deep.'

Becky made a gurgling noise in her throat. 'Are you saying she isn't as lovely as she looks or something different?'

'I'm not sure what I was trying to say.' She sighed. 'She's the spitting image of her mother.'

'That can't be easy to live with,' said Becky.

Kitty grimaced. 'She told me that a lot of women don't like her and I can see why. Mick's already besotted.'

'What about Teddy?'

Kitty glanced round for a sign of her second son but could not see him. 'I'm not so sure. He hasn't asked her out anywhere. Doesn't make a fuss of her.'

'That mightn't mean anything,' said Becky, her eyes wandering the room. 'He mightn't want to show his feelings but he'd have to be blind not to feel something. I mean her turning up the way she did is like something out of a novel.'

Kitty smiled. 'You're right. I never looked at it like that.'

'I think Davy's feeling the attraction, too,' said Becky thoughtfully. 'But of course he's far too young for her and it won't do him any harm just to look.'

'Do you think age has anything to do with it?' said Kitty. 'Ben's offered to polish her shoes along with the guests' and told her at least three times how he sang along with John when he was a busker.'

'And was she impressed?'

'She said she wished she'd been there to see it.'

'So she's not ashamed of that part of his life?' said Becky.

'She doesn't appear to be. I'll give her that.' Kitty saw a couple of her neighbours enter the room and excused herself. She introduced them around before going into the dining room where a buffet had been laid out. She found Celia and Hannah there and scolded the girl for hiding herself away and told her to join the party.

'I feel a bit out of place,' said Celia, running her hands down over pleated skirts and looking anxious. 'Besides I've got used to being on this side of things.'

'If you meant that you wouldn't be wearing that frock,' said Kitty frankly. 'You look really nice in it.' The frock was blue and was buttoned from the neck to the waist, showing just what a shapely figure Celia had. She had done something with her hair too, and her freckles were not so prominent because she had given them a dusting of face powder. She looked very different to how she had appeared earlier in the day.

Celia flushed with pleasure. 'I bought it in the January

sales with my Christmas box off the doctor, but I haven't had much chance to wear it.'

'Now you have, so don't waste your chances,' said Kitty, taking her arm. 'You can come in with me in case you're feeling shy.'

Once in the Smoking Room Kitty took Celia around and introduced her as John's goddaughter. She could sense her blossoming and felt pride in that. Groupings had changed. Mick was now in one which included Jeannie, and Teddy had made an appearance and was with Becky who was talking cars. The Irish great-uncles were telling Ben and Sarah how their horse had been beaten into second place by one owned by the wife of film star Randolph Scott. Kitty slid Celia into the group with Mick before going to where John and Daniel were idly talking and within watching distance of Siobhan and Jack.

Daniel looked up as she approached. 'You're looking a fair treat, Kit darlin'!' he said.

She gave him a quizzical look. 'Ta! I was feeling a hag among all these fresh young faces.'

'Never that,' he said. 'I like a mature woman.'

John eyed his wife. 'She's fishing for compliments.'

'Of course I am,' said Kitty, sotto voce, glancing at her husband. 'Jeannie seems to be a hit.'

'Aye,' he said simply. 'You're not jealous?' His eyes mocked her.

'Is there any reason why I should be jealous?' she murmured.

'No, but women can be funny.'

'Only women?' she retorted, instantly vexed with him.

'What is this?' said Daniel, his gaze going from wife to husband. 'Kitty has no need to be jealous. She's as gorgeous as a Wicklow morning with the mist just off the ground.'

Kitty gave Daniel her full attention. 'What have you been drinking?'

'Pure velvet,' he said, saluting her with a glass of Guinness. 'It helps me to put my worries aside for a moment.'

'Worries? What worries?' She was concerned. The O'Neills were good friends and she hated the thought of anything going wrong in their lives.

He smiled. 'Nothing for you to worry your head about. This is a celebration, isn't it? So let's be happy.' He clinked glasses with her and they drank to each other.

'Food in half an hour then some music?' she said turning to John.

He nodded and she left them to circulate among her guests.

It was not until the dancing that Kitty had a chance to see Mick with Jeannie at close quarters. They were dancing to *Honeysuckle Rose* and she felt a swell of pride considering what a nice mover he was. He had been taking dancing lessons and it showed.

'They make a nice couple but she's not as good a dancer as he is,' said Daniel, who always asked Kitty for at least one dance when John was playing.

'Poor Celia,' she murmured, aware that she was not the only one watching them. 'I think she could still be carrying a torch for him.'

'John said she's coming to work for you again.'

'Yes.' Kitty glanced around, hoping to see Teddy so she could tell him to ask Celia to dance, but there was no sign of him.

'D'you think that's wise?' asked Daniel. 'If she's still hankering after Mick she could get hurt.'

'She could,' said Kitty calmly. 'But then it could be that Mick might get hurt and she's ready at hand to console him.'

Daniel shook his dark head at her. 'I never realised you were so devious.'

'Me! I'm sure I'm not. But don't you think that nice young doctor would be ideal for Jeannie? And he'll be living so close too.'

'Devious,' he repeated firmly, his arm tightening about her.

'They could all be happy,' she said, and smiled up at him.

He returned her smile and pulled her close as they danced on to the strains of her husband's violin with the familiarity of people who were comfortable with each other.

Teddy had been watching his brother and Jeannie so he noticed when she left the room and followed her out. He found her sitting on the stairs fanning herself with her hand. 'Would you like to dance?' he said.

She looked up at him. 'I'm having a break. And besides you're only being polite in asking me,' she said with a sigh.

He looked relieved. 'You're right. I can't dance,' He rested a shoulder against a wall and gazed down at her, searching for something to keep her attention. 'Our Mick's good isn't he?'

She nodded. 'Too good for me.'

'That doctor bloke's good too.'

'Not as good as Mick.'

'You like our Mick.'

'Who wouldn't? He's nice and he's friendly.' She hugged a knee and Teddy could not help noticing a couple of inches of shining silk-encased thigh as her skirts fell back.

He glanced away and said morosely, 'You're thinking he's nicer than me.'

'No. I'm asking myself why you've asked me to dance if you can't dance.'

'It seemed the only thing to do to get close to you,' he said gruffly, tapping the bottom stair with his toe. 'I'd much rather take you for a spin on my motorbike.'

She smiled up at him. 'I've been warned against going on your motorbike.'

He sighed heavily. 'By the big fella, I suppose. So you won't come?'

She stood and gazed down at him. 'I don't always heed warnings.'

He could scarcely believe what he had heard and it took him a second to digest that she really meant it. 'It's a lovely night. All starry.'

She smiled and looked at him in a way that sent tiny tremors of shock through him. 'Show me.'

He did not waste any more time. 'You'll need a coat.'

'I'll get one.'

'Come out by the front door and I'll meet you up the road. And hurry!' He released her hand and headed for the kitchen, trusting her to do as he asked.

Jeannie raced upstairs feeling marvellously excited as she fastened her coat and pulled on a hat and gloves. Her week had been a bit dull. Too much like life with Granny and Aunt Emily and working at the hotel in Brighton, fetch and carry, be nice to people. Not that she wanted to be horrible to people but she wanted something different.

She nearly walked into her father as she reached the bottom flight of stairs but stepped back noiselessly onto the first landing and waited until he went back inside the dining room. Then she skipped downstairs and outside. When she saw the motorbike she almost changed her mind. It had no pillion seat, only a cushion strapped to the back mudguard.

'Is it safe?' she asked.

Teddy grinned. 'If you want safe, kid, walk. This bike's for thrills and going places. Are you getting on?'

Jeannie felt her spirits soar. He seemed different, more confident somehow, and that made her feel that she had done the right thing in agreeing to go with him. He looked the part in a long fawn gabardine coat and a woollen scarf and gloves as well as a close-fitting leather helmet. She glanced down at her stockings and shoes and remembered she had on her new frock. *Don't let me come a cropper, God*, she thought, hitching up her skirts and sitting on the cushion.

'Get a grip,' said Teddy.

She gripped the cushion as he kick-started life into the

engine. But the next moment the bike seemed to slide from beneath her and she was on the ground. He slowed down, glancing over his shoulder. 'Sorry. But you should have held on.'

'I did hold on,' she said indignantly, getting to her feet and rubbing her posterior.

'Do you want to try again?'

'Yes! But how do I stay on?'

'Grip with your knees and move with the bike.'

That did not sound too hard, she thought, and climbed back on. This time they got as far as Hope Street before she fell off. He parked the bike and ran back to her. 'I think I'd better give up,' she groaned.

'No, don't do that,' he pleaded, helping her up. 'Once you get the hang of it you'll be OK.' He smiled at her as he brushed the back of her coat. 'What you have to do is become part of the bike and when we turn a corner go with it. I'll take you the rest of the way along Hope Street, past the old cemetery and then come back. It's nice and straight. Another time I'll take you down to the river but that might be a bit too much this evening. Are you game?' His eyes challenged her.

She nodded, thinking the river bit sounded exciting. This time they had no mishaps and she felt a definite regret when they arrived back at the hotel and it was over.

By unspoken agreement she went in the front way and he went round the back. She put away her coat and brushed her hair and went downstairs. Immediately Mick claimed her for a dance and when Teddy arrived in the room she knew he was not pleased. He stood, leaning against a wall glowering at them for a few minutes before going out again.

Sunday morning and Teddy was in the yard tinkering with his motorbike when he heard the *tap tap* of heels and glancing up saw Jeannie dressed for outdoors.

'Something wrong with your motorbike?' she said.

'Er – yeah. Nothing much but . . .' He stared at her shapely ankles. 'Where are you off to?'

'To chapel. Your mother said none of you go regularly but I wondered if—'

'Sorry.' He smiled and held up oily hands.

'I suppose you haven't got time to get cleaned up?' she said regretfully.

'Nope.' He had no intention of changing the habits of a lifetime however much he fancied her.

'I'll see you later then.'

He stared up at her and the chestnut curls beneath the shabby hat undulated in waves. He had an urge to catch a handful of that shining curtain and pull her head down and kiss her. Instead he fumbled for a spanner and did not even say ta-ra.

A couple of hours later, singing heralded Jeannie's return as she came down the yard. 'You still busy? Your mother said to wash your hands. Dinner's ready.'

'Fine. How was church?' He did not look up. He had told himself he had no chance against his tall, dark and handsome brother.

'I like a good sing – and the preaching was powerful,' she said dreamily. 'Gran heard the great Sankey in London once and set great store by preachers who give the gospel all they've got. I was told they get some good ones at the Central Hall.'

He glanced up involuntarily. 'You went there? You're a Methodist?'

She smiled. 'You make it sound like a deadly disease. Don't you know anything about John Wesley our founder? He converted thousands and had a real exciting life riding about on horseback all round the country telling people about the Lord and upsetting the Church of England.'

Oh Lord! thought Teddy, his ears going red with embarrassment. He had never thought about her being holy. In fact he had started to believe the opposite. 'I suppose they did that kind of thing in those days,' he muttered, wiping his hands on a piece of rag.

'Obviously,' she said, still smiling as she prodded one of the bike's tyres with the toe of her shoe. 'Have you fixed it? It would be nice to go for a spin.'

'Not quite.' He still had not forgiven her for dancing with Mick as soon as she got back from being out with him.

'So you won't be going for a spin later?'

'Probably not.' Determinedly he cut his nose off to spite his face.

'Right.' Her smile had vanished and she turned away. 'I'll tell your mother, shall I, that you'll be in in a minute?'

'Fine.' He watched her go up the yard, her skirts swaying with the swing of her hips, and threw down the rag and swore.

When Teddy went inside he found Jeannie sitting next

to Mick at the dining table deep in conversation and he felt real sick about it. 'How's Celia?' he asked as he sat opposite them.

Mick looked up in surprise. 'OK, last time I saw her. Why, did you want her for something?'

'You used to walk her home that's all.' Teddy fiddled with his knife and fork. 'I wondered whether you did last night.'

'It was years ago when I walked her home,' said Mick, scowling at him. 'When we were kids.'

'She'd still like you to walk her home, though.'

'Well, that's hard luck on her,' said Mick. 'Now shut up, I'm talking to Jean.'

'I don't want to shut up,' said Teddy, resting on his elbows. 'Beside Jeannie mightn't want to listen to the way you go on and on about every subject under the sun.'

'Don't be rude,' said Kitty as she placed plates in front of them. 'And get your elbows off the table, Teddy. I don't know what Jeannie must be thinking of your manners, but I'm forgetting she's part of the family now. And you can keep your eye on Jack.'

'Why me?' protested Teddy.

'Because you're the nearest.'

Mick grinned and Teddy wanted to clock him one. 'But I wanted to have a serious conversation with Jeannie,' protested Teddy, smiling across at her.

'About what?' asked Kitty.

'About the Lord,' he said with all the reverence he generally kept for the worship of the combustion engine.

He succeeded in silencing them all for a moment. Then

Mick said, 'You're taking the micky!'

'No, I'm not,' said Teddy seriously. 'Jeannie made religion sound – different. I thought that maybe we could have a talk after dinner.'

'Sorry,' said Jeannie, her gaze sliding slowly over his face. 'But I've promised Mick I'll go for a walk with him and I can't break a promise.'

'Perhaps,' said John, looking at Teddy across the table, 'if you're so keen on religion you can go to church with the pair of us next week and see how interesting it is at first hand.'

Teddy did not know what to say. He gazed at Jeannie with his heart in his eyes and she gazed back at him. He almost promised he would go until he remembered she was going walking with Mick, so he kept his mouth shut. Why turn religious when it was obvious she was a two-timer.

Teddy left the table as soon as it was polite and tinkered some more with his motorbike. He felt restless and all mixed up. He waited until Jeannie had gone out with Mick before trundling out his motorbike and heading for the Mersey tunnel.

He went to Eastham where he stopped to enjoy a cigarette and gaze over the Mersey towards Liverpool. To his right were the Eastham Locks and the entrance to the Manchester Ship Canal. The tide was out and several feet below him was thick mud. He watched the ships, thinking about Jeannie and how, if he'd had less pride and more sense, he could have been walking in the woods with her right now. He determined that as soon as he could he would ask her out. If she refused at least he would know where he stood.

Teddy managed to catch Jeannie alone on her way to bed. 'I've fixed the bike,' he said. 'D'you want to come for a ride tomorrow evening?'

Eyes the same colour as the big fella's smiled into his. 'Can you guarantee I won't come off this time?'

'No. But I can guarantee you something more exciting than a walk,' he said boldly. 'But you'd best make sure you wrap up. We'll go further this time.'

'OK.' Her mouth turned up in that smile which sort of twisted his heart. 'It'll have to be after the evening meal, though,' she said. 'Your mother's told me I've got to help her if I'm stopping on a bit.'

He grinned. 'Right. We'll meet at the same place.'

They gazed at each other, both lost in a magic moment, and then she went into her bedroom and closed the door.

Teddy grinned when he saw Jeannie the following evening. She was muffled up as if she was going to the Antarctic. Her eyes reflected his amusement. 'I'm making sure that if I come off it won't hurt so much.'

'Don't think of coming off,' he said, wheeling the motorbike through the back gateway. 'Just think of yourself as part of the bike.' She mounted and he kicked the starter and they were off.

Jeannie managed to stay on until Teddy had to swerve to avoid a dog and hit the kerb. He almost lost control, only managing to prevent the motorbike from toppling over by skidding along with one knee on the ground. The next moment Jeannie was there helping him get the motorbike upright. 'Are you all right?' she asked anxiously.

'Are you?'

She nodded. They smiled at each other and he knew he was hopelessly hooked for better or for worse.

He took her along Hope Street, past the cathedral, and shouted at her to hang on tight. He heard her quick intake of breath as they plunged down Parliament Street and his own excitement rose as he felt her body press against his back. Her chin rested on his shoulder as they roared towards the Mersey which glistened shiny black as newly-hewn coal below them. It was exhilarating and when she whispered against his ear, 'It's beautiful,' his cup of pleasure was full to overflowing.

He slowed down and turned into Wapping and they sped along beside the river. 'What I aim to do this summer is get out of the city as much as I can,' he shouted. 'Get into Wales or over the Pennines into Yorkshire.'

'You like the country?'

'I love it!' he yelled. 'You can come with me if you like. That's if you're really aiming on stopping?'

'I'm stopping,' she said positively. 'Although I'm not sure your mother's pleased about that.'

'Ma's OK,' said Teddy. 'You being the big fella's daughter was a bit more than she reckoned on.'

'I'm not sure if she likes me.'

'Me and your dad didn't when we first met. Remember Mick mentioning me hanging from a railing? Your dad made me feel a fool by plucking me off it.'

'How d'you feel about him now?'

'I can stand him most times,' said Teddy frankly. 'He bought me my first fishing rod and I've never forgotten that.' He turned his head. 'There's the Custom House where Mick works. I'll take you right along the dock road as far as Seaforth before we head for home. If you're missing too long the big fella might ask questions.'

'And that's the last thing we want,' said Jeannie,

'Definitely,' he said.

It was not until they arrived home that Jeannie realised her stockings were torn and there were grazes and dried blood on one of her legs. Her coat had also picked up dirt from the gutter. She tried to creep upstairs but was caught by John as he was taking in the supper drinks. 'What's happened to you?' he asked solicitously.

'It's nothing,' she said swiftly.

'You've cut your leg.' He frowned. 'You'll have to wash that.'

'I'll do it!' She smiled reassuringly, although she felt irritated over his fussing. 'Don't worry. I know something about first aid. I wanted to be a nurse once.' She carried on upstairs.

'Jeannie, you didn't say how you did it,' called John.

'I slipped – uneven pavement!' She did not look back.

John stared after her. For some reason he could not explain, he felt she was not being quite open with him and that disturbed him. He went into the Smoking Room before returning to the kitchen and Kitty.

'Jeannie's had a fall,' he said abruptly, standing in the middle of the room.

'Is she OK?' Kitty came over to him drying her hands on a tea towel.

'She says she is.'

'Then what are you worried about?'

'She's cut her leg. Perhaps you could have a look at it, Kit? You know what young ones are like.'

'You're probably making a fuss over nothing,' said Kitty.

The back door opened and Teddy entered.

'Just look at it, Kit, and don't argue,' he said irritably. 'Don't you understand I feel uncomfortable asking my own daughter can I look at her leg.'

Kitty sighed. She was tired and wanted nothing more than to get to bed. 'OK. I'll do it. But I don't think she'll thank me for it.'

'I don't care about that. Neglect can kill. Just get on with it.'

'What's neglect going to kill?' asked Teddy, taking off his gloves and coat.

'Jeannie's cut her leg,' informed his mother, taking the first-aid box from a drawer. 'You make yourself a hot drink, son. You look cold. I bet it was freezing on that motorbike.'

'Not too bad.' He avoided looking at John as he put the kettle on.

Kitty left the kitchen with the box and Teddy sat down.

John stared at him and said, 'What have you done to your knee?'

For a moment Teddy could not think what to reply when he saw the tear in his trouser leg. He had become aware of his knee throbbing five minutes ago. Cold had a habit of freezing out pain and he had almost forgotten how he had done it. 'I skidded and had to put my knee down.' He could feel the blood rushing to his face and ears and hated himself for being unable to deal with any embarrassment or trouble in a cool calm manner.

There was a silence and then John said in a hard voice, 'She was with you, wasn't she? Where did you take her?'

Teddy realised there was no use in lying. 'Not far.'

'Where?'

Teddy eased his throat. 'Along by the cathedral and down to the river and along the dock road.'

John's breath hissed between his teeth. 'You're mad! I bet you went too fast down Parliament Street and that's when she came off. You could have killed her!' He towered over Teddy.

'No!' cried Teddy, getting up but having to lean on the table because of the pain in his knee. 'Do you think I'd take chances with her? It was a dog! I had to swerve to miss it in Hope Street. I wasn't going fast.'

'So you say,' said John in a voice he could barely keep under control because it came as such a shock that Jeannie had lied to him. 'You don't take her for a ride on that motorbike again. It's bloody dangerous.'

'She was game,' protested Teddy. 'She enjoyed it!'

That made it even worse in John's eyes because hadn't he warned her not to go on Teddy's motorbike? But maybe she wasn't to blame. Teddy had probably talked her into it and she was her father's daughter and would have enjoyed the excitement, even so the thought of her coming off the bike and being injured made his blood run cold. 'You don't take her on that motorbike again! Do you hear me, Teddy?'

Teddy stared at him tight-lipped. There was a long silence.

'I asked you a question,' roared John. 'And you won't leave this room until you give me your promise, or I'll get rid of that motorbike.'

'You've got no right,' said Teddy furiously.

'Don't talk to me about rights,' said John in a low voice. 'I'm the boss here, laddie, and don't you forget it or you'll rue the day.'

There was a loaded silence and then Teddy yelled, 'OK! I bloody promise.'

'Now you're showing sense,' said John, and flicked him across the cheek. He left the room as Mick entered it.

Feeling as if he was going to explode Teddy dug into his pockets and took out his cigarettes and matches.

'What's wrong with your face?' said Mick. 'What's going on? I could hear the big fella in the lobby.'

Teddy lighted up and scowled at him through a haze of smoke. 'Mind your own bloody business. I have enough people poking their nose into my life.' And he limped out of the room.

Chapter Twenty-Five

Very early the next morning Teddy went down the yard to check his motorbike. He was having trouble bending his knee and knew he would not be able to ride to work and would have to walk. He felt all knotted up inside, not only because of his knee but because of the big fella forbidding him to take Jeannie out on the bike again.

'Are you all right?' said a husky voice behind him.

He turned and saw Jeannie and held out a hand to her. 'My knee's giving me hell but I can take that. What sticks in my throat is that I promised not to take you out on the Rudge again. I wish I hadn't.'

She took his hand between both hers and held it against her breast. 'Poor you.'

'Did he make you promise?' he asked.

'Not promise. But he was so understanding and sympathetic that he made me feel terribly guilty. He said I was a sensible lass and he knew I wouldn't do it again.' There was a wistful expression on her face. 'Just as I was getting the hang of it, too.'

'The fall hasn't put you off?'

'No. But if I ever did get to ride on a motorbike again I'd like some proper clothes like yours.' She gazed into his eyes and Teddy raised one of her hands and rubbed it against his cheek before kissing her knuckles. 'What are we going to do? He said I wasn't to go out with you anywhere again.'

Teddy's anger threatened to choke him. 'Bloody swine! He's got no right!'

'He's not a swine,' she said thoughtfully. 'He's nice and kind and generous but now he's coming the heavy father and it's not what I want from him. It reminds me too much of Granny and Aunt Emily. They were always worrying about me, thinking a man was going to carry me off. They treated me like I hadn't a ha'p'orth of common sense. There has to be a way round your promise. We can't go places without transport and I want to go places with you.'

He lifted his head and they smiled at each other. 'I'll find a way,' he said. 'We'll have to be careful, though, or he'll have my hide.'

'We need to put him off the scent.'

He nodded. 'We'll have to go out separately and meet up elsewhere.'

'Yes, and I could—' She hesitated.

'What?'

'Be really nice to your Mick and young Doctor Calhoun to make him believe I'm not that fussy on you.'

Teddy did not like that idea but he could see she thought it would work. 'I hope our Mick's not really in love with you,' he said with brotherly concern.

'He's just in love with my face,' she said assuredly. Teddy knew he had to believe her or else he would have all kinds of reservations but he wanted to be with her so that settled it. He knew now as he looked at his Rudge exactly how he was going to get round his promise. It might be splitting hairs but love had to find a way.

He began to peruse the advertisement columns in *The Motor Cycle* magazine, as well as the *Echo* in search of what he wanted.

Come Sunday, Teddy discovered that the big fella and Mick were going along to the Central Hall with Jeannie so he decided it might be to his advantage to go. He did his best to appear to be hanging on to every word the preacher said but most of the time he was too aware of Jeannie sitting between Mick and her father to take much notice. Even so, Teddy made out he was interested and asked her to explain a few things to him on the short walk home. She behaved coolly towards him and was nice to Mick, but despite that Teddy got to walk next to her. He guessed he wasn't fooling his stepfather by his apparent interest in religious affairs but he had decided that if he made out he had already given up all interest in Jeannie on John's say-so, he would be acting out of character and the big fella might become suspicious. Teddy gave no thought to what his brother was feeling. At least not until they went to bed later that evening.

'Why did you have to go?' Mick said in a furious voice as he undressed. 'You're not holy!'

'I'm not pretending I am! But since when did you get a halo?' said Teddy. 'Admit you only went to get in with Jeannie.'

'I do have some interest in religion. I believe in God!'

'So do I! And the Ten Commandments.'

'Well, remember the one about not coveting and keep your eyes off Jeannie. She's too old for you.' Mick slid into bed.

'I like older women,' said Teddy loftily. He had not given a thought to Jeannie's age.

'Just find somebody else,' muttered Mick presenting him with his back. 'Or me and you are gonna fall out.'

So what, thought Teddy, and pulled the covers over his head. The battle lines were drawn and no longer would he worry the least little bit about his brother's feelings.

Kitty, who was aware that her two eldest sons were vying for Jeannie's favours, wondered if she should do anything about it. She knew that John had forbidden Teddy from taking the girl out on his motorbike and they had had words on the subject. There was a definite atmosphere between her husband and son and how Kitty managed to keep her mouth shut and not rush to one or the other's defence when they spoke to her about it, she did not know. Nor could she help wanting to lay the blame on Jeannie's shoulders for such a serious falling out. Kitty felt she walked an emotional tightrope to keep the peace and that one innocent but wrong word from her could only make matters worse.

It would have helped Kitty if she could have spoken to Jeannie like her own daughter but however hard Kitty tried she could not. She had never nurtured her as she had her own children. There were no shared memories to look back on, only the thought that this girl was Margaret's and John's daughter and she had no part of her.

Easter came and on the Sunday afternoon John suggested they went out as a family for a picnic to Sefton Park. It was soon obvious to Kitty that Mick and Teddy were out to impress Jeannie in the games they played, hogging the bat and giving Jeannie more second chances when caught out than her being a girl warranted. It was not fair on Jack and Ben who got fed up hanging around and wandered off. Jack fell in the lake and Ben had to go in after him, and the afternoon ended in an argument between Teddy and Mick, with John storming off carrying a sopping wet Jack, blaming *her* sons for what had happened.

The atmosphere in the private quarters of the Arcadia was still fraught when the Galloways left for Canada.

John, Kitty, Jeannie and Jack went to the landing stage to wave them off. Nancy and Malcolm tried to persuade them to leave England. 'Hitler's not going to be content with just Austria,' said Malcolm. 'And what about Italy and Abyssinia? Hitler and Il Duce are already in cahoots. They'll be marching into somewhere else next.'

'We'll think about it,' was all John would promise but, thinking of her sons, Kitty thought that perhaps they should. Several weeks passed and during that time Teddy made out that he was losing interest in Jeannie and religion. He also got rid of his Rudge motorbike.

The O'Neills came to see them. Daniel was cock-a-hoop because the economic war between Eire and Britain was finally over after six years. 'Hopefully it'll improve relationships.'

'It won't if a member of the Dáil carries on suggesting dropping poison gas on Ulster,' said Kitty.

Daniel sighed. 'Crazy. But de Valera did condemn the idea.'

She agreed he had more sense.

Celia came to work for them – a washed-out looking Celia with lank hair and a waist that could be spanned by a man's hands.

'You look like you need a holiday,' said Kitty, shaking her head.

'It's Ma. And it's been hectic at the doctor's the last few weeks,' replied Celia, straightening her shoulders. 'I'll be all right now I'm here.'

Kitty decided what Celia needed was feeding up and she made sure that was what the girl got by standing over her and making her eat. She was rewarded for her efforts and bought Celia a new frock and bullied Mick into taking her to the Laughter Show at the Pivvy.

Jeannie and Teddy narrowly missed bumping into them because they went there on the same night. 'I told you Mick wasn't in love with me,' said Jeannie, looking relieved. Teddy was not so sure but he kept his mouth shut.

At last, one night in June, he saw what he had been looking for and although it was not the most auspicious of days when he set out he was determined to get what he wanted. Gales had swept the country, bringing down telephone lines and ruining the punter's hopes of a Derby winner because of wreckage on the course. But as soon as Teddy saw the second-hand 1932 Ariel he fell in love with it and his thoughts turned to days out in the country. Without telling his family, he kept it at a mate's house and after a couple of practice runs he felt competent enough to take Jeannie out on it so arranged for them to meet at the Pier Head one Sunday afternoon.

'Yes, yes!' she exclaimed with a rapturous expression on her face when she saw him astride the Ariel. 'A proper pillion seat! You have gone up in the world.'

'I had to.' He glanced over his shoulder as she climbed up behind. 'I promised the big fella I wouldn't take you on the old Rudge but I didn't say anything about a different motorbike.'

'Big improvement.' She marvelled as she found the foot rests and settled herself. 'Let's go.'

The early gales of summer had passed but Teddy was taking no chances, so he did not take her through the Mersey tunnel and into Wales. She needed to get used to the feel of the bike so they went out for a spin along to Otterspool, just past the Cassie Shore.

It was the first of many outings and she bought herself a coat similar to his, along with leggings, gloves and a helmet, which she kept at his mate's. They were so wrapped up in each other that it was difficult to pretend that they did not particularly care for each other at home, but as the weeks passed it became even more difficult to pretend that there was no possibility of another war and their being parted.

Suddenly the newspapers were filled with headlines about Germans in the Sudeten regions of Czechoslovakia demanding self-determination, and of Herr Hitler's promise to help them get it. Hitler was getting too big for his boots and Germany too powerful, blazoned the headlines. Britain and France had to do something to stop the Nazis invading other countries, But France and Britain did not want another war.

Anxious crowds gathered outside 10 Downing Street and Mr Chamberlain went to Munich on a mission of peace. Everybody held their breath.

He returned with a piece of paper and waved it about. It was Herr Hitler's promise of peace but it had been gained at a price. Sudetenland was now part of Germany but Britain and France guaranteed Czechoslovakia they would uphold their new frontiers. Most people breathed again. John said grimly that there could be a next time but Kitty did not want to believe it.

The fear that there might eventually be another war crouched like some horrible demon at the back of Teddy's mind and made his outings with Jeannie all the more precious. It was a week or so after the Munich crisis he persuaded her to skip chapel and have a whole day out with him. 'It'll be winter soon and then we won't be able to get out and about the same. Let's go to mid-Wales.'

'I'll have to think up an excuse,' she said.

'Say you've got a sick friend.'

'I haven't any girl friends I'd need the whole day to visit.'

He racked his brains. 'What about that girl who stayed at the hotel a few months ago who lives near Chester and said you could visit any time?'

Jeannie smiled. 'She phoned me up a short while ago. She'll do.' John accepted her reason for being missing the whole day without a quibble. As for Teddy he told

Kitty he had to work. There was an increasing demand for aeroplane engine parts and it was true enough the boss was saying they were going to have to pull out all the stops.

The leaves on the trees were just turning the colours of autumn but Teddy and Jeannie were full of the joys of spring as they travelled along narrow winding roads between hedges bright with haws and hips. They stopped for a picnic near Bala Lake.

'One day soon,' said Teddy, as they lay on a towel on the grass, 'we're going to have to confess we've been seeing each other and want to get married.'

'You haven't asked me yet,' murmured Jeannie, rolling over on her side and gazing at him.

'Will you?' His face was close to hers.

'Yes.'

Their lips met and he pulled her against him, kissing her with an exhuberance that matched her own. They kissed and kissed. It was not enough for how they felt about each other but they both knew when to call time. They drew apart and stood up, both reluctant to leave what had now become a very special place to them.

'We'll come back here,' said Jeannie.

'We'll come for our honeymoon,' said Teddy, lacing his fingers through hers.

'Yes. I'd like that,' she said softly.

They left, still caught up in a kind of enchantment and not ready to head for home. They travelled on, enjoying the countryside and each other's company. When they rounded a bend and the giant pig came towards them it was so unexpected and happened so fast that Teddy had no time to brake. Before he could take action to avoid it, they hit the pig. He was flung into a hedge whilst the motorbike skidded out of control before falling on its side, pinning Jeannie beneath it.

Fear was uppermost in his mind as he dragged himself out of the hedge and staggered towards her with blood running down his cheek where a hawthorn twig had ripped open his face. He tried to lift the bike but it was too much for him and the scream from Jeannie would have made him stop anyway.

'Thank God, you're alive,' he said hoarsely, getting down on the ground so his face was on a level with hers. There was a bloodied graze right down her left cheek. 'What is it? Where does it hurt?'

'My leg, my leg really hurts,' she groaned and attempted to lift her head again but it was too much effort.

Teddy took off his coat, folded it and placed it beneath her head before attempting to see that part of her beneath the bike. It was all in shadow. He got up on one knee and glanced about him just in time to see the sow lumbering away. 'It must belong to that farm we saw back there. I'll go and get help, love,' he said.

'Don't leave me,' cried Jeannie, reaching out a hand to him.

He took it and held it tightly. 'I don't want to leave you ever,' he said unsteadily. 'I wish we were married right now.'

'I want to marry you, too,' she whispered. 'But get me out from under here first.'

He nearly smiled then but was too upset. He released

her hand and moved away from the bike. It was then he heard the sound of an engine and, suddenly frightened that a car might come round the bend and run into the bike and perhaps kill Jeannie, he ran into the middle of the road and waved both arms and shouted.

A car came round the bend and braked suddenly, narrowly missing him. It stopped and two men got out. 'Are you suicidal, boyo?' said one of them.

Teddy swallowed and blinked back tears. 'I ran into a pig,' he gulped. 'My girl's in pain and I can't get the bike off her to see what's wrong.'

'You're in luck, Scouse,' said the other one, a big, broad heavy-set youngish man. 'My friend's a doctor. Let's get her out from under there.'

The three men set about lifting the motorbike, only to freeze when Jeannie screamed piercingly. 'You two hold it just there whilst I see what's causing the trouble,' said the one who was the doctor.

Teddy and the other man braced themselves whilst the doctor lowered himself to the ground. When he got up again his expression was serious. 'One of the foot rests has gone into her calf and out the other side.'

'Oh God!' gulped Teddy, and felt as if all the blood had drained from him.

'Keep a grip on yourself, boyo,' ordered the doctor sternly. 'You'll have to hold the cycle while I see what I can do to separate them.' Teddy took a deep steadying breath and did exactly as he was told.

Afterwards, as Teddy sat in the farmhouse parlour sipping hot sweet tea and smoking a cigarette with shaking fingers, he wondered how he had not screamed himself when the doctor managed to get his fingers into the sides of the wound so they could pull out the foot rest. They had brought Jeannie here in the car but Teddy had been turned out of the makeshift surgery in another room because he and Jeannie were not married. It had seemed ludicrous in the light of what they felt for each other.

The door opened and the doctor came in. Teddy shot to his feet. 'How is she?'

'I've cleaned the wound and put in a few stitches but I'll have to get her to the cottage hospital in Welshpool.'

'But – but we've got to get home to Liverpool tonight,' stuttered Teddy, only now thinking of his mother and the big fella.

'Out of the question,' said the doctor briskly. 'She's not fit. She has a slight concussion and cuts and bruises, but most of all that wound needs attention as soon as possible from someone more expert than me. We'll take her in the car. You can follow us on your motorbike.' Teddy saw that he had no choice but to fit in with what the doctor said.

He was, at least, allowed to carry Jeannie out to the car. 'Keep your chin up, love,' he whispered as he placed her down on the back seat.

She smiled up at him drowsily and he wondered if the doctor had given her something. He did not wait to watch the car drive off but went in search of his motorbike.

He had not travelled far when the engine died on him and he discovered the return pipe from the crank case to the petrol tank had been flattened. He could have wept but instead he wheeled his motorbike to the side of the road and began walking. It was beginning to get dark and it was now that thoughts of the big fella and his mother crowded in. His stepfather was going to be furious. God only knew what he would do to him. Only now did Teddy admit to himself that he was scared stiff of telling him what had happened to Jeannie, but it would have to be done.

At that moment he heard the noise of a car engine and turned to face it. He waved but the car carried on. In desperation he ran after it shouting and it stopped. When he caught up with it a man stuck his head out of the window. 'I'm in a hurry, lad. Where are you going?'

'Welshpool Hospital,' gasped Teddy. 'My motorbike hit a pig and my girl's been taken there.'

The man smiled. 'Get in. If I'm not much mistaken it's your girl I've been called out to.'

'You're a doctor?' Teddy could barely credit it.

'That's right.'

Teddy began to laugh. He couldn't believe it! But it seemed someone up there was keeping an eye on them.

He was allowed in to see Jeannie for only a few minutes. 'Sorry, love,' he said, gripping her hand tightly as he gazed down at her pale injured face.

'It wasn't your fault.'

He knew that but, even so, he felt he was to blame.

A nurse came in and told him he had to go. The doctor wanted to see the patient. He kissed Jeannie and left, only to slump down on a chair outside with his head in his hands.

'I think you could do with some attention,' said a kindly voice. He lifted his head and saw another nurse. 'Come with me.'

Teddy felt as if he was in a dream as a doctor stitched the gash in his face. He was given a pill and told to undress and get into bed. He was asleep almost as soon as his head hit the pillow.

It was not quite light when he woke but he could hear noises. Instantly he knew he was in deeper trouble. His mother and the big fella would be sick with worry and might possibly be putting two and two together. Without speaking to any of the nurses, he dressed and left the hospital to find a telephone box and put a call through to his mother. Then he went back to the hospital to ask after Jeannie and wait.

The big fella came in person and met Teddy outside the hospital. Before he could even open his mouth to say he was sorry, John said harshly, 'You'll go home right away. There's a train leaving for Crewe in a couple of hours and you can get one to Liverpool from there.'

'No,' said Teddy, his face white. 'I'm not a kid anymore that you can boss me around. I know she's hurt and we've deceived you but I wasn't to blame for the accident.'

'You broke your promise.'

'That's a matter of opinion,' parried Teddy. 'I bought a different motorbike. A better one! If that pig—'

'I want no excuses!' shouted John. 'You knew what I meant. I don't want you having anything to do with her ever again.'

'But I've asked her to marry me and she said yes!'

A muscle in John's cheek tightened. 'Marry you! She must be mad! She's under twenty-one and there's no way I'll give her permission.'

'We'll wait then,' said Teddy, his face white with strain. 'You won't be able to stop us then.'

'You'll wait for years because I'll see your mother doesn't give permission either. When I think my Jeannie could get septicaemia I could strangle you with my bare hands.' His long fingers clenched into a fist.

Teddy swallowed and backed away. 'She saw a doctor right away. Honestly she's going to be OK.'

'She better had be,' said John icily. 'Now you get off home. There's a train leaving in an hour.'

'But I want to stay here,' said Teddy desperately. 'She'll want me.'

'I'm here. She doesn't need you,' said John scathingly, towering over Teddy. 'Now go before I do something your mother might make me regret.'

Teddy saw there was nothing for it but to leave. He walked away, but not in the direction of the railway station. He only had a few pennies in his pockets and he'd be damned before he would ask the big fella for money. He felt desperate, angry, guilt-ridden as he wandered along a wide street, thinking of Jeannie and how if she had been with him she would have liked this place. It had some nice old-looking houses and there was a castle up on a hill. He passed a garage, remembered his motorcycle and without thinking twice went in to see if he could get a piece of piping that would do for a temporary repair. After a search the mechanic came up with just what Teddy needed and told him he could have it for nothing.

It was dusk when Teddy arrived back in Liverpool, having travelled via the Runcorn Transporter. He was exhausted as he wheeled his motorbike into the yard of the Arcadia. He slumped against a whitewashed wall wondering what to do. He was no longer a kid that he could expect his mother to rescue him from this fix.

Chapter Twenty-Six

Kitty, who had been in the kitchen and had been roused by Nelson yelping and scratching at the back door, came down the yard with her arms held wide. 'Thank God you're OK, Teddy. I've been out of my mind.'

'Ma!' He went into her arms, burying his head against her neck.

She said soothingly, 'It's all right, son. You're home now. I see you came home on your bike after all. Jeannie told John you had no money for the train. Why didn't you ask him for some?'

Teddy lifted his head and drew away from her. 'Ask him!' he spat out. 'I'd rather die.'

Kitty was silent, knowing she should have guessed that was how he would feel and could only hope he would get over it. 'Come inside. You must be tired out.'

He nodded and went with her.

Celia and Hannah were in the kitchen and as they entered Mick and Monica came through the other door. 'So you're back,' said Mick, his expression hot and angry. 'Bloody fool!'

'That's enough of that,' said Kitty sharply. 'He's been through all that with the big fella! Now give it a rest. He needs food and sleep, not recriminations.'

'You're too soft. You always have been with him,' said Mick.

'No way,' said Teddy, glaring at his brother. 'You're just saying that because you're bloody jealous!'

'Bloody jealous of what? Not you, you little pipsqueak!'

'That's enough!' Kitty turned on them both with a wrathful expression. 'Mind your language. Do you want the guests to hear?'

'Guests! I'm sick of guests,' lashed out Mick. 'Why can't we live in an ordinary house?'

'What's that got to do with anything?' said Teddy. 'This isn't about guests! You're just in a mood because you are jealous of me and Jeannie, whatever you might say.' Suddenly the colour drained from his face and he sank onto a chair and closed his eyes.

'The lad's bone weary,' said Hannah in a surprisingly gentle voice. 'He needs his bed. I'll put a hottie in it.'

'Look at his face,' said Monica, who was growing more like her sister Annie in appearance every day. She had her bright red hair and sharp little chin. 'It's all cut and he's got stitches in it.' She carried the tray over to the sink. 'How did yer do that, Teddy?'

'You're as thick as two short planks asking him questions like that,' said Celia scornfully, wiping her hands as she moved away from the sink. 'It's obvious he did it in the accident.'

Teddy blinked at his mother and said, 'I wish you'd get them to all stop talking about me as if I wasn't here.'

'Never mind them talking about you,' said Kitty,

worrying about him all over again. 'Bed! That's where you're going, me lad!' She seized hold of his arm and chivvied him towards the door.

Those left behind in the kitchen exchanged looks. 'The missus is real upset,' said Hannah. 'And the big fella was in a right twist when he went out this morning.'

'D'you blame him?' said Mick, folding his arms across his chest. 'I feel like hitting our Teddy.'

'You're hard,' said Celia, staring at him. It was an accident. An enormous pig came round a bend and they crashed right into it. He's your brother! You should be glad he's OK.'

Mick reddened. 'I am glad he's OK. But he's been seeing her on the sly and that really gets my goat.'

The door opened and Ben came in with a relieved expression on his face. 'Our Teddy's home. Aren't I glad! I was worried in case he might have really hurt himself and died.'

'No chance of that,' muttered Mick, brushing past him and slamming the door on his way out.

He went outside and stood on the front step, looking up at the sky. The moon appeared to be covered by a veil and he wondered with a tiny part of his mind how far away it was and if men would ever get there. He was deeply hurt and angry, not only with his brother, but also with Jeannie, his mother *and* Celia for turning on him. He felt if it had not been for the need to know how Jeannie was he could have walked out the hotel there and then and never come back.

'Mick Ryan?' A figure in the uniform of an able seaman of the Royal Navy had stopped at the bottom of the step.

'Pete Curry?'

'That's right.' Pete grinned. 'Haven't seen you since way back.'

'Infants.' Mick shook hands politely.

Pete stepped back and looked up at the hotel's frontage. 'How's yer ma doing? I heard she got married again.'

'She's fine.'

'And your brothers?'

'OK.' Mick did not want to talk about them. He did not want to talk at all but he forced himself. 'How are you? How's life on the briny?'

'Not bad. Yer gerrabout and see places. I've been to Singapore.'

'You'll have to tell us about it one day.'

Pete's bony face lit up. 'How about the present? If yer gorra minute how about cumin' for a pint?'

Mick was lost for words a moment and then he glanced up at the hotel frontage just as Pete had done and hated it. 'You've twisted me arm,' he said, and followed him down the Mount.

Kitty watched them go from the attic window, having heard their voices as she drew the curtains. Her heart ached for both her sons and there was a core of anger deep inside her which was directed against Jeannie. How she wished the girl had never come but it was too late to do anything about it now.

She moved away from the window and over to the bed

where Teddy lay with his eyes closed. She looked at the stitches in the gash on his face and her mouth tightened. It seemed to her that John had not spared a thought for how he had suffered but only cared about Jeannie. The girl had been trouble, just as Hannah had prophesied.

Kitty went downstairs, hoping that nothing else would go wrong that evening but now she was also worried about Mick.

Her eldest son returned a couple of hours later and by then everyone else was in bed but Kitty. She sat in reception, making out a couple of bills. She eyed his unsteady figure as he came towards her up the lobby. He said with extreme care, 'I'm not drunk.'

She put down her pen and came out from behind the reception desk and took his arm. 'Let's go upstairs.'

'I'm not drunk,' he repeated.

She smiled. 'No. But I'd like your arm. I'm feeling tired out with everything that's being going on and I don't know if I can make it upstairs.'

'You're having me on,' he articulated carefully.

'Not in a thousand years,' she said sadly and accompanied him upstairs and put him to bed.

The next morning Mick obviously had a head like nobody's business, thought Kitty, having decided that she was not going to be soft with either of them. She mixed them both a glass of Andrew's liver salts and handed it to them. 'You're both looking liverish,' she said. 'Drink this, have some toast when you come down and then get out to work.'

They groaned but she gave them a steely look and

hissed, 'Are you men or mice? Get working and think twice before you go behaving like idiots again.'

'I haven't done anything,' moaned Mick. 'Not compared to what he's done.'

Kitty gave him another of her looks. 'Don't argue with me.' She went over to Ben and Jack and shook them.

Teddy gulped down the fizzing drink before getting out of bed. 'I don't know what you were doing getting kaylied,' he said to Mick. 'It's me that should have been getting drunk.'

'Me heart bleeds for you,' said Mick, holding his head up with one hand as he drank. 'You're a two-faced sod. Kidding us all that you didn't have a motorbike anymore.'

'I had to. The big fella would have put his oar in. He hates me.'

'I don't blame him,' said Mick, shuddering as the liver salts reached his gut.

'It's a waste of time talking to you. For tuppence I'd leave home.'

'Do that! The sooner the better,' said Mick, pouring cold water from the jug on the washstand over his head into the basin and effectively bringing the conversation to an end.

All that morning Kitty expected to hear from John that he and Jeannie were coming home but just after lunch she received a telephone call from John saying that they were not discharging Jeannie yet and he would stay around until they did. Kitty told him to give Jeannie her best wishes and left it at that.

It was to be a week before John and Jeannie arrived

back in Liverpool and she was taken straight to the Royal Infirmary.

'She's got septicaemia,' said John, looking drawn and tired as he sat in front of the fire in the basement. 'So much for your son's reassurances that she was all right.'

'I'm sorry, John.' Kitty put an arm around his shoulders and rested her cheek against his hair. 'It was an accident, though. He wasn't to know that pig—'

'Don't mention that pig to me again,' interrupted John. 'For months they've been meeting behind my back. She told me so!'

'I'm glad she's taking part of the blame,' murmured Kitty, moving away from him. 'She deceived you as much as he did.'

'I knew you'd stick up for him!' said John, firing up. 'Well, it's not your daughter who's lying in the Royal with blood poisoning. You might feel different if it was.'

'I'm glad she's not my daughter,' retorted Kitty. 'But it's my son who's moping around worrying himself to pieces because he loves her! Anyone would think you've led a spotless life instead of the one you have!'

He paled. 'You don't have to rub it in. I know I was to blame for Margaret's death.'

'Rubbish!' exclaimed Kitty. 'I'm not talking about that. I'm talking about young people being young and going their own way. About having fun!'

There was a silence and they stared at one another. Kitty's heart softened. 'Anyway, surely there's something the doctors can do for Jeannie?' she said in gentler tones. 'Otherwise they wouldn't have sent her to the Royal.'

'They're going to X-ray her leg. They can't understand where the blood poisoning is coming from. What if she loses her leg, Kit? Or she dies? I'll never forgive Teddy. Never!' he said in a choking voice.

'That's unfair,' she cried. 'I know you're upset but think how he'll suffer if that were to happen.'

'He probably won't die of it, though, will he?' said John bitterly, and getting up he walked out.

Kitty slumped down into an armchair and hoped that Jeannie would not die. What hope would there be of their family being united then?

When Teddy arrived home from work Kitty told him that Jeannie was back. Without waiting to eat, he went immediately to the hospital, hoping they would allow him to see Jeannie. 'You're too early for visiting,' said a nurse. 'Come back in half an hour.'

Teddy decided not to go home but walked as far as the Wesley chapel in Moss Street. He was so depressed the only thing he could think of doing was to pray, but when he got to the chapel he did not have the nerve to go in. He went back to the hospital only to be informed that Miss McLeod's father was with her.

Teddy waited, watching other people going in and out of the ward. Twice he went and looked round the door and caught sight of the big fella sitting beside a bed but he blocked off any view Teddy might have had of Jeannie. Teddy felt angry and resentful but he did not want to make a fuss or cause Jeannie any distress by having a confrontation with her father. After another five minutes he tired of waiting and opened the door and walked swiftly up the ward.

Fortunately the big fella had his back to him and Teddy could see Jeannie in bed, propped up by several pillows. Her eyes were closed and there was a flush on her cheeks. Teddy was scared out of his wits. She couldn't really be dying, could she? 'Jeannie!' he said loudly.

Her eyes opened and she pushed herself up on her elbows.

'Out you!' said John, getting to his feet and blocking them off from each other's vision. 'Haven't you caused her enough pain?'

'I love her!' said Teddy desperately. 'Didn't you ever do anything you regretted? I didn't want her hurt!'

'But you have hurt her! She's got blood poisoning and you know what that means.'

'Let me see her,' said Teddy, trying to dodge round him, but John grabbed him by the back of his collar and forced him the other way about.

'What's going on?' The ward sister came rustling up.

'Nothing for you to worry about, Sister. I'll deal with this.' John frogmarched a resisting-all-the-way Teddy out of the ward.

'I've never known such behaviour!' said the sister in a horrified voice. 'Now if you don't mind leaving—'

'I'm leaving,' said Teddy, finally managing to wrench himself out of John's hold. 'But I'll be back.'

'No, you won't,' said John, his expression uncompromising. 'I'll see to that.'

'Neither of you will be allowed in,' said the sister, quivering with rage. 'Upsetting my patients. Now out!' She waved her arms in the direction of the exit.

'But, Sister—' began John.

Teddy did not wait to see the outcome of John's war of words with the sister and left.

He went back the next day but the same sister was there and he was not allowed in. He was down in the dumps, not knowing what was happening to Jeannie but too scared to ask. It was Kitty who told him that she had had an operation.

He collapsed on the sofa, pale and shivering. 'They haven't taken her leg off, have they?' he stuttered.

'Of course not!' Kitty sat beside him and covered his hand with hers. 'Calm down, son. The X-ray found what was causing the infection trapped between two bones in her leg.'

'What was it?'

'A scrap of fabric. Wasn't she wearing leggings?'

Teddy nodded, imagining the foot rest going into Jeannie's calf and his fingernails dug into the palms of his hands. 'They removed it?' he said.

Kitty nodded. 'She'll get better now, you'll see. Everything's going to be all right.'

Teddy made no answer, convinced his mother was being over-optimistic.

A week later Jeannie came out of hospital, leaning heavily on a stick. When Teddy saw her his instinct was to rush over and carry her anywhere she wanted to go but John was there watching over her like a bulldog and would not let him get near. She looked tired and her face was drawn with pain. *I've done this to her*, thought Teddy, and his heart felt as if it was being squeezed in a nutcracker.

How can she go on loving me? Perhaps she no longer did because she had not looked his way once. If that was so, he wasn't going to be able to go on living here anymore, so close to her yet so far away.

Over the next few days Teddy toyed with the idea of leaving home. He saw little of Jeannie and when he did the big fella always seemed to be hanging around, making it impossible for them to have a conversation.

It was the advertisement in the enlisting office in Lime Street that finally decided Teddy and, not giving himself time to have second thoughts, he went in and signed on the dotted line.

When the day came for him to leave he went out at his normal time as if he was going to work, but it took all his willpower not to keep glancing over his shoulder as he wheeled his motorbike out of the yard for the last time.

Chapter Twenty-Seven

It was Mick who found the note when he came home from work. It was tucked under the box containing Teddy's fishing reel on the chest of drawers by their bed. He read it with mixed feelings before going downstairs. Jeannie was sitting behind the reception desk reading a book. She looked up and gave him a faint smile. For a moment he hesitated, considering showing it to her but then he changed his mind.

He found Kitty in the kitchen where she was making custard. 'Ma, I think you should read this.'

'Not now, son,' she murmured, not taking her eyes off the milk that was about to boil.

He waited, leaning against the table wondering how she was going to take the news. He felt partially to blame. Hadn't he told his brother to go?

'Lost a shilling and found a farthing?' said Celia, as she passed him with a tray.

'Not me,' he said.

She took a few steps back. 'It's not me mam, is it? Only she's worse and it's getting that way I'm thinking of going over her head and calling in the doctor.'

'Not your ma, Cessy,' he said shortly.

She stared at him. It was such a long time since he had
called her by her nickname that it stirred those feelings for
him which had never completely died. For a moment her
knees went weak. Then she pulled herself together and got
on with her work.

Mick watched her a moment, thinking what a neat waist
she had, before giving his attention to his mother who
was now stirring custard. He waited until she poured it
into jugs. 'You can take them in for me,' she said, licking
custard from a finger.

'I will. But have a gander at this first.' He held the note
out to her. 'It's from our Teddy.'

Kitty felt the colour drain from her face, went hot and
cold and had to grip the table. 'He's gone, hasn't he?' she
said in a low voice.

'How did you know?' His face showed surprise.

'The way he's been lately.' She took a deep breath,
straightened and took the note from him, spreading the
single sheet on the table. It was much worse than she had
thought and for a moment the words went fuzzy on the
page. 'He's joined the air force,' she whispered.

'Perhaps it's for the best, Ma!' said Mick in an excitable
voice, resting his hands on the table next to hers.

She stared at him, thinking what a terrible thing jealousy
was. 'For who?' she said tartly. 'If you think Jeannie's
going to have eyes for you after this, then you're kidding
yourself!' She hurried out of the kitchen in search of John
but the first person she saw was Jeannie in reception and
for a moment she could have hit the girl. This was all her
fault! If she hadn't come then Teddy would still be here.

'He's gone,' she said in a stony voice. 'Teddy's gone!'

'What!' The girl's eyes flew wide and she slammed shut the Agatha Christie she had not been able to get her head into because she could not get Teddy out of it. 'Where's he gone? Why's he gone?'

'Because of you, of course! He left a note saying he couldn't bear loving you and seeing you suffer anymore.'

'Oh no!' Jeannie slumped against the desk and her face crumpled. 'But I love him! Why did he have to do that? Why?'

'To get right away, of course! He's joined the air force!'

'Oh Lord!' Jeannie straightened and limped out from behind the desk. 'Let me see the note?'

Kitty handed it to her and her attitude towards Jeannie softened. It was obvious the girl was distressed and did really care for Teddy.

Jeannie read the note swiftly and then folded it carefully. 'It's Pops' fault! I told him I loved Teddy and wanted to marry him. I told him that I knew we'd have to wait because we were under age! But he wouldn't listen. He just kept saying it was out of the question, that I'd get over it. That I didn't know Teddy like he did. I kept saying that I did know him and I loved every bit of him but Pops would get this expression on his face and I just knew he wasn't listening.'

'He was listening all right,' said Kitty bitterly. 'He just wasn't hearing! He's just been too possessive of you and wouldn't see a thing right about Teddy.'

'What are we going to do?' asked Jeannie, her eyes on Kitty's face.

She looked at the girl and suddenly was deeply sorry for her. She remembered what it was like to be young and in love and to be parted from that person you were mad about. She eased the constriction in her throat and said huskily, 'I don't know if there's anything we can do. Teddy's signed up and that's that.'

Jeannie's eyes filled with tears. 'Pops put it into my head that Teddy kept his distance from me because of my limp.'

Kitty could scarcely believe it. 'Did your father say as much?'

'He said, "Maybe Teddy's keeping his distance because of your limp?"' Jeannie took out a handkerchief and dabbed her eyes. 'I didn't want to believe it but Teddy *was* staying away so I didn't have the chance to tell him it wasn't permanent. Now I know why he stayed away. He'd been warned off and all the time he loved me.' A sob escaped her as she struggled to keep back the tears.

'Don't cry, love.' Kitty patted her shoulder. 'Let's do something instead. Let's go and have a word with your father.'

Jeannie stared at her and suddenly her expression changed, became resolute and she wiped away her tears. 'I'm going to give him a piece of my mind.'

Kitty forced a smile. 'So am I. He'll be sorry he ever tried to keep the pair of you apart.'

They went in search of John and found him sitting on Jack's bed reading a book on railway engines to the boy, which threw Kitty for a moment but she guessed Jeannie was leaving the leading to her and so she said, 'Can we have a word, John, outside?'

John's hazel eyes lifted to their faces and there was a sudden stillness there. He handed the book to Jack and said that he would be back in a minute.

Kitty closed the bedroom door and looked at him, no longer able to keep the hurt and anger under control. 'How could you?' she said. 'I thought you had heart and tolerance but instead you've behaved like a bloody Victorian father!'

His eyes darkened and he said, 'What's happened?'

'Teddy's gone,' cried Jeannie, 'and it's all your fault! You lied to me!'

'Read this!' said Kitty, thrusting the note at him.

He read it.

'I hope you're satisfied,' said his daughter in a quivering voice.

'Yes, I hope you're satisfied,' echoed Kitty.

John's face set in uncompromising lines. 'You mightn't believe this, the pair of you, but it'll probably do him good. He's shown more sense than I would have credited him for.'

'You've never credited him with any sense at all, though, have you?' said Kitty bitterly.

'Can you blame me after what happened?'

'Yes! You've always thought the worst of him! You didn't give him a chance!' cried Kitty, almost in tears. She put a hand over her mouth. 'And now,' she added in a choking voice, 'you've chased him away.'

'You wouldn't listen to me when I said he wasn't to blame for the accident,' yelled Jeannie, banging her stick on the floor. 'Now I don't know when he'll be back and it's all your fault!'

'Don't speak to me like that and keep your voice down,' said John, frowning at her. 'It's a father's right to protect his daughter.'

'From my son?' retorted Kitty furiously and poked him in the chest. 'She didn't need protecting from him.'

'Don't do that!' John seized her hand and crushed her fingers so hard that she gasped. 'Get some control over yourself,' he hissed. 'What's Jack going to think with you making all this row?'

'Jack'll know what it's about soon enough. He's not daft!' whispered Kitty, struggling to free herself. 'He loves his brother, unlike you. You've always hated Teddy.'

'That's not true,' said John, looking shocked. 'There's been times when I've liked him well enough. He just doesn't know when to stop – when to use a bit of sense.'

Kitty gasped, 'And what about you? Have you always been sensible? He's eighteen, John, not a hundred!'

'I was protecting my daughter.'

'I didn't want protecting,' said Jeannie, attempting to thrust herself between them. 'I've suffered from people trying to protect me all my life! I thought you'd understand! You lived a free life. I wanted to do what I wanted for a change but you wouldn't let me.'

John freed Kitty's hand and stared at Jeannie with a pained expression. 'I was trying to protect you, to be a real father to you.'

'Well, you're idea of a father and mine were different,' she said in a trembling voice. 'An-an-and now you've ruined my life!' She sniffed back tears. 'I'll never forgive you.'

Kitty put an arm round her and said quietly, 'Don't upset yourself, Jeannie. Teddy'll be back and when he does you can get married.'

'Over my dead body,' said John.

They ignored him. 'The-ther-there could be a war and I'll never see him again,' said Jeannie.

Her fear was Kitty's fear but she did not admit to it. 'There's not going to be a war,' she said bracingly.

'Mick said there's a wine merchants not far from the Custom House which has turned one of their cellars into an air raid shelter and Teddy told me the government were giving the air force more money to build planes.'

'He's done the right thing then, hasn't he?' snapped John, exacerbated. 'More money – engine parts. That's where they'll stick him. He's not going to be a bloody hero!'

They stared at him. 'There's no need to swear,' gasped Kitty sounding affronted.

'You swore before,' he cried. 'Besides this family would make a bloody saint swear! I've had enough. I'm going for a walk.' He thrust past them and thundered down the stairs.

The two women looked at each other. 'Well!' said Kitty. 'There was no need for him to go thumping down the stairs like that!'

'It's childish,' said Jeannie. 'It was us that were in the right.'

'Too true,' said Kitty, hugging the girl's shoulders. 'But you can bet he's not going to admit it.'

'Well, I'm not going to say I'm sorry and be nice to him,' said Jeannie.

'He'll have to say it first,' said Kitty, who was nowhere near ready to forgive her husband for causing Teddy to leave.

But John did not consider himself in the wrong and, besides, he was deeply hurt, as well as furious with Teddy for leaving and making it appear that he *was* in the wrong. In his opinion he had behaved exactly as any sensible husband and father would.

So over the next fortnight the atmosphere in the McLeod household was strained and cool between husband and wife, and father and daughter but the two women in John's life drew closer together because of their love for Teddy. They all behaved amicably, of course, in front of the guests but behind the scene emotions simmered and threatened to boil over.

'So your Teddy's joined the air force,' said Celia, polishing the knob at the bottom of the stairs.

'News gets round,' said Mick, brushing past her and going upstairs. He did not want to talk about his brother.

'It's left the field open for you, hasn't it?' She peered through the bannister railings at him.

Mick frowned and leaned against the wall staring down at her and thought how pale the skin was surrounding her freckles and what a pity she didn't have Jeannie's looks. 'What's that supposed to mean?' he drawled.

'You and Jeannie – as if you didn't know.' She gave him a barbed smile.

'You must know there isn't a hope in hell of me getting

off with Jeannie now,' he said impatiently. 'You can cut
the atmosphere in this place with a knife because of Ma
and her ganging up on the big fella. I think it stinks that
a man isn't allowed to be boss in his own home and lay
down the law.'

'So you're on his side,' said Celia promptly. 'You think
he's right to keep two lovers apart.'

'Lovers!' Mick snorted. 'Teddy's too young for her.
And they probably only imagined themselves in love.'

'If you say so,' she murmured. 'So what are you gonna
do about making up to Jeannie?'

'It's none of your business,' he said. 'So keep your nose
out!'

That's very nice,' she said, giving a railing a desultory
flick with the duster. 'Not very gentlemanly.'

He flushed. 'I've never claimed to be a gentleman.'

'No, but you used to have nice manners. Always saw
a girl home after taking her out and enquiring after her
family.'

'How's your Ma?' he said.

She smiled. 'I wasn't fishing for you to ask, but she's
not much better really.' Her smile faded. 'I think—' She
stopped.

'Think what?'

'Nothing. You get on with your courting.' She turned
her back on him and continued polishing the newel post
with extra vigour.

Mick carried on upstairs, annoyed with Celia because
she had made him feel uncomfortable. He paused to pass
the time of day with Mr Spencer, who was still peddling

his patent medicines. Then he had to stop and say hello to the little Czech Jew, whose name he couldn't pronounce and whose English was that thick, one had to listen hard to make sense of what he was saying. He was only staying a couple of days and then was off to America.

Mick came to Jeannie's room, which was the one she had been given when she first arrived. She had told Kitty she liked being up there in the roof with the family so had not been moved. He knocked on the door.

'Come in.' Jeannie glanced up from her sewing and showed him a woebegone face, which looked pale against the thick red cardigan she wore. 'Oh, it's you, Mick. What d'you want?'

'Only to see how you're doing and whether you feel fit enough to go for a walk.'

'No thanks. I've got to get this done.'

There was a silence and she kept her head down over her work. He was unsure what to do. He was not used to being completely ignored by the opposite sex. He wandered over to the window and looked out. There was frost on the roofs and several pigeons huddled against a chimney stack. A seagull perched on another. Bad weather at sea, he thought vaguely, trying to pick up his courage to speak. He turned and said abruptly, 'I know this must be hard for you to believe but you'll get over it.'

'You'd like me to, wouldn't you?' There was a sharp edge to her voice and she did not look up but worked another stitch.

'Of course I would!' He thrust his hands into his

pockets. 'I know how it hurts. I was only young at the time but I haven't forgotten.'

'Spare me the details,' she muttered. 'I imagine my case is a bit different.'

That irritated him but he reminded himself that she had been through a bad time. 'I know. You could have died from the accident.'

'Yes.' She sighed and put down the stocking she was darning. 'But it wouldn't have been Teddy's fault. Pops says Teddy's irresponsible, but he's no saint. You know what he said to me not long after the accident?' Her tone was indignant. 'That Teddy upped and left me in that hospital in Wales and only cared about his motorbike. Do you believe that?'

Mick did not in all honesty but could not bring himself to say so. Even now when Jeannie was thinner and paler she was still lovely. 'The big fella probably believed it when he said it,' he murmured.

She nodded. 'What was your father like?'

He wondered at the change of subject but answered her. 'He was ill all the time. Ma and Gran were in charge of running things as far back as I can remember. There was my uncle but he didn't really prepare us for what it would be like to have a stepfather.'

'You make Pops sound a monster.'

He said bluntly, 'He had me by the throat once and I was terrified. Although Cessy was never scared of him.'

'Do you think Teddy's scared of him?'

Mick's eyes met hers. 'Now or when we were younger?'

'Now. Do you think that's why he left home?'

Mick did not want to talk about his brother. 'No. Now can we change the subject? Would you like to go to the pictures tonight?'

Jeannie ignored the question. 'Perhaps Pops is a monster? Perhaps he wears a mask and all the time he isn't nice at all.'

Mick stared at her incredulously. 'Come off it! The big fella's OK. He's been good to us. Our Teddy is no plaster saint.'

'I don't want him to be a plaster saint.' She smiled at him. 'Is Cessy Celia?'

He looked surprised. 'Who else could she be? You do know she's the big fella's god-daughter?'

'I had heard. Why don't you ask her to go the pictures?'

That did it for Mick. What girl would suggest to a bloke that he went out with another girl if she felt anything at all for him? Without a word he left the room and went downstairs, thinking that maybe he would take her up on her suggestion.

There was no sign of Celia but as he reached the lobby he heard a car draw up. He went outside and saw that it was the O'Neills – at least the female members of the family and they had come bearing gifts. He felt a lifting of his spirits as the three of them smiled at him.

'Hello, Michael,' said Becky. 'How's Jeannie?'

'You're best asking Ma,' he said cheerfully. 'Our Teddy's joined the air force and the pair of them are down in the dumps.'

'Wow! Is he going to be a pilot?' said Sarah who was now twelve, as tall as her mother and growing more like her every day. 'They reckon if there's another war it'll be fought in the air. We're going to need pilots.'

'There's not going to be another war. Forget about war!' said her mother. 'Just take that basket of fruit and give it to Jeannie. Siobhan, you can take the flowers whilst I go and see your Aunt Kitty.'

As they entered the lobby Kitty came out of the Smoking Room carrying a pile of ashtrays, already having heard their voices. 'I'm glad you've arrived now, Becky. It gives me an excuse to make a cuppa.'

Rebekah looked at her with concern. 'Mick said Teddy's joined the air force.'

'That's right.' She smiled brightly. 'He left a note and upped and left. We don't even know where his training camp is.' She turned and went ahead of Rebekah into the kitchen.

'You must be worried.'

'I can't bear thinking about it.' Kitty cleared her throat. 'If there's another war I'll probably go to pieces.'

'If-if-if! There's not going to be another war,' said Becky firmly, taking her arm. 'Peace in our time! You heard Chamberlain.'

'I heard him! But I don't trust that Hitler. I don't like his haircut and I don't like him marching into other people's countries,' she said briskly. 'The government acted like a scared cat over Czechoslovakia, although I can understand why. I don't want war! I hate war!' Kitty's fingers trembled as she placed the ashtrays in the sink and ran water on them. 'All these years rearing them only to—'

'It hasn't happened,' interrupted Becky, turning off the

tap and sitting her friend down. 'Hitler got what he wanted so stop thinking about it and tell me how's Jeannie taken it?'

Kitty sighed. 'She really loves him. We've got closer because of it. We're not exactly friends and we're not exactly like mother and daughter. It's different.'

'Is she the one to take over your hotel, though?' murmured Becky.

'I don't know about that,' said Kitty soberly. 'I don't think her heart's in it. And once her leg's better and we hear from Teddy I'm not sure if she'll stay. He doesn't like the hotel life and if he did, could he and John get along with each other? At the moment him and me, and him and Jeannie are barely speaking. It's his fault Teddy's gone off. He came the heavy father, overprotective and blaming Teddy for everything to do with the accident when it was the pig's fault.'

Becky smiled. 'Poor pig! John acted just like any father would in the circumstances. I'm sure Daniel would have been the same. If Teddy had only been patient, John would have calmed down eventually.'

Kitty was not so sure and decided to change the subject. 'How is Daniel?'

Becky was silent a moment then she said slowly, 'He's talking about going to live in the Republic. I know I said not to think about there being another war but he believes that if war comes, then Liverpool will be a prime target because of its position and it being a port. He wants the children out of it.'

Kitty groaned. 'I don't blame him but I wish you weren't

going. Let's hope and pray there isn't a war.'

'I want that as much as you do,' said Becky, and she seized her friend's hand and held it tightly. 'But if war comes, Kit, think of letting the younger boys come to us. I know you wouldn't leave England with Teddy in the air force, but let them be safe. There'll be air raids and maybe gas attacks.'

Her words caused a shiver to race down Kitty's spine. 'You don't have to tell me,' she said in a low voice. 'It doesn't bear thinking about.'

'But you've got to think about it,' insisted Becky. 'Think about Mick, too. We're all fond of Mick. Ask him if he'll come as well.'

Kitty stared at her. 'You'd have to ask Mick. I'd like him safe but he'll be twenty-one come spring. The decision will be his then, if the army hasn't got him already.'

Becky sighed. 'I just pray it doesn't come to a war and I won't have to leave. I love Liverpool and Sarah'll hate living on the farm.'

'But if it comes to it,' murmured Kitty, 'you'll all have to go.' She squared her shoulders and said more brightly, 'Let's forget it. All I want at the moment is to hear from Teddy and then perhaps I might just be prepared to forgive that husband of mine.' She was not yet willing to admit that maybe she might also have got some things wrong and needed forgiving herself.

Chapter Twenty-Eight

It was the day after Boxing Day that they heard from Teddy, but even then it was only a card sending his best wishes for Christmas and the New Year.

'I can't believe it,' said Mick, squinting at the postmark but unable to make it out. He placed the card on the mantelpiece. 'I thought he would have at least told us where he was and how he's doing.' He glanced at his mother and Jeannie, remembering how annoyed he had been every time he felt they were treating the big fella like something the cat brought in. He did not know how his stepfather had kept his patience because Mick had wanted to shake them until their eyes rattled in their heads like one of Siobhan's dolls. He was of the opinion that some of the women's anger should have been directed at his brother for his selfishness in not relieving their anxiety over the last few weeks, but his feelings were tinged with guilt because he still felt in some way to blame for Teddy leaving.

'He's scared of saying too much,' said John, not looking up from the newspaper.

'What d'you mean?' Kitty caught his glance and for the first time in weeks she did not turn from it. 'If you can give me a good reason for his sending us one measly card I'd like to hear it.'

'He'll be homesick. Most lads get that way at first,' said her husband in mild tones. 'He'll be missing his home comforts but he's not going to whine about it and upset you. He'll be a man when he comes home.'

'You seem to know all about it,' said Jeannie in a small tight voice. 'Perhaps you can explain why he hasn't written to me?' Her hands trembled on the table.

John glanced across at her and said quietly, 'I don't have all the answers. You'll have to work that one out for yourself.'

'Are you saying he doesn't want me?'

'No. I don't know what's going on in his mind but if he's the person you think he is then have some faith in the lad. He must have his reasons and I'm probably one of them. Maybe he thinks I'd rip his letters up before you get a chance to read them.'

'And would you?' she cried, starting to her feet and staring at him with an anguished expression in her eyes.

'What do you think?' he said quietly.

They continued to look at each other for several long moments before she turned and left the basement.

Nobody said a word but Kitty's heart felt heavy. Not only was she vexed with Teddy for not letting them know where he was, just placing him somewhere would have eased her mind, but also because she was imagining him unhappy and lonely and as living a spartan life.

Still, Teddy's card was the cause of a relaxing in the strained atmosphere between John and Kitty because she had been touched by her husband's apparent understanding of how Teddy might be feeling and also by his telling Jeannie to have some faith in him. No apologies were made but when she spoke to him her tone was much warmer and, instead of ignoring him when they were alone, normal conversation was resumed. She would also touch him affectionately in passing.

It was different with Jeannie who, though perfectly polite to John, showed him no warmth of feeling. Kitty tried to talk to her, to reason with her and to get her to understand how parents felt about their children and how they worried and wanted them safe. Jeannie laughed in her face, 'Safe,' she said. 'There's going to be a war!'

'No,' said Kitty, feeling chilled to the bone. 'It'd be madness.'

'The world is mad,' said Jeannie in a hard voice. 'If families can't live together in peace, then why expect countries to do it.'

'We're only human! Everybody falls out at times,' protested Kitty, feeling that Jeannie's remark was slanted at her family. 'Most families get together again.'

'This one hasn't,' said Jeannie and walked out.

Two days later Kitty went to wake her and found her bed made and all her clothes gone. She hated having to tell John and when she did, did not like it at all when his only response was, 'Well, that's that! She's another person I've let down.' Before she could say anything to reassure him he went downstairs and somehow the moment was lost for her to say anything that she considered might be of the remotest help.

In March, Germany annexed the rest of Czechoslovakia

and Kitty could no longer pretend that war was not imminent, but France and Britain dithered over what action to take so that in the end nobody seemed to know what was going to happen. The following month Italy invaded Albania and it became obvious to most thinking people in the light of the alliance between Germany and Italy that the situation in Europe was grave.

In May, the O'Neills came to say goodbye. 'Remember you can send Jack and Ben to us,' said Becky, pressing John's hand and gazing up at him with sad green eyes. 'We'll take good care of them.'

'We'll think about it,' said John quietly, keeping hold of her hand. 'Thanks for all you've done for me. I've appreciated it.'

Kitty and Daniel were handfast too. 'I'll never forget the way you came to my rescue over Charley,' she said in a shaky voice. 'I don't know what I'd have done without you both.'

'Mary, mother of God!' he exclaimed, looking exasperated. 'We will see each other again! This isn't goodbye forever. We'll still have ships docking here.'

'It feels like we're going forever,' said Sarah mournfully. 'I don't want to go. I hate the countryside.' She hugged Kitty and the boys in turn and added to Mick, 'If you go and fight you will be careful, won't you?'

He nodded and ruffled her newly cut and waved hair, feeling a bit choked himself. He told himself that of course he would see them all again. Hadn't that gypsy told him he'd return safe? 'I'll be careful,' he said, adding in a teasing voice, 'And you be good.'

'I'll try,' she said, and hung out of the window as the car drove away, waving madly and blowing kisses.

In June, the newly launched submarine *Thetis* sank in Liverpool Bay and the city was plunged into mourning with the loss of so many men. Kitty wondered if it was a taste of things to come, when the day finally came and war broke out. Teddy was never far from her thoughts and she longed for him to get in touch. She felt certain it was the same with John but neither of them would mention Jeannie or Teddy to the other.

John decided to turn the back basement room into a shelter and somehow that made her feel better about things. Lately she had feared he might just take off into the blue. The ceiling was reinforced with sheets of tin and extra wooden beams and an extra layer of brick all round strengthened the walls. There were already two perfect escape exits, one to the yard through the door into the back area and another leading three ways, upstairs into the lobby or along into the front basement room or into the coal hole opening in the pavement.

With Mick's help John made four sets of bunk beds. Whilst that was being done, Kitty began to lay in a stock of household goods, including linen, crockery and cutlery, as well as clothes all bought at the summer sales. She also stocked the basement with tins of fruit, vegetables and meat and dried goods.

The moment she had been dreading arrived and Mick received his call-up papers and chose to serve in the Royal Navy. It was the Spanish fortune teller with her talk of crossing the water all those years ago which influenced him. Anyway, for better or for worse, he decided to be a sailor. When it came to saying his goodbyes to the family, he realised why Teddy had left like a thief in the night.

'Keep your head down,' said John, shaking hands with him.

His mother did not speak at all but hugged him tightly, her eyes shining with tears. He was near to tears as well and did not know how he managed to control himself. She had always been there for him, part of his everyday life since the day he was born. Ben was silent like his mother. Hannah said that knowing Mick he'd be back in one piece just like a bad penny, but by now he knew her ways and guessed she was going to miss him. He was unsure how to say his goodbyes to Celia. Maybe if they had been alone he might have kissed her properly, as it was they shook hands and kissed cheeks. As for Jack, who was now five, he waved cheerfully and rode down the Mount part of the way with him on the tricycle and told him to blow the Germans out of the water. Then he was on the train and had left them behind.

In August, with mass evacuations of children from the cities on the way, John decided that Jack would be better in Ireland. He was handed over to Daniel with his tricycle and small suitcase and his parents watched his furiously waving figure as the ship departed until it was out of sight. Then they blinked back their tears and, holding hands as they had not done for a long time, they went back home.

Ben had been asked did he want to go to Ireland but he had just glanced up from the aeroplane he was making and said no thanks. He had his gas mask and there was the cellar. In an extremely adult voice he had added that he would take his chances with them.

In September Hitler's air force bombed Poland and his armies marched into that country. It was the start of the Second World War.

Those early months of the war seemed unreal to Kitty as she waited for the prophesied air raids. There were sandbags with their smell of damp sand and sacking piled up against the outside walls and the windows were criss-crossed with sticky tape and hung with ugly black curtains. John joined the Red Cross and when Ben left school he told Kitty he wanted to make money and do something for the war effort. She could not deny him the opportunities she had given to Mick and Teddy. So Ben started work with a local builder who was commissioned to build air-raid shelters. When he came home he regaled Kitty and John with stories of surface shelters, whose faulty design caused them to collapse. The designers had to think again. There was also a shortage of bricks which meant the city quota of one hundred and forty-two thousand shelters would probably not be met for a long time, if ever.

For a while business was slack as several of Kitty's regular sources of income dried up. The younger ones among her travelling salesmen were conscripted or volunteered. Fewer visitors ventured in from Wales and Lancashire and the man from the Home Office closed down all cinemas and theatres. He soon realised his mistake and they reopened because Britain needed its escapism.

Christmas came, bringing with it love and God bless from Jack and the O'Neills, as well as from Annie and

Jimmy in Ireland. There was also best wishes from Teddy
and a proper letter saying he was a maintenance man,
keeping the RAF mobile and travelling around the country.
That was the reason he could not give them an address. A
sealed envelope for Jeannie was enclosed which Kitty put
carefully away, hoping that the girl would get in touch
one day.

There was no card from Mick but he had written as soon
as he had joined the *Dunloughie Castle* depot ship as a
naval rating and was now serving on a cruiser somewhere.
It did not seem a bit like Christmas despite them going to
the Pivvy where Old Mother Riley was starring in *The Old
Woman Who Lives in a Shoe*.

On New Year's Eve, Celia did not turn in for work. 'It'll
be her mother,' said John, putting on his overcoat and cap.
'Cessy's worried about her on and off for the last year. I'd
better go and see how things are with them.'

Kitty looked at him and thought his face looked pinched
and cold so fetched a scarf and wrapped it about his neck
for good measure. 'Bronchitis, do you think?' she asked,
kissing him.

'Who knows?' He shrugged.

She asked no further questions but suggested he call out
the doctor if things were bad. He nodded and left.

When John returned Kitty knew from his expression
that matters were serious. She made two cups of tea and
put plenty of sugar and a tot of whisky in them. 'Well?'
She sat opposite him at the kitchen table, glad for once that
the hotel was almost empty. They had a lone English guest
from America who had come home to volunteer.

John bit into a slice of Dundee cake and gulped down half his tea before saying, 'I should have gone ages ago. I feel bad because I've neglected them.'

'You've been busy with the Red Cross and we've had other things on our minds,' soothed Kitty.

He shook his head and his expression was austere. 'That's no excuse. I just don't like the woman.' There was a short silence. 'I'm pretty sure it's consumption. Celia's suspected for ages it might be. She just didn't know what to do because her mother was so set against seeing anyone. Besides, they couldn't afford a doctor. I tore a strip off Celia and said we'd have paid. I've told her she's to see the doctor as well.' He looked across at Kitty. 'We should be checked over, too – and Ben and Hannah and Monica, just to make sure. Although I don't think there's any danger. Celia's experience with Geraldine Galloway made sure she was careful.'

'What about the boys before they went away and Jeannie—?' she began.

He shook his head. 'I doubt it. Have you ever heard Celia coughing?' Kitty shook her head. 'There you are then! Quickest way to catch it but she hasn't been coughing over anyone.'

Kitty's mind was relieved somewhat but she knew she would not know real peace until the doctor gave them the all clear.

Within twenty-four hours Celia's mother was moved to the Consumption Hospital on Mount Pleasant where she died within a few days. To Kitty's horror Celia proved to have the disease but John reassured her that it would probably not be fatal as it was in its early stages. Celia was found a place in Cheshire, where the patients were kept in isolation in little wooden cabins where fresh air and good food was the main form of treatment.

Two more letters came from Teddy for Kitty and Jeannie. In Kitty's he asked whether Jeannie had received his first letter and this time he enclosed an address where she could get in touch with him. Kitty had to write back and tell him that Jeannie had left.

Life went on with Kitty missing her boys and the two girls. She was certain that John felt the same but he never mentioned them. Still the air raids did not materialise during those early months of 1940. The expected rationing was also delayed. It did mean that people from out of town began to make appearances and so did several theatricals and newly married couples on one-night honeymoons, but the Grand National was scrapped and its supporters from the Republic of Ireland were greatly missed.

Kitty decided to open her dining room to the general public. John did her a couple of boards which she displayed in a front window and outside, offering substantial but plain meals such as shepherd's pie and carrots for eight pence and fruit tart for threepence. It was slow at first but business gradually built up.

Germany began its *Blitzkrieg* across Europe, forcing the British Expeditionary Forces to retreat to the sea. It was a worrying time for everyone, even Kitty because although neither of her sons were in the army she knew that they could still be caught up in Dunkirk somewhere. There was no news from either of them afterwards but Jeannie telephoned wanting to speak to John.

Kitty watched his face as he held the receiver, trying to make something of the conversation from his monosyllabic answers, waiting for him to mention Teddy's letters, but he replaced the receiver without saying a word. Immediately Kitty jumped on him, 'Why didn't you tell her about Teddy's letter?' Her tone was accusing.

'It wasn't the right time,' he said shortly. 'She's upset. I didn't want to upset her further.'

'It mightn't have upset her. It might have been just what she needed!'

John looked at Kitty but she could tell he was not seeing her. 'She's been training as a nurse down in Oxfordshire,' he murmured, 'and has just had to cope with some of the wounded from Dunkirk. She thought I would understand how she was feeling because of my experiences from the first war. Men with their limbs blown off and the like. It's really distressed her.'

It'd distress anyone, thought Kitty, feeling sad, but still uppermost in her thoughts was Teddy. She touched John's arm. 'Did you get her address?'

This time he looked at Kitty as if he was really seeing her. 'No. I didn't think,' he said simply. 'Besides she said she'd ring again.'

'Oh John!' Kitty shook her head at him. 'What if she doesn't? What about Teddy? There's a war on. What if he never gets the chance to sort this out? You should have thought!'

His face altered, hardened. 'Well, I didn't. And that's all there is to it. I had more on my mind than your son with his cushy little number with the air force. She's seen men dying! Who's to say they both won't have changed and see nothing they want from each other if they ever meet again?' And he walked away.

Kitty felt as if he had slapped her in the face. *Love, John!* she wanted to shout after him. Love doesn't change. Give them their chance. So it's young love but that can be true! But then she wondered whether there was some deeper meaning behind his words and he was referring to him and her. But had they changed so much from the people they had been when they first met? It was something she did not have the time to think about and, besides, she was unsure how profitable it would be if she did start analysing her feelings and looking back over the last eight years. So it was something else that was pushed to the back of her mind.

By July of 1940 the British Isles had become fortress Britain and Liverpool's Lord Mayor was asking women to sacrifice their jewellery to provide guns and aeroplanes for the country's fighting men. Kitty fingered the locket which had been her mother's and did not allow herself to think too much before joining a queue of women outside the town hall in Dale Street. Perhaps if she'd had a daughter to pass it on to she might have had second thoughts about sacrificing it but, of course, she didn't.

London began to suffer heavily from air raids and, in the Atlantic, merchant shipping was being sunk at an alarming rate. Kitty's heart bled for all those mothers and wives who had lost sailor menfolk. Mick was seldom out of her thoughts. 'Spanish fortune teller,' she found herself muttering one day. 'Is that really supposed to make me feel better?'

'What are thee chunnering about? Talking to thyself is the first sign of madness,' said Hannah, suddenly appearing in the kitchen doorway. She was getting old and bent now but Kitty did not have the heart to get rid of her.

'I was thinking aloud. Do you believe people can foresee the future, Hannah?'

'It says in the Good Book that there's prophets.'

'I don't know if that's quite what I meant.' She sighed. 'At least I've still got Ben home,' she murmured.

'Thou's worrying about them lads.' Hannah wiped the top of the table with a dishcloth. 'Doesn't thou know it's a sin to worry.'

'You've never had children, Hannah. And war is something a bit different.'

'It's an abomination in the sight of the Lord,' said the maid. 'And that devil Hitler'll pay for his lust for power and his greed.'

'I should hope so!' Kitty peeled a last potato and dropped it in a pan. The evening meal was served earlier now, just in case there should be any raids. There had been several false alarms and a couple of brief raids with little damage. Guests and passing trade continued to mingle. At the moment she had a couple of theatricals staying, two newly married couples, or not as the case might be – Kitty never asked to see their marriage lines – and four seamen from Norway and Holland. These were classed as aliens and had had to fill in a special form and report to the office at the bottom of Lord Nelson Street. She had a soft spot for them because she saw her own father in each of them.

One afternoon towards the end of August she was in the dining room. Ruth, Hannah's niece who had arrived a few weeks ago, was there but not Monica. Suddenly Kitty heard voices in the lobby and she stilled, recognising one of them. She fled into the lobby and froze when she saw the back view of a man in the uniform of the Royal Navy.

'Mick!' she cried.

He turned and it *was* him, looking a bit older but healthy enough. His eyes creased at the corners in his well-loved smile. 'Hello, Ma.'

She hugged him, needing the assurance that only holding him could bring. At last she found her voice. 'You look in the pink. What have they been feeding you on?'

'Nothing as good as you could dish up,' he said promptly.

'I suppose that's why you've come home,' she said, linking her arm through his. 'A bit of home cooking. There's a war on, you know, so don't be expecting cavier and peach melba.'

He grinned. 'One of your steak and kidney pies'll do, Ma.'

'As it happens . . .' She laughed. 'What are you doing here?'

'Our ship's in dock at Newcastle being repaired.'

'What happened to it?'

He shrugged. 'Nothing much. We had a brush with a mine. No one was hurt.' He glanced around. 'Where's Ben and the big fella? Where's Celia? Your letters told me nothing important.'

'That's because they're censored and we're told careless

talk costs lives. As a member of His Majesty's forces you should know that.'

He smiled. 'Well? Where is everybody?'

'John's a first-aid officer. Ben's building shelters and helping out. As for Celia she's in an isolation place in Cheshire somewhere in Delamere Forest. She has TB, Mick.'

'What!' He leaned against the reception desk, looking flabbergasted. 'How serious is it?'

'She has a good chance of recovering because they caught it early, but you know what it's like with that disease. We went to see her a few months ago and she looked a bit down in the dumps.'

Mick was not surprised. He'd be more than down in the dumps if he had the disease. He found himself remembering Celia sticking by Geraldine Galloway and how she had died. He hated to think that Celia might go the same way.

Kitty bombarded him with questions, which he answered in monosyllables. She managed to glean out of him that his ship had helped with rescuing those from Dunkirk but more recently had been in the North Atlantic on convoy duty. 'Any news about our Teddy's whereabouts yet?' he asked abruptly.

She told him about Teddy and Jeannie and then suggested he went upstairs and had a rest. He shook his head. 'I'll just get a wash and brush up and then give you a hand, if you like.'

She accepted gratefully and within the hour it appeared to Mick on the one hand that he had never been away, but on the other everything had changed. He missed his brothers and the girls and the banter between them all. Although it was Celia he could not get out of his mind. He decided if it was fine tomorrow he would get out his old pushbike and go and visit her.

Mick had become so used to not having to answer to Kitty for his whereabouts that when she asked him where he was going he did not tell her. He felt certain she would come over all protective if he said he was going to visit Celia, so he was vague about his destination. 'I'm just going into the country, Ma. I've been away from ol' England for a while and just want to enjoy looking at trees and fields.'

She nodded, sensing that reserve in him, and she realised that he was growing away from her. She knew she had to accept it, but still could not resist saying, 'If it rains come home.'

He said lightly, 'I've been in a force-nine gale, Ma. A bit of rain's not going to hurt me.' He kissed her cheek and set off.

Mick enjoyed the ride but especially he liked being on his own for a while after months spent on a ship in close confinement with hundreds of men. He went out Widnes way and across on the Runcorn transporter and on to Delamere where he found cabins under trees, which seemed so green after so long at sea that he felt a positive joy. He was directed to Celia's cabin and felt his stomach tightening as he approached. How would she be? He had been imagining her thin and drained of colour. It was a pleasant shock to see her looking so well.

It was nothing to the shock he gave her. 'Mick! I can't believe it!' She rose from the chair and for a moment she swayed and he thought she would fall. He seized her arm and sat her down again, picking up the book she had dropped. 'I thought you were at sea,' she said.

'I'm on leave. How are you?' He reddened. 'Daft question. You wouldn't be here if you were OK.'

She smiled then. 'I'm much better. They're saying I'll be able to leave soon. You can't imagine how that makes me feel, Mick. I thought I might die at one time. And now I'm feeling better I feel completely out of things here.'

'I can believe it,' said Mick, propping his bicycle against the cabin wall.

'I miss the sound of the trams and the kids playing in the street. I miss the lamplighters,' she said fervently.

'You're forgetting the blackout.'

'So I am!' She groaned. 'See what I mean. What I don't miss is Ma coughing! It was terrible, Mick, at the end.' For a moment she looked like a little girl lost.

He reached out and squeezed her hand. 'You did your best. If she didn't want to see a doctor you couldn't make her.'

There was a silence. Mick was remembering the past and how thoughtless he had been towards her. She cleared her throat. 'We were only just scraping by, Mick. You've no idea of the times I couldn't afford to put the gas on and we had to sit in the dark. Sometimes we couldn't even afford coal and had no fire after Ma's fancy man left.'

'You should have told Ma and Pops earlier. They'd have done something and you mightn't have had to come here.'

'They've been kind.' She smiled at him. 'And now you're here. How is everybody? How's Nelson?'

'He's still as spoilt as ever. Not much of the guard dog,' he said ruefully.

'I wish you could have brought him with you.'

'Don't be daft! He could hardly ride on the crossbar!' He grinned at her, thinking she was not as beautiful as Jeannie but he felt relaxed in her company and knew he did not have to put on another side. He could be himself.

She asked him about his life at sea and he enjoyed talking about it and told her things he would not have told his mother. When it came time for him to make a move she looked so sad that he decided to stay a little longer. If it got dark he could always sleep in a hedge or a field, he decided. They talked some more and she suggested a walk.

'It's ages since we had a walk together,' said Mick.

'Ages,' she said softly, thinking how glad she was that Jeannie had gone and that he did not seem to care. 'Remember the old days when we first went out with each other?'

Mick took her hand. 'Bela Lugosi carrying his coffin around and you being scared stiff. It's not that long ago.'

She smiled. 'It was a different world.'

'I was hurt you preferring to look after Geraldine Galloway to being with me. Now I realise how noble you were and what a selfish little sod I was.'

'I'd rather have been with you,' she murmured. 'But you just didn't understand.'

'I was only a kid.'

She nodded and they walked on in silence through the thinning trees.

They came out onto a field of wheat which had been newly cut and continued to walk along the edge of it, watching the sun sinking towards the horizon. It was quiet except for the sound of birdsong. Neither of them wanted to disturb the peace of the moment. It was not until they reached the end of the field that they heard the aeroplane.

They stilled and looked at each other. Celia went to speak but Mick shushed her. *Is it one of theirs or one of ours!* he thought, listening intently. Then he grabbed her hand as the heavy sound of its engine translated into the word *Dornier* and ran with her towards the woods, keeping in the shadow of the hedge bordering the field. When the bomb exploded they were caught on the edge of the blast and flung through the air to land face down in the shorn field.

Mick picked himself up and spat out bits of stalk and soil. He looked round for Celia and saw her a few yards away. For a moment he thought the shock of the blast had killed her. 'Cessy!' he croaked.

She moved and he felt an enormous relief and began to make his way towards her. By the time he reached her she was sitting up. Her hair was standing on end and her face was covered in soil and bits of plant. 'Bloody hell, Mick!' she gasped, holding out a hand to him. 'They nearly got us.'

'Bloody hell's right,' he panted, and abruptly his legs gave way and he fell onto the ground beside her. 'Bloody, bloody hell!' He rolled over to lie flat on his back despite the prickly stalks. He closed his eyes and opened them again. 'I can't believe we're still alive.'

'Why pick on us?' she cried, lying flat beside him.

'Target practice and they bloody missed!' He began to laugh.

'Swines,' said Celia with feeling.

'Bloody swines!' he spluttered.

She giggled. 'It's not funny.'

He shook his head and put his arm around her. 'No, but you can't help laughing, can you?'

She giggled and suddenly they were both laughing. They laughed and laughed until it hurt. 'Stop it,' wailed Celia, clutching at him. 'I've got a pain! Stop it!'

'I can't! I need a shock! That's what I need, a shock! Like you give people with hiccups.' The tears were streaming down his cheeks. He gazed at her, attempting to get control of himself and suddenly found himself kissing her even as the laughter still bubbled in his throat. They were alive, alive!

Her hands were suddenly on his chest attempting to push him away. 'What the matter? Don't you want me to kiss you?'

'Germs!' she cried, looking worried. 'Germs. Have you forgotten I'm here because I've had TB?'

He had. He'd clean forgotten but as he looked at her he could not believe she still had the disease. 'What the hell?' he said in a hard voice. 'Bloody hell, Cessy! We've both just nearly been killed. There's a war on, yer know! A war!'

'Oh God!' she whispered. 'You're a sailor. You could be killed tomorrow.'

'Not tomorrow,' he said unsteadily, still feeling slightly hysterical. 'And not right now.' He kissed her again and kissed and kissed and his passion rose until it was a raging urgency inside him. She muttered words in her throat, that he could not catch but felt sure she was telling him she loved him. He told her that he loved her and he did in that moment. She was warm and her body yielded against his in a way that said, 'Take me!' His fingers found the buttons on her dress and he undid them rapidly. He was not surprised to find that she had little underwear on beneath. His mouth found her breast as the lower part of her body bucked beneath him. He removed her knickers and pulled down his pants. Then he was easing himself inside her and they were both gasping and thrusting. He could scarcely believe in the glory of the moment because she was his first, but it was all over too quickly.

They drew apart to lie panting on their backs and only now did Mick become aware once more of the prickliness of the shorn wheat. Above him the sky was midnight blue and scattered with stars.

They walked back hand in hand to her cabin and both seemed stunned into silence by what had happened. Mick had not meant it to happen and his feelings towards Celia were a hotch-potch of gratitude and love and awkwardness, but lurking in there somewhere was a fear which he did not want to analyse.

They kissed before she went inside and she suggested he sleep beneath her cabin. She would see him in the morning. Mick nodded, intending to do exactly what she said. He slid underneath the cabin and lay on the grass but he could not sleep. Did he really love Cessy? He had loved her in the past but had got over it. Had that moment back in the field just happened because they had been so glad to be alive? He had mates who had married in a rush and some were glad and some were not. He did not know what to do. Would Celia expect him to marry her right away? How could he? She was in this place and he had to go back to sea. He would write to her, he decided. After all she mightn't want to marry him. Yeah. He would write to her and if they both felt they wanted to get married when he got his next leave, then they could. Somehow that decision made him feel guilty, so he decided not to wait and see her in the morning but instead rose as soon as dawn touched the sky and rode home.

Chapter Twenty-Nine

The air raids intensified and the acrid smell of burning and the inconvenience of debris and craters in the streets became a part of Kitty's life, along with the constant worry about food, guests and her family's safety. Still she managed to get through the days, seeing to the linen, shopping, cooking, swopping stories with the guests and ushering them into the shelter and feeding them down there.

Teddy's twenty-first birthday loomed and she hoped and hoped he would get home for it, but there was no word from him and she had to send his card and present. Christmas came with cards from Mick, Jack and Jeannie, which made John's eyes brighten until he realised she had not written her address inside the card. Kitty could only make a guess as to how he felt. His daughter had not telephoned since that first call and it could be that she had omitted the address deliberately.

Kitty felt sorry for him but she dared not say so. The air raids just before Christmas had proved a drain on both their physical and emotional strength. Neither of them dared mention Jack to the other, worrying about him growing away from them despite all that Becky wrote to reassure them that he was well and fit for mischief. They would much rather their son was playing his tricks on them than on Daniel's brother Shaun and the girls. If it had not been for Ben's cheerful presence they could have got really down in the dumps. Although Kitty worried about Ben if he got caught away from home during a raid. She was also concerned about Teddy who had not written for a couple of months.

It was after a visit from the Luftwaffe in the New Year that Kitty opened the door to find a man in RAF uniform sitting on her doorstep. A curl of tobacco smoke rose in the air, tickling her nostrils, and she noticed there was a car parked at the kerb. Her heart seemed to stop beating. 'Teddy?' she whispered.

He stubbed his cigarette out on the step and rose to his feet with a certain stiffness. 'Any room at the inn, Ma?' he said.

Kitty came to life and seizing hold of his sleeve dragged him inside before cuffing him lightly across the head. 'You deserve that,' she said, then flung her arms round him and allowed the tears to flow.

'Hey, hey!' Teddy said uncomfortably, rocking her in his arms. 'It's me that should be crying. That clout brought tears to me eyes.'

'Why haven't you written?' she sniffed. 'Not a thank you did I get for that parcel I sent you – and no Christmas card.'

'I sent you a card,' he protested. 'As for the parcel – I didn't get it for ages. I've been at different airfields down south and in the Midlands and as busy as hell. I haven't had time to turn round. I didn't get the parcel until I went to Stranraer last week. Now I'm on my way to Salisbury Plain and I can only stop for an hour.'

'That's all!'

'Sorry, Ma.' He looked regretful. 'But I'm late now.'

'I'll forgive you,' she said, slipping her hand through his arm and hurrying him into the kitchen.

'Where's the big fella?' he asked, glancing about him as if expecting John to pop out of a cupboard or down the chimney.

'He hasn't come home yet. He's attached to a first-aid post and there was a raid last night, in case you didn't know.'

'Tell me about it,' said Teddy sardonically. 'It held me up. Some copper treated me like an idiot and wouldn't let me through the streets for ages.'

She looked at him. 'It hasn't been much fun here. He was right to do it. We never know when the Jerries are going to pay us a second visit.'

He nodded and lit another cigarette. 'How is everyone?'

She told him, adding before he might ask, 'We had a phone call from Jeannie last June. She's nursing in the south.'

His expression was instantly alert. 'Did she ask after me?'

'John took the call. He didn't even get her phone number or address.'

He was silent and looked quite haggard and her heart went out to him. 'Anything else?' he asked after a few moments.

'She sent a card at Christmas but there was no address again.'

Teddy frowned. 'Does she know I wrote to her?'

'John didn't have time to tell her. The pips went.'

'Is that true or did he just not want to tell her?' muttered Teddy.

'I don't know, son.' She placed the frying pan on the range. 'You should have written sooner,' she said.

'I know. You said so in your letter.' A heavy sigh escaped him.

'There was an unholy row after you left.'

'So you said.'

'She was on your side. She blamed John for you leaving.'

Teddy grimaced. 'I shouldn't have left the way I did but I was blinkin' desperate. I thought there was no hope. It was only later I decided to give it another go because I was that blinkin' miserable.'

Kitty could imagine. 'Do you still care about her?' she murmured, placing several rashers of bacon in the frying pan.

'I've never forgotten her,' he said simply. 'I'd need to find out if there's anything still there for us.'

The kitchen door opened and Hannah and Monica entered. They both stopped and stared. 'So thee's home,' grunted Hannah, sending him a stern look from beneath twitching brows. 'I hope thee's asked forgiveness. Thou leaving caused a load of woe.'

Teddy smiled faintly. 'You haven't changed, Hannah.'

'She still has too much to say,' said Kitty. 'I'm just glad you're here. Now you rest and tell us what else has been happening to you.'

Teddy began to talk but Kitty could tell he was keyed

up and she could guess why. She too was expecting John to walk in any moment. As it was the big fella had still not arrived home when Teddy was getting into his car. As he slid behind the steering wheel, he said, 'You said Jeannie was nursing in the south. Do you know what county, or the name of the hospital?'

'Oxfordshire. That's all I can tell you,' said Kitty.

'Thanks, Ma. Take care of yourself.' He gave her one of his smiles, waved and drove off.

John arrived home ten minutes or so later, looking weary and drawn. She waited until she had given him breakfast before telling him about Teddy's visit.

'I suppose you told him about Jeannie ringing,' said John.

'He asked after her.' She leaned towards him, resting her hands on the table. 'He hasn't been having it easy, John. He's been here, there and everywhere to different airfields, in the south as well as the north. Now he's off to Salisbury Plain.'

'Wiltshire,' said John automatically. 'It borders Oxfordshire on one side.'

'Does it now,' said Kitty softly.

He looked at her from beneath drooping eyelids. 'Why are you saying it like that?'

She smiled. 'I told him she was in Oxfordshire.'

'And you think he can find her from that?'

Kitty did not answer him but she was thinking, where there's a will there's a way. 'He's twenty-one,' she murmured.

There was a taut silence before he said, 'And Jeannie's twenty-three.'

'They can do what they want now,' said Kitty. 'We can't do anything about it.'

John got up and took the whiskey bottle (Irish, from Daniel) from a top shelf and poured a capful and drank it down. 'If he can find her,' he said carefully, 'he deserves her, but the odds are he won't.'

Kitty smiled. 'You'd like to bet?'

'What are you putting up?' There was a faint smile in John's eyes.

She shrugged. 'We'll decide that shall we when it's settled?'

'Agreed.'

It was a daft kind of bargain. But it felt as if they had arrived somewhere after being in a wasteland for a while, thought Kitty. Maybe everything would start to improve from now on.

Chapter Thirty

The wind buffeted the car as it headed towards Oxford and fingers of icy air managed to find their way through the narrowest of cracks, chilling Teddy's neck and ears. He dragged his scarf higher and would have given a lot for a cup of scalding hot tea. "'The north winds will blow and we will have snow,'" he muttered. But the last thing he wanted was snow. Snow slowed things down and he had spent enough time since leaving Liverpool searching fruitlessly for Jeannie. Not sure whether she had joined the forces and become an army nurse, he had tried a couple of military hospitals; one set in a manor house in lush parkland and another in a group of Nissen huts, but without any luck. He had turned on the charm and asked a nursing sister for help. She had checked records and performed a few phone calls but with negative results, so he had switched his attention to civilian hospitals. He'd had little time to visit more than a couple before, much to his delight, he received orders to go to RAF Brize Norton, which was not far from Oxford.

The city of dreaming spires was the centre of the car-manufacturing empire of the creator of the Morris Cowley four-seater, which had ousted the Ford Model T from its position as the biggest selling car in Britain. William Morris

had been made Viscount Nuffield not long before the war
and Teddy admired him greatly. Even so, as he entered
the city he was not thinking of motor cars but of Jeannie
and hospitals. There were two he had been informed: the
Cowley Road Hospital and the Radcliffe Infirmary on the
Woodstock Road. He chose to visit the latter first.

As he drove up the driveway of the infirmary and
stopped not far from a fountain of Triton and accompanying
dolphins, he felt a sudden sick apprehension. What if he
was at the wrong place again? What if Jeannie had moved
on and was in another county? Perhaps she had gone south
to Sussex where she had been born? He locked the car
(Watch out! There could be a Jerry about!) and was aware
his hands were trembling.

He took a deep breath and made his way towards the
hospital entrance but as he reached the doorway a nurse
came through. Immediately he seized his opportunity.
'Excuse me, luv! Can you help me?'

Short and dark-haired, the girl stopped and sneezed.
She pulled a hankerchief from a sleeve and dabbed her
nose. 'What d'you want?' Her tone was nasal. 'But hurry
up I'm dying of cold.'

'Jeannie McLeod. D'you know her?'

'Sure.' She looked at him with interest and then sneezed
again. 'You've missed her by about half an hour but if you
hurry you might still find her. She said she was going to
the Indoor Market on the High Street. If she's not there, try
the Nurses' Home.'

Teddy thanked her and left hastily. He drove round
past historical buildings and cobbled streets, remembering

with half a mind an officer whose car he'd fixed and who'd been a student at Brasenose College, which was on the High Street. He'd said it had been taken over by the army and that most students had been billeted in Christ Church meadow. As Teddy looked about him his interest was stirred as he realised the place was just up Jeannie's street with her love for all things historical.

Jeannie! Soon he would see her again and the misunderstanding between them would be cleared up. He could tell her how desperate and hopeless he had felt his case to be. How he had believed the only thing to do was to get clean away so he would not be a reminder of the accident which had crippled her! No, that wasn't right. She wasn't crippled now but she had suffered and the big fella had said— He went over again in his mind trying to decide the best way to put things. Then suddenly he saw her.

He pulled up with a squeal of brakes part way along the busy High Street and his heart began to pound like a piston. There was no doubting Jeannie still had the power to make him feel that she was the only girl in the world for him. She was standing outside what had to be the entrance to the market with a basket on one arm. She was wearing a cloak of some dark fabric and a nurse's cap on her beautiful hair which was cut short and curled about her pinched-looking face. There was a droop to her mouth as she gazed about her – that mouth, which he had dreamed he was kissing so many times as he tossed on his narrow pallet.

He jumped out of the car. 'Jeannie!'

She stared at him blankly and his spirits plummeted.

'Marry me, Jeannie!' He seized her hand and squeezed it tightly. 'I've never stopped thinking about you! I've never stopped loving you! The last two years have been bloody awful without you.'

She took a deep breath and he was aware she was shaking. 'Have thee, Teddy?' There was a husky note in her voice. 'Then why didn't you write?'

'I did! But you weren't there to get my letter. I know I should have written sooner but I was all mixed up and miserable. I believed I'd crippled you for life and that you must hate me,' he babbled. 'Oh Jeannie, marry me! I can't go on living without you.' He pulled her against him and kissed her and went on kissing her and felt her yield for a moment before she pushed him away and gave vent to a volley of sneezes.

Teddy handed his handkerchief to her. 'Well?' he said anxiously.

She gazed at him from watery eyes above the khaki fabric. 'I'll think about it.'

He felt sick. 'Is there someone else?'

'It would serve you right if there was,' she retorted in a muffled voice. 'I went through hell after you left and gave Pops hell as well.'

'But did you stop loving me?' he demanded.

There was a pause and into that pause dropped an unfamiliar voice. 'Is this your car, corporal?'

Teddy and Jeannie glanced at the policeman. 'Yes, officer. I'm sorry,' said Teddy, trying to look as if he didn't want to strangle the man.

'It shouldn't be here,' said the officer in severe tones.

'I know. I'm sorry,' repeated Teddy, hoping he wasn't going to end up getting fined.

'He was just in the middle of proposing to me, officer.' Jeannie smiled at the man. 'We haven't seen each other for ages you see and—'

The policeman thawed slightly. 'Just get him to move it, nurse, and we'll say no more about it.' He nodded and strolled away with his hands clasped behind his back.

Teddy turned to Jeannie. 'Well?' he repeated.

She blew her nose and pocketed his handkerchief. 'Get in the car. You heard the officer,' she said briskly.

He did as he was told. 'Well?' he said for the third time.

'Drive on.'

He drove on under her direction until he parked in a wide tree-lined road. 'Talk,' she said, taking a roll from her basket. 'Tell me everything. Where you've been, what you've been doing.' She bit into the crackling crust.

He would rather have held her in his arms and kissed her, but he knew when to keep his distance. He talked, conscious of her eyes on his face the whole time, as if she was determined to read what was going on in his thoughts as well as his voice.

When he finished she leaned towards him and pulled his arm round her and immediately began to speak of her loneliness, of her fear, of her pain, in a hesitant manner which showed just how raw her emotions still were. His heart ached with love, sympathy and regret. They had both suffered, more than they would have if he had not run away.

'Forgive me?' he said awkwardly.

She nodded.

'You'll marry me?'

Again she nodded and smiled as she snuggled up to him. 'A proper wedding,' she said.

'When? Where?' Teddy could hear that anxiety in his own voice again. A proper wedding took time and planning and he didn't want to wait, and said so.

'I meant in church not a registry office. I don't want a big fuss but there's a lovely Methodist church here in Oxford – the Wesley Memorial Church. Remember me telling you about John Wesley not long after we met?' Now Jeannie's voice was soft with remembrance. 'He was a student here at Oxford.'

'When?' he repeated, tugging off her nurse's cap so he could nuzzle her ear and neck. 'In the eighteenth century.'

'I didn't mean him! I meant us – married. When?' She chuckled, a warm, throaty chuckle. 'Soon. I was there only yesterday at a meeting of the Women's World Day of Prayer Movement. I'll have a word with the minister. But it definitely won't be until I've got rid of this cold.'

Teddy sighed heavily but it was more from a sense of relief than anything else. He had waited two years. He could wait a bit longer.

They were married a fortnight later with just a few of their friends attending. After much debate, they did not inform John and Kitty until the knot was tied because they were still unsure of the big fella's reaction. Even so the young couple did miss the parents being there and said so in the letter they sent on their two-day honeymoon in Wales.

Chapter Thirty-One

Kitty's feelings were mixed when she received the news about the wedding. She was pleased that Teddy and Jeannie had found each other but disappointed that they had not let them know about their plans earlier. John was sore about the whole thing and Kitty said so when she sent them her congratulations.

But Teddy's and Jeannie's affairs were soon banished from their minds when news came that Mick's ship had vanished. Until they heard to the contrary it was presumed it had been sunk with all hands. Kitty could not take it in. She kept telling herself that it couldn't possibly be true. The fortune teller had said Mick would return! But then, said the rational side of her, who believed in fortune tellers?

John did his best to be positive. 'Men went missing in the Great War and they turned up again.'

'Not all of them,' she said woodenly, her heart like lead inside her.

He had to admit that was true.

Ben was terrible upset and took to wandering. He found it soothing going down to the river and watching the balloon barrage ascend into the sky. There was something about the sight that lifted his downcast spirits. Afterwards he would walk through the streets, noting what damage the Luftwaffe had done the night before, wishing he was old enough to join up and kill more than a few Germans for his brother. He wondered what Mick would have made of the Custom House being bombed. There were other buildings of note which had also suffered from the air raids. The unfinished Anglican Cathedral had damage to its stonework and glorious stained-glass windows, and St George's Hall had been set alight, but the blaze had been quickly brought under control. It was the bombed houses that angered Ben the most. They had been someone's home and now it looked like a giant scythe had sliced through them.

So the months went by without any news of Mick, and Kitty refrained from telling Teddy or Jack about his being missing. She was determined to keep her hopes alive but it was hard to do so as the days lengthened and she often wondered why she was working so hard to keep everything going. Perhaps it was for Ben, whose presence continued to be a blessing to them – so much so that she feared for him every time he was absent for any length of time, but she tried her hardest not to smother him.

So it was that on the evening of the first of May, Ben was walking home from a mate's house who lived not far from the river, when he saw Celia hurrying along the other side of the street. He watched her for a moment just to make sure he was not mistaken, remembering that first time he had met her with Mick. The thought of his brother made his heart sore but he crossed over to speak to her. 'How are you, Celia? We thought you were still in that place in Cheshire.'

He must have surprised her because she jumped before smiling and saying, 'Hello, Ben.' She sounded tired. 'How is everybody?'

He hesitated. 'Our Mick's missing. Ma lives in hope but—' He shrugged his shoulders.

Celia paled. 'I had no idea.'

'Why should you have? You haven't been around for ages. Are you cured now?'

'So they say.' Her smile was weak.

'What are you doing with yourself?'

It was a few moments before she answered. 'I've a job working shifts in the Royal Ordnance Factory in Stopgate Lane. I'm a welder. I help make Sten guns. It's good money. I can't believe it about Mick,' she said in a dazed voice.

'Me neither,' he said dolefully, shoving his hands in his pockets. 'He was a good brother.'

'He was good altogether,' she said in an uneven voice, tears shimmering in her eyes. 'See you around maybe, Ben. Give me luv to your mam and the big fella.' She began to walk away but at that moment the sirens began to wail.

Ben stared after her, realising just how upset she was and how his ma would go mad if he did not find out where she was living. She had always been fond of Celia. He ran after her. 'Where do you live?'

'Does it matter?' She sniffed back tears.

'Yeah! Ma'll want to know.'

She waved a hand. 'I have a room here in Grafton Street.' She told him the number. 'Now leave me alone, Ben, I want to get in before the bombs start falling.'

'Aren't you going to a shelter?' he said worriedly.

She shrugged. 'If your number's up, it's up,' she said, and carried on walking.

Ben could not believe it and ran after her. In that moment he heard the sound of the *ack-ack* guns and the drone of engines. He seized her arm and dragged on it.

'Don't do that!' she said, trying to brush off his hand. 'Leave me alone.'

'No,' said Ben. 'You're gonna come with me. It's not safe round here so close to the docks.'

'I don't care about safe,' she said angrily. 'Just go away and leave me alone.'

He shook his head and dragged on her arm. 'You're coming home with me. Ma's got a shelter. She'll be pleased to see you.'

Celia managed to free herself and came to a halt. 'Why should she? I'm nothing to her now. I haven't been in touch. She hasn't been in touch.'

He looked incredulous. 'That's because she's busy as hell and grieving and worried sick most of the time. She'd be real pleased to see you.'

'Why should she be pleased?' she said with a touch of breathlessness. 'She's not my mother. She's not even an aunt. Even the big fella hasn't come looking for me.'

'Where would they look?' he demanded and then nearly jumped out of his skin as a bomb exploded further along the street.

Celia dived into the nearest doorway but Ben seized hold of her arm. 'Let's make a run for it.'

'No,' she cried. 'I'm staying here. I can't run.'

'I always thought you had sense,' he said frankly and suddenly gave up on her and headed towards Parliament Street. Somewhere in the distance to his rear he heard another bomb explode. He glanced over his shoulder and saw Celia running up the road towards him as if all the demons from hell were after her. She caught up with him and he grabbed her hand and they ran for their lives.

'Oh God, oh God,' she kept saying,

'Shut up and save your breath,' he yelled.

She shut up as they dashed up Parliament Street, only to cry out when they were only halfway up. He stopped and looked at her. She shook her head, her chest heaving. 'A pain! I've got a pain,' she gasped, putting a hand to her large stomach.

'It's only a stitch,' he said.

She shook her head again and sagged against him. He was uncertain what to do as he stared down towards Grafton Street and the docks. Already flames were leaping into the air as houses caught fire and he could see more bombs falling. If he had not been so scared he would have thought it a spectacular sight. He glanced at Celia and realised she was making some kind of recovery. 'Can you go on?' he said.

'If we walk,' she groaned.

They carried on, past the Anglican Cathedral and on up Hope Street until at last they came to the Arcadia. Ben helped her down the area steps through into the basement shelter where he found his mother dispensing cocoa. Her hand stopped in mid-air as she caught sight of Ben and Celia, sweaty and out of breath and covered in dust.

'Thank God,' she said, putting down the jug and going over to Ben and hugging him.

'Ma-aa!' He pushed her away and pulled Celia forward. 'Do you recognise her?' he said.

Kitty stared at the young woman and said in surprise, 'Celia!'

'Ben said you'd be pleased to see me,' she said in a trembling voice. 'But I'm not so sure you are.'

'Of course, I'm pleased to see you,' said Kitty, making a recovery and putting an arm round her. 'You're looking fit. You've put some weight on at last.'

Celia's face crumpled and she rested her head on Kitty's shoulder. 'I'm having a baby,' she said on a sob.

Kitty had guessed as much. 'When did you get married?'

'After I left Delamere. He was a sailor and he was killed. It probably wouldn't have lasted anyway,' she sniffed.

Kitty, aware of the interest shown by guests and employees alike, drew Celia aside and told Ben to pour cocoa for them. She sat the girl on a lower bunk. 'When's the baby due?'

'Next month,' said Celia in weary tones, dragging off her headscarf and pushing back a handful of hair. 'I've been working and saving. I've had no one to turn to.' There were tears in her voice again. 'His mother – she was killed, as well. There was only him and her.'

'You should have come to us,' said Kitty, sitting beside her and squeezing her hand.

'I couldn't,' said Celia. 'I thought you might be angry with me. I thought Mick—' Tears welled up in her eyes again.

'Ben's told you about Mick,' said Kitty with difficulty.

Celia nodded. 'He came to see me in Delamere,' she said, raising her face to Kitty's. 'Did he tell you?'

'No.' She was surprised.

There was a silence which Kitty found difficult to fill. The all clear went and immediately the guests began to make their way upstairs. Kitty and Celia did not move.

'We were very close once,' said Celia, wiping her face with the back of her hand. 'When we were young.'

Kitty stared at her and could have wept herself. 'When we were young,' she echoed softly. 'Love! You're still only young! It's just this war. It's aging us all. It's the fear and the worry.'

Celia nodded and said abruptly. 'I won't stay. I'm only taking shelter.'

Ben approached with the cocoa and Kitty took a cup and handed it to Celia. 'You can stay as long as you like. You're among friends here,' she said firmly.

Celia stared at her and burst into tears.

Kitty let her cry. She felt like crying herself. 'It's the shock,' said Celia a few minutes later, after she had drank her cocoa. 'You ask your Ben. We were nearly blown up. I got an awful fright.'

Kitty said nothing but patted her hand, convinced there was more to Celia's tears than nearly being blown to Kingdom Come.

'I'll go home in a minute,' added Celia. 'I've got work tomorrow.'

'There's no need to rush off,' said Kitty. 'It's gone midnight. Why don't you put your feet up and have a rest.

When Mr McLeod comes back he'll see you home.'

'I'd like to see him,' said Celia in a shy voice. 'Perhaps I will have a little rest.'

Kitty patted her shoulder and left her.

John arrived home an hour or so later. Kitty was waiting for him in the kitchen and as soon as he entered she stirred herself and put the kettle on. 'Celia's here,' she said, and paused, her fingers curling on the edge of the table.

He stared. 'And?' he murmured, taking off his tin hat and gas mask.

'She's pregnant,' said Kitty swiftly. 'She says she married some sailor after she left that place in Delamere and he's dead.'

'It could be true,' said John quietly. 'Why do you make it sound like it isn't.'

'I just don't believe her,' said Kitty, slipping a hand through his arm. 'John, she says she wants to go home – that she's got work tomorrow but I don't want her to go. I don't think she's fit enough.'

He was silent a moment, his hazel eyes holding hers. 'Why don't you believe in this husband?'

'I didn't say I didn't but . . .' She paused. 'She says Mick visited her when she was ill.'

John's eyebrows rose. 'He never mentioned it.'

'No. Maybe it was because she had really met someone else and she was going to marry him, but perhaps she never did. Maybe he died before she could. Poor Mick, if he really cared for her,' she said in a choking voice.

John put his arms round her. 'You're only guessing it was like that. It could be that he just didn't mention it because he thought you might worry. She did have consumption after all.'

She wiped her eyes on John's shoulder and lifted her head. 'You're probably right. She and Mick hadn't had anything to do with each other for ages.'

They were both silent a moment and then he said, 'Where does she live?'

'Grafton Street.'

'Well, she can't go home there then,' he said positively. 'There's a whole row of houses down and the fires are still burning.'

'You tell her that,' said Kitty, looking relieved. 'She's still down in the basement in one of the bunks.'

A weary John went downstairs, only to reappear a few minutes later. 'She's asleep so I left it. I'll have a word with her in the morning.'

But when they rose in the morning it was to find Celia had gone, much to Kitty's disappointment. 'I thought she'd have stayed around to see you,' she said to John.

'I'll nip down to Grafton Street afterwards if you like,' he said, 'and see if she's there. I'll take Nelson for a walk.' It was a lovely bright day with a clear sky.

Kitty nodded. 'And bring her back if she is.'

But when he returned he brought only the news that where Celia had lived was now a crater half filled with rubble and charred beams. 'So she might be back,' said Kitty brightly.

John looked at her. 'Perhaps. But don't mention Mick to her. You'll only upset yourself. Work, Kit, that's the panacea for what ails us.'

Kitty agreed and got on with her tasks, remembering how seemingly carefree her husband had been when they had first met and of the fun they had shared over the years. Nothing was fun anymore, she thought sadly, with Mick missing and the other three away. It would be nice to have Celia and a baby living with them and cheering the place up.

Celia did not return but the Luftwaffe did, and in several nights of terror they rained down destruction on Merseyside. The city centre and the docks were in chaos. Troops were drafted in to demolish buildings and the fires burned for days. All but one of Kitty's guests deserted her but she did not blame them. If it had not been for John's refusal to leave his post, she fancied she might have upped stakes and left herself, taking Ben and Hannah with her. She wondered what had happened to Celia. Whether she was alive or dead.

There were a couple of nights of minor raids and people were starting to think that maybe this was the end of it, when just before midnight on Wednesday the sirens wailed again. Immediately a weary John got out of bed and Kitty, who had only been dozing, slid out after him. They went downstairs and she saw him out. They hugged and kissed each other, scared all over again that they still might lose the other.

'Take care,' she said.

'And you.'

She closed the door and made her way upstairs to rouse Ben. Hannah was already awake. Kitty knocked on the door of her one guest but, as he had done in the past few days, he told her he would stay where he was, thank you very much.

Kitty had just put the kettle on and Ben had slid under the blankets on one of the bunks when the door to the back area burst open and Celia, carrying a brown paper bag, almost fell in.

Kitty could hardly believe her eyes. 'Where've you been?' she asked, hurrying to close the door so that no light would show in the yard.

'Work,' she said unsteadily. 'I've been staying out in Fazakerley but when the raid was only light last night I decided to come into Liverpool and see if I could get a few bits and pieces. I thought there wouldn't be one tonight and I went the pictures to try and forget about things!'

'Weren't we all starting to think that,' said Kitty, pressing her down into a chair and seating herself close by.

'I lost the little I had,' said Celia, visibly trembling. 'Although luckily I had my ration and saving book and identity cards and things in my handbag but I didn't even have a spare pair of knickers to me name.'

'You should have come here,' said Kitty.

'I couldn't! I didn't feel right about it,' said Celia in a low voice, her expression strained. 'I lied to you. I was never married.'

Kitty leaned towards her and took her hand and squeezed it. 'It happens. You're here now and I'm glad about that.'

'Thank you,' whispered Celia.

There was silence in the room but for the now familiar sounds of gunfire and explosions penetrating the basement. 'You get to bed and have a rest,' said Kitty. 'I'll bring you a cup of tea, and then I'm going to try and have a rest myself.'

Celia did as she said and they drank their tea. Then Kitty tried to settle herself to sleep, but Celia's return and the barrage going on overhead made that impossible. It was obvious to her that this raid was not a light one. She was aware that Celia was restless in the bunk opposite. It was not that she was jumping at every noise but she kept tensing and then breathing deeply. Occasionally she gasped. At last Kitty could bear it no longer but got off the bunk and went over to her.

'Are you all right, love?' she asked.

'No!' whispered Celia, and seized her hand. 'I think the baby's coming,' she added in a panic-stricken voice.

Kitty had begun to suspect as much. 'Well, we can't get you to the hospital that's for sure, but don't you worry. I'm sure we'll manage,' she said, sounding much calmer than she actually felt.

She squeezed the girl's hand before leaving her and going over to Hannah who was snoring. She shook her. The old woman started awake and looked up at her, immediately alert. 'What is it, missus?'

'Celia's baby's started. And there's nobody to help but us.'

'Us,' said Hannah, and she shook her head. 'Yous needs a midwife, missus. I'm not going to be much help.'

Kitty was vexed. 'You told me you were there when your mother gave birth several times. We should be able to manage it between us.'

'I was only a kid then,' said Hannah. 'It's fifty years or more.'

Celia groaned. 'I'm going to die!'

'Don't be silly,' said Kitty sharply, turning on her because she was frightened of that very thing.

'Perhaps she's had a premonition,' said Hannah with relish.

'Shut up!' said Kitty. 'If you can't help I'll – I'll have to manage without you.' Her heart sank at the thought but she told herself it was only a simple matter of remembering the times she had given birth. She knew the baby's air passages had to be cleared and the cord cut carefully; tied up in two places and cut in the middle, or else the mother might bleed to death. Again her heart seemed to plunge into her stomach.

'Why don't you get Great-Aunt Jane?' said Ben's wideawake voice.

Kitty looked up at him. 'And who's going to go out there on a night like this? Don't make daft suggestions,' she said crossly.

'Just you get up and put two mattresses on the floor. We're going to need light on this subject.'

'Shouldn't I be putting the kettle on,' he said, sliding down from the bunk. 'That's what they do in the films when a woman's having a baby. They boil kettles and kettles of water.'

Kitty groaned, thinking she could do without his daft remarks.

'I'll go and get thy Aunt Jane,' said Hannah, who had got out of bed and was staring down into Celia's sweaty, pallid face. And before Kitty could stop her, she was across the room and out of the door to the area in the yard.

'Hannah!' she yelled, but the old woman was gone.

Ben crossed to the door in two long strides and would have gone after her if Kitty had not pulled him back. 'Get those mattresses off the beds. She's going to have to rely on God to look after her.' She went over to a cupboard and took out a tablecloth and then she hurried through into the front room and found her sewing basket which contained a pair of scissors. She returned and began to cut the cloth into strips, aware that Celia was breathing deeply and making little moans. Kitty wished John was there and prayed Hannah would get through, but whether Aunt Jane would come out while the raid was on, that was another thing. Kitty soothed herself with the thought that first babies generally took some time to arrive.

Half an hour passed and suddenly there came an ear-shattering explosion and the ground seemed to shake. Celia screamed and Ben shot to his feet. 'That was close. I think I'll just go and—'

'No!' yelled Kitty, throwing down the scissors with a shaking hand. 'You'll stay exactly where you are. No one else is leaving this shelter until the raid's over.'

He sat down again but she could see he did not like doing as he was told. They waited, their ears alert for any sound of crashing overhead, but nothing seemed to be landing on the floor above them.

Another hour crawled by and another and still there was no sign of Hannah or her aunt, and Kitty's time was now completely taken up with keeping Celia calm. Her pains were getting closer together and Kitty had visions of having to deliver the baby on her own, and of Hannah lying crushed somewhere by falling masonry.

Grey fingers of pre-dawn light were beginning to appear along the edge of the blackout curtain when the all clear sounded and Ben was out of the basement like a rabbit chased by a dog.

Kitty looked down at Celia and was torn in two. She did not want to leave the girl but she had to see what Ben was doing. 'I'll have to go,' she said to Celia. 'He's my son.'

'No!' cried Celia, grasping at Kitty's leg.

Kitty smiled. 'Let go. I'll be back in a few minutes. It's not going to happen that quick.'

Celia released her and flopped back on the mattress.

Kitty climbed the steps to the yard. The sky was red with the reflection of a new dawn and in its light she could see Ben at the end of the yard which was littered with shrapnel and masonry. 'We've been hit, Ma,' he shouted. 'It's a good job we weren't in bed.'

Kitty climbed over the debris and did not look back until she reached the end of the yard. It was then she was able to see that the top right hand corner of the Arcadia had been blown clean away. It gave her a terrible shock. Somehow, having escaped damage for so long, part of her had believed they would never be hit, but now she had been proved wrong and there was an enormous lump in her throat. Although by some strange fluke of providence, if there had been a fire it had gone out. 'One of the guests was upstairs,' she said abruptly. 'We'd better see what's happened to him. Besides it's not safe to hang around here. Some more might come down.'

The pair of them went back inside. 'Is everything OK?' asked Celia, stretching out a hand to Kitty.

'It's fine,' she said, forcing a smile. 'I'll just go upstairs and get some towels. We'll need one to make a nappy for the baby.'

Before Celia could say anything, she was through the inside doorway and upstairs, followed by Ben.

The first floor was not too badly damaged but several doors had been blown off. and when she went inside the room which had been occupied she found it empty. The window had been completely blown out and the bed was missing. She and Ben dashed to the opening and looked out, and there was the bed in the street with its occupant still lying on it covered in debris. 'Are you OK?' she shouted.

He raised a hand and she gave a sigh of relief. Having discovered that the flight of stairs to the second floor was blocked with debris, she forced Ben downstairs, remembering to pick up some towels on the way.

Kitty and Ben had only just reached the basement when Aunt Jane and Hannah arrived. 'What a night!' said Jane, shaking her head, and putting down a bag. 'This woman of yours needs a medal, Kit, or confining to Rainhill. I don't know which.'

Kitty hugged them both, relieved more than she could say by the sight of them. 'I thought you'd never come!' she said, tears in her eyes. 'We've been hit. Did you notice?'

'Aye,' said Jane. 'It's going to put you out of business for a while, luv, but then I suppose you could do with a rest.' She took a snowy-white apron out of her bag, put it on and went over to the sink.

Kitty hurried over and poured hot water into the bowl. Jane washed her hands and dried them before going over to Celia. 'Now let's help this babby into the world. Not that it's much of a world at the moment. Let's be having a gander at yer, luv. Let's have yer drawers off and open yer legs.'

'I'm going to die,' groaned Celia. 'I should never have done it.'

'We all feel like that, luv,' said Jane soothingly. 'Every time without fail. Isn't that right, Kitty? It won't be long now.'

'If I die—'said Celia.

'You're not going to die,' said Kitty, kneeling on the edge of the mattress and taking her hand and putting all thought of her hotel out of her mind.

'If I do,' said Celia. 'Will you look after the baby?'

'Of course, I will,' said Kitty without hesitation. 'But you're not going to die.'

An hour later Celia's daughter was born and whilst Jane took care of the mother, Kitty carefully wrapped the baby in a towel. 'Oh, oh, oh, aren't you beautiful,' she whispered, rocking the child in her arms as its first cries echoed round the basement shelter. As she looked down at her, she had a strange feeling that Mick's spirit was somehow with her.

Chapter Thirty-Two

It was several days before an official declared it safe for Kitty and John to venture further than the first floor and during that time they had moved Celia and the baby into the Smoking Room, Ben and John having brought down beds from the first floor. They slept in the dining room.

The Luftwaffe, having done its worst, had gone away. Viewing the damage – their bedroom and the boys' had been completely destroyed and so had several guest rooms – Kitty realised that the hotel was going to be closed for months. Perhaps even a year! There were going to be more urgent calls for repairs than her hotel. Although, with Ben's link with the building trade, she had hopes that maybe it might happen sooner. Fortunately they had money put by which had been intended for hot and cold water in all the rooms. She smiled grimly, then eased back her shoulders. As it was she had more on her mind than repairs to the hotel. What was she going to do about Celia and the baby?

'I want to call her Katherine after you,' said the girl later that day, having got out of bed far earlier than Kitty thought wise. Celia looked defiant. 'And I want to go away.'

'Go away where?' asked Kitty bewildered. 'You've got

nowhere to go. And you know you can stay with us as long as you like. I'll help you with the baby.' Kitty had already lost her heart to Celia's daughter and was helping feed and change her, Celia's milk not having come through. Perhaps through shock or because the baby was premature.

Celia's bottom lip trembled. 'I can't bear staying here. There's too many memories.' She moistened her mouth. 'I'd like to join one of the forces. Hit back at the Jerries.'

'But you can't!' cried Kitty. 'What about little – Katherine.' A thrill raced through as she said the name and glanced down at the child in a drawer lined with flannelette,

Celia cleared her throat. 'You said if I died you'd look after her. Pretend I've died. Part of me feels dead anyway with Mick . . .' Her voice trailed away.

For a moment Kitty stared at her, not knowing what to say. She sensed the girl was not far off breaking point. Perhaps it would be best for her to go away. Kitty touched Celia's arm and said, 'You do what you feel you must, love. Don't worry about little Katherine. I'm going to have some time on my hands now.' She walked out of the room and went in search of John.

She found him boarding up windows upstairs and without preamble told him what Celia had said and what she had decided. She finished by saying, 'I should have asked you first but she was in such a state.'

He put down the hammer and said, 'I know you mean well, Kit, but it's not natural a mother wanting to leave her baby.'

Kitty wanted to say, 'Not even with its grandmother?' but thought he might think her mad and accuse her of wishful thinking. 'What should I have done then,' she said wearily. 'Told her never to darken my doors again. I couldn't offer her a job and she needs to earn a living.' Her hands curled on the corner of a chest of drawers. 'She feels strongly about money. Being penniless and dependent on someone else frightens her and I can understand that, John.'

'She can go back to that factory until we open up again. Tell her that, Kit.' He picked up the hammer again.

'OK.' Kitty left him to it and went downstairs, but she could not find Celia in the Smoking Room and when she looked in the kitchen and elsewhere she was not there either. Kitty ran out onto the pavement and looked about her but there was no sign of her. She walked to the bottom and as far as the bombed out Lewis's building, but saw no sign of her there either. With a sense of fatalism she went back home, made a cup of tea and fed the baby before going upstairs and telling John that Celia had gone. He went out and looked for her himself but did not find her. They waited all that day for her to return. Kitty knew she was not going to come back, but it took John a couple of days before he would believe it.

A week later two letters which had been delayed in the disrupted postal services arrived. One was from a Scottish solicitor saying that John's grandfather had died and left him his house and little else besides. The other was in Mick's handwriting. Kitty went dizzy when she saw it and John lowered her to a chair swiftly. He took the letter from her, opened and read it.

Kitty watched him, her heart hammering so fast that she still thought she would faint. His throat convulsed and she saw there were tears in his eyes. 'What is it?' she whispered.

'He's alive,' said John huskily. 'The ship never went down. It took shelter in a fjord in Norway because there were that many U-boats skulking up there in the Atlantic. His ship's in dock now in Newcastle but he won't be able to get home.' He handed the letter to her and went outside.

Kitty read the words greedily with the tears rolling down her cheeks and then she followed him out onto the step. 'If only Celia had waited,' she said.

John nodded and put his arm round her and they stood there for some time just savouring the news in the two letters and taking the fresh air.

They were about to turn and go indoors when a car drew up at the kerb. They watched as a man in a casual jacket wearing a tweed cap stepped out. At the same time the door on the other side opened and a beautiful chestnut-haired woman in a green suit and hat emerged. Kitty could not believe her eyes. It was as if God had presented her with a huge gold platter with all her dreams on it.

'Thank God, you're both alive,' said Jeannie in a heartfelt voice. 'We feared the worst when we couldn't get through on the telephone.'

'The lines were down and we told them not to bother getting them reconnected,' said John in a surprisingly normal voice.

'You were hit, though,' said Teddy, stepping back and looking up at the damaged facade of the Arcadia.

'It looks like it,' said John.

At that moment Hannah came out and stared at the

couple and did a double take. Kitty had still not said a word.

Jeannie stared at her father. 'You're not still feeling sore that we're married?'

John shrugged and there was a slight smile on his face. 'After what we've been through? I'm just glad nobody else is dead.'

'Why who's dead?' asked Teddy, paling as he looked at Kitty. 'Not our Mick?'

She smiled. 'He was but he's alive again. It's John's grandfather up in Scotland. As for you two being married, of course John's pleased. Sometimes it just takes a parent a bit of time to realise just how grown up their children are.' She slipped a hand through his arm, kissed his cheek and noticed he had shaved off his moustache. 'Come on inside. We've a surprise for you.'

'A nice surprise?' said Jeannie, taking John's arm.

'Depends which way you look at it,' he said, leading her into the dining room and over to the drawer which baby Katherine still occupied.

Teddy's eyes went from his mother to John's and he said in faint voice, 'Not yours, is it?'

Kitty laughed and picked up the baby. 'I suppose she is in a way. At least she is for now.'

Jeannie lowered her head to take a closer look. 'She reminds me of our Jack.'

'She's Celia's but we don't want that talked about,' said John, glancing at his wife. 'To all accounts and purposes she is ours.'

Teddy murmured, 'She does look a bit like our Ben. Although all babies look the same to me.'

'I hope you won't say that about your own,' said Jeannie, giving him a mischievous look.

'When?' cried Kitty, thinking suddenly it was all too much. She would be a grandmother twice!

'Christmas.'

There were more congratulations and John got down the last of the whiskey and they all had a tot. Then Teddy said, 'Let's have a tour of the damage then?'

Kitty said she would do them something to eat and the two men went off but Jeannie stayed behind. The two women looked at each other and smiled. 'So how did he find you?' asked Kitty, making a guess at the reason why Jeannie had stayed behind.

'It was like something out of a film,' said her daughter-in-law softly, toying with the wedding ring on her finger. 'I'd just come out of the market and he was there. I could hardly believe it. I'd been on nights and thought that perhaps tiredness was making me see things. I really believed I'd got him out of my heart but when I saw him I knew it just wasn't true.'

'It was that easy?' said Kitty incredulously.

'Not easy,' responded Jeannie, remembering how she had struggled with so many different emotions in those first moments. Maybe if she had been in bed catching up on some shut-eye and he had come enquiring after her she might have refused to see him but there had been no time for such things and he had sounded so very, very desperate and still in love with her. She smiled at the memory. That first kiss had sealed everything. Whatever had gone before, one thing was for sure the magic was still there for them. 'We talked and got things sorted out. I'm sorry you couldn't be at the wedding but we were frightened of something going wrong again. We both felt awful and then the news filtered through to Teddy that Liverpool had copped it badly. He managed to wangle some leave and so here we are.' Her eyes glistened. 'The poor Arcadia! What are you going to do?'

Kitty smiled and squeezed her hand. 'We'll work something out. Now you go and join your father and Teddy just in case they've fallen out already.'

Jeannie left and Kitty did get as far as putting some liver and sausage in onion gravy in the oven before picking up the baby and going outside. There was probably a long road ahead before the war would be over but for now her boys were safe and she was content with that. *What was a building and not being at a wedding?* she thought as she looked up at the damaged Arcadia. People being together and content were what mattered.

Ben came whistling up the Mount and stopped next to her. 'Whose is the car?'

She told him about Teddy and Jeannie, and how Mick was alive. He hugged her and rushed inside. John passed him on the way out and said to Kitty, 'What are you doing out here?'

She smiled. 'Savouring the moment.'

'You're happy.' He returned her smile and kissed her.

'Aren't you? Our children are safe *and* they're happy.'

He nodded and looked up at the Arcadia. 'What about this place, though? All your dreams were once wrapped up in it.'

'Some still are,' she said, and glanced down at the baby.

He shook his head at her. 'Celia'll want her back one day.'

'Maybe. But in the meantime,' her arms tightened about Katherine, 'she's mine.'

He was silent, hugging her to him and she knew that whatever went wrong between them at times, they would always love each other. 'I've got a yen to go travelling. You and me, Ben and the baby. It's time you saw some other place besides Liverpool.'

She looked up at him. 'Scotland?'

'It's long overdue.'

'OK.' Perhaps it would be good to get away. 'I'll pack tomorrow. Now let's feed those children of ours.'

She handed the baby to him and they went indoors.